NATURAL VICTIMS

NATURAL VICTIMS

Isabel Eberstadt

Alfred A. Knopf   New York   1983

THIS IS A BORZOI BOOK
PUBLISHED BY ALFRED A. KNOPF, INC.

Copyright © 1983 by Isabel Eberstadt

All rights reserved under International and
Pan-American Copyright Conventions. Published in
the United States by Alfred A. Knopf, Inc., New York,
and simultaneously in Canada by Random House of
Canada Limited, Toronto. Distributed by
Random House, Inc., New York.

Grateful acknowledgment is made to The Welk
Group for permission to reprint an excerpt from
OL' MAN RIVER written by Oscar Hammerstein &
Jerome Kern. Copyright © 1927 T.B. Harms Company.
Copyright renewed (c/o The Welk Music Group,
Santa Monica, CA 90401). International Copyright
Secured. All rights reserved. Used by
permission.

Library of Congress Cataloging in Publication Data

Eberstadt, Isabel.   Natural victims.

I. Title.
PS3555.B486N3   1983   813'.54   82-48730
ISBN 0-394-52951-0

Manufactured in the United States of America

FIRST EDITION

For Nick

and

for Nenna

Contents

Part Three

REASONS TO BE CAREFUL

Part Four

GIRL FROM NEW YORK

Part Five

VIE DE BOHÈME

Part Twelve
GONE WEST

NATURAL VICTIMS

MONEY FROM HOME

1

A Family Meeting

A YOUNG WOMAN, dressed in black, stood on the corner of the rue de Rivoli and the rue Cambon. It was the first Sunday in August and the heat was intense. She was wearing a long-sleeved black shirt, buttoned to the neck, and black trousers. Her feet, in battered sandals, were caked with dirt; but her toenails had once been painted silver. Her hair was chopped off close to the skull, like a convict's, with a brutal disregard for effect. She was standing absolutely still, her unblinking gaze fastened at a point just above the trees in the park across the street.

The tourists did not jostle her, but flowed around her, eyes averted, as if she were a kind of street accident in which they might become involved. From time to time a Parisian shopkeeper would stroll out onto the sidewalk and study the sky with anxiety. It was the forty-first day without rain.

Mrs. Melmore sat in the back of her car, alternately fingering her pearls and touching her temples with eau de cologne. She didn't notice when the little flask was empty. She had asked Williams to turn the air conditioning up to high. Now she countermanded the order and began twisting the rings on her left hand.

"Williams, I told you to creep," she said. "Please creep! Can't you go any slower?"

They had started off at the far end of the rue de Rivoli, twenty minutes before noon, at this snail's pace. Mrs. Melmore was beset by conflicting superstitions. To be so much as a minute late for this meeting would be unthinkable. To be too early would be disastrous. To come in the car might be bad luck, since to stand on that corner in the blazing heat, alone and fearful, might be the exact sacrifice demanded of her by her daughter.

Mrs. Melmore looked at her watch and said, almost whispering, "Slower please, slower." This uncertainty was terrible, but they were moving toward the moment when there might well be no further room for suspense or grounds for hope.

As they inched toward the rue Cambon, Mrs. Melmore stopped fidgeting and grew rigid. Suddenly she leaned forward and clutched Williams's shoulder. "Stop," she cried. "She's there! It's Sarah!"

Not waiting for Williams to park, she jumped out of the car and ran toward her daughter, arms outstretched.

"Sarah!"

The young woman in black barely turned her head. Scarcely taking her gaze from the middle distance, she managed to fend off her mother's embraces and hold her at arm's length.

Now people stared. It was not only the strangeness of the encounter. People always stared at Mrs. Melmore, although she was no longer young. She had the indefinable stamp on her of one forever photographed and reported on; one who would always be met with a car, waited on first, given the best table, the room with a view. She gave the impression, this slender bejeweled woman, of being someone whose name must be familiar, even famous, so that it was anticlimactic to discover that she was someone banal, the widow of an American tycoon.

Mrs. Melmore was used to being stared at, but she detested scenes. She dropped her arms to her sides. As if making an equal concession, Sarah lowered her eyes.

Sarah's eyes, the huge wide-set eyes of her mother, trapped in her face like an archeological mystery. Sarah's gaze was directed toward her mother now, but she didn't seem to see her.

Sarah's eyes reflected neither hostility nor anger. They reflected nothing at all. "Sarah, darling!" Mrs. Melmore felt sure that if Sarah would only let her touch her, hold her, she could say what she meant. But what could she do with this frozen body, those empty eyes, and the lips pressed together as if they would never open?

Suddenly, shockingly, Sarah spoke. Her face hardly changed. Only the lips moved. The words she said were: "How's Toddy?"

Mrs. Melmore, startled, lifted a hand as if to touch her daughter, then dropped it.

"Toddy! Oh, darling! Oh, Sarah! Why, you don't even read my letters! I wrote you months ago—poor Toddy—he was run over. It was so sad. He's buried with the rest of the dogs. I haven't done the stone yet. You know, I wrote and I asked you what you wanted. I mean, you can't expect—"

She stopped herself. There must be nothing resembling recriminations.

"Is anyone else dead?"

"No, no, no one. Sarah, please—"

"Who's left alive?"

"Oh, Sarah, I . . ."

"Never mind."

Mrs. Melmore's skin, like her pearls, remained translucent, her gray eyes glowing, her slight smile intact, but moment by moment she seemed to fade, even shrink, before her daughter, while Sarah gathered her strength and light.

Mrs. Melmore whispered, "I love you, Sarah. You know I would do anything for you."

The young woman stretched her arm out stiffly, in a hieratic gesture suggesting various religious tableaux: the expulsion of the moneychangers from the Temple, Moses parting the Red Sea. "All right," she said, "all right, then. If you love me so much, there's one thing you can do for me. You can leave me alone. Just go away and don't look back. Just leave me alone. You may think I'm your daughter, but you're not my mother."

"Sarah, please!"

"I know who and what you are. Please, just leave me alone. Just leave me now. Now."

Her eyes followed the direction in which she was pointing, high above the gardens of the Tuileries.

Mrs. Melmore managed to grasp her daughter's hand and bring it to her cheek, which was wet now with tears. The girl recoiled and snatched her hand away. Mrs. Melmore turned and walked back to her car. She was trembling. The chauffeur, standing beside the car, his eyes discreetly lowered, held the door open for her.

The young woman's last word, low but very clear, followed her: "Murderer!"

Mrs. Melmore sat erect on her side of the car, but she grasped for her compact and held it in front of her, her hand still shaking, looking not at her face but at the corner behind her. The rue de Rivoli was crowded with foreigners. There were tourists with cameras, tourists with guides, tourists with packages, tourists of every race and nationality, but the figure she was searching for had disappeared.

Mrs. Melmore put her head between her hands. She sat quietly for a few minutes. Then she sat up very straight, patted her face with a handkerchief, took out her gold cigarette case, opened it once, then twice, then leaned forward.

"Williams, d'you have a cigarette?"

"Yes, madam."

"Well, thank God for that. Would you light one for me?"

He took out a cigarette, pressed it to the lighter, and passed it back. She took a deep drag.

"Williams, you *are* bad. You know I'm not supposed to smoke."

2

Sarah Melmore Meets
a Young Man with Some Flowers

SARAH MELMORE WALKED in a zigzag fashion, stopping abruptly and turning on her heel, stepping occasionally into doorways, where she examined the names of tenants, or stopping at small cafés, where the only customers were playing pinball. Sometimes she watched the games. She never played. Sometimes she spoke to the people she passed on the street.

"I know who you are," she said to a Japanese gentleman in a business suit. He bowed politely. She gave a ragged laugh, and walked on.

"You don't fool me," she told a man with a mustache, wearing blue jeans and sneakers. Sometimes she simply talked to herself.

"The point is, I *know*," she said. "You may have all the power, but you're not fooling me, so in the end I win. I know you're not dead. I never believed that. I only pretended. I know you think you can fix everything. You think you can buy and sell everybody. You think money can do everything. But it can't. You can torture me and kill me and keep me in hell forever, but you can't ever change what I think."

She stopped and watched a traffic light turn green, turn red, then green again. There was no traffic anyhow. Instead of crossing the street, she turned left.

"That was pretty clever this morning. That was a really good job. You made her look almost like my mother. You even told her about Toddy. Why don't you just make up another demon like me? Keep it for your daughter, and leave me alone."

Then she drew a long breath and stood still, her hand to her lips. "Demons can't cry."

She frowned and began walking along slowly, staring at the sidewalk. "You can't fool me," she said. "Look, I know you're dead. I know you can kill me any time you want. I know you have the power. You think I'm going to hell with you and you can punish me forever. Well, maybe not."

A crucifix was hanging around her neck. She pulled out the cross and held it up. Then she began looking through her pockets for something she had forgotten. A photograph. That was a bad sign. She always carried it. It was a small photograph of her with her brother Jimbo, dead many years now—that is, if he was dead. The picture of the two of them together as children, faded now and torn, seemed to suggest a time before everything had become so terrifying and confusing, when they were both alive and real and cared for each other. She must go back to get it.

Sarah stopped to read the words on a sign. "Go to the rue de Vaugirard." She wanted to laugh. How could they think she would fall into such an obvious trap? Sarah sometimes laughed when she saw people reading billboards in the street or on the Métro. No wonder they looked so puzzled by them: all the signs were addressed to her, and only she could decipher them.

One thing she had been puzzled and disturbed by: the huge signs around Paris lately which said "Apocalypse!" Surely that was going too far. Anyone could understand that. But she had watched people reading those signs with total indifference. It seemed as if they didn't care. People so stupid almost deserved what was coming. But what did it all matter? There was nowhere to hide anyway. She stopped.

That sign about the rue de Vaugirard. She had given it one swift scornful glance. It had said something about Hans, something about lessons on a stringed instrument. Maybe she was being too clever. A stringed instrument. Maybe it was a message from the other side. She tried not to think about the angels. She wasn't absolutely sure about angels. She knew there were devils, but that didn't mean necessarily that there were angels. She'd never seen one. But it could be true. And if it was true, she might have been disregarding their messages. She couldn't remember the number on the rue de Vaugirard. She retraced her steps, but then when she reached the billboard where the note had been tacked, it was gone. And she couldn't remember the number. Just Hans on rue de Vaugirard. She'd expected that really. She'd known it would be gone. "It doesn't matter anyway," she said aloud. Nothing mattered really. Only that she must be strong and show them that she wasn't fooled.

She started across the street, then made another quick turn and chose another direction. A tall man actually bumped into her. Bumped right into her!

"Oh, I'm so sorry. *Excusez-moi, mademoiselle.*"

She stared at him, astonished.

He was a tall, blond American in jeans and sneakers. He was holding a bunch of flowers. Anemones. This hadn't happened to her for a long time.

"You're American," he said slowly, looking at her. Then he put his hand on his chin and his head on one side and studied her. "Why, you're gorgeous!"

She looked around her in a dazed way.

"Here—take these. They're for you." He thrust the flowers into her hands.

"You don't know me," she said. "You must have me mixed up with someone else."

"Have you ever done any acting?"

"Have you?" she said quickly.

"Yeah—sort of, but I hate it. Actually I'm more of an artist. A sculptor or something."

"Do you know James Melmore?"

"Huh?"

"Never mind. Listen. I hate flowers." She was still holding them at arm's length.

"That's okay. Give them to someone else."

She looked around her for a moment, then went and put them head down in a trash can.

He followed her. He didn't seem angry. "Listen, child," he said, "do you live around here?"

"Where do you live?"

"Not too far. It's really simple. Five floors up, but real light."

His face had all the same colors in it: yellow hair, tan skin, yellow eyelashes, yellow eyes.

"Have you got any of your stuff there?"

"Yeah, lots. Would you like to see it sometime?"

"Yes."

"Great. But, well—maybe I could walk you home."

"I'd like to see it now," she said.

"Well . . . okay."

"It doesn't matter either way," she said. "It doesn't matter to me. I don't care who you are."

"My name is Jack," he said.

"Sarah," she said slowly.

"Mind if we take the Métro, Sarah? It might be a little too far to walk."

3

Mrs. Melmore
Pays a Surprise Visit

THE CONCIERGE in Harriet Milbanke's building was a slattern. Her hair was rolled up in curlers and her stockings were rolled down and full of runs. When Mrs. Melmore asked about her sister, she pretended not to understand her French. Mrs. Melmore pointed to her sister's name opposite the bell. The woman shrugged and said that she was not at all sure Miss Milbanke was at home or, if at home, that she would welcome visitors. She indicated to Mrs. Melmore that she could wait outside.

"Heavens," said Mrs. Melmore. The French people she had known were usually only too anxious to be of help to her. She probably looked like a lunatic after that scene. A witch. The Witch of Endor. But she mustn't think of that scene.

She strolled across the street, her eyebrows raised, to examine her reflection in a shop window. She arranged her hair a bit. Who was the Witch of Endor, exactly? Harriet would know, of course.

She turned as she heard a window across the street being thrown open. A dusty reddish mop of hair, and then—oh my gosh! She was gazing up into the pouched and speckled face of her sister Harriet.

"Oh, where's her red hair gone?" she thought.

Harriet was staring aggressively down at her. "I don't think you're on the right street, madam," called Harriet.

"Harriet! It's Sis!"

This was ridiculous! Maybe Harriet had gone blind after all these years.

Harriet shook her head again and squinted. "That old beast only told me some visitor was here. I thought it was another of her tricks. She wants me out of here, you know."

"Please, Harry! Let's not shriek about it in the street."

"What do you want, anyway?"

"Harry! For God's sake!"

"Oh, well. Come on up if you like."

Mrs. Melmore drifted up the stairs. Three flights. She was met by her sister, who was barefoot and wearing a nightgown with a shawl thrown over it.

"Well, Sis, as you see, my staff is *en vacances*."

Mrs. Melmore put out her hand, wary of being rejected

twice in one morning. This ended by their exchanging a firm handshake (Mrs. Melmore's idea) and a clumsy kiss (Miss Milbanke's).

All at once, Mrs. Melmore burst into tears. She curled up on Harriet's big sofa and covered her face with her hands.

"Bad as all that?" Harriet's voice was rusty with embarrassment. "D'you want to tell me about it?"

Sis shook her head, speechless. Harriet turned her back and looked at herself in a cracked and blackened mirror. "My goodness, I'm covered with ink. I've been working all morning. In weather like this, I just stay in my nightgown till it gets a little cooler."

"I'm so sorry," said Mrs. Melmore unevenly. "Really—awfully—sorry. I'm not used to—being kissed anymore. Isn't that absurd?"

Harriet Milbanke padded back and patted her shoulder in a random way. "How about a brandy?" she said. "That might help. What do you drink these days?"

"Harriet, you make me sound a positive drunkard."

"Oh, no, no. But, Sis, I've never seen you cry. Not since you were a baby. Please stop."

"I can't seem to stop today," Mrs. Melmore apologized. "A few more hours and they'll turn me into a *monument historique*. Niobe, or something."

"Huh. They're doing that with every piece of rubbish these days."

Mrs. Melmore started to giggle, but turned it into a cough.

Harriet had a selection of brandy. Indifferent, good, and Delamain, the one she always drank herself. She considered a moment, then poured her sister an inch of an inferior brand.

"No, no. I'm all right," said Mrs. Melmore. But she drank down the brandy like medicine, wiped her eyes with her wet handkerchief, and looked up. "Harriet, I hate to be so importunate, but this is too disgusting. I don't actually need a handkerchief. Just a towel or toilet paper or something."

Harriet brought a box of Kleenex from her bathroom,

but by the time she had returned, her sister, looking immacu-
late, her face dry, her composure restored, was standing at
the end of the room, gazing as if entranced.

Harriet handed her Kleenex anyway.

"My God, Harriet, Mama's portrait! It's such years since
I've seen it! Oh, thank you, darling." She put the Kleenex
box down on a round table. "Why, it never occurred to me
you'd have it here."

"She left it to me. What'd you think I'd do? Sell it?"

"Oh, no, no. Of course not. Store it, I guess. It's so huge.
Why do you think they liked everything so big? Mama was
little. He makes her look a perfect Amazon. I mean, she
could step right down and wrestle us both to the floor."

"Well, I like it."

"Oh, well, yes, I see what you mean—but gosh, Harry,
after all those years you spent with Mama, and those last
years, they must have been—well—absolutely Godawful. . . .
And then to have that giantess staring at you day and night!
And, come on, you two did fight like tigers! Admit it!"

"What did any of you know about us or what we did? My
goodness, you beauties— You beauties just sailed away, sailed
away into the golden sunlit sea, and never looked back."

"That's just not true, Harriet."

Mrs. Melmore had always loathed it when Harriet referred
to her three older sisters, Cottie and the twins, as "the beauties" in that sarcastic way. And even more when she had
begun including her with them. Harriet had always had a
way of making her feel guilty about everything. Anyway,
Harriet didn't need to be so plain and frumpy; there were
lots of things she could have done with herself—could do,
even today. No, she preferred being a living reproach.

"Of course, you were the best, Sis. You were always better
than the others, better in every way. You actually wrote. You
actually called. But you never really knew. Mama didn't tell
you. I was there."

That was Harriet's other favorite theme. "They," "the
beauties," had gone off and abandoned her and left her all

alone to take care of Mama. Of course it wasn't true, but even if it were, Harriet could have done something with her life. With all her talk of independence, she had taken no risks. She must have wanted to stay at home. But the last thing Mrs. Melmore wanted now was a silly quarrel.

"Well," she said, "I suppose that was because Mama loved you the most. You're the one who got her red hair. Gee! I always envied you that."

"You envied me? Come now, Sis. Sometimes I used to look at you girls and then I'd look in the mirror and slap my face, I hated it so for being ugly. But that was a long time ago, dearie. Hard to remember the silly things that annoyed one. Looking back on it all today, I wouldn't change my lot for anything."

"No, no," murmured Mrs. Melmore. "I can see your point. So now it's just you and me, Harriet."

"You and me, yes. Well, Sis, you were always the pick of the litter. You actually had a heart and soul. Not like the other ones—whatever they called themselves."

"Whatever they called themselves? What on earth do you mean, Harriet?"

"Why, the minute the twins left Charlottesville they changed their names. You know they did!"

"Well, Louisa—"

"That's exactly what I mean. Her name was Louise."

"Oh, Harriet! The thing was, everyone called her Weezie and Weasel, and that was so dreary."

"She was like a weasel, too. Sly and nasty. Unless she was like a mink."

"Please, Harriet. You're talking about your sisters."

"They weren't particularly sisterly to me. And then Ann."

"Well, she didn't change her name."

"I beg your pardon, Sis. I can still read and write. 'Anne,' with an 'e,' she called herself."

"Good Lord! That's the way everyone spelled it. It was just more practical."

"Ann is good enough for the Bible."

"For heaven's sake! The Bible is in Hebrew, if you're such a stickler! They probably spelled it with a little squiggle." Harriet scowled.

"And Cottie, she never changed her name."

"She changed her last name often enough."

"Harriet, don't be so horrid. Look, how do you think I like going down through the ages as 'Sis'? If anyone was entitled to change their name, it was me."

"Hmmmf. Well, it suits you."

"Oh, really, Harry. Let's not argue."

"Mmmm. I've gotten awfully grumpy, Sis. It comes from living alone, I suppose. It's mean of me when you're in some sort of trouble. I'm sorry, Sis."

"Oh, Harry, remember? We used to be such friends."

"You know, Sis, I'm dead wrong. In the Bible it's Anna, I think. Ann was after Ann Aldrich."

"Oh, darling, let's just forget it."

"I wouldn't have let Cottie or the twins up here today! Not if they'd stood in the street and caterwauled! They were shallow as plates, and mean as barracudas. Even if they are dead, I can't say otherwise. Now isn't that the truth?"

Mrs. Melmore twisted her long fingers and began to move, slightly swaying, around the apartment.

"Oh, Harriet, that's pretty harsh. They had hard lives. And all those husbands—they didn't add up to one man. Things went wrong for them. Nothing ever turned out the way they hoped. You've chosen an unworldly life, Harry.

"Well, at my age, I can see there's a lot to be said for it. It can give you peace of mind. But our world, their world, it's a hard world, Harriet. Oh, not financially, of course, but every other way, don't let anyone tell you otherwise. It's dog eat dog, and devil take the hindmost." She stopped and picked up a piece of lacquer.

"Gosh, Harry, this is a real treasure! What is it? Japanese eighteenth century? I've never seen one like it."

"They chose their lives themselves, didn't they? I'd like to know who forced them!"

"Oh, look, Harriet— This—this is Mama's. Now I remember— it was on her dressing table. Isn't it divine? No, well, Harriet—it's sort of you get on the roller coaster, and you're young, and everybody's laughing, and it looks like fun. But then it just keeps going and going. Some people still pretend it's terrific, but actually it's stopped being fun. It starts being scary, and still it keeps going and going, on and on. You can't ever get off once you're on. Not till you're dead." She sighed.

"Oh, look, what a marvelous way to use mother of pearl! Gee, what wonderful, wonderful things you have, Harry! The best of all of us. I hope you don't mind my poking around like this. It's just that—well, what a fantastic eye you have!"

Harriet looked at her with a slight smile. "Never bought a thing, dearie. Never had any cash."

"You'll hate me for saying this, but you'd have made a fortune as a decorator."

Harriet made a funny face and sipped some of her special brandy. Then she laughed. "Everything in this room belonged to Mama. Except for a few things from Cousin Emma. Everything except the books I read," she said.

"Really? Really? Oh, gosh, how stupid I am. It all looks so completely different here. The piano, of course. But, it all looks so—so personal."

Of course Sis had remembered the room the moment she had stepped into it. It was as long and narrow as a railroad car. There were two large windows at one end and a hall that opened from the side at the other—an almost classically difficult room to decorate, Sis had noted.

Harriet had solved the problem charmingly by ignoring it. Certainly there was nothing French about this room. One long wall was bookshelves, crammed with books. The windows were hung with crewelwork curtains. Between the windows was Papa's old Governor Winthrop desk with a Chippendale chair behind it. Rising from the desk, which was littered with papers and books, was a bronze maiden holding a lamp.

At the other end of the room was a small piano covered with a paisley shawl. The big sofa, facing the bookshelves, was slipcovered with that same familiar chintz.

"Oh, God," Mrs. Melmore had thought, "Charlottesville! Charlottesville!" Sometimes she had nightmares, never about the important things in her life, but about Charlottesville— that she was young and helpless in Charlottesville, that she was trapped there on the veranda and could never get away. This room even smelled like the house in Charlottesville.

Harriet watched her, smiling.

Mrs. Melmore was very agitated now. She was twisting her rings, her sodden handkerchief, longing for a cigarette. She even picked up the Kleenex box, then put it down again. Once more she stopped in front of her mother's portrait, searching her mother's face, as if Mama might give her a clue how to reach Harriet.

"Gosh, just a little more of this, Harriet? It does help."

Harriet took her glass.

4

Sarah Melmore Meets a Young Man with a Scar

"HEY, M'REEZ." Jack began knocking on the door. "M'reez, can you open up? I've got someone with me." There were sounds of scuffling inside, then silence.

"Oh, Lord. Sounds like M'reez must have got someone in there. What do you think we should do?"

Sarah sat on the top stair, her head between her knees. She didn't answer.

"Sarah, are you okay?"

She didn't feel like answering.

"Are you on something?"

"On?"

"Dope. You know. Drugs."

She considered the question. "I don't think so. I mean I was. On. Everything. Things no one else ever heard of."

He looked at her with interest. His tan face with the wide flat cheekbones was almost without expression, but his long, narrow eyes were pretty and glittering, like topaz.

"Like what?"

"Oh, grass and coke and dope, all that stuff. Oh, and uppers and downers. But I mean the new drugs. They test them on crazy people. They're still experimental."

"D'you have any left?"

"Why?"

"Then I could take some, and we could see if we felt the same."

He sat a step or two below her.

"I don't take anything now. They wanted to make me but I won't, because everything I took stayed in me and never ever goes away," she said.

Sarah drew her hand across her forehead, trying to remember something.

"Are you rich?" she asked finally. It was so long since she had asked a personal question.

"Rich? Lord, no. I know a lot of rich people though."

Her head sank between her knees again.

"I'm really sorry I can't get you something to drink. M'reez, he's probably not going to open up now. But I'd have liked you to meet him. He's really smart. Been on his own since he was eleven years old. He's gorgeous too. But he's vain about it." He paused. "I don't like to get involved, though. I finally learned not to get involved with people, any sort of people, I'm working with. It always makes the most terrible trouble."

Suddenly the door at the top of the stairs opened and a stocky man in a dark suit pushed past them, barreling down the stairs.

Standing in the doorway, unshaven, dressed in blue Jockey shorts, was a young man with black hair and green eyes cold as the March wind. A jagged scar ran across his forehead. He was very beautiful and absolutely furious.

"For God's sake, Jacques, what a way to behave!"

"I'm sorry, M'reez." Jack made a vague gesture to include Sarah.

"You stay out all night. You forget your key like always. Then you come banging at the door, a time everybody decent decides to sleep. You should learn how a gentleman behaves."

Jack got up and said to Sarah, "Come on in. There's coffee and vodka anyway. I guess we've got wine, too."

The room they entered was very large and flooded with light. There were three tall windows looking out over the rooftops. The white-washed walls were hung with blueprints, covered with jottings. A trestle table, with a small architectural model on it, stood in front of one window.

On a pegboard on another wall hung calipers and other instruments. In its whiteness, in its lightness, in its dedication and efficiency, it all reminded Sarah of an operating room.

Another table, with four chairs around it, was heaped with newspaper and magazine clippings. There was a paper construction, about three feet high, in the center of the room. Sarah couldn't tell what it was supposed to be.

Maurice took a look at Sarah, then went into another room and slammed the door. Jack cleared some papers off a round table. "Sit down," he said. "There are some of my sketches all around, and models. Would you like a vodka?"

"Yes," she said automatically.

On top of the pile of papers Jack had moved, along with a lurid picture of a hotel fire in Naples and a color page of the moon shot, had been a clipping from an American newspaper. A photograph of her mother and father, very dressed up. It must be three years old now. She didn't really look at his sketches.

5

Mrs. Melmore
Is Herself Surprised

"You know," said Mrs. Melmore, "when I was a little girl I just loved that portrait. I'd forgotten. I think he must have been in love with her, don't you?"

"Mama had a terrible tongue and a worldly mind, but she was a very chaste woman," said Harriet. "She nearly burst an artery when Cottie got her first divorce. And then Ann! But Mama was funny. She had all that tidewater blood, money-loving blood it was. And the beauties, they just left one rich man and married a richer one."

"But, Harriet, that really wasn't so! What about poor Cottie!"

"Oh, Cottie was round the bend. Never cared who she went to bed with. I can't imagine why she bothered with all those formalities. That last one of hers, the dark one, were they married? I never even knew."

"You mean the prince?"

"He called himself a 'prince'? Cottie was always so drunk when she called Mama, Mama stopped taking her calls. But make no mistake, Sis, you girls—in her heart, Mama didn't like any of that behavior. She didn't make that sort of choice herself. She married for love and she stuck with it. All those divorces! She believed in marrying for life. She thought all that carrying on was 'carnal.' "

"For heaven's sake, Harriet. I was just looking at that portrait and thinking—good Lord, I certainly didn't mean Mama had an affair with him. I just meant he was probably in love with her. I can feel it, in that portrait. Anyway—I never got divorced."

Harriet squinted at her. "Divorced? No, Sis, but that man was married. He was courting you while his wife was dying, and he didn't even try to be circumspect. We weren't so far out in the sticks we didn't hear all about that—it was a public scandal. You know Mama begged you to come home, again and again. She ordered you, Sis."

"Oh, God, Harriet. And do what? Who could I have seen? All Mama cared about were those 'nice' southern boys. And you know those boys were such creeps, weren't they? The only one of our husbands Mama ever liked was Francis, and I don't understand why Louisa ever married him, he was so dreary. No, worse. He was a real toad. Anyway, I was in love with Jim."

"So it seemed. You got married on about ten minutes' notice. No family. Nothing. Like a shopgirl. You could have waited."

"Actually, Harriet, we *had* waited. We'd waited a long time. Anyway, Jim was really killing himself down in Washington. Did all those people making those snide remarks realize all Jim was doing? You must know Jim was the youngest man ever to hold that position, and Roosevelt was awfully tricky. And you think we should have been engaged for a year or something? I just wanted to do anything that would make Jim happy. The rest of his life was so awful."

"No, Sis, it wasn't that, but Mr. Melmore was a man with a reputation and he was a Jew. Mama's father was a bishop, after all. Not that Mama had anything against Jews. But Mama didn't like that behavior. And she didn't like that man. Mama didn't like anything about that marriage."

"Every woman in the world wanted to marry Jim!" cried Mrs. Melmore.

"Maybe so. But you see, Sis, Mama and I, we always thought you were special."

Mrs. Melmore bit her lip, and the tears came to her eyes again. "She might have said something to me," she said, "instead of just freezing me out. Mama was just so cold. Isn't there a time to—to forgive? Not that there was anything to.

. . . But I hardly saw Mama again, Harriet. Not to really talk to. That was hard, Harry."

"Well, Sis, Mama and I were living in Charlottesville, right in the same place. We weren't hard to find. You were the one who was always traipsing around. We never saw you, Sis. Only your picture. People used to ask me how you were, and I would answer—just like Will Rogers—all I know is what I read in the papers."

"Oh, that's too unkind. It's simply not fair. I asked Mama over and over to come and visit. And you too. And stay as long as you could. God knows I tried!"

"Oh, you know Mama. She just didn't like New York or New York ways."

"But for God's sake! I was her daughter!"

"She was never comfortable staying in that man's house."

"And Sarah was named after Mama! What more did she want? Do you know she never said a word to me about it? Not one word."

"Well, my goodness! You know I wondered about that, myself. But Mama had it set in her mind that man would never name a child after her! No sir! She thought it must be after someone in his family."

"My God, Harriet! Now that's too much!"

"But, Sis, if you'd wanted to call her after Mama, why didn't you call her 'Sarah Brooks'? So there'd be no mistake?"

"Oh, God."

They were both silent.

"Sis, do you still ride?"

"*Ride?*"

"Well, that's what you always did. Don't you, anymore?"

"Ride? Harriet, I haven't ridden, not what you'd call ride —I mean, just sort of ambled around maybe—not for years. Why on earth do you ask?"

"Well, why don't you?"

"Harriet, you're being *odd!* Why should I start riding again, all of a sudden? I'm no debutante."

"For heaven's sake, you're a child, Sis. And you always

loved riding. The last time Mama and I came to stay, we looked at all your cups. I remember it very well."

"Oh, Lord. That shows you how long— Well, it took up so much time. And anyway it bored Jim."

"But it was something you were good at. You won all those cups."

"Oh, Harriet, that was the least, just the least—"

"You should have stuck to it."

"Oh, Lord!"

They both sighed at the same time.

"D'you call her Sarah then? Just plain Sarah?" Harriet said.

"Yes." Mrs. Melmore sighed again and coughed. "Oh, well, what's the difference now? I see. Mama really didn't care for me at all anymore, after I married Jim. I see. Do you know what she left me when she died? A little cat's-eye ring. Not a letter or a book or anything personal. I'd never even seen that ring before, and God knows I used to go through her jewelry drawer every chance I got."

"I think she felt you were the woman who had everything, Sis."

"What about my children? Her only grandchildren, after Louisa's poor little baby. . . . She didn't leave my children anything. Well, Jimmy was dead then. So there was just— little Sarah."

"Sis, you're making it too complicated. You were all so rich and I wasn't. I was the one who took care of her, who bathed her, who took her to the bathroom in the night. All those indignities, growing old. And then, later, I was the one who gave her those shots when she was screaming with the pain. Do you know I had to wait until she was actually screaming? Doctor's orders. It seemed so cruel. Well, I was the trained nurse she married. She wasn't thinking any further than that."

She paused and sighed. "It's funny, Sis. I never think I want to see you. I always think of you stepping right out of a bandbox. Coming from a foreign world—foreign clothes, foreign scent, foreign friends. And I think, 'What's that

woman got to do with my little sister from Charlottesville?'
I couldn't believe it when I saw you out there on the street.
But once you're here—I can't help but remember that I
always loved you. You were always special, Sis. I think I was
letting my mean tongue run away with me.

"Mama always loved you, you know. Right to the end.
Truly she did. You were her baby. In fact, I'll tell you something. After she died, I found this whole book of pictures
and clippings. Every word and picture she ever saw about
you. All cut out and pasted and painted around. Done so
beautifully. You know nobody but Mama could make things
like that. It was so pretty, and I was so jealous—you know
what I did? I threw it away. I never thought I'd tell anybody
that. Now, wasn't that mean?

"My word—so now there's another Sarah. How is little
Sarah? Living in Paris, I heard somewhere. Of course, there's
no reason she should have called me."

6

Cocktail Hour

"THERE'S SOMETHING about these drawings I don't understand," said Sarah.

She had had two vodkas, maybe more. They were warm
and tasted funny. But Jack had had at least twice as many.
Probably there was nothing poisonous in the bottle. If it
mattered. Maybe they were both dead already. Somehow he
gave her that feeling.

"You don't have to understand them. You can just look
at them."

"Well, these ones look like—um—architectural—um—
drawings of buildings."

"Yes," said Jack, nodding his head, encouragingly.

"But then, what's this?" she said.

"Well, that's the same building. Totally destroyed."

"Oh . . . why?"

"I just like to do that," he said.

She looked at the pictures some more. Something about them bothered her, so she stopped. "Do you believe in demons?" she asked.

He put down the drawings and looked at her. "I believe I can cure people of demons," he said.

"Oh . . . Well, I feel very tired. Can I sleep for a while on your sofa?"

"Sure. Do you have any money?"

"Um-hum. Not that much. Wanda thinks I shouldn't carry much around, because I'm not very responsible. She sticks all our cash in this place inside the mattress. Literally. I always thought that was a joke."

She turned out her pockets. She had about a hundred francs, her I.D., and the key to her apartment. She wished she could go back there and get that picture of Jimbo.

Jack took the money. "I'll be needing this," he said, "okay?"

"Okay," she said.

She must have gone to sleep and dreamed, for she heard the voices of many men talking around her and they were talking English with a funny accent, saying over and over again something like "pig slop." It had been like that sometimes in the hospital.

When she opened her eyes, no one was in the room but Maurice, astride a chair, staring at her even more malevolently than before. "What're you doing here anyway?" he said. "You passed out, or what?"

"I guess."

"Why you gotta go around doing that here? Why the hell not leave us alone by ourselves?"

She opened her eyes very wide and smiled. This might be

a good day after all. If this boy wanted her to get out, then he was a person she could trust. Someone who really didn't know her father. Her smile seemed to annoy him even more.

"*Putain*," he said.

"I don't think you really do like girls," she said.

"You think not liking you is not liking girls!" he said, furious. "You're crazy and ugly and dirty and behave disgusting! You're the last thing to have anything to do with liking girls!" She was still smiling, then suddenly her face was serious.

"Why does he have a photograph of my father and mother here?"

"Who, Jacques? He does what he likes. You never mind what he likes! What the hell you mean, anyway—your father and mother? Who do you think you are? Patty Hearst?"

"No, I'm not Patty Hearst," she said.

"Huh! Don't I wish you were! God! Jacques he's one strange guy. You got terrible clothes, you don't even clean your feet. You're crazy and you got no money! Why'd Jacques bring you the hell here, anyway? What d'you do, anyway?"

He stopped suddenly, gave her a long reflective look and went into another room. She went back to sleep.

When she woke up, Jack was there. He was shaking her by the shoulder very gently. He had a bowl with some soup in it.

"Take some of this," he said. "You'll feel better."

She shook her head.

"I bet you're thinking I must be a real terrible cook," he said and laughed, "and you'd be right. 'Cause I hardly taste the difference in food myself. But M'reez made this soup. He's just incredible, so you'll like it."

Maurice was sitting at the table, cutting something up. He turned and flashed her a big grin. "Okay, kid," he said.

Sarah took a mouthful of soup. It was good, but she pushed the spoon away. "I don't feel like eating," she said.

She knew there was something she had wanted to ask Jack. "Jack, are you an angel?"

Jack laughed. "An angel? Well, maybe if you think I am."

"Oh. Um. How do you know my mother and father? It doesn't matter," she said under her breath.

"Your mother and father." Jack paused. "Well, everyone sort of knows your mother and father, Sarah."

7

Mrs. Melmore Is Candid

SARAH. Mrs. Melmore gazed at her sister. She felt it was almost too late to talk about Sarah now. "Sarah," she said finally. "Oh Harry, that's the reason I'm here, actually. For help."

"About Sarah?"

"Yes."

"Dear child, I've seen Sarah twice in my life. I know she had a Mainbocher christening robe, and I was told by God knows whom that she was driving her father wild. She'd joined the Black Panthers or one of those other problem groups. But, dearie, I don't know the first thing about Sarah."

"Yes, yes, I understand. It wasn't the Black Panthers or anything like that. That's a total falsehood. But I see what you mean. God knows she had—has—plenty of problems. Oh, God, Harriet, *Sarah!* I don't know where to begin. It's all so awful, just awful. Well, maybe at the end. Do you know, Sarah called me a murderer this morning! A murderer. That was just before I came over to look for you, Harry."

"Hmmm," said Harriet. "I presume you were having a fight."

"No, no. Actually, I'd been telling her how much I loved her. Harry, I hadn't seen Sarah for months and months. Oh, you can't imagine what she looks like now! Just like a skeleton, and no hair at all, just ghastly!"

"What was she talking about, anyway?"

"I don't know. Nothing. Nothing at all. Oh, well, you see she had this very serious nervous breakdown, and she had to go to the hospital, and that whole time it was—well, she thought everyone was trying to murder her. It was all just horrendous. I suppose it's something to do with that. But actually, Harriet, I think the hospital was the thing that did Sarah the most harm. She came out of the hospital ruined, just ruined. They're never going to put her back there again. Over my dead body."

Harriet shook her head. "I don't know, Sis. She sounds like a pretty sick girl."

"No, Harry, no. Basically, she's not at all. That's the point. So many people have messed Sarah up, they've almost destroyed her. But underneath it all she's—she's quite different. She's strong.

"But they did one thing for Sarah, those doctors. They found out that the thing that's really wrong with her, it's physical, not mental. And they have these pills now, and if she takes them, she's perfectly fine. It's just like diabetes, you see. All she has to do is take the pills. But she has to take them—oh, all the rest of her life, probably. And obviously she must have stopped taking her pills."

"Let me get this straight now, Sis. Sarah is living here in Paris?"

"Yes."

"All by herself?"

"Yes, but, when she came over here I thought she was much better. I never thought she'd stop the pills, you see. Oh, Harriet, I can't go over it all now. I'm just too much of a wreck."

Harriet handed her sister a Kleenex. Mrs. Melmore took it and dabbed at her eyes.

"So this morning," said Harriet, "you and Sarah had a fight."

"No. It wasn't a fight, I keep telling you. But she said she never wanted to see me again. Never wanted to speak to me."

"Hmmm." Harriet frowned. "That's what we used to call a fight."

"Well, it wasn't. Anyway, I told you Sarah wasn't herself. But, Harriet, listen, Sarah would talk to *you*. I know she would. I was thinking it over. It's providential you're living here in Paris now. I'm absolutely sure you and Sarah would get along. I know you would."

"I don't know what makes you think so, Sis. Don't you realize what an old fossil I am? I daresay Sarah is very modern. I don't know a thing about life today. Drugs and sex and all the things they care about today. I don't know, and I don't want to know. The classic old maid. I'm just glad I'm as old as I am—I don't know, and I don't want to. Put it on my tombstone."

"Gee, Harry, if you knew how little I know, you'd faint!" Mrs. Melmore grimaced. "Some worldly life! But, Harry, you don't understand. I mean sex and drugs. That's not the point with Sarah. The thing is, you and Sarah would get along. Sarah's very serious. She's not a bit like me. And she reads a lot."

"What does she read?"

Mrs. Melmore paused. Her mind was blank. All she could think of were the old children's books in Sarah's room: *Bob, Son of Battle*, and *Helen's Babies*, and *Prince Prigio*, and *Diddy, Dumps and Tot*. She wasn't going to tell Harriet that.

"Oh, all the classics," she said. "But, Harry, Sarah hasn't really lived at home for years now. Actually, she really loved nonfiction. History and so forth."

Harriet gave her shoulder a pat.

"Oh," said Mrs. Melmore suddenly, "I just remembered. She had—has, I guess—a real thing, a fixation, about Papa.

"One of the very last letters I got from Sarah that was lucid—I mean, sort of lucid—she was going on and on about Papa. Did I understand the implications of one of his last experiments, and so on. Well, I didn't. And Jim said they'd proved years back, those things Papa was working on led nowhere. He took the letter to her doctor, the doctor she had then."

"What utter rot," said Harriet immediately. "I'd like to know how much *he* knew about physics! Did he know Papa got a very nice letter from Dr. Einstein? For the child to take an interest in her grandfather may be unusual these days, but hardly certifiable."

"That's what I thought. I'm convinced, Harry, really convinced, that everything they do for you in the hospital you can do better at home. Certainly in Sarah's case, when it's just a question of her taking the proper pills."

"So you have to persuade Sarah to take those pills. I see. Sis, I'll help you any way I can, but I'm not at all sure I'm the proper person. I'm not tactful with very high-strung people."

"Sarah's not very high-strung. She acted that way with me, but I know she wouldn't with you."

"I suppose you know best. All the same Sis, it seems to me what's essential is to get hold of a doctor, a good one, not some quack. I know a good one, for a wonder—"

"No, Harriet. Absolutely not. That's absolutely out of the question."

"For heaven's sake, why?"

"Sarah doesn't trust doctors, and who knows what he'd do? I don't want any ghastly French doctors involved."

"This man is Scottish."

"No. I don't care. No doctors, Harriet. You've got to promise. Anyway, I don't even know where Sarah is exactly."

Harriet stared at her. "I don't understand. You saw her this morning."

"Yes. I have an address from the bank, but I think it's just sort of a mail drop. Oh, Harriet, I'm really about to collapse. I'm sorry. Could we talk it over another time?"

"Dearie," said Harriet, "I really do have a cook, and she really is *en vacances*, but I can make us a plausible omelet, and I have some pears and cheese and a *crème caramel*. You

don't look as if you could eat much more than that, anyhow.
You're much too thin, of course."

"Oh no, I mean, Harry, that's fabulous of you but I'm too
tired even to eat. But you've been unbelievably kind and
good to me. I was so scared when I came here, and you make
me feel so safe. Can't we be best friends again? I'll be here
till I work things out with Sarah, and with you to help me,
I know we can get things straight."

"Sis, you're white as a sheet, you look as if you're about to
pass out. Do you want to lie down? Maybe I gave you too
much brandy."

"Oh, Harry, I'm not drunk. I'm just tired. I ought to go
back to the hotel."

"Where are you staying?"

"The Crillon. I know you don't approve."

"Sis, there's a daybed I can make up in my library, if—or,
actually, you can take my bed, you're so tall."

"No, no, Harry, that's sweet, but you know I have all this
paraphernalia. And my maid, and so on."

"Stupid waste of money."

"I know, I know. But I really couldn't. But I love you for
asking. I feel so badly coming here and scattering all this rue
and rosemary and thyme all around. Just seeing you, well,
you make me feel so much better. So much saner. But I
think I'd better go back and lie down now. If you'd call *me,*
then?"

Harriet had walked over to her desk and seemed to be
looking for something. She came up with a scrap of paper
and a pencil. "Drat. My pen's leaking on everything," she
complained. "Now would you like me to see if I can get in
touch with Sarah?"

Mrs. Melmore paused. "Oh, would I! But, darling, I don't
even have her real address, just that one I told you about.
The bank sends her checks there. She cashes her checks, but
I think she just tears my letters up. But I keep turning them
out: tragical-comical-historical-pastoral, or however it goes.
. . . Oh, well."

"Have you thought—of talking to the bank?"

"No. I would never do that. And it's her money, anyhow."
Harriet shook her head in disapproval.

"Oh, Harry, you and I—we'll work it out now. I know
we will."

Mrs. Melmore gave her sister a warm kiss goodbye, and
ran down the stairs. She gave the concierge a dazzling smile.

Williams was standing by the car, waiting. Mrs. Melmore
gave him a hug. "Oh, Williams, Miss Milbanke's going to
help us. I just know it's going to be all right now."

The concierge came out to stare at them.

"Oh, look, Williams! Just look at her face! She thinks
we're Lady Chatterley and friend!" She clasped her forehead.
"Poor Williams. 1 really am a little goofy right now. Jet lag,
I guess." She climbed into the back seat. "What an incor-
rigibly frivolous creature I am," she thought. "Or does one's
heart not break all at once, but just break down, bit by bit,
like one's other organs?"

Part Two

PROBLEMS
OF THE RICH

1

Cecil Is Curious

MRS. MELMORE opened the door of her sitting room. It smelled ever so faintly of sandalwood. Good Lord! What was all this? She hadn't told a soul she was coming to Paris, but her rooms were full of flowers. (Had the hotel circulated the news? Had there been a photograph?)

Cecil, Mrs. Melmore's maid, who had thoroughly assimilated her way of doing things, was looking disdainfully at the formal, spiky arrangements. Then she looked at Mrs. Melmore, her eyebrows arched.

"Oh, Cecil," Mrs. Melmore said, "please don't let's get serious about these flowers. It may look like a mortuary, but maybe that's where I belong. If you could just stick them over there, out of the way. Don't try doing anything dazzling with them. The scent's divine. I don't know how you do it so quickly. But, oh Lord, I'm so tired. What I'd really love is a bath and a backrub, Cecil. Then I'll just pull on my nightgown and crawl in bed with a book. I don't care what time it is over here, I've got such jet lag you wouldn't believe it. It's even worse today."

She knew Cecil was voraciously curious about everything that was going on. Any break in her normal routine made Cecil writhe with curiosity. Cecil knew that she was coming to Paris to see Sarah. But that was all she knew. Now she was waiting for some familiar things to happen: telephone calls to or from friends, visits to the collections, trips to Normandy, the South of France.

No, actually Cecil could tell a good deal from the things she'd been told to pack. She hadn't packed for the South or for the mountains or for the country. It was unkind of her, she knew, but she never felt like confiding in Cecil. She felt it was very important that their relationship remain professional.

Cecil had come to work for her at a chaotic time, and Mrs. Melmore had known from the first that she would never want to discuss with Cecil the things that were happening in her life—Jim, Jimmy, Sarah. Maybe it was just as well. "A lady keeps her troubles to herself," Mama always said.

Cecil had run her bath. Now she helped her with her clothes. Mrs. Melmore stepped into her bath. Absolutely perfect temperature. She could count on Cecil: the right amount of bath oil, the square white towels with the crocheted fringe, her cassette of Maria Callas, her castile soap.

"Cecil, where's my pumice?"

Cecil rarely forgot anything. She was a first-rate lady's maid, and after all, that was what counted, wasn't it? She knew it was a weakness in her, this longing for affection. She had sized Cecil up immediately as someone who would never have a grain of affection for her—nor for anyone else, for that matter, unless it was for that niece of hers. Cecil's concern for her niece was virtually the only thing that made her seem human. But did she actually have a niece? Mrs. Melmore had grown more and more dubious.

Oh, well, what she admired was Cecil's total commitment to her job. She knew Cecil was gratified by the effect Mrs. Melmore created. It was a business relationship.

"Cecil!" she called out. "I can't find my pumice stone!"

Cecil must be woolgathering, a pastime in which she seldom indulged. Mrs. Melmore was sure she knew exactly what Cecil was doing: staring resentfully at her white linen sheets.

The question of sheets and towels was the only serious divergence of taste between the two women. Five or six years before, Mrs. Melmore had decided that she was tired of all the flowered linen from Porthault, and had begun using white linen sheets made by nuns in Portugal. Cecil hadn't liked that. Of course she liked the new economies even less. When they had had Jim's company plane, Mrs. Melmore had been able to bring over as many trunks as she liked. All the linen was sent home to be laundered, and sometimes Mrs. Melmore replaced what was necessary at Porthault in Paris. Now she insisted that Cecil pack more rigorously, and as a consequence, when they were traveling, Cecil had to iron her sheets twice a day. Naturally, Cecil didn't do this sort of work at home.

Mrs. Melmore felt she'd done her best. With the advent of the white linen, Cecil had said, "I'll miss the Porthault, madam."

Cecil seldom voiced an opinion.

"Oh, Cecil, I'd forgotten you loved it so. Well, look, I'll give you all you want. Sheets, towels, whatever. Just leave us enough for the guest rooms in the country."

"Oh, madam! I couldn't do that."

"Oh, come on, Cecil. Don't be silly! Or, look, why don't you give them to your niece?"

That was satisfactory to Cecil. Mrs. Melmore was really certain that Cecil had no niece. No letters ever seemed to be

exchanged, no snippets of news from this single, beloved
relation. Cecil's niece was a convenient fiction, Mrs. Melmore
decided, the recipient of many gifts Cecil was too ladylike
to accept for herself. Mrs. Melmore pictured Cecil's little
apartment on Seventy-eighth Street piled to the ceiling with
sheets and towels and other loot.

"Cecil!" Mrs. Melmore switched off the cassette. "What
about my pumice?"

Cecil came in with the pumice, looking very cross. "I'm
sorry, madam. I couldn't hear you with all the racket."

Racket! Maria Callas singing "Casta diva"! And Cecil
acting as if it were an imposition about the pumice. Cecil
seemed to be getting a little careless.

Of course, Mrs. Melmore had no doubt that if she were
to become unfashionable, "uninteresting," Cecil would find
another job. Well, she hadn't gone downhill. Even since
Jim's death, she had the same prestige. She was still treated
like a reigning beauty; her taste was still the standard. And
Cecil still enjoyed their collaboration, even though it was
disappointing to her that Mrs. Melmore did so much less
shopping these days. And of course Cecil was curious. She
took a definitely ghoulish pleasure in all the tragedy she had
witnessed. Cecil wanted to be there for the grand finale.

Goodness! Why was she being so morbid? Was it because
the windows of her suite were the windows of the old Hôtel
Crillon? They had looked over the place de la Révolution,
and the guillotine would have been standing right where
the shadow of the obelisk fell today.

Of course, Jim had relished all that mandatory gore. How
he had loved describing it to the children: the tumbrils jolt-
ing their way over from the Conciergerie, through the howl-
ing mobs. Down the rue St. Honoré, the rue Royale, to the
place de la Révolution.

Marie Antoinette, white-haired and icy. "*Pardon, monsieur.*" Madame du Barry, clinging to the last vestiges of life:
"*Oh, ne me faites pas du mal.*" Well, she probably would

have behaved like Marie Antoinette, herself. Not through
pride, but through shock and self-consciousness. But she preferred Madame du Barry. Heavens! She only wished the
Ritz weren't so full of rock stars and Arabs. And the Plaza-
Athénée even worse.

When Mrs. Melmore went back into her bedroom in a
dressing gown and slippers, she said, "You're an angel, Cecil,
but maybe no backrub. We're all too tired, I should think.
Why don't you go and rest? I hope your room is nice and
cool. And let Williams know, too, please. I'm just going to
sleep for sixteen hours."

"Yes, madam." Cecil would certainly ask Williams what
they'd been doing that day. Williams wouldn't tell her a
thing, bless him.

2

Miss Milbanke Is Perplexed

HARRIET MILBANKE KNEW she wasn't going to get any more
work done that day. She, too, had watched Sis embrace the
chauffeur. Good Lord! What would people think? Did she
always kiss him? Could that really be the way everybody
behaved in the set Sis saw? She remembered old Mrs. Van
Arsdale saying to Mama, "My word, Sarah, your girls have
a lot to answer for! They just go around kissing everyone they
see. The worst part is, everybody is copying those Milbanke
girls. I hate going out these days. I'm afraid I'm going to be
kissed by my dentist!"

Mama had just laughed. "They don't get it from me,
Susan."

No, Mama wasn't one to kiss or let herself be kissed. Just
a goodbye kiss before a trip, and welcome back when one

came home. Harriet looked over her glass at her mother's portrait. Sis was right, it did fill the room with her presence.

"Well, Mama, what are we going to do?"

Mama stared back with that quizzical expression—he'd caught that, all right. Well, Mama would be glad Sis and Harriet had gotten together at last. But, my goodness, it was going to take a lot of getting used to. Harriet remembered Mama's scrapbook. She hadn't wanted to look at it—just chuck it out, she'd thought. But in the end she'd read it, feeling somehow wicked, as if she were reading a bad book, or sitting down to eat a whole chocolate cake.

The pictures of Sis were all right—but the writing! She remembered: "Mrs. Melmore designs each and every detail of her life like a latter-day Cellini. In her patchwork garden, the rows of bibb lettuce are vertical, the romaine horizontal, and the radishes are planted on the bias. . . ."

"Radishes planted on the bias." That stuck in Harriet's mind.

And another bit about her "fun" jewelry—all designed by some man with a Jewish name: golden seashells, golden oysters with a pearl inside, golden seaweed necklaces for the seashore.

And her country jewelry: all flowers and vegetables—a lily with a tiny ruby bug inside its leaves. God knows what her "serious" jewelry was!

What on earth had Mama made of all that? She just wished they had discussed it together. It was mean of Mama doing all that on the sly. Maybe Mama secretly liked that sort of thing. She'd never know.

After a certain date, the text pieces stopped and there were just pictures. Sis must have stopped giving interviews. Some of the photographs were lovely, especially that one of Sis with her hunter, Mogh Ruith, but some were just grotesque. They must have been tampered with. There was one of Sis where her neck was as long as a giraffe's and she seemed to have no shoulders at all, like the Loch Ness monster.

Yes, Sis must have stopped giving interviews. There were a few color spreads of her house in Florida, the fishing camp in Canada. No photographs of the house in the country or her apartment.

The last picture Mama had pasted in was from some newspaper. Sis was wearing a full-length fur coat. Oh no, she remembered now. The very last was titled "Pants Are Here to Stay. Sis Melmore on her way to lunch." It was some restaurant with a French name. Sis had been wearing a pair of pants and a shirt, with a long chain around her neck. Beside this picture, Mama had written in her spidery hand: "My little Maud."

Mama had known she was going to die. She had been too weak to color and paste and paint around this picture— certainly not without Harriet's help. But Mama was so orderly. At the bottom of the page she had written *Finis*. She'd been able to write that word the way she liked, beautifully embellished, like a word in a medieval manuscript. Then, at the bottom right, she had written in small plain script: Sarah Brooks Milbanke, and the date, and then on the inside leaf:

> *If this book from me should roam,*
> *Give it a kick and send it home.*
> *Sarah Brooks Randall*
> *Rural Hill*
> *Richmond, Virginia*
> *U.S.A.*
> *North America*
> *The World*
> *The Universe.*

This was written in a child's handwriting. Mama must have been in one of those states when she thought she was a child again, living in her father's house. Well, she was not such a child that she hadn't been able to jump out of bed and hide that book, so that Harriet wouldn't find it! It hurt her so much—as if Mama were leading a double life really, a sort of betrayal.

Harriet walked into the kitchen. How was she going to get along with someone who planted radishes on the bias, kissed her chauffeur and had "seashore" jewelry? They had those first twenty years in common, and that was about all. Would Sis have a young lover and smoke drugs? Sis had seemed very sweet, but of course Sis had always been very appealing. She still didn't seem hard or worldly. But that daughter! If she wasn't barking mad, she certainly sounded terribly unattractive. And Sis didn't seem a bit sensible about her. What had she let herself in for?

Harriet rinsed out the two glasses and put them on a rack to dry. Then she went back and stared at her mother, the way Sis had done.

"All right, Mama," she said, "so here's your little Maud in trouble. I'll do what I can, Mama."

3

Family Portraits, Family Skeletons

WHEN CECIL HAD GONE, Mrs. Melmore opened the small bag she never let Cecil touch, the bag that held her photographs. She decided she didn't want all of them out right now. Just the one of the four of them, Jim and her with the children, the summer they had tried taking a house in Bar Harbor. What a disaster that had been! This must have been the one moment all summer when everyone was at least trying to look cheerful. She didn't know why she liked that picture, but she did.

Another picture of her own family: Papa, Mama, and the five girls, just before Louisa's wedding. Louisa and Anne were really the beautiful ones. Cottie was making a funny face. Harriet was staring down at the ground, looking disgruntled, and *she* was eleven, twelve? She certainly didn't look very pretty. Too fat that year. She hadn't reached her full height. The hair so unbecoming, and that pouting expression.

And Mama, now that she looked at her closely, Mama had a strange smile on her face. Slightly sarcastic? Back in the bag, that photograph.

The darling pictures of Jimmy and Sarah when they were babies. And here they were still very young—Sarah on Jimmy's lap, five and nine they would have been? Both of them smiling as if it were Christmas morning.

Those were the pictures she wanted near her. And the snapshot of Jim that she loved.

Jim had liked the glamour pictures of her that all the "great"—that is to say, "fashionable"—photographers had taken. A couple of them were always on his desk, a couple in his bedroom. She liked the snapshots where she was mugging. Just as Jim had liked the Bachrach picture of himself behind his desk, looking like a Supreme Court justice. She liked the snap of him eating a hot dog at a ball game.

She ended up, of course, putting her little folding case of three next to her bed: Jim, Jimmy, Sarah.

Jim—he was a little bit fat by then, but anyone could see he was a powerful man, an intelligent man, and at the same time a man who was sexy, and full of vitality and fun. His eyes were wrinkled up and he was grinning. It was plain to see he wasn't thinking about anything either good or platitudinous.

God, she had loved him! But, oh God, he had been a handful!

The times he was supposed to be in London or Phoenix or Chicago. She knew he wasn't. But still he would come home, shameless, not even remembering his lies.

"What's on for tonight, Sis? Nothing? Well, I'm bored, I feel like being entertained. Call up some people who can make me laugh. Nothing educational tonight.

"And what about dinner? Christ, I'm bored with fish and chicken. I've lost three pounds, anyway. How about the soup we had at Daisy's that night? I hate all that 'secret recipe' shit. You can get Paulette to make it even better. Have that first. I'd like to see Daisy's face, so ask Daisy. Otherwise I don't care—just, please, no fairies. Or those barrel-of-laughs curators of yours, okay? Well, I think I'll take a nap until everyone's here. Wake me up about the wine."

Dear God, to put that together at four o'clock and make it work! And his fury if it didn't!

The things he expected from her! Menus and place settings and flower arrangements and gardens and gazebos that no one had ever imagined. They had to be completely original, but at the same time cool, classical, and in perfect taste. All at a moment's notice, and without any appearance of effort.

Then, calm and composed in the center, never revealing her feelings, would be Sis, with a gentle smile, only trying to anticipate whatever might be demanded. Mrs. Kubla Khan, dressed by Givenchy, growing ever more beautiful as she grew older.

He was enormously pleased by what he thought of as calculated effects—when her hair became slanted with a gray that was virtually the same as the silver of her Rolls-Royce. When her nails happened to be lacquered the color of the soup bowls.

He kept track of everything she wore—he had a better memory for this than Cecil. "Sis, didn't you wear that suit to the theater before?"

He loved showering her with furs and jewels, so that, as he said, she could wear a new coat or a new set of rocks every day of the year.

"Christmas is coming," he used to say, "time to be piggish. Now, Sis, there's only one thing. You can burn your old clothes, or you can give them to the museum. But don't let me catch you ever again—understand me, ever again—giving anything to that bitch of a sister of yours. I don't ever want to see anything you've worn on anyone else."

Jim was so strange about her family. Her sisters were her closest friends, Anne and Louisa that is. Sis adored her sisters. She was so pleased when Jim had seemed to enjoy having them around. He flirted with them outrageously, of course, and naturally they were crazy about him. But then behind their backs he referred to them as Imprudence, Intemperance, and Incontinence. That was Louisa, Cottie, and Anne, respectively. When he got tired of them, one by one, he told Sis they were cheap and greedy. He didn't even like her visiting them. It was difficult.

Of course they'd never seen much of Harriet. Jim had never paid attention to Harriet, except for an occasional public speculation as to whether she'd ever been laid. He decided not, and that Harriet wasn't even a lesbian, and he lost interest.

But, Mama! Gosh, that was another story. He really seemed to respect Mama, and for a long, long time he was fascinated by her—almost obsessed. Of course, everyone usually ended up in Mama's thrall.

It was funny. Mama had never been a beauty, like the twins, except for her coloring, that dark red hair and white, white skin. She was beautifully made, of course, small but delicate, and she was very quick and neat and graceful, a pleasure to watch. And she had a beautiful voice, and an extraordinary imagination. And, well—an even more extraordinary temper. She was like a cat, Mama. You'd think she was purring, but the next minute she'd scratch your face. She'd be affectionate, and then walk away and never look back. And she was funny. Of course Mama could be very, very funny.

Sis knew that the older girls didn't like bringing their beaux home. They were scared that Mama would steal them, and sometimes she did. Sis could remember some of the young men just sitting and talking to Mama, bewitched, while her sisters were fuming. Oh, Mama was a great seductress all right, though, as Harriet had said, chaste, of course. Good Heavens, yes.

Even Jim must have fallen under her spell, although she was so brusque in her rejection of his advances. He didn't like it one bit that Mama never came to visit. She supposed he really wanted Mama's blessing, her approval; and he blamed Sis when it wasn't forthcoming.

"For Christ's sake, Sis, why don't you ever ask your mother here?"

"But, Jim, you know I have. She really doesn't like to travel."

"But I notice she does travel. To other people's houses."

"Hardly at all, Jim."

"There's little enough I ask of you, Sis. I think you might try to please me when I do. Particularly when I'm only asking you to do something that's in your own interest."

"I'm sorry, Jim."

"I think it looks wrong, never seeing your mother. It looks strange."

"But I'd like to see her."

"Then for Christ's sake, fix it up!"

But Mama was always evasive. "Tell Mr. Melmore I'm sorry, Maud, but I hardly ever travel." Mama was the only one who called her Maud. Or "Maud, you know in the summer I always go to Maine." Or "It wears me out just going in to the city, to do my shopping."

It was Jim's idea to call their daughter "Sarah." She wouldn't have dared suggest it. He must have thought that would be the final breakthrough. But, when Mama never responded in any way, he gradually stopped talking about her, although Sis knew he held her to blame for the failure.

It was after that that he got bored with her sisters. Yes, it was really Mama he wanted. Sometimes Sis thought he wanted Mama more than he'd ever wanted her. Mama's intransigence and, well, rudeness intrigued him. He never discussed it directly with her, just forbade her to visit her mother, unless her mother visited them first. And, of course, every so often he would make a snide remark.

At the beginning he had found the things Sis had learned from Mama "cute" or "funny."

Mama had believed in proper accounts and had drilled her daughters accordingly. From earliest childhood, Sis had known to the penny where she stood, and she never dreamed of any extravagance she couldn't afford. In fact, when she had gone to stay with Anne and her second husband, she had decided Anne was almost "wicked" when she crowed to Sis she was never going to have to keep accounts, ever again.

"It simply doesn't matter in Alex's bracket," she had said. The idea had horrified Sis.

After their marriage, Jim had told her there would be a sum for household expenses, a sum she found absolutely staggering, and another for her allowance—smaller, but still princely. And every month Miss McMillan would come to the apartment and they would sit in the library while they went over the books together.

When they were first married, Sis had tried to make a budget based on a report she had read in *Time* magazine of Jim's salary as president and chairman of his company. Although his salary was one of the ten highest in the country, it still didn't seem large enough to Sis to justify the way they were living, with no thought for the morrow. She revised their budget drastically, not forgetting to subtract ten percent for charity and twenty percent for savings. Jim whooped with joy and told her not to worry—they weren't over the hill to the poorhouse yet, and if she'd take care of the household, he would worry about charity and savings.

Even after all these years she still didn't understand about dividends and straddles and royalties and lease-backs and futures and the various financial dealings that she only glimpsed when Miss McMillan brought her the papers to sign, or when she signed the tax returns. But she had learned very soon that Jim's ideas about money had nothing in common with Mama's.

Whatever Jim wanted, they bought. Jim never told her they couldn't afford anything, and he all but despised Sis's economies. Occasionally he objected to the expense of something he didn't care for. Jim seemed to have a sixth sense that led him to flip through a few pages of figures, hardly looking, and then put his finger on one item.

"What's this, Sis?"

"This" might be a trip to Europe for Cottie, after George Barking ran off with his secretary.

"Well, it's out of my allowance, Jim."

"My God, Sis, have you got no sense about money at all? You're going to start endowing every tart and wastrel in the Western Hemisphere! Look here, it may be, as you so crudely put it, 'your' allowance, but please remember 'your' allowance comes out of my hide."

"I'm sorry, Jim."

Gradually Sis accepted Jim's ways, but they were always foreign to her. It was like conversing in another language.

Jim liked to talk to Sis about clothes and taste. But anything personal? God forbid! His first wife had been dying of a rare sort of blood disease when Sis met him—she seemed to have been an invalid for years. Sis had never seen her, and thought of her as very old, but what would she have been? Thirty-eight?

Young people are so heartless. Well, *she* had been heartless, anyway. And Jim had never seemed to mention Marcia —she hardly seemed real. If he ever did, it would be to say that if she hadn't been so sick he would have divorced her years ago. But now it would look bad.

Jim had told Sis on their very first evening together that he was going to marry her. And the doctors had told him ("promised him," he said) that Marcia couldn't last until Christmas. So his wife had been in the hospital dying— dying, maybe, for love of him—and Sis really hadn't given it a thought. Marcia had been dying, while they had been making love. So frivolous, so frivolous. Harriet hadn't really needed to rub that in. Because, yes, frivolous as she was, she'd known how bad she was, and she wouldn't have dreamed of telling Mama. When Marcia died, there was no emotion but relief, just relief and joy.

They'd gotten married in a civil ceremony within the month. Well, Jim's parents hadn't liked that much either. It had taken her a long time to realize how guilty she really felt about Marcia. Guilty, or maybe frightened? Someone was going to pay her back for that someday. Someone would pay her back in the same coin. She knew it. She would be the one lying in the hospital, waiting and waiting for Jim to call. She already knew what it was like to suffer in the same way. She became more and more curious about Marcia. What had this woman, her predecessor, been like?

The first evening she had dinner with Jim in his apartment, she had seen the huge portrait over the fireplace. A pale woman, with great dark eyes and black hair drawn back in a classic knot—a slender Semitic beauty, in a pailletted dress, with a Siamese cat lying on either side of her. And in the library there was a large photograph, a white face peering soulfully out from a black background, on the hand by the side of her face a diamond the size of a walnut. And a smaller photograph of Jim and Marcia sitting on the ground —Jim grinning, Marcia looking more haggard, more than a little sad, as if she knew what fate awaited her.

But the next time Jim brought Sis back to his place, after the theater, all the pictures of Marcia were gone, even the portrait. In its place was a Matisse interior. Sis had never asked Jim about this, even after all their years together. But she had wondered. Maybe he had given the portrait to the Hochschilds, or even to his parents.

Jim's parents had "approved" of Marcia. His family was richer; hers was German, a cut or two above the Melmores socially. Marcia had been a talented musician, a cellist, with a promising career which she gave up to marry Jim when they were both very young. And intelligent—most of Jim's interesting books were Marcia's.

Sis had begun by despising Marcia's taste. Marcia liked Louis XV furniture. Marcia wore only diamonds and pearls. Soon after their marriage Jim had offered her Marcia's diamond-and-pearl earrings, but she had declined them. It would have been so much easier if Marcia had had a daughter. But all her jewelry was in the vault. Every three years when the insurance was renewed, Sis would see "Blue White Marquise Solitaire, Blue White Diamond Rivière, Black Pearl Necklace with Diamond Rondelles." She had paid no attention at first, but later on she had become obsessed by Marcia's jewelry. Jim had been annoyed that Sis wouldn't wear it. Someday he might find someone more appreciative.

One thing Sis envied Marcia was her relationship with Jim's family. Marcia called Jim's parents Mother Melmore and Father Melmore. Father Melmore in particular had loved Marcia. It was he who had been at the hospital with her when she died. Jim had been in bed with Sis.

In spite of all Jim's talk about family feeling, he really didn't want Sis to be close to his parents. The Melmores hardly ever came to stay, and when Jim visited them in Santa Barbara, he never invited Sis to go along. "They'd just bore you, Sis. What's the point? And they don't really want to visit us in Locust Valley, either. That would bore them just as much."

Sis knew that Jim had made his parents think that she was too snobbish to have them around. But there was nothing she could do about it—Jim did what he liked. She knew by now how touchy he was about everything Jewish. He had no close friends who were Jewish, no girlfriends, either—at least none she knew of. Of course, there was a lot she didn't know.

She learned that whenever Jim suddenly referred to a woman he'd seemed to like as a "slut," she was a girlfriend on her way out, and should be crossed off the list of extra women. Those girls! She hadn't wanted to know about any of them. He could have managed that, left her some dignity.

But the bills! Every few months when she went over the bills with Miss McMillan, she would get a shock. She always had to pretend that she knew about the mink shawl, the amethyst ring, the color television set—things like that were what he called "nickel and dime" presents. But why couldn't he be more discreet? Why on earth didn't he pay for those things out of his own account? Either he liked to humiliate her or he just didn't care. She never said a word. But every month she feared that accounting. Most of all, she dreaded the day Jim would buy someone something substantial.

Then there were the dinner parties that she'd planned with such care—to give Jim everything she thought he demanded: beautiful women, important men, perfect food, marvelous wine, entrancing conversation (or the kind of music he liked), and she would glance over at Jim, to draw pleasure from his approval, and—oh, God! his hand was on the knee of the girl next to him. That girl—was that the girl who was going to replace her?

Of course, Jim used to be jealous, too. That was the thing about her riding. Jim had been very proud of her nerve and skill as a rider, she knew that. But it had drawn her into a world where he couldn't follow her, a world she thought of as one of physical camaraderie and simple relationships, but which he viewed as full of shadowy, unclassifiable figures, out of his control.

She had fought quietly over this territory, losing inch by inch, until suddenly, the year Sarah was thirteen, Jim had said to her, quite casually: "Sis, why don't you ever go out hunting with Sarah? You don't ride at all anymore." And she had realized, with a drop of her heart, that he didn't care. He wasn't jealous anymore.

But all the same Jim had loved her too. She knew it. "Sis, you're the only broad in the world with any class." "Sis, I wish I could live a million years, just so I could get a real good look at you." "Sis, you're the only one I could never get tired of."

Jim had always wanted her to be above the whisper of a rumor. He wanted her to be cool and perfect and untouchable. But he had liked his own way of having fun, which was coarse and lowdown and raunchy, sometimes outrageous. Sis liked having fun too, but he didn't like their two worlds to meet.

Sometimes, she wondered how much fun it all was. More often than not, when Jim came home late—so late she'd be having her breakfast—with his eyes all bleary and his suit looking as if he'd slept on the beach, he would give her a hug and say, "Oh, God, Sis, what a dreary evening I had. Oh, Christ, was I bored!" And go to bed for thirty-six hours.

Well, that might be part of a man's life. She could have accepted that willingly, if only Jim could have talked to her about his business, his daily triumphs and defeats and worries. She had to read the *Wall Street Journal, Barron's,* and the financial pages of the *Times,* and all of it in secret, because it made him angry. He would never tell her a thing.

"You think I want to come home to Helen of Troy and talk about 'my day at the office' like some little clerk? Come on, leave me some illusions."

Or when he was tired and surly, "Shut up, for Christ's sake, Sis. You worried something's going to happen to your meal ticket?"

He wanted her to be unique, unattainable, and incurious. He wanted to be mysterious and omnipotent, to lead many lives. So all the time she had to follow his career like a spy, trying sometimes to tell him, but never succeeding, how feverishly interesting she found the workings of his mind, his manipulations, his maneuverings. But of course she was never an equal partner—never a partner at all.

He was a real man, anyway. Maybe she just wasn't a real woman. She had grown up in a house of women, Papa a gentle shadow. All the tall, courtly beaux, treating her as if she were so fragile she would break in the real world. Her

sisters' husbands, spoiled, silly, petulant, self-pitying old boys
—and promiscuous, too, always trying to make love to her in
the end.

No, she was lucky, no matter what anyone thought. And
if Jim had lived, who knows, they might have had a tranquil,
even happy, old age together.

Now she had traveled back to that scene out by the poolhouse in the sun. Jim in his striped T-shirt and bathing
trunks. His hair thinner, his belly bigger, than in her photograph, very tan, his curious light eyes wrinkled up, his
voluptuous mouth loose. He had just realized what had
happened. Realized. Couldn't believe it. Believed it. She
was holding his head in her arms. The blood on the neck—
just a little spot. It didn't look bad—as if he'd cut himself
shaving. . . . A little blood running down his neck onto the
green and purple shirt. Or was she imagining it? There was
very little blood, actually. And in the end what did he do
but smile?

"Well—I'll—be—damned." It was a hoarse whisper. "Give
me a kiss, little bird." More blood on her than on him. "My
little girl. You've been a good girl, Sister."

But that was the Jim nobody understood. The love and
generosity underneath his roughness. It ran through and
through, and it was right there at the end.

He had always had this gift for reducing things quickly to
their essential components. Now the essential was time. How
much time? Thirty-five minutes? Call the doctor, and take
the helicopter into the city. Fifteen minutes? Call the doctor,
an ambulance, some first aid. Five minutes. Commands and
instructions for the future. One minute. Tell your wife you
love her. That she's been a good wife.

She didn't want to think about the children, but the room
was full of ghosts. She really hadn't understood about Jimmy.
He was more like her, she supposed. At least he had nothing
in common with Jim. Emotional, secretive, moody, imagina-
tive, brilliant—a poet, she thought, and he might be a good
one—though a dunce in school.

"Oh, why argue about it, Sis? That's the bottom line, after all," Jim had said. Jimmy had such a craving for affection. "Weak," Jim said. Yes, probably he was weak too. Jim didn't believe in spoiling children. (That is, not until Sarah.) "You're just going to ruin him, Sis, letting him lie around in your room all day looking at ladies' magazines and writing so-called poetry. You've already made him a fairy by the time he's seven."

Of course, Jim had had very little time for Jimmy when he was young. Occasionally, Jim would decide to take Jimmy on a trip by himself, from which the boy would return white-faced and speechless. He never spoke about those trips to her. When she asked Jim what they had done together, he would say something vague: "Trying to make a man of the little guy."

The only description she remembered was of a trip to Chicago to the slaughterhouse. "Any other kid would have eaten it up," said Jim.

And her closeness to Jimmy had evaporated under that constant barrage.

"Don't hang around your mother's room, Jimmy. You're making a goddamn bore of yourself." "Don't write your mother so often, Son. You just worry her." Or "Why don't you read the newspapers, Son, find out about what's going on in the world. Otherwise you're better off outdoors. Take a swim. Play some tennis. It's not as if you're a scholar."

On and on. And then school after school. The fantasy of Groton or St. Paul's had been dropped. It would have to be a military academy.

Jimmy had come to his mother's room a week before he was supposed to leave for school. They hadn't had a real talk in months, it seemed. His hair was clipped down to his skull, which made his ears stick out even more, and he looked pathetic and desperate.

"Mummy, I swear this is the last thing I'll ever ask you to do for me. Please don't let me down, Mother. You've got to stop me from going to that school. I'll do anything else you want. Anything. Or if there's nothing I can do, I'll go away and you won't ever have to see me again. But I'll need a little money—about seventy-five dollars anyway. Because Dad's right. I can't do anything. I can't do anything at all. But, if I had a little money, I could go away somewhere where nobody had ever heard of you or Dad, and I know I could find something simple to do. And it wouldn't matter. But if you send me to that school, I'll kill myself. I swear to you, I'll kill myself!"

Sis had thrown down her needlepoint and hugged him. "Jimmy darling, please, baby, don't talk that way, I know you're exaggerating! We all hate going away from home."

Jimmy shook his head sadly. "No, Mummy, I don't hate going away from home."

"Darling, that's a terrible thing to say. You know how all of us here love you and will miss you. And you know Dad chose this school for you because he looked at dozens of schools and decided this would suit you the best."

"He did not, Mother. He looked for the most cruel school he could find, to punish me."

"Baby, that's crazy. You're his son. He loves you."

"Mother, everybody doesn't love their sons. He certainly doesn't love me and you know it. Mummy, please, you're my last hope. Please don't tell me the same lies Nanny does. Can't we just talk about the truth, for once?"

Sis put her head in her hands. "Darling, everything you say is terrible, just terrible. I know it's not true about Daddy, I promise it's not. Jimmy darling, I don't doubt you're feeling that way now. Listen, sweetheart, give me time, give me some time. Suppose I could persuade Daddy to wait a little bit? Wait till next year?"

But Jim had been furious. "How the hell do you think I feel, Sis? Do you ever give any consideration to my feelings? Now you're telling me he's a sneak and a coward on top of everything else, and you're as much as saying he should get a reward for it! I suppose you're so involved in your own social life that you've never given a thought to what it means to a man like me—having a son who can never succeed him. How it fills me with shame!

"You've taken me for quite a ride, Sis, you know? I really fell for all that shit—those old southern families, and their quality and character. It's not a mistake I'd have made if I'd gotten a good look at those sisters of yours! A regular genetic cesspool!

"Now let me tell you something. The men in my family may have been poor, but they were men and they kept right on climbing up the ladder; someone might put a foot in their face, but they kept right ahead. There's never been a male in my family anything like that boy. He should have been a rabbi, for God's sake, that's all I can say. Now, Sis, if you ever come to me whining about Jimmy again—Sis, I've spoiled you, I know I've been weak with you—but I always thought you were on my side. But, Sis, one more word about Jimmy, and you'll find out what it's like when someone crosses me!"

Jimmy never asked her any questions. He said nothing more to his mother until the day before he was due to leave for school. Then, when she was walking around the garden with the dogs and her basket of flowers, he came and walked with her for a while, in silence, the way he always used to.

Finally, he said, "I don't blame you, Mummy. I know you can't help it. And Dad treats you in just as beastly a way as he treats me. But you did choose him."

"I love him, Jimmy."

"Do you?"

"Of course. I love you, too. Very, very much."

He stared at her for a while. "Did he who made the lamb make thee?" he said. "Mummy, I'm going to miss you all my life."

They'd hugged and kissed and she'd thought he'd resigned himself after all. But that night he'd disappeared.

There were the discreet calls to friends. And then the increasingly urgent ones to the police.

"Probably the kid's gone off on a hike. You know kids today. No sense of time."

But after twenty-four hours the local police were read a lesson and the Governor was consulted. Sis didn't know what to do. She didn't want to tell Jim about Jimmy's threat— she was afraid it was exactly the sort of thing that would make Jim harder on the boy when he was found. And she was sure they would find him. The police were sparing no efforts now. They were picking up every hitchhiker; every boy near Jimmy's age without proper identification was questioned. Of course it was more difficult because Jim would tolerate no publicity, so no description could be given out.

On the third evening Jimmy was found. He was lit up by the headlights of a police car as he was walking along slowly, a little off the road, weaving a bit. He tried to run, but stumbled and fell, and hallelujah, who was it but Jimmy Melmore! He said so, straight away, but he pleaded to be left alone. He wasn't doing any harm, he said. He wasn't drunk, just hungry and thirsty and dead tired.

The captain of police had scrambled out of bed to deliver the boy personally to Mr. Melmore. They had driven up to the house just after midnight. Jim was in his wrapper and slippers. Sis had been standing a little behind him. Jimmy dragged himself along behind Captain Rizzuto. Jimmy wouldn't look at her. He kept his eyes on his feet.

"You'll see I know how to take care of my friends," Jim had said, shaking the captain's hand. He didn't say a word to Jimmy. He scarcely seemed to notice him.

"Jimmy," Sis said. Something prevented her from kissing or hugging him. She couldn't. Not in front of Jim. "You really ought to go straight to bed. You look so exhausted. But I'm sure you need something to eat, first."

"The boy should go straight to bed," Jim said. "We'll be starting early tomorrow. We need to be at the airport by nine o'clock."

"Tomorrow?"

"Well, naturally tomorrow, Sis. Jimmy's already a day late for school. And I'll have to take him myself, evidently, since he can't be trusted, and I haven't time for any more complications."

Jimmy didn't say a word. He just walked upstairs, his eyes averted. And the next day he flew west with his father.

Jimmy didn't kill himself, but he was sent home within three weeks. And then it was school after school, and drugs, delinquency, God knows what—until that call in the middle of the night. And Jimmy was dead in a cheap room down on Avenue A, his arms full of needle marks. Nineteen years old.

And there was his face, in the little shrine by her bed. Sixteen maybe. Big eyes, big ears, crooked nose, and crooked smile. Sarah on the other side.

Mrs. Melmore got up and, contrary to her habit, took a sleeping pill. She was going to think about Sarah. She was going to think about nothing but Sarah. But not right now.

She had made up her mind she was not going to let her last child walk away into darkness. She had come to Paris intending somehow to bring Sarah home. But the Sarah she had seen today—dear heaven, she'd never expected that! She had never seen Sarah so crazy, not even in the hospital.

The year before, when Sarah had asked if she could visit her friend Lavinia Talbot in Surrey, it had seemed like a safe step, even a step forward. Lavinia was one of the few friends from school Sarah kept in touch with. Mrs. Melmore liked the girl, she seemed to have a happy marriage, it would do Sarah good. Lavinia and David Talbot were interested in art. The plan had been that after two weeks in the country they would go to Paris to see the "fabulous" Picasso exhibit, then to Rome, where David's sister lived, and then on to Athens—Lavinia's cousins had chartered a boat. Sarah wasn't very keen on the idea of the boat. She didn't like strangers, and said she might come home from Rome.

After a few days Mrs. Melmore had called Sarah at Lavinia's place in the country. Sarah had sounded a little impatient. When she called a week later, Lavinia said Sarah
had gone out for a walk, but she would tell her to call her
mother. Sarah never called back. Mrs. Melmore had to fight
the impulse to call again. Sarah probably disliked her mother
hovering over her, treating her like an invalid. She supposed
that might even be a good sign.

When another week passed, she felt impelled to call. She
got no answer. Of course, they must have left already for
Paris! She didn't even have an address. Sarah had said she
would let her know, and she'd forgotten to ask Lavinia.

When a few weeks had gone by, she decided Sarah must
have gone on that cruise. How long was it supposed to be?
Ten days? Well, sick or not, Sarah was very inconsiderate not
to let her know. Lavinia, too. Of course, she had no idea how
much Lavinia knew about Sarah's "nervous breakdown."
Still, even if Sarah hadn't mentioned it, Lavinia must have
noticed that her friend was very fragile.

And then one morning she had gotten a call from Mr.
Gilchrist at the bank. He had received a letter from Sarah.
Sarah had asked him to transfer her income in the future to
their Paris branch; she intended to stay in Paris indefinitely.
Mr. Gilchrist made this statement in a neutral tone.

"What ad-duh-duh-dress?" Sis thought she had left that
nervous stammer behind her, with her childhood.

"I beg your pardon?"

"What address did she give you in Paris?"

"She writes that as yet she has no apartment. She asked
that all letters and funds be sent to a mailing address, care of
Advent, 10 rue Minou, Paris."

"Telephone number?"

"The place she is staying has no telephone. I think I should
read you the letter in full, Mrs. Melmore."

She hardly listened. The letter sounded much more businesslike than she would have imagined.

"I thought I should call you. Naturally, we'll send you a Xerox of the letter."

"Yes, I see. Well it comes as a surprise to me; I had no idea she intended to stay abroad so long. She'll probably call me soon. Sarah's so—absent-minded."

"So we'll act on these instructions?"

"Sarah's not a minor."

"No-o-o."

She had hung up the phone and called Lavinia. Still no response. Good God, she'd been mad to let her daughter stay with this irresponsible ninny.

But the very next day Lavinia Talbot called her. Called Sarah, that is—but talked to her.

"What on earth have you done with Sarah?" Mrs. Melmore was trying not to sound too shrill.

"Sarah's not with you?"

"Of course not. She was supposed to be with you. Where is she?"

There was a long silence on the phone. Then Lavinia said, "I'm very sorry, Mrs. Melmore. I was worried about Sarah too. You see, we just got back and she's left most of her things at our house. I mean we were just going to hot countries so—"

"But where is she now? I got some insane message about Paris. What does it mean?"

Again Lavinia hesitated. "Actually," she said, "Paris was the last place we saw Sarah."

"You left her!"

"Just a minute, Mrs. Melmore. Let me think. . . . Okay. We had planned to be in Paris about a week. Well, the second day Sarah took some film to be developed, and she met—she met this woman who apparently was a very good photographer, and had a lot of interesting ideas." Again she paused.

"I guess I'd better tell you the whole thing. We weren't getting along very well at all. I mean David and Sarah. And

I was sort of in the middle. Sarah's changed a lot, you know, and she can be awfully difficult. Do you think, maybe, she's sick? But, you see, God knows when David is going to get this much time off again, so he resented—"

"Yes."

"Actually, after she met this woman, the photographer, she said she was going to move out of our place to a place this woman told her about that was much nicer and much cheaper. I asked her to stay and so forth, but she said no, she couldn't get along with David—which she certainly couldn't. Sarah's awfully different now. And I said what about her things and everything? And she said, never mind, she'd pick them up sometime. And, well, if it hadn't been for David, I'm sure it would have worked out between the two of us but—"

"So you just abandoned her with a stranger in Paris."

"Oh, that's honestly not fair, Mrs. Melmore. Sarah decided she wanted to leave us."

"You didn't even try to meet this woman? Find out anything about her? Her name even?"

"All I know is that she's a photographer. Oh, and she's not French, she's Czech or something. I'm sorry. I honestly don't even remember that—maybe that's not even right. I'm really sorry, I don't even know what photo lab they met at."

Later the postcard came—a banal postcard of Paris. All it said was, "Hi, from Sarah." It was definitely Sarah's handwriting. She had studied it carefully.

Mrs. Melmore had written letter after letter begging her daughter to call her, to tell her about her life, her friends.

Every few weeks came the ugly postcard. The Eiffel Tower. The Arc de Triomphe. Sacré-Coeur. Notre-Dame. "Hi, from Sarah."

Mrs. Melmore's letters grew more frantic. She wrote her daughter that she must see her, or at least talk to her on the phone. She didn't want to sound threatening—she had a terrible fear that Sarah might disappear altogether. She waited now for each post, started at each ring of the phone.

She felt nailed in place. If she went away, even for a day, that might be the day Sarah's call came.

Then she had gone over Sarah's accounts. Sarah's income was really colossal—Jim had never changed his will. Funny, for someone so meticulous. Before Sarah left for Europe, she had seemed totally uninterested in her money. Her income simply accumulated, gathering interest. So what was Sarah doing with all that money? Or rather, since Sarah was such a very rich girl, what was someone else doing with all that money?

Mrs. Melmore considered her alternatives. A private detective? She only knew about them through thrillers. If those books were the least bit accurate, private detectives were a money-mad, corrupt, sex-crazed lot. That was the very last thing Sarah needed in her life; it was out of the question.

But what could she do? She knew she must do nothing to draw attention to Sarah in any way. If Sarah was frightened or put under too much pressure, God knows what might happen! Sarah might be locked up for good!

So she must tell no one, and derive what comfort she could from Sarah's unsatisfying scrawls.

But finally, after months of anxiety and distress and scores of unanswered letters, it had all been too much. Too much time had gone by. Too much time. Mrs. Melmore had composed a wire to Sarah, faintly ominous in tone, demanding a meeting as soon as possible, if "steps" were not to be taken. To her surprise and relief, she received an answer a few days later. She was given a date, a place, and a time. But the cable wasn't even signed. And the date was the following Sunday. My gosh, that gave her no time at all. Never mind. Juliet Sands, her secretary, could pull everything together fast. Cecil would come with her to Paris. Williams was an extravagance—she didn't really need a driver, but he was on her side. It would give her someone to talk to, someone to support her, or if Sarah wanted a little trip . . .

Williams had been her legacy from one of her old lady

friends, Alison James; he had been Alison's chauffeur and butler, although in Alison's house, after her dandified father had died, everything was focused on the garden, and "butler" seemed perhaps too formal and limited a designation for the office Williams filled.

Sis had always liked Williams. She found him tactful, discreet, and, in a funny way, a gentleman. "If I were a servant," Sis thought, "I would try to be a servant like Williams."

When Alison had died, quite suddenly, it had been Williams who, together with Sis, had arranged the funeral. She had asked him about his plans for the future.

"I've spent my life in service, madam. Old Mrs. James. I came to her when I was quite a boy. Then Mr. James. Then Miss James. They were my life."

"And I know how much you meant to them, Williams." Sis hesitated. "If you ever wanted to work for me . . . I know you love the gardens, Williams, and that is so rewarding. . . ."

"No, madam. That was only because of Miss Alison—Miss James, that is. I'm not a gardener, madam." Williams stared into the distance. "I was always the chauffeur, madam. Everything else was piecework. Mrs. James didn't trust anyone else to drive her. That was my education, madam."

"It's too early to make plans, I know. But, Williams, if you ever wanted to be my chauffeur . . ."

"Madam."

"Oh, Williams, but do think it over. It isn't the same quiet life. . . . You know it."

"Madam, I've thought it over."

"But take your time, do. This must have been such a shock. And your responsibilities . . ."

"The James family was my responsibility, madam. Miss James was the last of them."

And so it was settled. Sis found Williams even better than she had hoped. Somehow, without a word, he could convey to her his admiration and approval, when she was looking particularly well, his sympathy and concern when she was tired or sad. The things he said were monosyllabic or banal, but they conveyed an enormous amount to Sis. And, unlike the other servants, Williams had never shown the least interest in Jim.

So many of the nice servants had left after Jim's death. Daniel—well, naturally, she didn't need a valet, but she missed Daniel. Paulette. She was sorry about Paulette. Paulette felt bored and unappreciated—Mrs. Melmore ate so little, and entertained so much less; Jim used to talk to Paulette for hours about sauces. Paulette didn't think Jim was fat; she thought he had a "fine figure." She wouldn't follow any of the orders Jim's doctors had given, even when Sis begged her.

"If you don't like what your doctor says, find another doctor, eh, Paulette?" Jim would say. And both of them would laugh. Sis was always "the enemy" with Jim and the servants. And with Sarah—he and Sarah used to have secrets behind her back as if she were an ogre.

Oh, my Lord! Sarah! She'd had her wish and it was like one of those frightening fairy stories. She'd gotten her wish, a meeting with Sarah, and what a nightmare! Sarah must have stopped taking her pills. That was evident.

But, dear heaven, how could she have been such a fool this morning! She'd actually run away. It was the shock. She just hadn't been prepared. She had assumed that probably Sarah had come to hate and despise her, the way she'd come to hate and despise Jim, but that figure, that creature, looking as if it had come up from hell on a visit. . . . How could she have turned her back on her? She should have followed Sarah, pleaded with her. She didn't have the kind of pride Jim had. She should have told her over and over how much she loved her, made every kind of fool of herself. Found out about this Czech woman, where Sarah lived, what sort of people she was seeing . . .

And now—well, she'd have to start all over again. If it

meant living here in Paris, she'd live here in Paris. She would put up with Sarah's rejections. She would haunt her. She would beg and plead, until she wore Sarah down. Nothing else in the world had any value, only Sarah. For Sarah she would pay any price. "I will pay any price," she said out loud. Then wondered what she meant. Financial? Emotional? Well, both naturally.

This is just what she didn't want to be thinking about. She was working against that pill. She wanted to be clearheaded in the morning.

She began to do what she'd been taught to do. She drew a long breath in through her nose, and then exhaled, saying the word, "Nerim. Nerim. Nerim. Nerim . . ."

4

An Unexpected Call

THE PHONE must have been ringing for a while. Mrs. Melmore was groggy. She picked it up.

"Yes?" She'd been in the middle of such a strange dream—a dream about Sarah.

"Is this Madame Melmore speaking?" It was a woman's voice with a funny accent.

"Yes, this is Madame Melmore."

"Madame Melmore, you must forgive me for calling you at this late hour of the night, but I have a question I must ask you."

"Yes?" The woman's voice was rough, and rather ugly. Maybe it was the accent. Balkan, it sounded.

"Is your daughter with you tonight, Madame Melmore?" Mrs. Melmore put her hand to her head. God, why had she taken that pill?

"Who is this I'm talking to?"

"Really, it doesn't matter who I am. I have this one question I must ask you. And it's urgent. Yes or no?"

"I'm afraid I don't want to talk about my daughter to someone who won't give me their name."

"Let's say I'm a friend of hers. Obviously. Names don't matter. But I've become very concerned. If you tell me there's nothing to concern me, well, that's that."

"Anyone close to my daughter is a concern of mine. Please tell me who this is?"

There was a silence. Then, "She's not with you."

Mrs. Melmore paused, knitting her brows. There was a click as the phone was hung up in her ear.

Mrs. Melmore was drenched with sweat, and shaking. She got up, threw open the double windows, and let the hot night air creep around her. She felt like walking, but whoever it was might call again. She went into the living room and opened a split of champagne—another kindness of the management. She had never liked champagne. She must ask Cecil to make up a mess of bullshots for her in the morning.

She looked out over the place de la Concorde toward the Seine. A river of blood. And this was the abattoir from which that blood had flowed. But the river looked innocent, silver and bland, in the early-morning light. The streets were bleached, the shadows pale. Semicircles of dolmens. A boneyard. They killed people. The obelisk, a bone in a boneyard. Mrs. Melmore picked up the phone and ordered a carton of cigarettes and a pack of cards.

When Cecil came to peep tentatively in at her door, long past her usual breakfast hour, the sun was blazing into the living room and Mrs. Melmore was still sitting by the window, smoking and playing patience.

5

Mrs. Melmore
Visits Her Bank

WHEN MRS. MELMORE ENTERED the bank, there was always a discreet, almost imperceptible ripple. It started with the doorman, spread through the cashiers; even the money stirred gently, as people tried not to stare. The American side of the bank, the French side of the bank—on paper so amicable, in reality so suspicious—seemed to draw together in the space of her visit into an actual *entente cordiale*.

The two men who had the right to address her personally hurried out. Mr. Northrop, who handled her account, "My dear Mrs. Melmore! What a pleasure! And a surprise! How well you're looking!" Monsieur Pelissier, who didn't handle her account, kissing her hand, playing the courtier. They exchanged insincere courtesies with each other. "My French friend." "*Mon cher collègue.*"

Finally, the miniature drama over, Mrs. Melmore found herself seated in Mr. Northrop's little paneled office, with a glass of Vichy water and lime. She could tell he was dying for a good chat. Mr. Northrop's father had been in the consular service—not in England or France, alas, but in more obscure and intemperate climes where "no one one ever heard of showed up, except in the most sordid circumstances." An only child, he had been educated, for the most part, abroad and spoke five languages, though without much pleasure. He had vaguely English clothes, a New England wife, and two sons, whose pictures dominated his desk.

"Mrs. Melmore, you won't be staying here in Paris in all this heat? It's absolutely unprecedented! You must be surprised I'm here, but I passed up my little 'summer' this year. Angela's been worried about her mother. Nothing serious; I think she'll last for years. Good stock. But I know Angela longed for a month in the States. It'll be good for her, poor girl. But what a summer to choose! They say there's never been anything like it! Not in this century! I only hope your place in Locust Valley—your beautiful gardens—"

"Oh, well, of course it's a wasteland. . . . My men are losing their minds."

"It will have to break soon, I suppose. Cigarette?"

"No thanks."

"These weeks, I always think Paris will be empty. Certainly, none of *my* people. But would you believe it? Old Mrs. Angleton came in last Tuesday and tried to cash a check for twelve thousand dollars! Thank God I was here. You can imagine how *they* would have treated her. My mother always told me that Mr. and Mrs. Angleton were the best-looking couple she'd ever seen. Of course he was a first-rate sailor too, you know—he won the America's Cup twice. The story is she used to roller-skate around the house in Brookline.

"Poor old Mrs. Angleton never really took in everything that's happened. Every once in a while, she forgets she's not living back in the twenties. Goes on a spree! Well, I told her there was some trouble about exchange, took her across for tea at the Ritz, put a call through to her son (at my expense, of course) and got the whole thing straightened out. That son of hers—not at all the same type. Not the fellow his father was.

"Then on Wednesday, who should come in but old Mrs. Devereaux. Ninety-three years old—can you believe it? Glasses a foot thick—she could hardly recognize me! And almost stone deaf! Tragic, with her passion for music. And still batting around Europe like a schoolgirl! She's off to Salzburg for the festival.

"Do you know what she said to me?" He doubled up with laughter. "I said, 'How are things in Northeast, Mrs. Devereaux?' 'Very tiresome, Jake,' she said. 'I was compelled to wait until my daughter's seventieth birthday party.' 'That must have been very gala!' I said, shouting of course. 'Gala!' she said. 'It was more like a wake. That girl has never learned to give an adequate party,' she said. 'That girl' is seventy years old! What a character!" He laughed some more.

"And now you, Mrs. Melmore. The apex of my unusually social week. Frankly, most of the people I see these days are those dreadful hippies living on trust funds." He paused. "I only hope there is some small way in which I may be of service to you."

Mrs. Melmore preserved her sweet faint smile. "Oh, Mr. Northrop, you just can't imagine how glad I am you're here. I'm an absolute idiot. I flew over from London, just on impulse, and I left my address book behind. I know you handle Sarah's account. It's so silly—I remember her address, but not her telephone number. I'm sure you have it, of course."

Mr. Northrop's face went through several changes of expression, but he only said, "Yes, yes, of course. I'll let you know in a jiffy."

He rang a bell. "I've never had the pleasure of meeting the young lady myself, unfortunately."

A girl entered, he spoke to her. She vanished as quietly as she had appeared.

"You're still at the Crillon, I imagine?"

"Oh, yes. I'm not very adventurous."

"The service hasn't gone downhill too much, I hope? It has everywhere, of course, but that should be one of the last bastions."

"No, no. I'm very comfortable."

The girl reappeared with a folder. Mr. Northrop put on his glasses and read it through carefully.

"Hmm, hmm, oh dear, I suspected as much. That's what I was afraid of, Mrs. Melmore. The only address we have for your daughter is a mailing address. No telephone at all, I'm afraid. Care of Advent, 10 rue Minou. That's been for almost

a year. She seems to have an account at the central branch of
the Crédit Lyonnaise. I must say she deposits her checks
very promptly. No problem there. It's a bit of a bother for
you, I'm afraid, in case she's out of town. Young people, of
course—they don't think of telephones and so on. Would
you like me to send someone around?"

"No, no," said Mrs. Melmore rising. "I really must stop
by, in any case. But, Mr. Northrop, you've been an angel, and
I'll be in touch. Maybe you and I will be able to find an
oasis in the Sahara where we can cool off."

Mr. Northrop blushed and chuckled. He followed her to
the door. He noticed she moved without any appearance of
haste, but yet so swiftly that that cad Pelissier didn't have a
chance to slobber over her again.

Well. He'd wondered about that daughter himself. He'd
have to ask around a bit. "Hippies with trust funds." He
could have bitten his tongue off.

6

Miss Milbanke
Engages in Espionage

MRS. MELMORE HURRIED BACK to the Crillon. Even though
Harry was standing by, she hated being away from the telephone. She could have slapped Cecil this morning when she
came in with that self-congratulatory smile, saying she had
told the switchboard not to put any calls through. Of course,
the phone calls had turned out to be nothing but garbage,
except darling Harry, whom she had asked to rush over.
What an exercise in futility it had all been! And now that
old fool Northrop would be gossiping about Sarah to everyone in town.

Harriet was sitting in the living room, looking down over the place de la Concorde, sketching on her little artist's pad. She raised her eyebrows.

"Nothing, Harry, nothing at all. Same mailing address I have already. And a lot of old-lady chat."

"Nothing here, Sis. Countess Dragtail heard you were in town. In and out, I said. An awful impertinent newspaper fellow—he wanted to know if you thought couture was dead. I told him where to get off."

Oh no! thought Mrs. Melmore. Oh, well, what's the difference now?

"It's hell," she said. "I can't tell them to screen my calls."

"What about what's-her-name? She seems dying to answer the phone. Very much underfoot."

"Oh, poor Cecil. I was unbelievably cross with her this morning, that's why. But never mind. Look—the first thing, as I see it, is just go on over to rue Minou. See what's there."

"Right-o. I looked it up. It's not in what you'd call a very grand neighborhood. Shall we go?"

"I'm in a dreadful quandary. I want desperately to go. On the other hand, if I go, and, God willing, Sarah's there—if she's Advent herself, I mean—she probably won't answer at all, if she sees it's me. God knows, she was unequivocal— never wanted to lay eyes on me again. And that woman who called, well, it may all be nothing. . . . God knows, Sarah's crazy enough so she'd have nothing but crazy friends. But if that's the woman Lavinia was talking about, the Middle-European photographer—and I'm sure it was—I mean how many Czech women could Sarah know in Paris?—well, she sounded a really nasty customer.

"And the point is, she didn't know where Sarah was either. But anyway she just might be at rue Minou. And she just might know what I look like. She sounded mean as a hornet, but she might talk to you. You see, you look so much—"

"Don't rub it in," said Harriet.

"Honestly, Harry, I was going to say 'brighter.' But if she's there, d.v., she might see you. She might talk to you."

Harriet considered. "I'll do it any way you want, Sis. Any way you think's best. Look here, I'm no Talleyrand. All I can do is try not to put my foot in it. And I can't say I have any special gift for the mentally ill. I may be off my rocker myself, but that doesn't give me any more sympathy for the other ones."

"Oh, Harry, I do trust you. Just use your instincts, and I know you'll do the right thing. Can you explain to Williams where this place is? Do you need a map?"

"What do I need Williams for? Of course I can find it."

"No, no. You must take him, or I'll be worried about you, too. Harry, please, please. Fast as you can. And I'll be saying my prayers every minute."

"And if it's Mr. or Miss Advent, I say I'm the aunt? Get in touch with and so forth?"

"Yes, yes."

Harriet paused in the doorway.

"Where's Sarah again?" Mrs. Melmore stared. "Idiot, I mean her picture. That's the most recent?" She examined the photograph in the light. "She's a good-looking girl, all right, but not a Sarah Brooks, is she? Well, I think I'll know her, anyway."

It was one-thirty. Cecil had been banished, sulking, to her quarters. Mrs. Melmore was prowling behind the door of her suite, jumping at every noise. At last she heard Harriet's tread in the hall, flung open the door, and with her enormous gaze knew, before she could even shake her head, that Harriet had not seen her daughter.

"Nothing?"

"Well, only a little something. May I come in?"

"Yes, yes, of course. She's not there?"

"I'm pretty sure not. I'm afraid it's all awfully unsatisfactory."

"But the people? Did you see anyone in the apartment?"

Harriet shook her head again. "I had the feeling there

might have been someone there, but let me tell you about it. First of all, it's not such a bad neighborhood. I had it mixed up in my head, or else—they do a lot of redevelopment here, you know. They have lots of those hideous-looking apartment complexes that seem to breed like rabbits in the States."

"Is that what it is?"

"More or less, yes. Very middle class—but clean. Lots and lots of tenants, of course. When that chauffeur drove me up to the building, I had a feeling I was being watched. Watched very closely. I'm not psychic and God knows I'm not used to being stared at in the streets, but there's an experience, a definite feeling. You get it with animals, sometimes. They're watching you, before you see them, you know?"

Mrs. Melmore nodded, "Did you see—who?"

"No, I'm sorry. I just looked up at this great blind façade of windows, but I didn't see a thing. I'm sorry. You see, you should have gone yourself, Sis."

"No, no. Please go on."

"Inside there were dozens of names, of all the different tenants, but none of the boxes said 'Advent.' So I was in a quandary. There weren't any boxes without names on them, either. Oh, of course there was no Melmore. I didn't know what to do. I knew those people must pick up their mail somehow, but I didn't know whom to ask—there didn't seem to be anyone around."

"Heavens. What did you do?"

"Well, I just picked a name at random, 'Charcot,' because it was a name I knew, I guess, and they buzzed back. And I went up. It was the third floor. There was a woman standing at the door—about my age, I suppose. A real Madame Defarge. And, not surprisingly, not much pleased when she found I was a total stranger. First off she thought I was a tax snoop. You know how the French are. I just barged ahead—asked if she knew a group or a person called Advent.

"That opened the floodgates. I think she had hopes I was a spy for the landlord, or a health inspector. She thought I was English, of course—for some reason, the English still represent decency to some people over here. Anyhow, I didn't have to say another word. All these young people, coming in, going out, how many people lived there anyway? It was against the law! It wasn't fair to the other tenants! She had complained!

"I just let her talk, and asked were they very noisy? It wasn't that. Messy? No, though what that place looked like inside she couldn't imagine. Twenty people in a two-room apartment. Boys and girls, I said? You bet! She thought maybe it was a den of vice—some sort of bordello. Or else a terrorist lair. All the comings and goings.

"I asked if she knew their names, if she could describe them. Oh, they were nice enough looking, she said. Polite, when you talked to them. But you could just imagine what they were up to! She described a few. None of them sounded like Sarah, Sis. A lot of blondes. It seems she'd written three letters complaining to three different departments. No answer yet.

"I'd gotten the apartment number by then, the fourth floor, and after I'd talked to her, I just pretended to look very businesslike. I always have this little notebook I carry with me, so I wrote in it and I thanked her. Then I went and took the lift up. I knocked and rang, but I didn't get any answer. There wasn't any noise inside, but I had the same funny feeling that there was somebody there. I tried for a while, but then there seemed nothing to do, so I went back downstairs. The name on the door is 'Persson,' by the way. I looked up at that window, once I knew where it was, but there was no one looking out. The apartment really might have been empty. It's just a feeling I had. I'm sorry, Sis. It's not much."

"Oh, God, Harry—no, that's fantastic! I could never have figured all that out. Persson. That's good to know. We could look in the phone book, anyway. Twenty people! Do you think Sarah lives with twenty people?"

"No, really I don't, Sis. That woman is some sort of a

crackpot. I wouldn't pay any attention to her fanciful ideas. I imagine a couple of people live there, and the rest visit."

"Oh, Harry, that's marvelous of you! How intrepid! I could never have done all that." Mrs. Melmore gave her a hug and kiss. At least she had another tiny piece.

Part Three

REASONS
TO BE CAREFUL

1

Mrs. Melmore Meets
a Strange Young Lady

MRS. MELMORE LOOKED DOWN at her hands—the hands of a stranger. Ringless fingers. She hadn't really coveted all that big jewelry at first, it seemed a bit garish, but, as it had accumulated, it had become a kind of ballast, holding her in place, explaining who she was.

Now, instead of jewels, she had those dark glasses. She almost never wore dark glasses, considering them pretentious, except on the boat, or if one had an eye infection. She was becoming another woman, a more furtive, shabbier woman, ordering a Campari and Schweppes in the back row of an outdoor café. It had been so easy to resume her old habit: lighting a cigarette, taking a few puffs, stabbing it out, and then lighting another. What other bad habits?

It had come exactly a week after Harriet's visit to Advent—
the telephone call. It had been both more and less alarming
than she had feared. It was a girl's voice—not like the rough
voice from the middle of the night, but a "nice" voice. It
could almost have been English, except for those very subtle
differences in intonation.

"Is this Madame Melmore speaking?"

"Yes, yes. This is Madame Melmore."

"Madame Melmore, my name is Anna. I am a friend of
Sarah's."

"Yes," said Mrs. Melmore, breathless.

"I would like very much to talk to you about Sarah. I
think you will find our interests are exactly the same. I know
you are concerned about your daughter, and I think perhaps
I can help you."

"You're a friend of Sarah's," Mrs. Melmore repeated.

"Have you involved any of the authorities?"

Suddenly Mrs. Melmore's throat seemed to close up. This
wasn't a friend of Sarah's. It sounded more like what she had
read about kidnapers and ransom. She paused a long time.
What would be the smart thing to say? What was her best
chance? Finally she whispered, "No."

"I'm very glad. I believe that it's very much in your interest. I would like to suggest that if you and I were to meet
soon and talk, you will not have wasted your time, and it
would help us both. I do not like very much talking on the
phone."

"Where is Sarah?" asked Mrs. Melmore.

"Madame Melmore, I entreat you to follow my suggestion.
I will meet you at a place outside, any café of your choice,
and I will answer all the questions I can." Mrs. Melmore
held the phone away from her as if it were a snake. She must
be cool. She must be careful.

"Please, Madame Melmore, I do not know what you may
believe of me, but I assure you, we all want Sarah's good. I
can only beg you at this time not to call the police, but I

cannot prevent you. However, I assure you that we will all benefit, including Sarah."

"That's what they always say," thought Mrs. Melmore. "Don't call the police. Don't tell the authorities. Someone may get hurt. Dear God, how much money will they want and how fast can I get it?

"Tell me," she said, "is Sarah safe? What do you want?"

"Please to meet me, and I will explain."

"I must know, is Sarah safe?"

"Madame Melmore, these phones at your hotel are not very good. I want to talk to you, and as soon as possible."

Mrs. Melmore looked at her watch and found she could not read the hands. "I can meet you in half an hour," she said.

"Where would you like it to be? I, myself, would prefer it to be in an open-air café on one of the boulevards near your hotel—for your convenience. Is that possible? It would be good if you would sit in the back row."

Mrs. Melmore searched her mind and could only come up with the name of a place she had often walked past. The Café de Paris.

"Very well. In half an hour. Meanwhile, I beg you to talk to no one about this. I cannot prevent you, but it's truly in all our interests. That I promise you."

"How will I know you?"

"I will know you, Madame Melmore."

Mrs. Melmore put the phone down. If she were drenched with sweat after each of these phone calls, how would she deal with these people face to face? She wanted desperately to talk to Harry ("Always keep your troubles to yourself, Maud"), but Harry had only started home half an hour ago. She'd refused the car. She'd be walking and most probably stopping and shopping on the way. Harry would be an hour or more, at least. And there were things she must do, and do quickly and well. She mustn't think too much or imagine anything at all. Over and over in her head was running a rhyme from a children's fairy tale: "Be bold, be bold, but not too bold. Lest your heart's blood run cold."

She threw off the dress she was wearing, pulled off her jewelry (How did one dress to meet a kidnaper?—or whatever this person was?), sat at her desk almost naked, and wrote as legibly as she could a description of the telephone conversation and her plans. Then she sealed it in an envelope addressed to Miss Harriet Milbanke, sponged herself off, put on a simple black dress and her dark glasses. Thank God Cecil wasn't anywhere around. God knows what she would think. Mrs. Melmore never left this sort of mess.

Then she hurried downstairs, told the concierge that she wouldn't be needing Williams that afternoon, but please to ask Miss Milbanke, when she called, if she would come over as soon as possible. And to give her this letter and the key to her room.

She reached the bank just before closing time. She was very glad Mr. Northrop was nowhere to be seen. When she had called last week, with an idea she had had to regularize Sarah's income, he had been disgustingly eager to play detective. A large withdrawal would provoke all sorts of speculation. Well, thank God; he had left early. She cashed a check for ten thousand dollars, in francs; after that, she'd see. The doorman at the bank found her a taxi almost immediately. Of course, it was no distance at all.

Had it been more than half an hour? She might be late. She still couldn't seem to get the time straight. Her eyes must be failing along with the rest of her faculties. She didn't dare go to the ladies' room. She had a bottle of Valium in her pocketbook, but she was frightened to take anything. She didn't want her mind to be any more addled. She didn't dare order a stiff drink for the same reason. Another cigarette. Then, almost mindlessly, she reached into her purse, played with the bottle of pills a moment, turned it round about, round about, slipped open the top and fished out a Valium. One wouldn't hurt. One and a half. She didn't want to be hysterical, either. "Find a very calm place," she told herself and tried to remember her meditation.

One of these remedies must be working. She no longer felt such total panic. She'd been very quick getting here after all—she couldn't have been more than five minutes late. She stubbed out her cigarette and ordered another Campari and soda.

She looked around. At the café where she was sitting, there were only two tables that interested her—a young blond couple—honeymooners? That was a little out of date, she supposed—but whatever they did today. Anyway, completely wrapped up in each other. They were very good-looking, really, in an old-fashioned way. The girl appeared to be without makeup, wearing a blouse and skirt. The young man had his hair cut short, no jacket, but a shirt that was neat and clean, khaki trousers, and he was actually wearing socks. They even resembled each other—the high color, the clean-cut features. Could they be brother and sister? No, the rapport was too intense. Well, she was all for love. Particularly with good-looking young people.

The other table, much nearer to her, was inhabited by a French couple. Tiny, both of them, and hunched with age, dressed as if there were no such thing as this brutal heat— he, in suit and tie, she, in a navy blue silk dress and jacket, pearls (small, but real, she decided), and a little hat. What could they be doing in a place like this, at this time? She was not close enough and it was too noisy to eavesdrop. Every once in a while, the old woman put out her hand, which seemed permanently curled up (perhaps arthritic?) and touched or patted the hand of the old man. What tragedy was she seeing? What aftermath? The death of someone dear? But no, they didn't look sad. They looked utterly con- tained in the little capsule of intimate space they had made for themselves. God, if they knew how she envied them!

"Grow old along with me. The best is yet to be." What awful poems Papa had liked. She had learned that for his birthday—oh, a million years ago—probably the year she was nine. Ten had been "Evangeline." Well, a lot of it, anyway. Oh, the agony!

Now, she began to scan the streets. What would Advent look like? Blue jeans, *de rigueur*. What else would those people wear? Certainly not the high-heeled shoes and cinched belts with which the French girls made their blue jeans attractive.

It must be almost an hour now. The blond young man had gotten up, said goodbye to his girl, not all that affectionately, Mrs. Melmore decided. Perhaps they were fellow students after all, having a good chat about calculus. The girl stayed on, writing in her notebook. The old Frenchman had asked for the bill. Did she dare order another drink? She certainly didn't dare leave the table, though she wanted desperately to call Harriet. Or at least go to the loo. But she must not leave the table. She turned and ordered another drink. She was aware that someone had spoken to her, just as she finished giving her order.

The blonde girl with the notebook had stopped by her table. To ask her where the ladies' room was?

"*Je m'excuse,*" she said to the girl, who perhaps had not been talking to her after all.

"Madame Melmore," said the girl, "I'm Anna."

Mrs. Melmore was only aware that she didn't drop the glass, didn't burn herself, didn't utter a sound. In fact, she was speechless, and humiliatingly she took a last large gulp of her drink instead of replying.

"May I sit down?"

"Yes, yes, of course. I'm so terribly sorry. I was so . . ."

"Yes," said Anna coolly and rather loudly. "I was afraid you wouldn't remember me. It's been quite a few years, but of course I'll always remember you and your kindness to me and my mother. I hope I'm not disturbing you?"

"No, please. Please sit down. Would you like a drink?"

"A *citron pressé* would be very nice, if you have the time."

"Of course."

The girl's total composure helped to make Mrs. Melmore calm. Also, she had to admit, her good looks. She always felt safer with good-looking people. The girl, Anna, was even prettier than she had thought, young enough with that fair, flushed skin to appear even more charming without makeup. Her clothes were simple and strangely becoming, what a nice college girl of the fifties would have worn—that white blouse with the round collar, and the skirt a little too long.

"I'm very happy to see you again," said Mrs. Melmore, as the waiter brought the *citron pressé,* falling in with the conspiratorial game, then feeling a perfect fool. Were there spies all about?

"I hope we can have a good talk here," she said immediately, meaningfully.

"Yes," said Anna. "That was a little silly of me, but I thought maybe I had frightened you, which I didn't want to do."

"No. I wasn't frightened. Just surprised."

Anna had a very faint smile on her face, as if she knew better. "I realized after our conversation that you might have misinterpreted what I said. I will tell you what must be first on your mind. We wish only good for you and Sarah, Madame Melmore. My friends and I can be of the greatest help to you. More than anyone. We have been very close to Sarah, although she does not live with us. She shares an apartment with a woman named Wanda, who lives with her and looks after her."

"That's where she is now?"

"No, that's the point, Madame Melmore. We don't know where Sarah is now."

"Oh, my God." Mrs. Melmore's stomach seemed to fall through her pelvis and down and down.

"Please, just be calm and listen, Madame Melmore. You saw Sarah last Sunday at noon. You did meet? That is correct?"

"Yes. Why? What is this?"

"Was there anything unusual about your conversation?"

"*Unusual!*"

"This is important, Madame Melmore."

"Well, naturally— Oh, Lord. Well, unusually crazy."

"Sarah was under a great deal of pressure that day. Undoubtedly she was quite disturbed."

"Pressure? What do you mean? She was certainly disturbed. Now, please let me know— Pressure? What is it that's happening? Where *is* Sarah?"

"Madame Melmore, Sarah has not been out of touch so very long. It is only five or six days."

"Eight days," said Mrs. Melmore.

"That need not be so very unusual. We have checked everywhere. Hospital admissions, accident reports."

"What do you mean? Do you think Sarah's been hurt?"

"No, Madame Melmore. Nothing of that sort has happened to her. So please don't worry. In fact, I'm convinced that we will have some positive news of Sarah very soon. Even today."

Mrs. Melmore swallowed again and lit another cigarette.

"You must realize, Madame Melmore, that your coming here to Paris is only a very small interval in your daughter's life. Forgive me for being so blunt. This could have happened a hundred times before. In fact, it has happened before.

"Sarah could have been missing for a month, two months, three months, and over there in the United States, you would not have known. Who would have told you? So you would not have worried. It is only that you are unfortunately here in Paris on a specific evening when Sarah does not come home to Wanda. And you have an unpleasant experience. Do you see what I mean when I tell you that your worries are irrational?"

Mrs. Melmore looked at her naked hands and took long deep breaths, the way she'd been taught.

"Wanda," she said. "Wanda was the woman who called that night?"

"Yes, Wanda. Wanda is also a very emotional, not very well-balanced woman. Her whole life has become centered

on Sarah. She has great fears that you will persuade Sarah
to go home with you. Against her will, so to speak. Or—that
you would arrange to have her kidnaped."

"I? Good God, no. Never."

"I'm sure. Nevertheless, I'm trying to explain to you
Wanda's paranoiac mentality."

"Yes, yes, I see."

"Have you received any other calls regarding Sarah?"

"Only yours. Please tell me what this is all about?"

"Madame Melmore, I don't like talking to you while you
are so disturbed. Tell me, am I the kind of person who would
wish to harm your daughter?"

Mrs. Melmore looked straight into her glacial blue eyes.

"How on earth can I tell?" she said.

Anna gave a short laugh. "Correct," she said. "How indeed? That is the most intelligent thing to say." Her hand
immediately flew to her mouth, as if to stop the words. It
was her first uncontrolled movement.

"Forgive me," she said. "I realize you must be in great
travail. But I must ask you to listen to me carefully, so that
you will understand with your reason that we are the last
people in the world, the very last, to do anything but follow
your wishes regarding Sarah to the very—letter, yes?"

Mrs. Melmore understood nothing, but she put her chin on
her hand and gazed at the girl, wishing she could see through
those light blue eyes into whatever darkness they covered.

"First of all, I must ask you again—and I beg you to tell
me the truth—have you talked about this matter of your
daughter to anyone official?"

"No."

"Forgive me, I believe you, but the fact is it would be
very much the worst action to take—not just for us, but for
you and Sarah."

"Why?"

"Please try to listen carefully so that you will be logical.
You know the name Advent, obviously?"

"Yes."

"It is not anyone's last name, as you may have surmised. It is the name of something. Of a group of people with similar ideals. A very dedicated group of people from different countries.

"No, we are not extremists, Madame Melmore. Madame Melmore, please! I'm sorry, but I could see what you were thinking. We ourselves oppose acts of terrorism. They are useless actions that only serve to separate the peoples of the world.

"I will not deny that the underlying basis of our thought is Marxist, although the pseudo-Marxists you would associate with us would disown us immediately."

("My God, so they *are* terrorists!" thought Mrs. Melmore.)

"Per guides our thinking. He is what you would call a good man, Madame Melmore. This you need to know. He does not believe one should drink, smoke, take drugs, eat meat, or toxify the body in any way. We believe in health, physical and mental."

Mrs. Melmore, almost unconsciously, took another sip of her drink and another drag on her cigarette. She nodded her head.

"Also, though we live in what might be called a commune, we live by very strict sexual mores. Per is totally unsympathetic to any lack of sexual discipline."

Mrs. Melmore nodded again. She wondered if she looked improper. "Always trying to please the teacher," said a little voice inside her.

"I'm telling you all this because it's necessary. And to introduce Wanda. Wanda is a woman with a very tragic political history, and an unfortunate lesbian orientation." She glanced at Mrs. Melmore and said, "I should say immediately that Wanda's relationship with your daughter is not overtly homosexual."

"No, no, of course not," murmured Mrs. Melmore. Anna looked back at her, she felt, a little ironically.

"It is passionately maternal," said Anna. "And so, perhaps, often not wise."

("Passionately maternal, therefore not wise," the little voice repeated.)

"In any case, we had encountered Wanda long before we knew Sarah." She paused and drank the last of her *citron pressé*.

"Wanda was drawn to Per and his precepts, but we concluded, after letting Wanda visit us, that she would never be able to play a decisive role in Advent. Wanda can be extremely successful at ingratiating herself. But she was too aggressive, too personalistic, too unstable, too adventurist. Her sexual orientation counted against her, and above all it was evident that her real wish was to involve herself with Per on a personal basis, using her supposed ideological conversion as an excuse. All this, naturally, made Wanda unacceptable."

"The hell with Wanda," Mrs. Melmore thought. "What about Sarah?"

"Because Wanda was constantly burdening Per with threats of suicide, he allowed her to visit us at carefully regulated intervals. In my opinion, and it has been borne out, Wanda tries to manipulate people with her hysteria in order to gain power; and when she is given it, she becomes irresponsible and vindictive."

Again she paused, and this time she let out a long breath and swallowed. Mrs. Melmore had grown calm enough to notice the fact that Anna also seemed to be having trouble with her throat. "She's scared of me, too." She decided not to offer her another *citron pressé*.

"This brings us to Sarah, Madame Melmore. And to a mistake, a tragic mistake in judgment, for which I and I alone am to blame. We had not seen Wanda for several months, when she approached Per on the street and he, with his customary compassion, invited her to come and share our meal with us. She came in the evening and brought with her a young woman. No one is permitted to bring strangers into our group, particularly without warning. However, I talked to this young girl and immediately discovered that she was not a young lover or a spy, but a frightened, deeply disturbed girl. That young woman was your daughter.

"I talked to Sarah for over an hour that night, Madame Melmore. As you know, your daughter has culture and intelligence. She possesses a remarkable strength of character, and, when her mind is not clouded, the most lucid insight. I was interested in Sarah. I thought your daughter had great potential. I thought with us she might fulfill herself. I knew with Wanda she would not."

Mrs. Melmore merely smoked and occasionally nodded her head.

"Sarah returned. She was very quiet, but the few things she said were cogent. Per was prejudiced because of her signs of mental illness. But what interested me most, Madame Melmore, was her fascination with our ideas, as opposed to her interest in the personal. It is what we look for, what we long for, the ideal we so seldom find.

"Per is a man who cannot fail to be recognized as a leader, wherever he goes. His philosophy, the complex concepts of a genius, he explains with such lucidity as to be universally comprehended. Although he is very strict, he is very compassionate. Also, he is exceptionally fine-looking. Many young women become over-emotional."

Again she paused and sighed, while Mrs. Melmore nodded and smoked. She wondered if that had been Per Anna had been sitting with earlier. She had never been keen on those fine-featured Nordic types. So this little girl was mad about a daft Swede and thought it was politics. God help us women!

"Sarah, although she had many problems, did not suffer from this confusion. She was drawn only to Per's ideas," said Anna.

Sarah had certainly been attracted to some horrible men, thought Mrs. Melmore, but she felt rather triumphant she hadn't fallen for this twit. She'd begun to think the one she would really have trouble with was the woman Wanda. She certainly sounded a harpy! If only Anna would get on with it.

"I believed, Madame Melmore, that your daughter was on

the verge of extreme sanity—as one might say, 'on the verge of insanity.' I watched and waited. We had known your daughter only as Sarah, a girl from New York. In our group, it is not necessary to know more. But it's not so simple, unfortunately; Sarah cannot be treated as just a girl from New York. Sarah had been spending several nights a week with us for some time when Wanda came to me with an extraordinary offer. She was half mad with jealousy and fear and wished to strike a sort of bargain. She told me that Sarah was a great heiress, Madame Melmore, rich on a scale we had never imagined.

"Wanda suggested that we, our group, use half of Sarah's income for our purposes, while she retained the other half for Sarah's use. She told me Sarah cared nothing for money —only justice and freedom, the work for a better social order. She told me that if she and Sarah were admitted to our group Sarah's money would be used for the advancement of our ideas.

"I suppose you were brought up a Christian, Madame Melmore?"

"And how!" Mrs. Melmore thought, but she merely nodded.

"You remember that the devil took Christ to the mountaintop to show him all the power and glory of the world? Madame Melmore, I am no Christ." Mrs. Melmore nodded.

"It wasn't personal, Madame Melmore. I need you to believe this. Personally, I need no more than food to eat, a place to sleep. But Per. For his ideas. For our ideas. I'm sure you can have no conception what even a little money means to people like us. How much it can do. It meant a printing press . . . opportunities for the dispersal of ideas . . . opportunities for mobilization . . . for the organization and defense of oppressed groups . . ."

Mrs. Melmore found she was not really listening. Obviously, this girl was telling the truth when she said she represented no direct threat to Sarah. In fact, she might be actively helpful.

"You can see the end of the story. I was tempted. I fell. I talked the matter over with our group (in Per's absence, of course). That in itself was in flagrant violation of our principles. But in the end we accepted, for Per's sake, although Per would have been disgusted by such an arrangement himself. We voted as a group to include Wanda and Sarah on an unprecedented basis. We agreed that Wanda and Sarah, while they would not live with us, would be free to come and go, use our resources, and be given some small measure of responsibility.

"Per was most unhappy and confused by this decision of ours. He knew our distrust of Wanda and so our explanations involved us in further deceptions. What we did was right neither in our world nor yours, Madame Melmore. I know. And we have suffered for it.

"All this time Wanda was manipulating us in ways we did not understand. She told us that Sarah did not like the mention or the touch of money, so that Sarah's checks should come to us. She gave us Sarah's signature card. It was not difficult to imitate. We followed her agreement, and out of Sarah's monthly income we gave back half to Wanda. A stupendous sum, as you must know, so that Sarah might live like an empress if she chose.

"The first few months, everything went smoothly. You may find it strange that Per saw nothing unusual in our change of fortunes, but Per is an idealist who believes that our ideas, presented logically, could not fail to gain recognition and support."

"What twaddle," thought Mrs. Melmore. "Per didn't notice all that money coming into his life?" But she was silent. Anna was going on about Per's great ideas. They sounded puerile and futile to her, and it was only Wanda's name which brought her back to attention.

"We did not understand how calculating and vindictive Wanda had been. It was only after these few months had gone by that she showed her hand. You see, she had put us in the position of replicating Sarah's signature. She was technically not to blame. At the same time, she began brandishing the whip. She had never forgiven us for rejecting her initially. Now she threatened that she would tell Per everything. She knew Per well, Madame Melmore. She knew that if she told him how he had been deceived by his comrades he would turn his back on all of us. And his great plan? What would have happened to that? It would have taken another hundred years maybe, another great leader. I am not making apologies, Madame Melmore. It is beyond that. I know it is a sordid story."

Mrs. Melmore gave a very small smile. "I've lived through worse," she said. It was a smile of relief. These people seemed more like cranks than crooks. Sarah was not in danger. Sarah was not in danger.

But how had Sarah gotten involved with this beast Wanda?

"But, we have just received a letter from Sarah's bank, or rather a letter addressed to Sarah. We have been handling Sarah's affairs, at Wanda's request, regarding Sarah's income. Certain inquiries are being made. May I presume this is your doing, Madame Melmore?"

Mrs. Melmore's expression did not change. Well! Northrop had certainly taken his time. What was today? Monday? He must have waited till Friday to write, or else the mail was awfully slow.

"They wish Sarah to appear in person in order to verify her signature."

Mrs. Melmore nodded. "That seems reasonable."

"Reasonable? Maybe. But, Madame Melmore, here is where you must cooperate with us. You see, we do not know where Sarah is all this time."

Mrs. Melmore felt a distinct pressure drop, as if everything around her were falling away.

"Well, where is Wanda?"

"From the day after Sarah disappeared, we have not heard from Wanda. For twenty-four hours she called us night and day. Threatening us. Making impossible demands. Delivering ultimata. Then—nothing."

"I see. So you believe . . . ?"

"We believe Wanda is with Sarah. Wanda would never have ceased to torment us unless she had found Sarah. That much is evident. I believe they have left Paris, Madame Melmore. Wanda did not feel safe in Paris while you were here."

"I see. But exactly what are you telling me now? Can you find them?"

"Madame Melmore, undoubtedly I should have contacted you before. But I thought Sarah would reappear in a few days. I believed so. I hoped so. Per's situation I have explained—he knows nothing and we would do anything to keep him ignorant of this matter. But now, with this notice from the bank, I realize you intend to use force."

"Force?"

"The force that people such as yourself have at your disposal. I don't blame you, Madame Melmore. It's your system. Only I think I can explain to you why we can be more helpful than the resources your world commands. That is, depending on your priorities."

"What do you mean?"

"Whether you are more concerned with Sarah's money or her safety."

"Are you serious?" said Mrs. Melmore very coldly.

"Don't be angry. I assumed as much. But I had to ask. If that is the case, you must cease every sort of pressure from every official source."

"You mean you want that money?"

"Not at all. But you are going to excite people's curiosity and suspicion, which may be dangerous."

There it was again—a touch of ice.

"We are the ones who can help you now. But it is not as easy as you may suppose. Here in Paris, every hand is against us—every political group in this political city. The right would like us deported. The left would like our bodies floating in the Seine. The French police would use any excuse to throw us into jail. That is not mere paranoia. I must tell you, Madame Melmore, the police in this country care nothing for justice."

"No, just about breaking the law," thought Mrs. Melmore.

"But perhaps you wonder why you should trust me, trust us, rather than the police. What is it, after all, in your life if we all rot in jail? It's true. But you see, Madame Melmore, we are in the best position of anyone to discover where Sarah is. It is we, not the police, who can find Sarah most quickly. We know where to look. We have stronger motivation. The police only want sensations. If Sarah is in a scrape, you have to realize it might be that the police—their interference—could cost Sarah very much, even her life."

"What!"

"You don't believe me? It's true. We have so many enemies. But it is only we who know who they are."

"What in God's name are you talking about!"

"I will tell you what I think the most probable. I think Sarah after meeting you, I think perhaps she couldn't face going home to Wanda and all her dramas. Who could blame her? Obviously, she spent the night somewhere else. The next day, either she returned or Wanda found her. As I say, Wanda's calls ceased, and in their apartment—we felt it necessary to enter their apartment at that time—in their apartment, everything was gone. Not only their papers and their passports, but I have good reason to believe they had a great deal of money, a vast amount, Madame Melmore, in cash. It was all gone. I think Wanda took Sarah very far away.

"Even so, it is not a question of endless time with Wanda. She does not know of this letter from your bank, so she will expect her money. Believe me, her talk about moral purpose was grossly deceitful. Even at this moment, Wanda may be calling us. In any case, there is a limit to the time. No matter what has happened, Wanda will call us when Sarah's next check becomes due."

"Which is when?"

"The tenth of September."

"The tenth of September? But that's forever!"

"Not so long, truly, Madame Melmore. But I am convinced that Wanda will call before then. She will call. She will want to know if you have left Paris.

"Furthermore, Madame Melmore, I am willing to offer my services as an intermediary between you and Sarah."

Mrs. Melmore thought this over.

"If this is the case, if Sarah returns, if I help you with her reorientation, Madame Melmore, could you be magnanimous? Could you allow us to go on our way without exacting legalistic reprisals? Sitting here with you, I have concluded that you are a kind and honorable person. A woman of integrity. When Sarah is safe, we will return to you what money remains to us, with the promise that neither you nor Sarah will hear from us again. This money—it has been a terrible curse."

Mrs. Melmore spontaneously took the girl's hand, which was as cold as the stone inside a church. "Poor child," she said. "You're really nothing but a child yourself."

The girl bent her head toward the table, as if under the weight of an enormously heavy crown.

"Why do I do things like that?" thought Mrs. Melmore. "I can't help myself, and yet in fact I feel no sympathy for this obnoxious and probably very dangerous young girl."

"You're very understanding," said Anna. "Your face is so kind. I feel it is only fair to tell you one other thing we must consider. It is Wanda. I've told you the demon Wanda has been to us. She calls us. She hangs up. In three minutes she calls again. The bright side is that if she had not found Sarah, Wanda would never have stopped calling us. Never."

"Yes."

"The dark side, I must say this to be fair, and because you have been kind to me, is that whoever has Sarah might have Wanda too."

"*Has* Sarah?"

"Yes, yes. There must be many people who have wondered how suddenly we have become so rich. We have tried to be discreet but on our level Paris is a little village. Everyone is very jealous of us. Naturally people spy on us. They have ways of knowing."

"You're suggesting?"

"I'm suggesting that some of our enemies, or even outright extortionists, could be holding Sarah and Wanda. Please, Madame Melmore, are you all right? Please take something to drink. Are you all right?"

"My God, Anna, what are you saying?"

"I felt I must be fair with you, even if it goes against our interests. But please, Madame Melmore, I don't believe it. It's not logical. You would have heard. We would have heard. And Sarah, if the worst came to the worst, no one would harm Sarah. That's the last thing anyone would do. Sarah, excuse me for being so crude, Madame Melmore, but she is the goose that lays the golden eggs."

"But what people are you talking about?"

"Madame Melmore, we are the ones who can find out. Not the police. It is only if the police become involved that Sarah might be in peril. Do you see?"

"You think that has happened?"

"No, not at all. I think Wanda and Sarah have taken a trip somewhere and that we will hear from them at any moment. I had hoped it would be much sooner than this. We might have avoided this scene—so painful for you."

"It's not the scene. It's the idea of what may be happening to Sarah that is so painful to me."

"Madame Melmore, whatever has happened to Sarah did not begin a week ago!" Anna softened her voice. "Forgive me. I believe that it's most likely that Sarah and Wanda are somewhere in Brittany. Wanda had wanted to go to Brittany; she had talked of it. They will come back, healthy, with a nice tan, and your worries will have been for nothing.

"We began to turn our attention to this matter seriously long before this letter from the bank. We will find Wanda and Sarah. Here, I'll give you a number you may call, at ten

in the morning and ten in the evening. Ask for Nadja or
Anna. One of us will always be there. I am sure, I am cer-
tain, that within forty-eight hours Sarah will be back in
Paris."

Anna handed Mrs. Melmore a piece of paper on which she
had scrawled a number. Mrs. Melmore stared at it. She said
nothing at all.

Anna heaved a truly enormous sigh. Then, out of a neat
schoolgirl's handbag, she drew a passport.

"Keep this, then, if you like. It's a guarantee."

Mrs. Melmore flipped through it fast. Anna Maria Bjorn.
Born in Stockholm. Three years younger than Sarah. Swiss
passport. She pushed it back and shook her head. "Keep it,"
she said.

"You're right. I could somehow get another. But I
wouldn't." She paused a minute, then dropped the passport
into her bag. "But what matters is that you believe. Either
Sarah and Wanda are on vacation, or, if things have gotten
. . . different, we can find out faster where she is and how to
help her. Of course, I'll let you know in that case too. Even
if it means the police. Do you believe me?"

"What choice do I have? If Sarah turns up as quickly as
you suggest, you can run away wherever you like and I don't
give a damn about the money you've taken."

"We are not running away, Madame Melmore, and Sarah
wanted us to have the money."

"Okay. Whatever. If I don't hear from you or her, or too
much time goes by, or I have reason to be alarmed—well, I
must do what I think best."

The girl watched her. "We are the best, Madame Melmore.
I believe we will have news for you very soon."

"Tonight?"

"Perhaps tonight."

"Oh, I'd like something else. My daughter's address and
telephone number."

"They have no telephone."

"And Wanda's name."

The girl wrote three lines. Mrs. Melmore stared at what she'd written, then put on her glasses. Seven letters—three consonants in a row. Could that be right?

"About Wanda," said Mrs. Melmore.

"Yes."

"She's a photographer?"

"She takes photographs."

"She's Czech?"

"No, Polish, Madame Melmore."

"Look, you're not telling me a thing."

"I told you that Wanda was a deceitful, self-interested, avaricious person, whose ideas—"

"No, I don't care about her ideas. What sort of woman is she? How old is she, for instance?"

"Wanda is no longer young."

"What age might that be?"

"Wanda is at least thirty-five."

Dear heaven, she was never going to learn anything from this horrid girl.

"I am afraid you will find Wanda a very formidable adversary, Madame Melmore."

"That's really the least of my worries. I'll call you tonight, Anna, and I hope for all our sakes you'll be lucky."

"Actually it's a question of logic more than luck," said Anna. She stood up abruptly and shook Mrs. Melmore's hand.

"It's been a great pleasure to see you, Madame Melmore. More than I can say," she said.

Then she walked out of the café and down the street in the direction of the Métro, very straight, like a Buckingham Palace guard; but, just before she was out of sight, her shoulders seemed to sag a bit, and her walk seemed not so brisk, nor so purposeful.

Mrs. Melmore continued to sit at her table, smoking and thinking. She ordered a Vichy, and sipped it slowly. It was curious. She hadn't sat like this since she was a girl. She hadn't sat at a café, all by herself, having a drink, watching the people. . . . Really, she had lived in a kind of purdah, hadn't she? "The money is a terrible curse," Anna had said. Well, not really, of course, but she did have a point.

If Anna and her group were some sort of terrorists, she hated thinking of all the time Sarah must have spent at their place. They sounded just the type to blow themselves up, making a bomb.

Particularly, if this Per was in charge. If that fellow really didn't notice such a spectacular change in his fortunes, he shouldn't be in charge of opening an umbrella. Imagine someone like that fooling around with letter bombs or whatever he did. Mrs. Melmore shivered.

How could Sarah stand all that hypocrisy and jargon? Because, as Anna said, she was very intelligent, beneath it all. If she was attracted to dreadful Per . . . but Anna had definitely said this was not the case, and had been watching with hawk's eyes. So it wasn't even that.

Oh, heavens, after the horror of Sarah's friends these last years, Anna and Per might actually be a step up. At least they were trying to do something, however stupid it sounded. Thinking over the conversation, Mrs. Melmore became more and more sanguine.

It's all right, after all, she thought. Anna is paranoid and a little hysterical about the police. Probably with good reason. There was no reason to think someone in Paris would kidnap Sarah, all of a sudden. God knows, she looked poor as a rat, and no one had asked *her* for a penny. So Sarah and the beast Wanda probably were off on a trip.

Anna was right. She had gotten unnecessarily overwrought. She had forgotten how erratic a life Sarah must lead. And now it seemed as if she might be in tremendous luck. This woman, Wanda—she looked at the name on a piece of paper —B-r-z. Was that possible? It was like one of those eye tests. But it might work out well, since the Advent group and

Wanda were obviously at swords' points, and it was in their interest to help her in every way with Sarah. Naturally the whole lot could go straight to jail. Probably Wanda's record wasn't spotless either. And if she'd been signing Sarah's checks too (wasn't that like Sarah—not even to endorse her checks?) . . .

Oh, Lord! She realized she had automatically been thinking of Sarah as a rational human being! Not endorsing her checks! That was the least of it!

What a fool she was, taking Anna's assessment of Sarah's sanity as anything but self-justifying delusion. Still, at the same time, what luck! So that ass Northrop hadn't done his homework on the signature. And the whole lot could be made to cooperate or go to jail. Sarah need never know.

"Sis," she thought, "you're thinking like Jim now. He'd be proud of you."

Of course she wouldn't go to the police. The last thing she wanted was a scandal, to draw attention to Sarah, have Sarah's name in the papers. There would be no way to prevent that here. But of course she must keep holding that club over Anna, until Anna had done everything she had promised.

Anna thought Sarah was on the "verge of sanity." How seriously could she dare take that?

But if Anna was really sincere? Anna had suggested that Sarah was unusually upset that day on the rue de Rivoli. . . . It was Mrs. Melmore's philosophy to try to believe in the best. It occurred to her that she was avoiding going back to the hotel.

She liked being here by herself. She felt that she had handled her conversation with Anna very well, and that it had turned out much better than anyone could have dared hope. And, well, there it was, she really didn't want to tell Harriet after all. With Harriet, she'd been acting like the clinging baby sister—it was so easy for her to fall into that role. Now, she wanted to handle this by herself. Make the decisions herself. She got up abruptly and went to the telephone. She called the hotel. "Has my sister, Miss Milbanke, telephoned?"

"Not as yet, madame."

"Oh, good. Because I'd like to change my message for her. When she calls, will you tell her I've gone for a walk and I'll call her later. We're meeting for dinner anyway."

"Yes, madame."

Mrs. Melmore smiled and went back to her table.

2

Sarah Melmore Learns There Is More Than One Sort of Education

JACK WAS FEEDING SARAH SOUP. Maurice was sitting at the table working. The next time she remembered, Jack was feeding her soup and Maurice was gone. Sarah wasn't hungry. It began to remind her of the hospital. "Am I back in the hospital?" she asked one afternoon. But no one was there.

"What day is it today?" she asked, but no one was there. She didn't know how much time had gone by.

"Have you ever been in the hospital?" she asked Jack. He was sitting beside her, trying to get her to eat. Maurice must have gone out.

"The hospital? Oh, Lord, yes. The first time, I was fifteen years old. Where I come from, they can sign you away till Judgment Day."

"I don't think they could do that with me, for some reason." He raised the spoon. "Jack, I just can't eat right now, please. Otherwise they would have. Did you feel you were crazy?"

"I sure acted crazy that particular time. Sarah, you should eat something. Otherwise you'll never get your strength back."

So she had been here quite a while. How long?

"Well, 'crazy'—that's just a word," Jack said. "Like the day you came here." (How many days? What day is it today?)

"You were talking about demons, remember? Now people aren't supposed to believe in demons today, so mostly they don't see them. People just see what they're taught to see. But I know every time somebody says they see something it's really there. And if it's scary, well, there's always something I can do. If it's demons, I figure out how to get rid of the demons. Like if it was rats, well, then I'd get rid of the rats. But rats, mostly, they don't do people any harm."

"Why did they put you in the hospital, Jack?"

"Oh, that's a long story."

"Your family?"

"Sarah, you're not going to eat, I'm going to turn off the light."

"But I can't go to sleep, Jack."

Sarah woke up in bed. She thought she was still on the couch. Jack must have put her there, but she didn't remember. She knew she had a fever. She was really burning up.

"Jack!" she called. There was no answer. "Jack!"

Maurice came in and stared at her. "What you want Jacques for?"

"Oh, nothing. Never mind," she said.

Maurice went away again.

She saw the little photograph of her with Jimbo propped up next to her bed. She must have asked Jack to get it for her. But she didn't remember. Time was always so different when you were sick. It didn't seem that long before Jack came back. But it could have been. He sat down beside her, and held her hand.

"What is it, Sarah?"

"I'm awfully thirsty. I'm sick, I guess."

"Mmm-hmm. I'll get you something. You'll be all right. I'll make you all right. I didn't spend more than three days in school, Sarah, but I know about things like that."

"Didn't you ever go to school, Jack?"

"Hold on, Sarah. I'm going to get you something." In a little while, he came back with a steaming cup.

"Now drink this, Sarah."

"Oh, Jack, I want something cool."

"Do what I say, Sarah. We gotta burn out the fever. Come on, right now. I mean it."

Sarah looked at him for a minute, then took the cup. It was hard to drink it down, but she managed. First, she felt even hotter, but then something changed, and she started feeling a little better.

Jack was watching her. "Okay?"

"Okay."

She knew Jack was getting ready to leave her. "Why didn't you go to school, Jack?"

Jack laughed. "Oh, Sarah," he said, "up to tricks, aren't you? You know I mostly never talk to people. I let them talk to me."

"Did you ever go to school?"

Jack laughed again. "Do I sound like I did?" he said. "Sarah, you got to know I'm a—well, functional illiterate." Jack had stood up. Now he sat down again. "Okay, Sarah. Well, you see, my momma died when I was a little tiny kid."

"How did she die?" Sarah said.

Jack's face changed in some way. He had a brown part in one of his yellow eyes. Now it seemed as if both his eyes were dark.

"Different folks said different things," he said.

"Oh," Sarah said. She was silent a while.

"After she died, it seemed like my dad went wild. He'd always been a rough man. Fast with his fists. If you looked at him sidewise, he'd beat you senseless. People used to use him like a bogyman.

" 'Watch out,' " they'd say, " 'or Old Man Straw's going to get you.' "

"That's your name? Straw?"

"Mmm-hmmm. Jack Straw. Anyway, my momma's mom, old Emmie, put the snatch on me. Old Emmie." Jack stopped and laughed. "That's what everyone called her. Her real name was too hard. My momma's folks were mostly Hungarian. They were good-looking people, but kind of wild. And they'd always had funny ways.

"Well, Emmie just picks me up and takes me back home to Reunion City. It wasn't any city, Sarah, just a poor little farm town. She had this little house there, right on the outskirts of the town. 'The witch's house,' everybody called it.

"That house hadn't been painted in years. It wasn't the money, Lord knows. She could've done it herself, if she wanted. She could do most anything. She just didn't care, once my momma left home. My momma was like a queen. Emmaline—that was my momma. Well, there were weeds growing up over the windows and all. That's why they started calling it 'the witch's house,' I guess. That's the way they thought out there.

"Old Emmie just didn't care. It was the inside of the house, you see, that was wondrous. That could keep a child like me in its thrall.

"You see Emmie, well, she believed kind of like I do, that there's lots and lots of worlds. And lots of spirits in all those worlds. And anything anyone ever saw or said or wrote down, just even in their wildest imagination, it was all true.

"Sarah, I forgot to ask: Are you religious?"

"I don't even know by now, Jack. Oh well—my great-grandfather was a bishop. And my father's Jewish. He never believed in anything. My old nurse was a Catholic, and I used to go to church with her a whole lot, when my parents weren't home. I guess that's what really took. I believe in God, and I believe in sin—and hell."

"Hmm," said Jack. "Sounds like you just picked out the worst parts. Well, I don't want to say anything that's going to upset you, Sarah."

"You don't believe in heaven, Jack?"

"It's there if you think it's there, Sarah."

"And hell?"

"Well, what do you think, Sarah? What kind of trick would that be, when all we do here is what's required?"

Sarah was silent. Then she said, "But your grandmother. Did she have a religion?"

"I don't know if you'd call it that, or not. She saw a lot of powers. She just sort of dealt with all the powers around. She was—well, she was kind of impartial."

Sarah stared at him. "But couldn't they hurt her?"

"Of course not, Sarah. Spirits can't hurt you. Only thing in this world that can hurt you is yourself. Other people, if you let 'em. But spirits are just there for use. If you can learn to use 'em."

"Did you ever—um—see any?" said Sarah.

"Well, Emmie had these funny mirrors you could see stuff in. And spirit catchers she had, too. You ever see them, Sarah? Maybe they're Hungarian or something. They'd be these little things, hanging from the ceiling, reflecting every which way. And pools of water in copper plates. Sometimes they had eyes in them. And inside the house she had a garden. Up in the attic window. The things that grew there! Well, you'd never believe me." Jack paused. His thoughts seemed far away.

"Sarah, I had the best time, just grooving out there in outer space with my crazy old granny. I just wanted Emmie to teach me everything she knew, or something. But you know how two people never can be pleased at once. Emmie loved me in her way, but I didn't really count. She hardly ever called me by my right name. It was 'boy' or 'Emmaline's boy.' That's what I was to Emmie. I wasn't any Emmaline.

"She kept my momma's room like a shrine. Everything in it so beautiful. I wasn't even allowed in for a look.

"It was old Emmie taught me about mother love, Sarah, with her love for Emmaline. That's about the strongest power, for the people feel it. Well, I'm not complaining. I had my share, and then some."

Jack paused, his eyes looking, but not seeing. "Those were the best years," he said. "I just wanted to stay right there in that house. Seems like the truant officer never learned my name.

"And my father. I guess he didn't ask any questions. He didn't like coming to Reunion City. Guess he just left well enough alone. So he never got to know the worst.

"Well, all the while, I was just having the greatest time. Home was school and play for me. If people had known what we were doing, they'd have locked us both up.

"Of course, old Emmie wasn't just a spiritualist. She was an herb doctor, too, Sarah. You know, a folk doctor? Emmie used to say the only thing she couldn't heal with her brews was a broken heart. But she had cures for that all the same. They were like charms, sort of.

"Only times we used to see the townsfolk much was when someone was ailing. Then they'd sneak out after dark, so nobody would see 'em come. It was mostly women, ninety-nine percent. They were leery of Emmie when they were well. I guess they were ashamed. But when they were sick, that was another story. Old Emmie was just the best nurse in the world. Sometimes I used to wish I was sick, so she'd pay me all that mind, but I was always on the other side, like her, and I knew I couldn't ever fake it. Not with her.

"Emmie wouldn't take money for healing. But she'd take eggs and butter, or a chicken, or preserves. Maybe a quilt. Stuff like that. But what she'd always say was, 'You come to my house in the morning, and you bring the kids along. They can play with my boy here. You do that, and I won't take nothing. I like the daylight healing.'

" 'Oh yes,' they'd say, 'I'll come,' but they'd get well, and that was the last we'd see of 'em until there was trouble again.

"But it worked out all right, all the same. People gave my granny her distance, but they gave her respect. Of course, Emmie didn't go in for bad spells. And not because people didn't hint around. I guess if she had, my old dad would've been first to go." Jack laughed, and shook his head.

"Like I said, it was too good to last. Old Emmie died, just like it was foretold. Lord knows I tried everything there was in the way of healing, Sarah, and truthfully, I was just as good as Emmie by then. I took care of her like she was my child *and* mother. But Emmie, you see, her time had come. She'd made up her mind to die.

"Old Emmie, when she died, she died so easy. She died just like a bird. I was sitting there holding her hand, and after I knew, I kept holding her hand all the same. It got real cold, even though I kept holding on. And finally I just had to let go. My hand was getting just as cold. I was thirteen that year.

"It had been foretold, so I shouldn't have been sad, but I was. I knew what I was supposed to do, though. I knew how to fix her body exactly right, from having been a death nurse. I did all that, and a few little things for her that were special.

"Well, Sarah, I fixed certain kinds of stuff, here and there and all over the house, and then I set the whole place on fire. You see, I did it such a way the flames would just swallow it whole. Nobody would ever lay eyes on Emmie or the insides of that house of magic again. No fire brigade in kingdom come could have saved a stick in that house.

"I watched it go, Sarah. Those flames went right up into the air. It was so hot, nobody could've even tried to get near. Then I beat it.

"I wasn't going to be around by the time they figured was I in there, or what. I never knew *what* they figured, to tell the truth. I'd just scraped up what money there was, and took off. I never did go back to Reunion City.

"How do you feel now, Sarah?"

He laid his hand on her cheek. Her face was cool.

"Mm-hm," he said. "You know something, Sarah? That fever's gone for right now, but I get the feeling you need to be sick, someways. Something's got to burn itself out in you, and I'm just interfering. Would you mind if I just let it finish itself off? See what the problem is then?"

Sarah felt scared. "Would I have to go to the hospital?"

"Lord, no, Sarah. I'll take care of you. You've been put in my hands."

"Well, okay then, Jack," she said. "But right now I feel sort of okay. I mean much better. Could I come out in the other room? I have to go to the bathroom, anyway."

"Okay, Sarah." Jack hesitated. "M'reez is out there, though. Okay?"

"Sure."

He helped her up. She had on nothing but her underpants, so she wrapped the sheet around her. Maurice was cutting something up—he always seemed to be doing something with a knife. It looked like a chicken. He hardly looked around. After she used the bathroom, Jack helped her get comfortable on the sofa. Sarah knew that something difficult was going on around her. There seemed to be trouble between Jack and Maurice. Maurice turned his chair so that his back was to her. She had the feeling Jack wanted to leave, but he didn't want to leave her alone with Maurice. She supposed maybe she should go back to bed.

But Jack went over and filled a glass with vodka.

"I probably shouldn't be giving you this right now, Sarah. It wouldn't be that good for you. But if you want?"

Maurice suddenly turned around. "Jacques!" he said angrily. He held out his wrist, and pointed to his watch. Sarah was surprised. Maurice had on one of those Cartier watches. She knew they were very expensive.

Jack sat down near her, and drank some vodka. Then he said, not really looking at Maurice, "Time is for us to use, M'reez. Not the other way around." Maurice just shrugged and turned his back.

"Okay, Sarah? You all right? Okay. I hate hospitals, too.

Anyone does, who gets to know them from the inside. Okay, Sarah. You wanted to know how I got put in the hospital. I'll tell you.

"After old Emmie died, I went to New York. By bits and pieces, sort of. Hitched most of the way there."

"New York? When you were thirteen, Jack? What happened?"

"Oh, all the kinds of things happens to kids, I guess. Kids on their own, in the big city."

Suddenly Maurice sprang up, threw down his knife, and went into his room, slamming the door behind him.

"I got hold of some money. I was doing lots of different drugs then. And I wasn't all that responsible. I'd started doing my first pieces, well, models. My first film bits too. When I could find the right people.

"But something happened. There was this old man I knew. He died. And it turned out he had two brothers and a sister. It was the sister was the worst. I think I must've tried to kill somebody, probably the sister. Anyways, someone must've got in touch with my daddy somehow, and the next thing I know, I was locked up in a loony bin in Little Rock. My dad hadn't wanted me too close to home. He just hoped the folks down home wouldn't hear of it."

"How'd you get out, Jack?"

"Just used my head a little."

"Where's your father now?"

"He died." He paused. "In the end, we weren't such bad friends. I helped him die. He wanted to."

Maurice suddenly threw open his door. "You going out, Jacques? Or you're not going out! One way or the other! I need to know."

"Okay, M'reez."

"But, Jack," Sarah said urgently, "did you kill him?"

"Oh, Lord, no, Sarah. See, my daddy had got to drinking a lot. Doing things real funny, like midnight plowing. That doesn't mix too well with farming, and the next thing I heard, he fell in the combine. Well, it chewed him up, and when it spat him out, his legs was just like cubes of Jell-O. I flew right on down home to see him. And he was in this poor little bit of a hospital there. He had a lot of life left, considering. But he was in such pain.

"All I could do was just hold his hand, try and help him a little bit. See, about morphine—they were real stingy about morphine, there. Afraid he'd get a habit." He laughed.

"I believe in herbs, Sarah, but I sure don't disbelieve in morphine. Well, I just sat with him. Maybe thirty-five, thirty-six hours was all. All I could do was keep hold of his hand, sometimes I'd pretend I was rubbing his poor legs. I made it as easy as I could for him. He was calling my mother's name. But she never came near. All I could do was help him die. But you know something? When he died there was a minute, just that one minute, when all the bad things just fell away. All that anger and pain. He looked just like a little kid."

"My God," Sarah said, "I killed my father. He didn't want to die, but I killed him. My mother said I didn't but he was dead anyway. But all the time he really wasn't dead."

Maurice put his head on one side, and flashed Sarah an ingenuous smile. "Sarah," he said, "you're quite a kid, Sarah. You ought to have your own TV show, Sarah."

"How do you know my name?"

"Sarah. Because you told us, Sarah. Is it supposed to be a secret, Sarah? Sarah. . . . That's a pretty name. You Jewish, Sarah?"

"My father is," she said, "so I am. But I don't want to talk about my family. It gives me a headache."

Jack walked over to Maurice and spoke to him in a low voice. He put something in his hand. Then Maurice put his hands in his pockets and slouched out of the apartment.

Jack sat down by Sarah again. "I really hope M'reez doesn't bother you, or something," he said. "He's very up and down sort of. He gets depressed and worries about his career. And then he worries about money and stuff. He has all this nervous energy, and sometimes it makes him kind of crazy and mean. You know, he didn't even have a father. And his mother—well, she was just a woman of the streets. You know—a whore. But I don't want anyone or anything bothering you here, because you're safe here with me. I have this very strong idea now we're going to be together at the end, Sarah."

Part Four

GIRL
FROM NEW YORK

1

Miss Milbanke Takes
Mrs. Melmore to Dinner

"OH, HARRY! How absolutely divine! How on earth did you ever find this little place? It must be right off the map!"

Harriet Milbanke, who ate at the little place whenever she didn't eat at home, said nothing. She was feeling distinctly angry with Sis, angry with herself, too, ever since Sis had called late that afternoon and told her, after those days of suspense and drama, told her that, after thinking it all over, she had decided there was really no reason to be so hysterical about Sarah. Sarah hadn't said she would keep in touch, after all, and that other woman—well, crazy people would have crazy friends, wouldn't they? So she thought they should just wait.

Sis had talked on, sounding cheerful and reasonable, while Harriet found herself getting crosser and crosser. Harriet was the sensible sister, after all. Sis made it sound as if it were Harriet who was being hysterical. How had she gotten sucked into all this? And why did she feel so angry? She had been exploited, that's why. Her sisters could always put one over on her, even after all this time.

And she had really worked, during that last week. It was she who called all the photographic laboratories trying to trace Czech photographers. She'd gotten nowhere—just the names of two Czechoslovakian men. Several of the little labs were closed for August. Sis had been indignant: how slipshod the French had gotten! No wonder they were going down the drain! They should take a leaf from the Germans, and so forth.

Harriet was surprised. She thought such rhetoric ill became a rich, idle woman like Sis. "I never heard you spent many of your vacations in Berlin, Sis. Is that a German dress you're wearing?"

Sis stared at her a moment, then giggled. "No, and I don't want bratwurst for dinner. Oh, Harriet! Haven't I gotten horrid?" she said.

It was Harriet who had followed the trail of Advent, and the name Persson. It was hard work too. Persson. She had tracked down four in Paris and the suburbs. All false trails. Persson must be another pseudonym. But still . . . She had talked to her friends at the Sorbonne about Scandinavian students. That hadn't been productive so far, either. But it might have been.

And Sis—Sis had just been sitting in her room at the Crillon, smoking cigarettes, and waiting for this problematical phone call. With her two servants. And what servants! That woman Cecil, what was she supposed to do? Look after Sis's shoes apparently. My goodness, what did she do all day long? Walk them around the block a few times? And that driver, as if anyone needed to bring a driver here. Sis said he was "wise and sweet." Harriet found him ridiculous. He wasn't even a good driver. He had a queer look in his eye, Harriet thought. Probably he drank.

She had done everything she could think of. She'd gone
back to the address on rue Minou. Never any answer from
Persson. She'd given Sis sensible advice but Sis wouldn't go
to the police.

"Never, never."

"I don't see why."

"Not yet, anyway."

"All right, then. Do you have a lawyer here? Could you
find a good one?"

Sis's eyes rolled back in her head. That meant she was
thinking. Actually, Sis could make even that look pretty.

"Actually Jim has a lawyer here, Donald Tremaine. But,
I'd really hate to call him. He was Jim's friend and I know
what he'd say. Bring on the CIA or Interpol, the Canadian
Mounties, or whatever. You know how those men are. And if
I said 'no,' he'd just go right ahead and do it anyway. And
do you know what would happen? They'd find Sarah, I suppose. But somehow or other they'd make such a mess Sarah
would be terrorized, and they'd end up putting her back in
the hospital. They're inhuman."

"Maybe. But maybe it's for her own safety. And what about
those pills you say are so important?"

"Harry, if it goes on too long, I'll call Donald—Donald's
one step better than the police. But he thinks like a man. All
they want is action, never mind the consequences. I don't
want Sarah put in a zoo. I've seen what that's done to her. I
want to find her and help her get well."

Actually, Sis had had the idea about the bank all by herself.
She had told that man there to write a letter to Sarah, telling her she must come into his office and verify her signature
before any more checks could be cashed. That was a good
idea. But what was this total reversal? She didn't know what
to think. Maybe Sis had just lost interest. Maybe Sis would
tell her at dinner that she was going to drop the whole thing
and go off on a North Cape cruise, or adopt a Vietnamese
orphan. She should have known better.

Harriet had to admit to herself that there was another,

baser motive to her anger: disappointment. She had actually enjoyed all this unfamiliar drama and excitement. It made her feel useful: Sis clinging to her, gazing at her with those great eyes, kissing her, hugging her, telling her that she couldn't get through the day without her. All that love and dependence and flattery. And Sis could be fun too. Sometimes everything was put aside and they acted like a couple of schoolgirls. It had been very seductive.

In return, Harriet had been circumspect. No snide remarks about James Melmore. She had a most unchristian curiosity about some of the incidents in the twins' lives; she had heard tales. . . . Sis would have known it all. But Harriet didn't ask her. They just talked about their childhood, or impersonal things—very occasionally about Sarah (never in any depth; Sis always shied away). And, of course, Harriet had been busy, very busy, on her sister's behalf.

Sis must have sensed her hostility because now she began to apologize profusely for all the trouble she had caused. Harriet couldn't help interrupting this by saying nastily, "But we still don't know where Sarah is, do we?"

"No." Mrs. Melmore paused. "But somehow I have this instinct that (God willing) it's going to be all right."

She looked at Harriet for confirmation. Harriet stared grumpily at her plate.

"You know what I'd really like to hear about tonight, Harry? This book you've mentioned to me. I mean the one you're writing about—sparrows. It sounds so interesting."

"Flowers, not sparrows. I loathe sparrows. I said a man named Bill Sparrow was working on it with me."

"Oh, I'm so sorry. How could I? I really *knew* that, Harriet. Remember, I said, 'How fascinating'? I've been so totally round the bend. . . . What a moron I am! Harry, you know I'm much, much more interested in flowers than sparrows. I only wish I could write. Anyway, I love to read."

"I don't think this is the kind of book you'd love to read."

"Oh, Harry! Relent! Why are you so cross with me? You should know if there's one thing I'm passionate about it's

my garden. (Oh, Harriet, my poor garden! You've no idea!)
And I do know just a little bit about flowers myself.

"Oh, darling! I've just had the most wonderful idea! You
know what I have at home? A portfolio of those fabulous
eighteenth-century botanical prints by Couvert, d'you know
who I mean? They're very, very rare, practically no one has
even heard of them. You could use them to illustrate your
book!"

Harriet sipped her wine. "I shouldn't think so," she said.
"My book is on the derivation of classical names of flowers,
and their mythological significance in different countries."

Mrs. Melmore frowned slightly. Gosh! That did sound
leaden. "Still, why couldn't you use my prints for illustra-
tions? That would help to make it an important art book, too.
They charge the world for them, and they sell like hot cakes!"
("And no one would have to read the text," she thought.)

"It would be much too expensive."

"Oh, Harry, that's no problem for us. Or . . . I'll give them
to you."

Harriet scowled, and shook her head. Why say anything
to remarks of that sort? Just get through dinner and go home.

Sis was appalled herself by what she had said. It was so
hard to remember, sometimes. Virtually all the people she
talked to were so very rich, or else if they were writers or
artists or anything, or sales people and so forth, naturally she
took their feelings into account. How on earth was she going
to retrieve herself now?

They ordered dinner. Harriet drank some soup. Mrs. Melmore pushed some *céleri rémoulade* about her plate in
silence. Finally, she said, "Harriet, I'd better tell you something."

Harriet was paying a great deal of attention to her roll.

"Harriet—listen. Something happened this afternoon. Not
that crucial, but, well, very important to me. The only thing
is—that I swore by all that was most holy not to tell another
living soul about it. And I was trying to take that literally.
I mean—I mean—by not even telling you."

Harriet began to attack her roll.

"You see—someone found out I was here in town, and looking for Sarah. Someone—probably someone heard we were looking for Sarah or for Advent."

Harriet still looked cross.

"And so this afternoon, well it was about a quarter past three and I was resting. This girl called me, because she didn't want me to worry. She was a friend of Sarah's. At least, she said she was, on the phone. And she wanted to meet me and talk. And I was scared, and wanted to call you right away, but you'd just left, of course. Anyway, I left you a letter all about it. It's back at the hotel, if you don't believe me."

Harriet stared at her.

"Harry, I was awfully scared. I mean, you can imagine. I thought somehow they wanted money for Sarah, or maybe she was dead, even. You know? But then, well, this turned out to be a really—a really very nice girl. I—I was so surprised. And she promised she'd help me—us—find her, and everything. She says Sarah's all right. And well, I believe her. That's why I feel so much better."

Harriet had stopped eating and had listened to her sister's story with complete attention.

"Why on earth did you have to swear not to tell anyone?"

Oh, God. Trust Harry. "Well, um—if I tell you, will you swear the way I did, never to tell a soul?"

"Sis, I think I'm getting in over my head. It's just a little too crazy for me. I'm not used to all this excitement, and I don't understand this world you're living in. I'm not going to swear to anything I don't know anything about. It sounds to me as if whatever it is must be against the law and I want no part of that. And I think you'd be an absolute fool to get involved in it yourself."

Sis could not control herself. "But, Harriet, I want my daughter back!" she cried.

Harriet looked at her *poulet à l'estragon*, which was cooling, but she didn't eat it yet. "Yes, Sis. I know," she said. "I know you want Sarah back. But I also think, from what you've just said, that you're going about it in completely the wrong way. You're trying to make bargains with criminals. That's what it sounds like to me. Don't expect them to keep their end of it. You should go straight to the police, with everything you know."

"But there's a very good reason I can't!" cried Mrs. Melmore.

Harriet simply shook her head. "There's never a good reason," she said. "Don't let anyone fool you. If you want to tell me about it, go ahead. I promise you I'll be as fair as I can be. But on the provision that I make no promises of any sort, and do just what I think is right."

Mrs. Melmore thought this over. It was just exactly as she had feared. And she had no confidence in bending Harriet to her will. Harriet would ruin everything.

"I understand, Harry. All right. I'd rather tell you everything, because you have such a good brain. But, in this case, I'm just going to have to follow my emotions and instincts, even if they're wrong. Anyway, these people are not criminals. They're just in trouble with the police about papers and things, so they're scared, you see? And they're not doing anything wrong. They're just frightened. You know?"

Harriet scowled back at her.

"And they've promised me they can find Sarah in a very short time, and that there's nothing to worry about. I have Sarah's address, she doesn't have a telephone, so—well, it's just a question of waiting.

"But, Harriet, please, you may think I'm totally wrong, you may disapprove of me terribly—I suppose you do. But won't you be my friend, anyway? Won't you be my sister again? You've been so marvelous to me. Won't you stand by me, while I'm waiting? I need you so. And then—well, then I'll need you with Sarah."

Harriet began to eat her chicken. It was a tiny bit tough. She wished she had chosen the fish instead, as Sis had done. Sis, of course, had no intention of eating the fish; she just wanted to poke at it. What a waste of good money! Harriet had arranged the bill herself in advance, not wanting her sister to pay for anything further. All the same, she felt somewhat mollified. She believed Sis's story, to a point at least. But the fact remained that Sis was totally incompetent to deal with any of the alarming possibilities inherent in this situation.

If nothing was wrong, why had this girl showed up today? The timing—sounded like pressure from the bank, didn't it? It could hardly be out of good will, since she hadn't been in touch with Sis before. Naturally they were using Sarah and her money. Naturally. But for what? And naturally they wanted to calm Sis down as quickly as possible, so that they could go on with whatever they were up to. Anyone could pull the wool over Sis's eyes. Yet maybe they would be frightened enough to throw Sarah out, and send her back to her mother. Wait and see. And Sarah—yes, Sarah. Even if they tossed Sarah out of Advent—whatever that might be— why on earth did Sis think that Sarah might go home with her?

Harriet had to admit that she had taken quite a dislike to Sarah, without having seen her. She sounded like a spoiled girl who wanted her own way and gave no thought to other people. And those pills. Harriet had never heard of pills like the ones Sis described. If it wasn't quackery, it must be some kind of dope. Maybe tranquilizers.

Well, Harriet had promised to do everything to help Sis find her daughter, but she decided that afterward she would probably only be in the way. A sensible doctor was what Sis needed, and one who didn't rely on pills. Someone like Dr. McGregor. Sis needed help herself—she couldn't even seem to decide whether Sarah was crazy or merely wayward. Probably both, Harriet thought.

"You know, Sis," Harriet said, "it's not easy for me to think like a mother. You believe Sarah will turn up soon. All right. Of course I'll wait it out with you, and help you if I can. But you know, with all this excitement we've had, I've missed a lot. For instance, I don't really know the first thing about

Sarah. I mean about Sarah herself. Except you seem to have been out of touch for a very long time."

Sarah herself. Who was Sarah? The angelic baby in her arms? The chubby little girl with the radiant smile? The lean, hostile adolescent? Or Sarah, the young woman with the clipped skull, on the rue de Rivoli? "Murderer."

"Do you mind if I smoke?"

"Not at all. But I thought you had given it up."

"Yes, but—well, when all this is settled—maybe . . . It helps me think." Sis lit a cigarette.

Harriet wished she could ask Sis whether she could eat her fish. Funny, such a little while ago she wouldn't have thought twice. Even reheated, that fish would be good.

"You see," said Sis slowly, "Jimmy was always the stormy one. Sarah was the sunny one. Jimmy was mine. Sarah was Jim's. Do you know what I mean, the way that happens in some families?

"Darling Jimmy . . . It used to seem as if he could never do anything right. I mean he wasn't very athletic, and he didn't do very well in school or anything, and of course Jim —well, naturally Jim was always impatient—and so, well, it drove him absolutely crazy. He felt, in a sort of a way, that Jimmy did it on purpose. To—to humiliate him."

"And so that made Jimmy do even worse?"

"Yes, yes exactly. Jimmy was always so frightened of his father. He never understood how much his father really loved him. But Jim's pride was involved—"

"Mmm-hmm."

"Harriet, look, please—I can't talk to you if you're going to be critical and sarcastic about Jim. Maybe you didn't like him, but for God's sake you didn't even know him! Anyway, I'm getting off the subject. It's just that Jimmy, well, you would have adored Jimmy, Harriet. Everyone who knew him did."

Was Harriet still looking at her quizzically? Damn her eyes!

"People who didn't know Jim may have thought he was a

tough, cold man. At least, I suppose they did. But no one knows what he had to go through, his whole life. . . .

"His parents were just horrible. Greedy and coarse and materialistic and—and—unloving and—undemonstrative. Jim had to struggle so hard to fight his way out of that world."

"I always thought his parents were rich."

"Oh, his father had made money, of course, but nothing like . . . And, well, they were just awful people. Jim had to do everything for himself and they never gave him any approval and he was such a perfectionist. He always worked ten times harder than any man in the United States, while his parents—all they did was play mah-jongg and try to decide what color mink coat they'd get next month. His mother, I mean. His father didn't do anything. Jim was brought up with no love at all, so it was very hard for him to show love and affection. Even to the people he loved best."

She gave her fish another poke.

"Sis, are you going to eat that fish?"

"This fish? Oh. Oh, no. It's delicious, really, but I'm not very hungry."

Harriet spoke rapidly to the proprietor, who nodded and took the fish away.

"I'm sorry I interrupted. You were telling me that Mr. Melmore—uh, that Jim, because his parents played all this mah-jongg and so forth, uh, that Jim couldn't love anyone?"

"Goddamn it, Harriet, I was not. You're twisting everything I say into something nasty. I said he was very loving, but sometimes—well, often—he had trouble showing it. What on earth is that?"

The chef was offering her something disgusting wrapped in silver foil. It was dripping.

"That's your fish," said Harriet.

Oh, my God! Harriet was going to make her take it home and eat it for breakfast!

"It's for me," said Harriet. "It looked so good. And some-

times I like to heat things up and eat them at home. I suppose you don't want any dessert?"

"Oh, I don't know. I might. Actually I feel like something
sweet. What about you?"

They ordered.

Sis sighed. "Look, Harriet, I've simply got to ask you not
to . . . I mean, this attitude of yours about Jim. Jim tried
with Jimmy. He really tried.

"For instance, when Jimmy was about ten or eleven, he
got absolutely fascinated by China. I forget why. But anyway he got this sort of obsession about going there. Of
course, no one could go to China then, and I didn't even
think Jim paid attention. But then one night, just out of the
blue, he brought Jimmy home about twenty-five books on
China. Everything he could lay his hands on. I mean history,
and art, and religion, and everything. Beautiful books, naturally. I was just—just moved to tears."

"What about Jimmy?"

"What? Oh. Oh, I don't know. Jimmy was funny. He'd
lose interest in things so fast. He had a mind like a grass-
hopper. Quick—but not—you know, tenacious. Jimmy took
all those books up to his room, but then I don't think he ever
even opened them. At least, they just sat there in a stack, and
some of them, they had that sort of cellophane wrapping. It
was still on. I took it off, and made them look a little—well, you
know, in case Jim ever went in there, which, thank goodness,
he never did. But actually Jimmy never really thanked him
or anything, Harriet. I mean that was really rude." She
looked at Harriet. "Don't you think?"

"Well, yes. Certainly."

"Naturally, if I'd known at the time, I'd have done something. But Jim didn't tell me for years. Sometimes—well, it
seemed as if Jimmy went out of his way to be provoking.
You know Jim loved sports. And he'd take Jimmy to the ball
game or ice hockey when he was a little boy. And you know
what? Jimmy would just take out a comic book or a movie

magazine and start reading it. Naturally that made Jim livid. It always happened when I wasn't there. And usually Jim couldn't blow up because there'd be guests, and he'd yell at him afterward, but . . . Well, naturally Jim stopped doing a lot of those things with Jimmy. You can imagine!"

"Hmmm," said Harriet, contemplating her plate, round-shouldered. It certainly sounded as if Sis had two nasty children. "Just like their father," she thought. But she did feel a little repentant, especially now that she had her fish.

"You know, Sis," she said, "I really am being mean and horrid. I admit it. I don't know why—just my nature, I suppose. But, as you point out, I didn't even know Mr. Melmore, and I really do want to hear about Sarah. I gather he was very—uh—undemonstrative with Sarah?"

"No, no, he wasn't, really. Not with Sarah. That's the whole point. Why, practically from the moment Sarah was born, he thought she could do no wrong. Of course she was perfectly adorable, a really adorable child. Terribly bright and oh—sort of funny and original, and well, high-spirited and mischievous. The fact was, Jim spoiled her terribly. I told him again and again he spoiled her perfectly terribly. He always took her side, and she could be awfully naughty. There has to be some discipline, I mean.

"But he would say to me—later on, of course, when I'd be complaining about Sarah being too spoiled—he'd say, 'By the way, Sis, how were Sarah's grades last month?' And of course they were always straight A's.

" 'And extracurricular'? Well, Sarah was a terrific athlete. Tennis team, basketball team, softball team. Rode like a dream. She just plain didn't like field hockey, who could? But anyway, she was always president of her class or editor of the yearbook or whatever. Tons of friends and so forth.

" 'Hm,' he'd say. 'Now let's look at how Jimmy's doing.'

"Oh, God, Harriet. The agony! Believe me, I'd have chewed those reports of Jimmy's up and swallowed them if I could have gotten away with it. After a certain point, I guess he didn't expect much anymore. He didn't get angry—he'd just listen, and shake his head. And then he'd say: 'Well, Sis, looks like whatever we're doing with Sarah must be the right thing. Wouldn't you say?'

"They were so close, Harriet. Honestly, you've never seen a father and daughter like that. I mean they really were one another's best friend. I know he told Sarah all kinds of things he never told me—lots of things, about his business, and well, other stuff, too. Their relationship was just fantastic. I mean —naturally I didn't play too much of a part in it—because they were just on an entirely different plane.

"And then after Jim, Sarah really absolutely adored Nanny —Nanny O'Donnell. Do you remember Nanny? She was my nurse at the Lying-in Hospital, and I brought her home with me, and just wouldn't let her go. She was a real darling, Nanny, and we just kept her, kept her right on through all of the mademoiselles and Fräuleins and so forth. What horrors they were! In fact, I think they're what ruin so many of these children."

She stopped and bit her lip. "Oh, Harriet!" she cried. "What am I saying? Of course I'm talking about a ruined child."

Harriet patted her hand. "Well, dearie, well," she said. "What do you think went wrong?"

"But, you see, I don't exactly know. It didn't have anything to do with Jim, though. As I said, he absolutely adored Sarah. Just spoiled her to death. Sarah always got everything she wanted.

"Oh, well, there was a time when she wanted to go to boarding school just because all the rest were going, you know. But Jim felt she was doing so well where she was, and, after Jimmy and all—it was that same year, that God-awful year, and Sarah adored Jimmy. Just adored him. And I really don't think boarding school would have been the answer. I think we three needed to stay together.

"And then, you see, Sarah changed. I mean we all did, after Jimmy. But maybe Sarah the most. She got much quieter, and sort of—well, more serious. Not so crazy—I mean 'fun' crazy, clowning around, and so on. Of course, first of all, she couldn't stop crying—but when she did, she would never mention Jimmy's name. It was just as if she had stricken his name off the books. As if she'd never had a brother. It was eerie.

"Maybe we should have had the sense to do something then. I mean that's really not natural. But you see Jim was the same way and Sarah probably picked it up from him. You know, I found it so hard. I needed so badly to talk about Jimmy. It was all I ever thought about, but naturally I wasn't going to babble on about it to some perfect stranger.

"I suppose I should have gone to a psychotherapist or a priest—but to tell you the truth, I don't believe in one or the other. But anyway, with Sarah the boarding-school thing wasn't really important. I'm sure of that.

"Of course, Jim used to take her out of school a lot, take her on trips and so forth. He couldn't have done that if she'd gone to boarding school. I know that isn't supposed to be good, but her marks did keep up, and Jim said, and I'm sure it was true, that she was gaining invaluable experience. You see, he trusted Sarah with everything. Everything. He really did. He always said Sarah had a brain like a man, you know. I know that from a certain point he decided—really, I mean it—Jim decided that Sarah was the only one who could take over his business. After—afterward. You know, Jim always had such trouble with the men he trusted. All they were really out for was themselves, and so they always let him down."

Harriet had finished her apple tart.

"But what happened with Sarah?" she said.

"But that's it, Harriet, nothing! Oh, normal adolescent rebellion, and so on. But I suppose the first thing—you see, Sarah was always a very attractive girl, and had lots of beaux and so on, and so naturally she fell in love. Like—like we all do. . . . Only the thing was, she was always, invariably—well, she always chose the most awful, ghastly, sinister people and then—the most terrible things happened."

"Like what?"

"Oh, actually her first serious beau wasn't that bad. Truthfully, he wasn't bad at all. At first I thought it was just fine. Jim never did, never, but he was very calm and relaxed about it all. More than I dared hope. You know, I'd always dreaded what Sarah's leaving home might do to Jim. Because he counted on her so.

"Well, this boy, Track—his name was Robert but they called him Track—Track Merriman, actually. Did you ever know the Merrimans? Of course we'd known them forever, and Track—Track Merriman—and Sarah had really grown up together. Same dancing class, same parties, same friends, everything. It should have been ideal. Oh, and Track was good-looking and a big football star and so on. Imagine how glamorous, for a young girl! And his family gave him this very snazzy sportscar the year he was eighteen. They always spent more than they could afford on Track. Sarah used to go up almost every weekend to see him. (Of course, we made sure she had a proper chaperone.) Or else he'd come down. And I sort of thought, well, this is perfect for a first romance. I mean I always knew Track wasn't as bright as Sarah, but I have to admit he was a nice boy—terrific manners, and so on. And I never thought it would last.

"And then, you're not going to believe this, Harry. Well, one Sunday night, Sarah came and told us they wanted to get married! Imagine—those poor children! I mean, Sarah was sixteen years old! And, Harry, they weren't talking about after college or something. They meant right away. I mean what could have possessed them? Well, naturally Jim and I thought the very same thing—we thought Sarah must be pregnant. And everyone knows now that that isn't a good basis for marriage. Sixteen years old, Harry! And there are things . . . But it wasn't even that.

"Jim handled it all terribly well. He pretended to take Sarah absolutely seriously. He never criticized Track to Sarah. I know he thought the boy was an absolute twerp and that Nancy Merriman was just trying to latch on to a good thing for him when she had the chance, but he never gave the least hint of his feelings.

"What he said was: 'Sarah, you know you're much too young to take this step. If you're as madly in love as you say, your relationship should stand the test of a little time. Now, Sarah, I promise you that if you wait a year, and you feel the same way, we'll announce your engagement, do everything properly, and you'll have my blessing.

" 'But, in the meantime, you must abide by my rules. You're still a schoolgirl. I want you to work hard and graduate first in your class. You've always been first, Sarah. I don't want your grades to slip. And, until you graduate, I want you to keep all the same rules and curfews you do now.'

"I was totally amazed. Sarah in a year would only have been seventeen. And even if Jim dragged things out as long as he could, well, she'd be married at eighteen or something! I mean it's so pathetic! But, knowing Jim so well, I always noticed his language. Of course, Jim began as a lawyer, so his exact words were terribly important. And you see, if the worst came to the worst, all he'd promised Sarah was that she could get engaged. Not married. Anyway, the poor things didn't wait. And something so very strange happened.

"Jim is—Jim had such a masculine mind, but he had this almost feminine streak of intuition. It was uncanny, totally uncanny. He would get these hunches—out of nowhere, it seemed—and they were always dead right. Well, one night Sarah was out on a date with Track. It must have been a Friday, because on school nights she had a really tight curfew. Jim didn't want her to go out at all during the week, but I said, 'Look, if she goes out with Track, she has to be home early, and she gets her work done. If she can't, they just sit and talk on the telephone for hours, running up a small fortune in telephone bills, and she doesn't get anything done.'

"Actually, it all happened so very oddly. Jim had just gotten home, just beginning to unwind, when in came Nanny, the way they do when you've only been alone a minute, and he's just got his slippers on, and his lip over a martini.

"Well, Nanny said to me, 'Excuse me, madam, but I can't find Miss Sarah's toothbrush or toothpaste anywhere. I've looked for them high and low. And, what's more, I can't find Raggedy.' She meant Sarah's old Raggedy Ann doll, that Sarah always slept with. Isn't that ridiculous! You know the sort of things servants do that make you want to strangle them? What on earth was I supposed to do about it?

"But Jim—Jim just leapt up in the air as if he'd been electrocuted. Then he grabbed the phone—I really thought he'd gone mad—and called the Merrimans. He got Nancy. And right away he asked if the boy was driving his own car. Well, he was. (Jim always thought that they'd bought him that car to help him hook poor Sarah.) So, next thing, he asked her for the license number. Just yelled at her! Made no effort to be polite. We've never really been friends since.

"Then he called the highway patrol and told them to stop this red Triumph with such and such a license number. Even then I didn't guess what was happening—I thought he'd gone completely berserk. And honestly I was too scared to ask what it was all about.

"But do you know they found that car way up on the Connecticut border. Those two little children, with these pathetic little suitcases and stuff—and Track had taken two of his football trophies with him—isn't that sad? And they had all this cash, about a thousand dollars. Track had opened up his parents' safe and just cleaned it out. Well, that was one story. Jim would always have it that Nancy Merriman just staked him for this little outing. But I never thought Track was scheming at all. I think they were both in love. Sixteen-year-old love.

"So it was true. Just as Jim had guessed, in one flash. They'd actually been running away to get married."

She gave a little laugh, looking at Harriet to see if the story was funny or sad.

"They brought Sarah home and she admitted the whole thing. Sarah was always very truthful. It was Jimmy who would make up all those wild stories.

"Jim was completely furious with her, of course. She'd broken her word to him. And of course Sarah was furious, too. She was used to doing whatever she wanted, and she was convinced she was mad about this Merriman boy and felt Jim had absolutely ruined her life. Things were just ghastly, for the longest time, at home. Just ghastly. They were both so stubborn. Nobody was speaking. Just glaring. Just like a Strindberg play.

"And I'd try to talk or something, and the silence would just fall. And fall. God.

"Jim wouldn't let Sarah out of the house alone, or let her have phone calls or anything without supervision. You see, he felt she had let him down so terribly that he couldn't trust her anymore.

"That fall the Merriman boy went out to some college in California, and then, well, Jim was always so right in these instincts of his. I mean the boy was nice and sweet and polite and so forth. But there was something really the matter with him. Anyway, his first year, his freshman year, he actually did get married, to some girl from Iowa or something. Imagine poor Nancy Merriman! I guess he was just desperate to get married. And by now—and he's only a couple of years older than Sarah—by now, I think he's been married two or three times. Maybe more," she finished. "We don't keep in touch."

"So you think that's what made Sarah so . . . so . . ." Harriet didn't quite know what word to use.

"Track Merriman? Oh no! Good God, no. Believe me, Track Merriman is the best Sarah's been involved with. In a way, looking back on it, I wish she'd gone ahead and married him. And found out right away how foolish the whole thing was. Better yet, I wish she'd just slept with him. Honestly, Harriet, I think that's all she really wanted to do. I'm just sorry she didn't."

"I didn't know girls still had such an old-fashioned point of view," Harriet said, "about marriage, I mean."

"Well, they certainly don't. And Sarah didn't stay that way for very long, herself. God, that was a bad time. But it passed, of course. It had to. Jim didn't stay angry with Sarah. He couldn't, he loved her too much, he loved her better than anyone in the world. Oh yes, way, way better than me. I didn't even mind. Do they want to close up here, do you think?"

"Well, maybe. It's early. But we are the last ones here. We could sit outside at that little place over there, if you like. Or you could come back to my apartment, unless you're tired."

"It looks awfully nice outside. That little breeze tonight. The check? Oh, Harriet, that's really bad of you. But thank you. It was marvelous. Don't forget your fish. Oh, but please, have them put it in something a little sturdier!"

They sat outside. Mrs. Melmore ordered a *décaffiné*, and Harriet a *fine*.

"Let's take a walk before we go home. It's nice tonight, and I've been talking much too much. I'm sorry."

"Well, I'm getting very intrigued with your Sarah."

"Really? I feel like the Ancient Mariner. Gee, let's just take a breather? Do you mind?"

2

Sarah Melmore's Transformation

SARAH HAD BEEN SICK. She had no idea of nights or days. Sometimes Jack would wake her up and give her soup and a sort of gruel. Sometimes it was dark. Sometimes it was light. His voice was always very soft and concerned. But in her dreams everyone was screaming and shouting:

"If you disobey me, I'll kill you!"

"You're crazy, crazy! I'm not going to stand for this!"

"You'll stand for it!"

Sometimes the shouting voice was Jack's, but in the day-time his voice was so low she had to lean over toward him to hear what he was saying.

Once, Maurice woke her up with the soup. "Hi, kid. I'm getting kind of used to you."

He looked different to her—very glittery and happy. Or at least excited.

"In fact," he said, "just make a few changes and you might be the kind of girl I'd go for."

He began to feed her. "You know what? To begin with. First place. You got to eat more. Thin is good. Too thin is not good. Not sexy. Look." He pulled up her shirt. She seemed to be wearing a man's white cotton shirt.

"No, come on, look! Lift up your head!"

"Ow, don't!"

"It's your body—just look what you do to it. Think that's pretty?" He went out and returned with some bread and butter, cheese and fruit. "Now, eat that."

"I'd throw up."

"If you throw up, I'll hit you so hard your whole stomach is going to come up."

She ate a little. It was pretty good.

"Are you going to throw up? No? Okay. Next thing, take a real bath. I'll fix it for you." He ran off. She closed her eyes. Back to the hospital.

"Okay. It's nice. It's got nice scent and everything. Can you walk? Okay, then I'll carry you."

He picked her up and dropped her into the tub, fairly hard. The water did feel good though, and smelled nice, and Maurice washed her so gently and expertly that she forgot about everything else.

"Don't I do this good?" he said. "Feels good, huh?"

"Mm-hmm. Hey, what are you doing!"

"What I'm doing is shaving off all those disgusting hairs."

"Don't do it. Stop!"

"Huh! You think that's sexy? Well, I don't like it. You shut up or I'll drown you."

Then he washed her hair with a rubber spray and a shampoo that smelled like lime.

"Shit! That's the ugliest job of hair cutting I ever saw," he said. "Who had that brilliant idea?"

"I did."

"What for?"

"I like it that way."

"Huh. What I can't figure out, Sarah, is are you crazy and stupid, or are you crazy and a cretin?"

"People where I come from used to think I was smart."

"No kidding. I just wish I knew those people where you come from. Then I'd be not just very handsome, but very handsome and very, very rich!

"Okay, now come on. Get out of the bath yourself. You're taking a lot of my time, Sarah, and my time is worth a lot of money."

He wrapped her in a towel, and sat her on a stool. It was daytime, because the light was coming in the window. He held out her hands.

"Okay," he said, "no sense doing anything about the nails, yet. We'll just have to wait. Just don't bite them. Same no deal about the hair. Maybe, a couple of weeks, we could do something. Don't you dare touch my scissors."

Now he held her face in the light and looked at her a long time. "Uh-huh," he said. "Well, kid, you look better for the rest." Then he began messing stuff over her face. It smelled nice though. Stuff on her eyes. Stuff on her lips.

"Hey, keep your eyes open! Think I can fix your eyes when they're closed? I'm not God. For God you pay more."

"Ow!" she yelled. "That's enough!"

"Shut up! That's all I'm going to do. I needed to do that. Makes your eyebrows more pretty."

Then he held her face in the light, moving it this way and that, squinting at it from different angles.

"Well, well," he said. Then he went away and brought back a short lavender dress, or maybe it was lingerie. It was satin—no, imitation satin.

He dropped it over her head, and forced her arms through the shoulder straps. Then he sat on his heels and looked at her for a long time.

"I'm awfully tired," she said.

"Then go to bed."

She stood up, feeling sick and dizzy. "Maurice!"

"So you want me to take you? Okay." He carried her over and laid her on top of the bed.

"You got horrible toenails," he said. "I wonder what's to do about that besides varnish?" He had cleaned off the silver lacquer long ago.

She was drowsy and wondered if she could just go to sleep when he wanted to talk.

"Hey, Sarah, do you think I'm very handsome?"

"Uh-huh. Very."

"And sexy?"

"I guess so."

"Would you like to make love with me?"

Sarah opened her eyes and looked at him. "Not one bit."

She thought maybe he would hit her, but instead he seemed pleased and laughed.

"So that's why I'm attracted to you, Sarah. Because you're not attracted to me. That's always the way. In fact that makes it perfect. Oh, wait a minute, I forgot, there's a secret I'll tell you." He hurried away and came back with a bottle of spray. It felt cool on her face.

"That's yours now. That's a present. Just put it on your skin after. It looks nice. It feels nice. And it's good for you. Skin needs a lot of water." He put it on a table next to her bed.

Maurice certainly had his ups and downs.

Later, she woke up when Jack came in, and she heard Maurice talking to him, very excited. She knew it was about her.

Jack came in, took a long look at her and shut the door quietly. Then she could hear him shouting. This time she was awake.

"What's the matter with you? Are you a total fucking idiot? Turning that gorgeous child into a little slut out of Pigalle?" There was a lot of shouting, but she didn't want to hear it.

Later that night, Jack came and sat with her. He washed her face very gently. They were both good washers, the two of them. Finally he said, "There," and laid his cheek against hers.

"I'm sorry," he said. "That was all so stupid and so unnecessary. And I hope you didn't get scared. Sometimes I get so mad at M'reez, and it's wrong, because he just wants to make people look like other people he's seen and admired. That's a boring way to think, and it makes me mad. But it's my fault too. I'm always interested in the beginning, because I always think I'm going to find something new. And then, after a while, I see I'm not going to find anything new, nothing that surprises me. It sounds awfully egotistic, but the only place I find something new and surprising, Sarah, is in my imagination. The trouble is it's so expensive. You wouldn't believe, Sarah, how terribly expensive it is."

She didn't understand most of this, but she felt very sorry for everyone. She knew Maurice was just trying to be nice.

3

Mrs. Melmore Tells
a Disagreeable Story

"SO SARAH AND HER FATHER were friends again?" Harriet persisted.

"Well, yes, in a way. Certainly on his side. And she must have seen that that boy was really an idiot, and his feelings for her were pretty shallow—and so on. But actually Sarah stayed fairly hostile—to both of us, I guess. But particularly Jim.

"I told you that Jim's big plan was to take Sarah into the business. Even at the worst moment of our lives—I mean, well, Jimmy's death, you know. Of course, Jim didn't say anything for hours. He could never express his emotions. But almost the first thing he said afterward was, 'Sister, I'd always planned to take Sarah into the business.'

"That was always what he'd intended to do. And of course he wanted her to have the proper training. They must have talked about it a lot.

"It was taken for granted she'd go on to college, particularly since she was a woman, and had a bit more to prove, and so on. They'd decided Radcliffe was the best. And Sarah's marks had kept up. She'd been accepted everywhere, including Radcliffe. So I'd thought, naturally, everything was set.

"But after graduation Sarah just wouldn't talk about it. Wouldn't mention college at all—when she was going up there, or what she was going to do about her room, or clothes, or books. Nothing. Just silence.

"Well, about the middle of July, Jim noticed a letter from Radcliffe, and it looked a little different. Handwritten or

something. And Sarah had been so odd. Just totally reticent.
. . . That night at dinner, Jim finally asked Sarah about it,
the letter. And you know what she said? She said, 'Oh that.
That was from the dean.' She'd written to say if Sarah
changed her mind—*changed her mind!*—that was the first
we'd heard of it, you see—they'd keep her place for her!

"In other words, that's how we learned she wasn't going to
Radcliffe. Sarah said she'd written back already (and Sarah
wasn't that fantastic a correspondent) to say she wasn't going
to change her mind.

"Harriet, our mouths were just hanging into the cold soup.
Jim was so stunned he didn't even blow up, or anything. He
wasn't even being sarcastic when he finally asked would she
mind letting us in on her plans. You just can't imagine the
shock.

"Sarah said, as a matter of fact, she would be going to acting class. She wanted to be an actress. Of course, that was
absolutely our first inkling. I mean one had to admit she had
a flair for the dramatic!

"Sarah didn't fool around, naturally. Once she made this
terrific decision, it was none of this 'I'll take a year off, give
it a try.' You know, nothing normal. All on her own, she'd
decided on this man who—well, I'd never heard of him, but
he was one of that 'Method' school apparently. I found out
more about him later. And they'd worked together a bit, and
he'd said he'd take her on in the fall. And, on top of that, he
was going to help her find a couple of girls to share an apartment with. In town! So the future was all taken care of,
thank you.

"You can imagine, that was one of our more memorable
dinners, though I have no idea what we ate. I guess we didn't
eat. Jim was so upset he just went off by himself after dinner.
Just shut himself up. I guess I went down to the stable.
That's what I always did. I told you I stopped riding, but I
still spent a lot of time with the horses. There were only
about four of them then, and Sarah's hunter, but I used to
like to go down and just be there, spend time with my babies.

At night, down there, it was the most peaceful thing—really, Harriet, I know you don't like horses, so to you it must just sound weird, but to me it was always so comforting. Like 'Little Town of Bethlehem.' So that was where I always went when things were tense. I always felt better. Jimmy knew that. He'd always find me there, even though he didn't like horses much. He had allergies. Sarah—well, Sarah was a terrific rider, but she didn't understand.

"Anyway, Sarah wasn't even eighteen then, so Jim could probably have done something legal, but it would have been pointless. In a way, the worst of it was that I was so sure it was less that Sarah had this mad passion for being an actress than, well, she just seemed to want to hurt Jim as badly as she could. After that, whenever we had friends over, she insisted on talking about her plans with them and asking their opinions about acting classes and so on. As if any of those people would have had any opinions.

"Jim said to her just once, at the first: 'I think you're making a great mistake, Sarah. I think you should at least keep your options open.' But after that he never said a thing. And that was unbelievable, too. I knew how much it must have shocked him and hurt him after all his plans for her. They were plans they had shared for so long, Harriet. But he never let it show. He had too much pride. He never said a word. I mean the three of us barely talked, unless we had guests. And then, of course, Sarah would go into her ridiculous drama-school spiel and embarrass everyone.

"Jim hardly said a word, and Sarah's manners seemed to be deteriorating daily, but I guess she felt everyone still wasn't miserable enough. So the next thing we knew, all of a sudden, well, she'd been dropping her old friends and so on, too square or something, and then, all of a sudden, she just totally took up—almost from one day to the next—with this bunch of 'townies,' you know? Those local kids that always live near you, wherever you go?

"Remember Willy and Mike and so forth, when you and I

were growing up? Well, Mike was kind of cute. I even had a crush on him one time.

"But the townies today, they're completely different. They don't go to college or work or anything at all. And still they seem to have money, so they can have all these cars and all this time on their hands and so forth. No wonder they get involved in dope and theft and all kinds of delinquency and —well—actual crime.

"So, that's the group Sarah started to go around with. First of all, Jim threw them all off our place. Then she began meeting them in town. When we tried to forbid her to see them at all, she just said in that case she'd leave home. She meant it, too. Oh, God, Harriet, life today.

"Well, she'd go off with them, and, Harriet, you can't imagine how disgusting they looked. All this greasy hair done up in this ghastly way, pretending to look so smart. And seeing Sarah with them. By then, she wore nothing but blue jeans, of course, but anyone could tell she didn't belong. It was just awful. And naturally I used to wonder if they were giving her drugs and so on. I didn't dare say that to Jim, he was worried enough.

"It must have been at that point that Jim lost confidence —confidence in his influence on Sarah, I mean. It was the very first time he'd turned to me. 'For Christ's sake, do something, Sis,' he said. 'She's your daughter.' He'd never said that before. 'My daughter,' that's what he'd always called Sarah."

"What did you do?"

"Oh, God, I felt so helpless. I knew I had no influence at all over Sarah; I never had. But anyway, one afternoon when I knew Sarah was in her room, I went and knocked on her door. I almost never did that, you know—I very much believe in people's right to privacy. Sarah said, 'Come in' and then, when I did, she looked amazed to see me. She gave me that look she'd perfected over the summer—that look as if I were some rather unusually disgusting specimen of bug that had crawled into her room.

" 'Mother,' she said, 'what a surprise! What do you want?'
"Oh Harry, I felt hopeless. I expected absolutely nothing.
But it's strange, Harriet, things are so strange. Once we
began to talk, we just went on and on. It was one of the
closest times we'd ever had together, even though a lot of
the things she told me were so terrible. I asked her how she
spent her time with those boys. She said mostly just driving
around, but a lot of the time they spent shooting. With guns,
you know. They would go down to the beach and shoot.
They all had guns. Mostly she went with this one boy,
Hooker. Sarah already knew how to shoot—Jim and Carey
had taught her when she wasn't much more than a tot. But
she said she'd gotten so she had a 'dead eye.' She was very
proud of that." Suddenly Sis stopped and looked around. "I
wonder where Williams is?"

"Right over there, see?"

"Oh, poor Williams. Where was I? Oh yes, talking to
Sarah. Actually, it seemed as if each time I asked her a question she would answer me quite simply and frankly, without
all that sarcasm and hostility. I asked her about Hooker,
about her feelings for him. She said she wasn't in love with
him, but she cared for him a lot. She felt sorry for him. 'Sure,
we go to bed together, Mother,' she said. She didn't use any
of those other words people use—I guess to protect my in-
nocence. God, Harriet, that's what things are like today.
Look, I don't understand it any more than you do.

"From the way she told it, she saw it as a sort of interval
in her life, a summer romance or something (if you can call
it that), where she and this boy would just, well, shoot—and,
well, make love, and drive around together. It all seemed
about equal. And in the fall, she said, she was really looking
forward to going to acting class. And she'd really enjoy the
independence of sharing an apartment with other girls.

"I said, 'But they'd be strangers, Sarah, and you'd only
just be eighteen.'

" 'They'd be strangers at Radcliffe, too,' she said. 'And I
wouldn't be any older.'

" 'But you'd know quite a few girls there, Sarah. And with the others, at least you'd share the same interests.'

"And she said, 'Mother, that's the point. At Radcliffe, they wouldn't share my interests.'

"It probably sounds rude, but it wasn't. She actually sounded rather sane about it all, everything considered. Even about this boy, Hooker. I mean, it was all totally unappetizing to me, but I guess I was just so terribly grateful she was so friendly, and that she hadn't gone completely over the edge. . . . And that she didn't seem to be doing the whole thing to spite her father. . . . Maybe it's hard to understand, but I felt a lot better about it all.

" 'If you really want to know what I'm doing, Mother, just ask me,' she said. I said I thought I understood a little, and so on, but I did ask her if she couldn't be a little less flamboyant about the whole thing, for her father's sake. 'Oh, did Dad send you here?' she said.

"And then she began looking at me as if I were a bug again and I just crawled on out.

"I didn't know what to tell Jim. I didn't dare tell him much. I did say that, after talking to Sarah, I felt things looked worse than they were. I said nothing awful was going on—the kids might be unattractive, but they were harmless. Maybe that was a little disingenuous, but it was more or less what I thought, and I didn't want Jim to go through the roof. I said I thought it would be a good thing to help her with an apartment (Jim had been very much against that) and her plans for drama school. Then she'd just go back to town and forget that whole group. I said the year after, I was sure she'd go on to college. It would be just like a—well—like a year off. Lots of children do that.

"But Jim was just icy. 'You don't know what slime you're dealing with, Sis,' he said. And you see he turned out to be right again. Something happened—oh, really awful!

"Jim had given me this big rock—it was some anniversary or other. He always did that. And I hardly ever wore it. It was so much trouble! You know—the insurance—signing it in and out of the vault—and a whole lot of extra things, because it was so expensive. Well, I'd taken it out for this huge dinner they were giving for Prince Bernhard, I think it was—Jim used to get hurt if I didn't wear it once in a while, though, actually, I almost never wore it in the country. Anyway, that night before I went to bed I put it in my little jewelry bag on my dressing table, just a soft little bag that didn't look important. It was there that night, and the next morning. Cecil checked too.

"The next day was Sunday and Jim and I were going out to lunch. Then we planned to stop back at the farm for some things and then drive straight on into town. In a way, the ring was a weight on my mind—and I had a sort of feeling about it. I almost wore it to lunch, but it would have looked too ridiculous. Anyway, I was going to put it right back into the vault Monday morning.

"We'd let most of the servants off, and most of them had started back to the city, all except Cecil, of course. Sarah, naturally, was roving around somewhere with her friends. We had seen her driving down toward the beach on our way to lunch. She didn't wave or speak.

"When we got back to the house, I was putting a few things together, when just with my forefinger I touched the outside of this little bag—and—well—suddenly I knew something was wrong. I just tore everything apart, and, yes, my ring was gone! It was just the most incredible thing. Of course, we turned everything upside down, but in my heart I knew there was no mistake. I remembered to the last detail, and so did Cecil. Obviously, someone must have stolen it.

"God, what a nightmare! You can't imagine. That meant the police, the insurance company, the papers! All that sort of hideous publicity that makes you a perpetual victim! Of course the insurance people are the worst. Because they have the most to lose.

"Well, we called the local police first. Actually, we were all great friends out there, so it's not really like 'police,' you

know. They all loved Jim so. They would have laid down
their lives for him.

"They came right over and we all sat down. Jim gave them
all a beer himself (strictly against the rules, you know) and
they had to hear all about my ring. When they asked how
much it was worth, I could have died! It makes you feel absolutely naked, you know. Jim had to tell them what it cost—
it must sound so vast to people like that! You'd think they'd
want to strangle you!

"Well, then they asked what servants had been in the
house. Imagine—poor Cecil, the chief suspect! And did we
know if any of them had records! Servants with records!

"I absolutely dreaded the hell everybody was going to be
put through. I wished I'd just swallowed that ring. And then
suddenly Jim said: 'Admiral' (he always called the police
chief 'Admiral' and the police chief always called Jim 'General.' I forget how all that began). 'Before we do anything
further, I have an idea for you. And I'd very much appreciate
it if you'd bear with the old man and his hunches before we
start bothering a lot of innocent people.'

"Then he told them Sarah had been running around with
a very rough, wild bunch of boys that summer, and that we
had seen them on our way out to lunch. When he said where
they came from, nobody liked it a bit. You see of course
they're townies too, so they stick together. They asked for
the boys' names and of course, we didn't know all their
names. Only Hooker.

"Then, at that very minute, in came Sarah. When she
found out what was going on, she got angrier than I'd ever
seen her.

"She began cursing her father and acting in such a totally
demented way, saying that now he'd really gone too far, and
she'd fix him forever and so on. From the way she was acting, I know the police were all ready to believe Sarah had
stolen the ring, not one of their boys. Anyway, after a bit,
Sarah got very calm and said, 'Okay. So you want their names.

I'll give you their names.' And she gave them the names and addresses and telephone numbers of about six boys.

" 'Go right ahead. Turn their houses inside out. Beat them up,' she said, and stormed up the stairs.

" 'Where do you think you're going, Sarah?' Jim yelled.

" 'To pack. I'm too ashamed to stay in this house a minute longer.'

"Well, the police went to the house of this boy Jay Hooker. No one was home, but they were able to turn up his mother. She was at a bar or something. She wasn't much pleased, but she didn't actually object to their having a look around. 'Nothing to hide,' she said. And—it's just unbelievable, but there it was. My ring! Under some dirty clothes in the boy's drawer!

"God, it was all just a nightmare! A nightmare! Sarah wouldn't believe it when she heard. She just began to scream and carry on and shrieked it was all lies. We were all lying. And later Jim told her (and me—he'd been protecting me too, you see) that he'd run a check on that boy Hooker and he'd found that he had a record. A record of theft. One, a car theft, when he was under age, so he could get off easy. All that under-age stuff is supposed to be a total secret, but . . . But there was another, car theft and drunken driving. And some other charge too—I forget now, but he'd weaseled out of all of them. So you see, naturally, Jim had suspected that boy immediately. I suppose that was really when Sarah started to go crazy. She must have felt so exploited and deceived. She kept saying the boy had never set foot in our house, that she'd been with him the whole day—which, of course, she hadn't—and if anyone contradicted her, she'd start to scream.

"It just got worse and worse. That horrible rat—well, after they caught him, he kept swearing he'd never heard of any ring. He'd never seen it in his life. He'd never even been in our house. Of course, he couldn't say how my ring came to be in his drawer. That was at first.

"The awful thing is, Sarah must have told him about it. God knows why—maybe to show how decadent we were, or something. Of course, she didn't know he was a thief. But she must have felt terribly guilty all the same.

"He probably knew it, because then, when he saw he wasn't going to get out of it this time, do you know what he did? He said Sarah must have stolen it and planted it on him.

" 'Why would she do that?' they said.

" 'To send me up the river,' he said.

"Thank God, the boy had one of those real hick lawyers. I mean a five-year-old could have made up a better story than that. He could have said she'd stolen it, and they'd planned to sell it and split the money or something. Probably a lot of people would have believed that—particularly out there. Sarah was acting so strangely that year.

"Anyway, naturally Sarah had to learn all about that, and then she got even more upset. In fact, that was when she had what I suppose was her first real nervous breakdown. She wouldn't talk to anybody. She wouldn't eat. It was really horrible. And I'm sure some of those people out there do still believe Sarah stole my ring. I know they do. Because of her breakdown. If a person is crazy, they'll blame anything on them.

"I said Sarah stopped talking and eating then, but I'm mixed up—actually, that came later. I mean she only comparatively stopped talking and eating that time. She said one thing, over and over: 'I've got to get away. I want a place of my own.'

"And when I say over and over, I mean it. I mean constantly. Those two sentences. I know she said them in her room, when she was all by herself. I'm sure she even said them when she was asleep.

"And her father would say every once in a while: 'You are not competent to live by yourself, Sarah. You don't even know how to protect yourself.'

"It didn't make any difference to her. Finally, we went

back to the city, and after a while I actually did arrange for her to take acting lessons. Not with that first man, of course —he'd really been the one to fill her full of those hopeless ideas. Just overturned everything constructive everyone had planned for her all of her life.

"Of course, I didn't know the first thing about acting classes and all that stuff, and on top of that it seemed absolutely futile, since she was almost a total zombie. And Jim was still completely against it. But I felt at least it was something positive. And something she still wanted. 'What harm could it do?' I kept saying.

"You see, the only thing she did on her own, after getting to town, was call that first man, to see if he would still take her. Naturally, he called us right away, since Jim had warned him what would happen to him if he ever tried messing around with Sarah again. I don't know what he said to Sarah, to put her off, but whatever it was, she just got more and more depressed.

"But I called her school, and they gave me the name of someone reliable, and I did what I could. And it was amazing. They did take her, and she did go.

"And miraculously, little by little, it actually seemed to help."

Sis found she was getting fidgety. Her story—she kept having the feeling that Harriet was interpreting it all wrong. Besides, it was now seven minutes to ten.

"Then what?" said Harriet.

"Just a minute, Harriet. Would you mind waiting here while I go to the loo? That place across the street looks cleaner than this one. I'll only be a minute."

She didn't give Harriet a chance to argue; she just jumped up and went off. Luckily, the telephone and the loo were both downstairs. She put on her strong glasses—the light was bad—and dialed Anna's number. The phone rang four times. God, had Anna been cheating her? Then she heard Anna's voice.

"It's Mrs. Melmore."

"Madame Melmore. Yes. It's Anna."

"Have you heard from Sarah?"

"Not as yet, Madame Melmore, but we have friends in the provinces. We have a good friend who is very much at home in Brittany. We are optimistic. We believe that we can find her there. It is to Brittany we feel sure they have gone. In that case, the puzzle would be solved. Would you wish to go to her there?"

"I would rather . . ." Mrs. Melmore considered. It might be a wild goose chase. Somewhere off in the provinces. . . . "I would rather you fulfilled your part of the bargain. I would like to have Sarah here in Paris."

"But we have not the authority to order Sarah to Paris. Per could perhaps command Wanda. But what reason would I give him?"

"Tell him Sarah's mother is desperate."

"Per is not very sympathetic to the bourgeois family."

"Then think of something more sympathetic yourself."

"It is difficult."

"Tell him the police are after him."

There was a silence.

"So you insist that Sarah be returned physically to Paris, Madame Melmore."

"Yes, I do."

"I do not think that is fair."

"You must know that capitalists are very unfair. Also, I think you said something about helping Sarah adjust. You said you would help."

"Yes."

"I think we should both stick to our agreement, then. I'll call you at ten in the morning. Oh, another thing. I would like to see Sarah and Wanda's apartment."

"Very well. I'll speak to you tomorrow, Madame Melmore." Anna hung up.

4

Tête-à-Tête

SARAH WAS AWAKE most of the day now. She thought Maurice must have left for good. Sometimes a man in black leather sat and sewed. He didn't speak to her at all, and she didn't speak to him. He brought her her food now and she noticed she was getting more to eat: bread and butter and sausage, cheese and fruit and yogurt. But then, one afternoon, Maurice was back—as unfriendly as he had been at the beginning. He hardly spoke to her, and when he did, he was mean. She didn't mind for herself, but she felt sorry for him. She had begun to associate him with Jimbo. Jimbo had acted awfully mean when he got so unhappy. She tried to think up something to say to Maurice, but it just wouldn't come. One afternoon when he brought her her tea and toast she asked, "How did you get that scar, Maurice?"

He glared at her. "Maybe I was so young and so dumb I asked somebody a nosy question like that. You're not that young, Sarah."

The next time she saw him, she asked him the only other thing she could think of. "Maurice, what's Jack doing all day?"

Surprisingly, Maurice unbent. "Who knows?" he said. "Getting money, I suppose. And at night he goes out with rich old cunts and gets more money from them. Money, money, money, and we live like pigs."

"Why does he need so much money?"

"Jacques? Jacques is a great artist. Do you think I'd live this crazy life if Jacques weren't the greatest artist? Jacques, he's a very kind man too. Like a saint. But then, little sugar, Jacques gets bored. He gets bored so quickly you can't believe it! And then, kid, he gets rid of you. Yes, you!" He looked at her. "In fact, you've been around here one hell of a long time."

"Well, I'm not hard to get rid of. I could leave today."

"I don't think that's his plan for you, Sarah."

"I don't think you know what his plan is yourself."

"Oh, you don't! Well, tell me this then. Where would you go?"

"Back to Wanda's apartment."

"Maybe she's not there anymore."

"She's always there."

"Nothing's for always, Sarah."

"Oh, shut up, Maurice. You don't know anything about anything."

He slapped her—really hard, so it actually went dark and light. She reached out for his hand and bit it as hard as she could. He began to yell at her in French, and they struggled a minute before he grabbed both her wrists. They stared at each other, furious.

"I ought to throw you out the window!" said Maurice.

She glared back at him.

Then suddenly he said, "Can I trust you, Suzy? If I let go your hands, you won't do anything bad?"

"Don't call me Suzy."

"You don't like it?"

"No. It's not my name."

"Okay, okay. Well—too bad. I always got a liking for the name of Suzy. Well—Sarah—we're both bad, it's true? And the funny thing is such a smart guy like Jacques don't understand people like you and me. You know something? I believe you killed your father, Sarah. We're bad people and there's nothing to do about it. That's what Jacques doesn't understand. So maybe that's why he's not bored with us yet, huh? What do you think?"

After that he was nice to her again, unless he was in a really terrible mood.

5

Sarah Melmore Chooses a Man

MRS. MELMORE actually did have to go to the loo.

Harriet was looking cross again. Or perhaps that was just her natural expression now. Maybe she needed different glasses?

"The loo over there was foul," Sis said, "but I called the hotel. They said I had no messages. I mean nothing important."

Harriet nodded and stared at her.

"Oh, God, Harriet, I've just been talking and talking and getting nowhere. Maybe I am tired."

Again, Harriet nodded. Then she said, "I gather drama school didn't work out in the end for Sarah? And she had— another nervous breakdown?"

"Oh, well—not quite that way, of course. It was another man, naturally. And the worst of the lot. I mean unbelievable. That was what gave Sarah that final breakdown."

"What happened?"

"Oh, Harriet, do you really want to hear? It's all so sordid. And you must be getting a little tired of hearing about Sarah."

"No, I'm interested in Sarah. After all, she was named for Mama and I never knew."

"Oh well. Sarah's next episode. Please, don't mind if I make this as fast as I can—I can hardly bear to go over it.

"After a while, as anyone could have predicted, Sarah got tired of acting class, but she did seem a bit better, a lot better. And then she did actually move in with a girl she'd met in class. Really, a perfectly nice girl. Of course, we still had to be careful. And then she got interested in this sort of half-baked political, mystical stuff. You said the Black Panthers, Harriet. I don't know who on earth told you that. Sarah never even had a close friend who was black.

"No, these were more like social workers, sort of. They brought books to prisoners and stuff, and Meals on Wheels and so forth. All very high-minded.

"We didn't see Sarah that much. Of course we always had to call her, and it was the greatest effort to ever get her to come to the apartment. And, when she did, it wasn't like Sarah. It was like, well, like having a social worker visit.

"You never knew Sarah before, but she was just so high-spirited and such fun. We used to laugh all the time. And she really abhorred those earnest, pompous people and all that pious hypocrisy, and so forth.

"So it was always uncomfortable and weird when she came those times, like a social worker—I mean, as if she was watching to see if we beat the dog or something.

"She used to go out to the country a lot—when we weren't there, of course. When I'd ask Nanny about her, Nanny would say she was just like her old self. But Nanny—you know. She always thought Sarah was perfect. 'Quieter,' Nanny said.

"Oh, somewhere along in here, Harriet, I really ought to show you the other side. Because my relationship with Sarah was so complicated, and I know I'm not very good at explaining that sort of thing. I certainly don't mean to give the impression everything was all black.

"You know, Harriet, maybe this won't make any sense, if you don't have children, but a lot of the time, you don't really view them from a normal perspective. Everything gets sort of exaggerated. One minute they can seem total monsters and the next like little helpless babies. Maybe you have to have children to understand."

"Mercy, Sis. What's so special about that? Everybody feels that about everybody. I felt the same way about Mama."

"Oh, well then. . . . The thing is, when Sarah was growing up, she seemed so strong and so bright, I was really in awe of her. And, her relationship with Jim seemed sort of a closed corporation.

"But then, even with all the trouble, sometimes she could be—well—thoughtful to me. You see, the year Sarah graduated from school, that was her coming-out year, of course. This was before the thing about Radcliffe and drama school and the theft—all that nightmare stuff that summer. But anyway, Jim had made me start working on her party years before. You really had to, back then.

"Jim had these two visions about the farm. He wanted to have a really spectacular coming-out party for Sarah there. And he wanted Sarah to get married from there.

"That was right in the middle of that so-called debutante rebellion, when all those girls would just pull on their St. Laurent trousers and jump into their Porsches and drive off to some poverty march. Probably you were spared all that, Harriet. Anyway, some people didn't know until the very day itself that their daughters weren't planning to attend their very own party.

"You might have thought Sarah would be up for that, especially after what I've just told you; that was certainly her point of view, more or less. But Sarah was always different. About six months before her party she said she wanted to talk to me. And she said I probably realized this sort of party was the kind of thing she most hated.

"Well, I thought silence was best. Then she said, 'Mother, I know you've been working for years on this.' Naturally, I had.

"Then she said, 'I know what a disappointment I've been to you, Mother. And honestly I'm sorry.'

"And then she said, 'If this will make a really big difference to you, Mother, I'll do it. But, please—I just want to be absolutely sure you really understand it's not for me. And it's not for Dad. If it's just for Dad, I'm not going through with it. It's just if it makes a really big difference in your life.'

"That's one of those packages Sarah had been delivering about that time—a dozen roses and a hand grenade—but I pretended not to notice, and just said I was really touched

(I know it sounds ridiculous, but things were like that, then) and I'd be very grateful. Pathetic, isn't it? Anyway, it was true that it had the greatest importance to me, even though the reason I cared most was because of Jim. I couldn't begin to imagine what Jim would have said. You see he had no inkling of what was to come.

"Anyway, the party was set for the twelfth of June, and she kept her bargain. Or sort of halfway, at least. She was there in body—I mean she stood around for a couple of hours shaking hands—not very festive, though, I mean definitely the skeleton at the feast sort of thing. And about an hour after the receiving line broke up, she just completely disappeared. Jim was furious. It spoiled the whole party for him. But I couldn't spend my time looking all over the place for Sarah, and nobody would really notice that much, unless we made a fuss. I'm not quite sure what I'm trying to say, Harriet, except sort of explain that Sarah would do things to please me, sometimes, that she just hated. (Never mind the logic, or the lack of grace.) And, Harry, it did mean something to me. And you see that party was just a month before she dropped the bomb about Radcliffe.

"Jim was usually a wizard about reading Sarah's mind, but that night I thought I could. When the party ended it was really morning and Jim and I had the most terrible fight. You can imagine! About Sarah's behavior. I didn't do any fighting exactly. I was more like the innocent bystander, or so I thought. But it went on a long time, and finally Jim had exhausted his vocabulary, and then he marched off to bed. I waited a little while, to make sure, and then I slipped out of the house. I was barefoot and the grass was all wet with dew. There were quail. . . . You know the way you feel sometimes when everything's simply horrible, and suddenly some totally irrelevant little thing like the smell of leaves or the salt air or something gives you a thrill which is just ridiculously out of context?

"Well, I mean it was such a beautiful morning—I can still remember the silver-bell. And I was sure I knew where Sarah had gone. Way down in the woods we'd built a playhouse that Sarah and Jimmy both used to love. Of course, it really hadn't been used for years, and I think Jim had practically forgotten about it, but I knew Sarah hadn't. Sarah and I spent a lot more time in the woods than Jim did.

"But, there was this little house, and inside it, there was Sarah. Just like Goldilocks, curled up on the couch in her slip, fast asleep. Of course, Sarah always looked more like one of those Arthur Rackham waifs than Goldilocks, but she did look so young and frail—these violet circles under her eyes. Just sound asleep. And beside her on the table was a pad, and pages and pages of her writing. I knew Sarah kept a diary. I didn't know if this was it, or something else she'd just written—I'm not one of those mothers who's tempted to read their children's secret thoughts. Actually, I dreaded to think what she might say, even then.

"I hadn't the heart to wake her up, and anyway, if I brought her up to the house, I'd be landing her right in the eye of the storm. So I just pulled a blanket over her. She never stirred. And then I tore a piece of paper off, and wrote: 'Dearest Sarah, I appreciate what you did for me, and I want to thank you.' And then I thought about it and added, 'Maybe you should stay away till Dad gets over being mad.' That seemed sort of treacherous to Jim, and I almost scratched it out, but finally I let it stand.

"Sarah didn't come home till lunch, and by then Jim had stormed off to the city, after he'd decided the one really to blame was me. About a week went by before he saw Sarah, and by that time all his rage was totally frozen over and he was just silent—silent and frosty—and he cut her dead. Me too, of course. He never mentioned it to her at all. He was like that. Well, I'm trying to show it had more than one side, Harriet, but I'm not sure I'm getting anywhere.

"Oh, dear, where was I? All the disasters. And the year and a half of acting class. She'd gone on to another class, and dropped out. And then she was sharing that apartment with

Miriam. I kept feeling she really would have liked to go to college, or at least take courses, but she was too stubborn.

"And then after another year or so, Miriam went off and got married, and Sarah stayed on in the apartment alone. Not very friendly to us, I guess, but she seemed competent. Of course, by then Sarah was no child anymore. But she had nothing to show for it—just these acting classes and all this social work.

"All that time, Jim wasn't quite as upset as I was. It was almost spooky to me sometimes, as if he had a timetable in his head, and he knew perfectly well when this whole ghastly business was going to be over, and he was more or less content to wait.

"Then one day Sarah called me at home. That was a complete novelty at the time. And she actually asked how I was, and what had I been doing, and so on. I was awfully pleased. Then she came to the real point of the call, which was—well, she wanted Jim to have lunch with a very smart man she knew, named Paul Donovan. I said would she be there? and she said no, it was about business. I had always thought Sarah ought to go into business, so I was sort of pleased and intrigued. And then she asked, well, when? And it was only then I thought how weird it was she hadn't called Jim herself. I said, 'Why don't you call your father,' and she said, 'All those secretaries get on my nerves.' Of course, he had a direct line, but I didn't like to use that any more than she did.

"I talked to Jim and he was awfully sweet about it and made an early date—which if you knew Jim's schedule— well, anyway. They fixed on a day for the next week—it was on a Wednesday, Cecil's day off.

"About two-thirty Wednesday, I was having my conversation class in the library when I heard the front door burst open and slam shut. And then I heard Jim banging and cursing his way back to my room. So I told poor Signora Leone *'più tarde,'* and rushed off to see what was wrong. Well,

Jim was just the color of a poinsettia, with these sort of lobster eyes—I was afraid he was having a stroke or something. But then he shouted at me—well, no, he didn't shout, he whispered (when Jim was truly furious, he always whispered), 'Sis, you'd better tell me right now what part you've played in this filthy game.'

"And, of course, I was totally bewildered. 'Paul Donovan,' he said, this whispery way. By then I'd remembered about his lunch and so on, but I couldn't imagine what had happened.

"I made Jim sit down, which was hard, and I brought him a drink, and I said if he didn't relax he was going to make me a widow—Jim was always joking about my longing to be a merry widow. It turned out Jim had gotten so enraged at lunch he couldn't go back to the office. That was a 'first,' let me tell you.

"Anyway, here's what happened. This Paul Donovan had insisted on taking Jim to lunch, which Jim didn't like for starters—Jim liked having lunch right there, because he had a terrific chef who knew just what he liked. And it all saved time, and so on. But Jim was doing it all for Sarah, so he didn't insist. I gather Paul Donovan had just gotten himself made a member of this business club downtown, and I suppose he wanted to show Jim off to the other members.

"Of course, Jim was the sort of person who would have been more impressed if Paul Donovan had presented himself just the way he was. I mean just a brash little mick from some little hick town, where his father was a bartender or an undertaker or something, and who'd gotten himself somehow through some crummy law school. That way, Jim might have had some respect for him, at least.

"So he started off on the wrong foot. And then he began being very familiar with Jim—putting his hand on his shoulder and so on, which Jim can't stand. But Jim was just doing all this for Sarah, and wondering what the hell it was all about.

"Apparently, Paul Donovan wasted no time. Practically right off the bat he said, 'I know you're a very rich man, Mr.

Melmore. And I think I can say in all honesty I'm the answer to every rich man's prayers.' Arresting, isn't it? Well, it turned out the prayers he represented were tax shelters—you know, not 'tax evasion,' 'tax shelter'? Only the shelters he was talking about, according to Jim, were very dicey, if not absolutely on the wrong side of the law.

"Jim was so totally taken aback he didn't say a word, just stared at him. Finally he decided, never mind Sarah, he'd better say something, or silence might suggest acquiescence.

"And he said he had no quarrel with the laws of the United States—he was happy to pay his taxes, and not at all happy some stranger would assume he might be interested in cheating Uncle Sam.

"Well, then this Paul Donovan got very mad—he was just unbelievably conceited, this man. I suppose he thought he was so smart and so smooth Jim would simply stuff some fat check into his hot little hand. And when he didn't, Donovan got insulting.

"And he said about not breaking the law—well, he said that was all an act, just totally fake. Apparently he'd gone over Sarah's trust agreement, and he claimed he'd found out Jim was illegally holding back money that was owed her. Can you believe it? And he said he could prove it in court!

"The truth of the matter was that Jim had set up a trust for Sarah, and it was true Jim controlled the income from it, but she certainly had enough to get by, and Jim thought that was the best way of protecting her from crooks and fortune hunters like this Donovan.

"Harry, you've never known anyone who had more of a horror of people poking around in his personal affairs than Jim. He told me there was a minute when he thought he was going to break the man's neck, but then he just jumped up and rushed out of the place like a madman, and came on home. He didn't know whether I had had anything to do with it. Thank God I hadn't—I hope I'd have had more sense.

"Well, I just prayed that was the end of that. I was sort of shocked by Sarah's behavior. Her only excuse seemed to be she was too naïve to understand. But the next morning Sarah called me as if nothing had happened. How was I, and so forth. Then she said, 'Did you hear what happened yesterday?' And I said well, I thought I had. I thought maybe she was calling to apologize. Not at all. She said, 'Mother, I wonder if you know the true version.' Well, what does one say? Then she said, 'Dad was terribly insulting to Paul Donovan.'

"So we talked about that for a while—she was saying how horribly Jim had behaved, while I tried to tell her Jim's side of it. We were at such cross purposes that after a while even Sarah saw it was pointless.

"Then she said, 'I'm very sorry to have your relationship begin on this note, Mother, because Paul and I are going to get married.' Bang! What a stomach drop that was! Finally I said that in that case I thought it would have been more prudent to say so first, and have this meeting afterward. Sarah said, if Jim hadn't had such a temper tantrum, Paul would have told him that that was the only reason he was looking at the documents for her trust, and that Paul was a very proud man, and wanted to prove himself to Jim before Jim knew he was going to be his son-in-law.

"Oh, my God! I said I was afraid that he was a very stupid proud man, then, because he'd approached Jim in the exact way—and, so on and so forth, till I realized how hopeless it all was, just like before.

"Finally I said to Sarah it was a great shock. She must know that her father was going to be very, very upset, and I thought she'd better give me a chance to break it to him and let her know if he cooled off, and so on. And I did say please to think over the step she was taking.

"Breaking the news to Jim was no treat, as you can imagine. I'm such a coward, I kept putting it off, day after day, till finally I began to get more afraid of Sarah calling Jim herself. So I told him. It wasn't quite as bad as I'd feared. I mean he didn't think I was to blame somehow. He just shook his head, and said, 'Sarah, Sarah,' very sadly. Jim never cried. Never shed a tear. He despised tears. I wish he could have cried, sometimes; it would have been better.

"Anyway, we had tickets to the fight that night, but instead we had a quiet dinner at home, and after dinner he went straight to bed. I didn't see him till the next morning. Then he asked me if Sarah had said anything about when she planned to marry this fellow. She hadn't, so I guess that was a relief.

"And that night, when we were going out, Jim said, 'Now, Sis, remember nothing's ever served as hot as it's cooked. Nothing's going to come of this stunt of Sarah's, I guarantee. Have I ever broken a promise to you, Sis?'

"Well, Jim was not a man to make empty promises.

"After a few more days, Sarah called. She asked if I'd told Jim, and I said yes, and there was a silence. And she said, 'I guess he was furious.' And I said yes. There didn't seem any point in saying he was heartbroken.

"Then she said, 'Mother, I'm sorry I've dumped all this on you. Really I am. But you see I'm fighting for my life, too.'

"I asked her what did she mean—her life? It suddenly struck me that maybe this big palooka was threatening her in some way.

"She said, 'That's melodramatic. But I mean my whole future. My right to lead a happy life with Paul. When you feel that way, you'll stoop pretty low.' I didn't know if she meant stabbing her father in the back, or what, so I just listened. Then she went on praising Paul, and I didn't say anything, until finally I said, 'What can I say, Sarah? I've never even laid eyes on Paul.'

"I guess that was what she was waiting for, because right away she said, 'Mother, that's the point. I'm dying for you to meet Paul. It's so terribly important to me. And please, Mother, please just look at the situation for yourself, through your own eyes. Not Dad's. Please. Please.'

"I had to say that I'd have to clear it with Jim.

" 'Mother,' she said, 'have some guts. Can't you do one thing without Dad's permission? We'd all feel better.' "

Sis paused and lit a cigarette and watched the smoke as it drifted around her.

"Well, did you?" asked Harriet.

"What? Oh, no. Of course not. I had to ask Jim. But when I asked him, the amazing thing was he said yes. He said I could ask them up for a drink the next afternoon. He was going to be in Pittsburgh. He said, while he didn't want to lay eyes on the little bugger himself, it might even be a good idea.

"Well, I called Sarah back, and she was very pleased, and a little after six o'clock—that was the time Sarah chose— Sarah brought this bright legal star, Paul Donovan, to our place. I was awfully nervous, I can tell you. I was sorry I'd had anything to do with the whole thing, because almost any move I made was bound to be wrong.

"I suppose I expected some werewolf, so I was surprised that Paul Donovan had the requisite number of eyes and hands and shoes, and so forth. And actually he was sort of good-looking. Very good-looking. Neither Sarah nor Jim had said anything about that. But of course, he was completely N.O.C.D."

"What? What's that?"

"N.O.C.D.? Well, it's—actually it's just a stupid sort of joke. It means common."

"Oh." Harriet could put more nuances of disapproval into one syllable! What was the matter with her now?

"I'm afraid this is pretty boring," said Sis.

"Not boring for me. No."

"I'll try to be quick. Let's see. Well, nothing came out of that little get-together, except I learned Paul didn't drink at all, nor did Sarah, which made it pretty sticky. So I had about five vodkas to even things off, I was so nervous having them just stare at me.

"In fact, they weren't doing much staring. They sat right

down on the sofa and started hugging; Paul was acting as if he hadn't seen a white woman in ten years. I was terrifically embarrassed. Remember Mama used to think saying 'dear' or 'darling' in public was common? I mean that's what the bedroom door is for. . . .

"Anyway, I guess they wanted to show me how much they loved each other. In fact, I think Paul said something of the sort to me—couldn't I see how much they loved each other. My gosh. Spare me the next installment! But, finally, they sort of got disentangled and said they had to go. I was so relieved. I felt undone."

"Of course, the next morning Sarah called up to see what I thought of Paul. Poor Sarah! She was so crazy about that creature. And she said, 'He really liked you, Mother,' very pleased and proud, and I thought that showed a lot of discernment, since I never said word one, and was looped to boot.

"And she said, 'You two really seemed to get along so well.' Dear heaven! So I was a coward again, and couldn't bring myself to tell her I thought he was loathsome.

"And she said, 'Mother, if you only stick with us, it will work.'

"Then I told her just how terribly opposed her father was. And she said, 'Well, Paul's stubborn too, and he can make miracles.'

"She said she was sorry about the bad start, but she asked if Jim wouldn't just see them together, so he'd get a better impression of Paul. And then they could talk things over together, and there was really no reason to fight, and so forth. I said I'd ask but I couldn't hold out much hope.

" 'Just ask,' said Sarah.

"Naturally Jim said no. I hadn't told him much about their visit, because nothing much had happened, except all that necking, which he would've hated even more than I did.

"When I told Sarah, she said then could I have lunch with her. Harriet, I would have jumped for joy if I hadn't known the only reason she wanted to see me was to make me do something or other that Jim would hate. And she said, 'I suppose you'll feel you have to ask Dad before you can have lunch with your own daughter.' I said I didn't have to ask him but naturally I'd tell him. That we told each other everything, and this was a pretty important thing.

"And then Sarah said, 'My God, your marriage must have changed dramatically since I left home.' In that very sarcastic tone. I said what was the point of meeting if she was going to talk that way. And she said she was sorry, and so on. Anyhow, it gave me a preview of what lunch might be like, so I ended up really dreading it.

"Sarah and I met down in some little health-food restaurant in the Village. The first place she wanted to go didn't even have booze—and, well, I'm making myself sound as bad as Cottie, but it's just that when I'm nervous I want something available—wine, at least.

"It was a long, long lunch, Harriet. At first, Sarah was very nice and even—well—affectionate.... She said, 'Mother, I have the feeling you think I never really loved you. But you're terribly wrong.' I was very touched, so I leaned over and gave her a hug and a kiss. 'I wish you'd done that before,' said Sarah. 'You were always so cold and aloof with me.' Well, cold and aloof is the last thing I am, you know? Sort of the other extreme I would think. But then she started the other business. 'I was always so afraid you would drag me down with you,' she said. That certainly sounded squalid and disagreeable, but I was still sort of in the dark. What she meant, apparently, was that I'd always sided with Jim against the children.

"I suppose, in principle, that may have been true—it's my generation, I guess. But in fact I never felt I was siding against the children. It was sort of one case at a time, you know. But the truth was, Jim was so bright he was usually in the right.

"Anyway, I said, I thought it was a little late in the day to talk about things like that; it seemed more important now for Sarah to make the right decisions in her life. Then, Sarah got positively sort of—well—you know how people are when suddenly they get religion, or join A.A., or stuff. I'd've thought she was on drugs except I knew she wasn't, because the one good thing about Donovan was he was very against drink and drugs.

"Anyway, she said in this really impassioned way, 'Look, Mother, it's not too late. Of course I know the women's liberation movement has marched on by you and you never heard a peep.'

"'*Au contraire,*' I said. 'One thing I hate about it is how noisy it is.'

"I could see Sarah was annoyed with me—she was big for every sort of liberation and thought I was being too frivolous.

"Anyway, I said, 'Sarah, I'm glad if it makes people your age happy. But in my case it's just not applicable.' And I saw she was going to ask me why, and start some pointless argument, so then I just said quickly, 'I'm not intelligent enough.'

"'Mother,' she said, 'let me tell you something. Now that Paul's met both you and Dad, he's decided you're just as intelligent as Dad.' Now doesn't that take the biscuit? I couldn't help but say, 'Do you believe that too, Sarah?'

"Then she did look a little uncomfortable, but she said, 'You were trained never to show your brains or your emotions, Mother. If you had ever gone into the market place to find your natural level, you'd have so much more confidence in yourself, and Dad wouldn't be able to act like such a tyrant with you.'

"Lord. I tried to think about my natural level, and pretty soon I realized that was exactly why I hadn't wanted to go into the market place. I'd be lucky to be making artificial flowers in some dank little cellar!

"Sarah was talking on about various things I could do, but it was all so silly I couldn't even concentrate. Finally Sarah said in this sort of despairing way, 'Look, Mother, didn't you ever want to *be* anything?'

"Well, I really tried hard. I said, 'When I was little, I used to think I was going to grow up to be a great artist . . . doesn't everybody?'

"Then she said, 'No, but anyway I mean when you were older. There must have been something, sometime, you desperately wanted to be.'

" 'Sarah,' I said, 'the only thing I wanted desperately to be was your father's wife.'

" 'Oh, God,' said Sarah.

"So then I said if the point of this lunch was to criticize my marriage, I resented it.

"So Sarah said my marriage was actually beyond criticism. And then she paused, and then she said she didn't see how anyone could even call it a 'marriage'—it should just go under the heading of cruel and unusual punishment.

"Sarah had never talked that way to me before, and I was really taken aback. Jim may have been a difficult man, I admit that, Harry, but all I can say is, my God, Harriet, it was worth it. As terrible as he could be, that's how marvelous he could be. He could be so funny. And, when he was in a good mood, it was so exhilarating your feet weren't even touching the ground. He had ten times the energy and magnetism of any other human being.

"Harriet, all the years I was living with Jim, I told myself over and over how lucky I was. So I said, well—I didn't say all this to Sarah, but I just tried to be calm and I said that her father was wonderful in so many different ways.

" 'Let me count the ways,' she said. I thought she was going to, but then I realized she was quoting from that drip Mrs. Browning; and in fact she was just saying it very sarcastically, as if she couldn't think of any ways. And it began to seem another pointless discussion, and I said so.

"Sarah said it hadn't been pointless for her; that she was glad to learn that I really loved Jim, because then my life hadn't been such a total washout. Dear Heaven! The condescension! She said she'd thought all I felt was fear of him. She said it was a great relief to her, because then I wouldn't be too frightened and revolted by what she wanted to tell me.

Oh, God. I said, 'Just a minute, Sarah,' and then I went into the loo and took two Valium."

"Is that what you did just now?"

"What on earth do you mean, Harriet? Right now? I mean this is an awful story, but I don't expect you to punish me or anything. At least, I hope not. Why do you ask?"

"I don't know. I just wondered."

"Actually, in addition to not being an alcoholic, I'm not a drug fiend, either. This was a special case. Anyway, I came back and I said to Sarah if she was intending to tell me anything about her father's private life, I didn't want to hear it.

"Sarah said there was certainly plenty to say about that, but it was all pointless. Anyway, she said she would spare my feelings, and not criticize her father, except in this one specific case, having to do with her.

"She said Jim always said or implied or something that while he might be tough or ruthless in business he had absolute integrity, that he never deceived anybody, and kept right to the letter of the law.

"I said, 'That's right.'

"She said, 'You mean *he* says that's right.'

"So then, she launched into her story about how her father had made a big deal with her about her trust fund—how much he was doing for her, and that he was making her independent and so forth, but in reality he was keeping most of the income for himself.

" 'Good Lord, Sarah,' I said, 'do you really think your father would try to cheat you out of a little bit of money?'

" 'It's not what I think. It's what the law says,' Sarah said.

"And then she went into all the same stuff Paul had, and she said Paul thought she ought to go to court and sue Jim. Of course, Paul would be her lawyer.

"I was just speechless. The treachery! But I tried not to get too emotional. I said, 'First, Sarah, you'll lose your case.'

" 'We'll win,' she said.

"And next, I said, she'd never see her father again.

" 'I'll take that chance,' she said.

"Well, I didn't think there was anything further to say, so I asked for the check.

"But then Sarah said, 'Please, Mother, I don't want it to come to that. If you just side with us, Dad wouldn't go against both of us. You don't understand. You're the one who has the real power.'

"Well, I certainly didn't. And then Sarah said, 'You probably don't even realize this, Mother, but you're one of the richest women in America.'

"I said she well knew I had no money at all; it was Jim's money.

"Then Sarah sort of laughed, and she said, 'What do you think all those papers you've been signing all these years are about? Paul says he's checked the proxy statements, and without your stock Dad doesn't have a controlling interest. It's sort of ironic, but Paul says Dad couldn't afford to have you side against him.

" 'Look, Mother. I wouldn't have found out all this business about my trust and so forth, if Paul hadn't been so smart; I was always psyched not to question Dad, too. But look, there's no reason you should believe Paul or me. Go to a lawyer of your own—not a lawyer of Dad's, though. They'll explain.'

"Well, I've never been so shocked. At her very worst, Sarah had never been hard or conniving.

"I couldn't help but say, 'Is that all you care about, Sarah? Money?'

"And then she said, 'Oh, God, Mother, you know that's not true.'

"And then I said that everything she'd been saying sounded as if it came straight from Paul, and it sounded to me as if she were totally under Paul Donovan's thumb.

"And then she said again, 'Oh, God, Mother.' Then she said the hardest thing she'd ever have to do was have this showdown with her father. And far from being under Paul Donovan's thumb, Paul was desperately trying to help her be independent, and specifically of her father, and not to be scared of him any longer. And proving Jim was in the wrong, and she was in the right, was part of the way.

"And I said, 'What do you mean, "in the wrong," Sarah? Where does that money come from? It all comes from your father.'

" 'Okay,' she said. 'Suppose we don't say "wrong." Just "illegal." '

"So then I said as long as she had that attitude toward her father, what could she expect from me?

"She said, 'Mother, I truly believe you've always cared about my happiness. Please, *show* you do, Mother. Please side with us. Then Dad would have to come around.'

"I couldn't say a word.

"And she said, 'At least, don't side against us.'

"Then I said, 'Sarah, you may think it's love you want, but you make it sound more like money. You must know I think disloyalty is the most rotten of all the vices. Could you really believe I'd go behind your father's back and plot against him? What a sorry opinion you have of me.' So I slapped down a twenty, which was the smallest I had, and got up to go.

" 'Please, Mother,' she said. 'Please, Mother. Don't walk out on me.' Her face was awfully white, and she looked as if she might burst into tears any minute.

"Of course, I couldn't leave her then.

" 'Don't think I like what I'm doing,' she said. 'My God, I know. But, well, you talk about loyalty. I know you're loyal to Dad. My God, do I know! But, Mother, don't you see? My first loyalty is to Paul now. Just like Paul's first loyalty is to me. That's why I've got to go through with it.'

"And then she said, 'Mother, even if Paul's not totally in the right, I've got to consider his feelings. He may come across as totally strong and confident, but with a man like Dad, Paul's not as confident as he seems. That scene with Dad really shook him up badly. He's too proud to say so, but I know. And I've got to back him up.'

"By then I was feeling sorry for Sarah again, because obviously this rat was pushing her to do all these horrible things.

And I had begun to realize this girl was over the edge, and what she really needed was not a lawyer but a doctor, so the thing to do was to try to stay calm and make sure she didn't do some sort of lunatic thing that would be irreparable.

"Meanwhile, I said, 'Sarah, you asked for my help. Look, here is the best help I can give you.' I told her she was doing everything totally wrong. That once Jim's back was up, he was inflexible, and that he would never, never give in to blackmail.

"I said, 'Sarah, please just let some time pass.' Then she could approach her father on her own, and if she was quiet and reasonable and made her peace with him, it was just barely possible everything might work out.

"Sarah said, 'That's the way you'd do it, Mother, but Paul would lose every vestige of respect for me if I behaved like that. He's a fighter. He's all the things Dad pretends to be—straight and totally honest. And with all kinds of integrity. He's the first human being in the world I've ever totally trusted. Paul is totally incorruptible.

" 'Don't you see, Mother? If it's money he wanted' (and I admit the thought had crossed my mind), 'he's no idiot! He knows this would be the worst way. All we'd ever get would be the capital from my trust fund. We know that! We know Dad would cut me off. But Paul refuses to compromise. If only you'd explain our side to Dad.'

"Harriet, by that time I was just totally befuddled. I only knew I certainly didn't want to be the one to repeat all those threats to Jim. I told her she must know that was impossible.

" 'Sarah,' I said, 'Paul is betting on the wrong horse.'

" 'But we're not asking anything,' Sarah said. 'Or anyway, just for you to tell Dad the truth. And back us up.'

" 'Sarah,' I said. 'What am I supposed to tell Dad the truth about?'

" 'About Paul,' she said.

"As little as I liked to, I felt I had to go on. 'What about Paul?' I said.

" 'That you think he's a truthful man with—with total integrity,' she said. 'I'm sure you do,' she added.

"Well, the silence was sort of deafening.

" 'That you like him very much yourself,' she said. I didn't say a word.

" 'Well—that—I love him.' She almost whispered it.

"I looked at Sarah, and suddenly I felt so sad. You know I said I had a habit of thinking of Sarah as a strong, competent girl, who was a formidable adversary, while all the time, she was really like a child—so very, very fragile. When she had come face to face with real evil, like Hooker I mean, she just went to pieces.

"I didn't know what to say or do. Naturally I would have loved to comfort Sarah. It was hard not to just hold out my arms to her. But it would have been false and misleading, and so it would have made it all the worse in the end.

" 'Mother,' she said. 'Don't you see, Mother? I want the half a loaf.'

"That was a saying we had in the family—Sarah and Jimmy and I, that is. It comes from the fairy stories I used to read them when they were little.

"Harriet, I know it's the most total bore—other people's pet names and family jokes and so on, what could be more tedious? But, in a way, I really do have to explain this. You know, a lot of those fairy stories began with a poor old woman who had three sons, and when they grew up, she had to send them out into the world to seek their fortunes. And she would bake a loaf and each boy had his choice—to take the half a loaf with the blessing or the whole loaf with her malison. The greedy older brothers always plumped for the whole loaf, and did that ever turn out to be a bad investment! The children, particularly Jimmy when he was little, would get so excited and say, 'No, no, take the half a loaf, take the half a loaf.' Jimmy, in particular—as if he could alter the whole course of the story. But of course all those stories, unlike life, had a happy ending.

"Anyway, for some reason, the children and I started to use that as a sort of shorthand sometimes, the way you do, you know. 'I'm taking the whole loaf' meant, go jump in the lake. And the 'half a loaf' meant, well—the opposite. But we stopped saying that after Jimmy died.

"So when Sarah said 'half a loaf' she not only meant she wanted my blessing—she was invoking all the most totally emotional, instinctive feelings. And, most of all, she was invoking Jimmy. It was the strongest thing she could have said. It was almost unfair. Because how could I give Sarah and Paul my blessing?

"I said, 'Sarah, God knows I love you.'

"She had been all drooped over, but she looked up a little at that.

" 'Please,' I said, 'hold on. I don't see how I can help you. You want me to tell Dad something I don't think is right.'

"She didn't deny it.

" 'Not because I believe it myself.'

"She never said a word.

" 'Not because I think it's the best thing for you.'

"Not a word.

" 'But just because you begged me.'

" 'Yes,' she said, 'just because your last child begged you.'

"Oh, Harriet, I hadn't thought she'd say that. Sarah always had so much pride. I'd counted on that. Dear Lord, Harriet. I didn't know what I was going to do then.

" 'Sarah,' I said, 'are you really planning to marry Paul?' I hated even asking, but I knew Jim would want to know. And Sarah was so funny. She was actually capable of making a big deal about the issue without really meaning to follow through. With her opinions, who knows?

"Sarah sighed and she said, 'Oh, Mother, you must know— I couldn't care less about that. But yes, we do plan to get married. If. The "if" has to do with me, Mother. The "if" is if I'm brave enough.'

" 'About marriage—well, Paul's a real romantic, you know.

I'm not. And he sees marriage as such a mystical final commitment. And then, of course, he's Catholic. So he can't get married more than once. So, if it's me, then that's it for him. Paul doesn't have much respect for relationships outside of marriage. He's old-fashioned, okay? The "if"—it's if I can win this battle with Dad.'

"And I said, 'Sarah, you keep implying you want family harmony, but it really sounds as if you want a battle royal.'

" 'But, Mother,' she said, 'I've been trying to make you understand. Right now, there's room for compromise. I know very well it'll be different once we haul Dad into court.'

"So there you are. The minute I weakened, she used threats. And I just wanted to get out of there before I got sucked in again.

"So I got up, put on my coat, and said, 'Oh, let Paul tell him then.'

" 'Paul can't get through to Dad. He's tried.'

"Well, I was back to feeling no sympathy for Sarah, I just wanted to go home, so I said, 'All right, Sarah. I'll tell him. It's your funeral.' And I left.

"My God, Harriet, it was all so ghastly. I know I'm probably not doing Sarah justice. I don't want you to think she was cheap or money-grubbing."

"I don't," said Harriet. "I'm glad you called her after Mama. She sounds like a spunky girl."

Sis lit another cigarette. "Well, maybe. So I guess you think I'm a villainess."

"I didn't say that, Sis."

"But you mean it."

"Well, what happened then?"

"Oh, God, Harriet, I didn't think you'd turn against me!"

"Heavens, Sis, I had no idea you were so sensitive to criticism."

"If you want to know, Harriet, aside from cowardice, sensitivity to criticism is my salient characteristic."

"Sis, I haven't criticized you yet. Just go on."

6

Conversation Class

"SARAH, who do you think is better-looking?"

"I don't know."

"Come on, Sarah. You must have some opinion."

"I don't even know who you're comparing."

"Me and Jacques. Who else is here to compare?"

"Oh. Well, you're both good-looking."

"Sarah, that's not an answer. You have to make a choice. Do you think Jacques is better-looking than me?"

"Um. No. Look, I don't honestly think about that sort of thing. I told you I think you're both good-looking."

"That's not an answer."

"If I absolutely had to say?"

"That's what I'm telling you."

"Well, maybe you. Because—um—you're more strange-looking."

"Strange-looking? 'Strange-looking' doesn't sound that good to me."

"Well, I mean Jack is more—um—well, when you look at Jack at first, he could be sort of the All-American—well, the ideal American boy, you know."

"Yeah. Jacques looks like the ideal All-American boy, Sarah. You're right. Like a football player, or a cowboy."

"Um—no. I was just going to say he begins by looking like that, and he can talk sort of like a farm boy. But then you notice he's got those strange eyes. And he's got broad shoulders. But he's really, I mean, you know he couldn't possibly be a football player. Not a cowboy, either. And he's not a farm boy at all, really. So you end up realizing he's strange-looking, too."

"Hmmm. 'Strange-looking'? Sarah, I actually got you talking even if you don't make too much sense. You see, strange-looking is how I think *you* look, Sarah, though you're getting over it a little. So you think I'm strange-looking. Do you think I begin strange-looking and end up strange-looking too?"

"Actually I do, Maurice. But I mean it as a compliment. You see people can be terrifically handsome, but so—um—insipid, it makes them dull. But I think you begin by looking —well—'strange-looking-interesting,' and maybe you—well, still you end up—still looking very—interesting. And well—um—strange-looking."

"I guess you haven't got much taste about good looks. Did you ever have any boyfriends, Sarah?"

"Um. Yes."

"How many?"

"That I really cared for? Oh, two, I guess."

"Were they good-looking at all?"

"I guess most people—um, most people—well, the answer is yes. Actually, they were both—um—very good-looking, but that was just a coincidence, because actually, being good-looking, well it's just totally unimportant to me."

"These very good-looking guys you loved. Did you think they were strange-looking?"

"Um. No. Actually I didn't. But you've gotten everything totally confused, Maurice."

"I'm not confused by you, Sarah. In fact, what you're saying is you don't think either Jacques or me is good-looking, but especially me."

"Oh, God, Maurice."

"Look, Sarah. I was just trying to think of something interesting we could talk about."

"Maurice, I think talking about how good-looking—well, you see that's about the most boring thing to me. The most boring thing I can think of to talk about. I'm sorry."

"Sarah, you're wrong. It's one of the most interesting things there is. But okay, you don't know anything about it.

And anyhow you're crazy. I wonder, will I ever know if those boyfriends of yours really were good-looking? Do you have any pictures of them?"

"Maurice, you would drive anyone crazy. I said talking about being good-looking is boring."

"So you think I'm boring without even being good-looking. Thanks a lot, Sarah. Oh, and by the way, I didn't drive you crazy. You were always crazy."

"Oh, Maurice. Please, please leave me alone. Just leave me alone. Leave me alone."

"Don't get so excited, Sarah. I'll leave you alone. It's my pleasure."

7

Sarah Melmore's Retreat

"HARRIET, do you really want me to go on? It's late."

"Just finish."

Sis lit a cigarette.

"In the end I told Jim almost everything," she said, "because he didn't blow up. And Sarah had asked me to, after all. He just listened, hardly said a word, and then at the end he said, 'Sarah certainly picks the winners.'

"There was nothing much to say to that. I hadn't thought Jim would get hysterical about Paul's threats or anything— I mean Paul was just like a little mosquito buzzing around his ankle. It was Sarah's disloyalty.

"Jim just stared at the fire awhile. Then he said, 'I saw that boy at '21' the other day. I left before he saw me. He isn't very prudent.'

"I was dying to know what he meant—obviously Donovan must have been with crooks or hookers or something. But most of the time Jim never satisfied my curiosity.

"Then he said, 'Sis, you're a woman of feeling and sensitivity.'

"Harriet, I was so moved I think I must have blushed. Jim almost never gave me compliments, except about—you know —how I looked. I could count his other compliments just about on one hand.

"Anyway, he said, 'What do you estimate Sarah's feelings really are about the young man?'

"I had to say that I thought she was crazy about him.

" 'No,' he said. 'Think carefully, and sort it out. How much does the man mean to her, aside from just liking to screw him while he screws her family?'

"Well, I certainly had thought about it seriously, and I had to say I really thought she was sincere. I thought this time she was really in love. I told him what Sarah had said about Paul's honor and integrity and so on, and he asked me to repeat that. Jim had this way of making you repeat things word for word. And I did tell him a little bit of how she criticized him, because it was really part of the story.

"Jim just listened, and then he shook his head, and said, 'Sarah, Sarah.' Like that first day.

"After a while, he said, 'Sis, I just can't understand. How can the girl have so little judgment?' Neither did I, so there wasn't much to add.

"Then Jim said, 'If I taught Sarah anything, Sis, I taught her that every man has his price. Some may be better, and some may be worse, but never trust the man who won't admit that. Of course the price doesn't have to be money.'

" 'Jim, I wish you weren't always so cynical,' I said. 'Anyway, you don't have a price.'

"Jim just laughed. 'You bet I do, Sis. And you're the one who knows just what it is.'

"Jim wasn't serious, but all the same, I couldn't help but wish he hadn't stuffed Sarah so full of ideas like that. I even said so.

"And Jim said, 'Don't worry, Sis. Sarah and I understand each other.'

"There didn't seem to be much evidence of that, either, but I held my tongue."

Mrs. Melmore shivered. "I'm cold," she said.

"Sis, that's a pure impossibility. It must be ninety degrees."

"It's the wind." It was true Sis had gooseflesh.

"Do you want to go home? Maybe you're coming down with something."

"No, I feel now as if I have to tell you the rest of it. We're almost there. But I don't see why you said I'd acted so badly, Harriet. I think that's very unfair."

"I never said that. I said I admired Sarah's courage."

"Isn't that more or less the same thing? Never mind. All right, here goes.

"Well, time passed. Then one day Jim said, 'Sis, the time has come to have all this out.'

"And he told me to call Sarah, and tell her her father wanted to talk to her by herself. Jim said to make it absolutely clear that under no conditions would he see Paul Donovan. Sarah said that in that case she wanted to make absolutely sure I would be there—'as a witness.' I knew that would be all right with Jim, so I didn't quote her.

"Sarah said she'd come after dinner. Apparently, she'd lived away from home so long she thought that meant about eight o'clock. Well, I decided we'd better have a really early dinner, because God knows what might happen, and I wanted Jim at least to have something to eat.

"Anyway, Jim got dressed very carefully, as if he were going on television or something. So did I, I guess. And then neither of us had much to say to the other. It was a mistake about dinner, because Jim hardly ate at all. After dinner, I asked if he wanted a cigar. That was silly, because cigars— Jim only liked a cigar when he was feeling relaxed.

We sat there, and then Jim said to me all of a sudden, 'Sis, I must be getting soft. I know you think I've always been soft with Sarah. Maybe you were right.

" 'You know what? I was just thinking what a great feeling

it would be if you and I were sitting here waiting because Sarah had found herself some really swell fella—a guy we could all respect. He wouldn't even have to be smart, just someone strong and decent, who'd love Sarah and be a good father to our grandchildren.'

"Jim always thought a lot about grandchildren. I think he fully intended to live long enough to have one grandson he'd bring up himself to take over the company.

"Then he said, 'But that's not the worst, Sis. You know, in a way I wish I'd never laid eyes on this Paul Donovan. Then maybe I could kid myself about the fella, just take him on Sarah's say-so. I think I could have done it, Sis. I truly think I could have done it if they'd played their cards right. This thing with Sarah has cost me more than you know.' And then he just gave a terrific sigh, and didn't say anything else till Sarah arrived. When Sarah came up to the apartment, she was actually wearing a dress, quite a pretty dress, not the usual trousers. No makeup of course. She looked a little scared. I didn't blame her. What she'd done was pretty low, and Jim could be scary.

"She just stood there. Didn't come over and kiss either of us or anything. And finally Jim said, 'Well Sarah, why don't you sit down?'

"And she did, but she still didn't say anything, so finally he said, 'You wanted to talk to me?'

" 'You're not making it easy,' she said. 'I didn't want to come here like an enemy. I wanted to see if we couldn't work things out.'

"Of course that was all Jim wanted, and he told her that. And he said he'd like her suggestions.

"Then Sarah opened up and began to talk about Paul. By then I could practically recite the whole thing with her, chapter and verse, except this time she said that she and Paul intended to get married, that she knew it wasn't a worldly match, but she and Paul didn't like worldly people and didn't care what they thought.

"And finally Jim said, 'Why did you come here to tell me all this, daughter? Can't you see that I am in no way interfering with these dreams of yours?'

" 'But you are,' she said.

"So he said, 'Sarah, please explain to me how I am standing in the way of your marrying this man. If you don't care about anyone's approval, you could have married the fella last month, or last week. Is there something I don't understand?' "

" 'Paul's a Catholic,' she said.

" 'So what?' said Jim.

"Then Sarah said, all in a sort of a rush, 'All my life I've been afraid of you, Dad. As long as that's true, I'm not fit to be anyone's wife. I'm just no use until I can actually stand up to you and have my way, for once.'

"There was a long silence. I couldn't even guess what was going to happen. But Jim didn't get annoyed, he was really terrifically patient and sweet. He told Sarah he was sorry to hear she felt that way. He said he had always felt they had a very equal relationship—like partners. Then he told her how very much he cared for her. And he said the most terrible thing that he had ever had to endure was this break with her. I was just amazed. Never, ever, had I heard Jim express his feelings so openly—never to me, certainly. Everything he said was so touching, really heartbreaking. And I thought even Sarah would have to melt.

"Finally, at the end, he said, 'But Sarah, if only you could have set your heart on something else. Sarah, that's a worthless man you've picked. He's worthless, Sarah.'

"Maybe he should have waited and let her say something first. Maybe it would have made a difference. But, whatever she might have been going to say, she stiffened up then, and said, 'Father, you know how I feel, so I won't repeat myself. It's interesting that the word you choose has to do with money. "Worthless." You see Paul and I don't care about money the way you do.'

"Jim shook his head and said, 'Oh, Sarah. Where's your

sense of proportion?' Then he said, 'You know something, Sarah? In spite of what I feel about Paul Donovan, if you'd come here tonight to say you liked the man for his looks and what the two of you did in bed, and didn't give a hang about his character, you know what, Sarah? I'd've been very unhappy about it but I wouldn't have gone against you. I would have thought, let my girl have her man for a couple of years, or however long it takes her to find him out. But, as it is, I can't let it go. It's a question of responsibility. I tell you, Sarah, I know as sure as I'm standing here, that man is a phony. He's false and greedy and cheap, Sarah. He'd sell you out for a song. He'd sell his mother for a nickel. You say all I talk about is money. Well, probably that's the terms I think in. But so does Paul Donovan. Except he's a hypocrite, which I'm not, and he's not as smart as he thinks he is. Sarah, I tell you that man's for sale, and the price isn't high.'

"Sarah said, 'What you're saying is so ridiculous it doesn't even make me angry.'

"Then he said, 'Sarah, whatever else you think, surely you can't think I'd lie to you about something this important to both of us? Sarah, I give you my sacred word of honor that what I say is true and I can prove it.'

"Sarah said, 'Then I'll be polite, and say I solemnly believe you're mistaken.'

"Jim said, 'The boy can be bought off, and I could tell you to the exact penny what it would cost.'

"Sarah said, 'Mother, I don't seem to be making much headway with Dad. Do you mind if I just talk to you?'

"Jim said, 'Sarah, I'm going to give you two alternatives. You can believe me, or you can take the painful alternative of having it demonstrated to you.'

"Sarah kept looking at me. She said, 'Mother, would you tell Dad it's ridiculous either way.'

"Jim said, 'Sarah, if you care so very much for him, it would save a world of suffering if you would take my word and break with the boy. And it would save you, among other things, your self-respect.'

"Sarah stood up then. She said she'd been a fool to come, and please understand he couldn't bully either her or Paul with his threats, and she left.

"Jim was angry and upset, the way he'd laid out his most private feelings for Sarah and she'd still trampled on him and as good as told him he was a liar. I knew how awful he must feel.

"He said to me, 'I'm not a cruel man, Sis, but you do see I can't let this farce go on.'

"And then he just sat there thinking. And then he said, 'The man's a moral idiot, as well as every other kind.' And then he said, 'In this case, it's being cruel to be kind.' And then he sort of sighed, and said, 'But the trouble is, Sis, when you open up a can of worms like this, you just don't know where it will all end up.'

"That had been quite an evening. I was worn out, and I felt so sorry for Jim. He was just as exhausted, and we—at least I—just dropped into bed and slept like the dead.

"I hadn't a clue about Jim's plans, and God knows, he practically never told me a thing. But I knew he wasn't one for idle threats, and I knew something was going on, because Sarah called me once, and said did I know Jim was calling Paul all the time, and she said she supposed he 'must be getting senile.'

" 'You and I should be that senile,' I said.

"That was the level of the conversation. I told you how my feelings about Sarah used to ebb and flow. I had felt sympathetic to Sarah when she'd said she was frightened of her father—I certainly used to be! But when I thought it over, it didn't make that much sense to me. Sarah was the one who never had a reason to be frightened of Jim, and she always said just what she pleased to him. Sometimes she was terribly rude. And she always set right out to get whatever she wanted, bearing Jim no mind—like drama lessons, and so on. Looking back on it, I was afraid she'd just been playing on my sympathy—play-acting, really—to get what she wanted.

"But about a week later, she called me in the morning,

sounding—well, quite hysterical. She asked me where Paul was. Naturally, I hadn't a clue.

" 'Dad knows,' she said. 'I want you to tell Dad if I don't hear from him in the next couple of hours, I'm going to call the police.'

"Harriet, by then I felt so totally worn out by Sarah's carrying on. I just hoped that man had taken off for the tall timber. I said, 'Do what you like, Sarah. Goodbye.'

"But then, just as I was going out, Jim called. He said to cancel whatever our plans were for that night. He said Paul Donovan would be coming up to our place about seven. He said to tell Sarah to be there too.

"So I did, and maybe it was just as well Jim hadn't told me anything more, because Sarah had about a hundred questions and I could just say, 'I don't know, I don't know, and I don't know.'

"Needless to say, I dreaded the whole thing. I couldn't imagine what was going to happen, except that it wouldn't be pleasant. Jim came home about six-thirty, and almost immediately he started working on some business stuff and hardly spoke to me. So I was all alone when Paul Donovan arrived.

"Curtis showed him in and then came the first surprise. Right away he asked for a drink. Scotch on the rocks. That was about the extent of our conversation.

"Sarah arrived about five minutes later, and obviously she still knew no more than I did, because she said, 'Paul, what in the name of God is going on? Where have you been?' And then she saw he had a drink, and she looked even more upset.

"And he said, 'Wait a minute, Sarah. We have to wait for your father.'

"She'd been about to sit beside him, but when he said that, she went and sat on the other side of the room, and just stared at him.

"Then Jim came in. And he said, 'Good evening, Sarah, Sis. We're all here? Mr. Donovan has something to say to you, Sarah.'

"Then I noticed how weird Paul was looking. His face

looked as if it had been put on all awry or something. He looked horrible. He'd probably been drinking all day, and I guess he wasn't used to it.

"Well, Paul stood up, as if he was going to recite the Gettysburg Address or something, and then he stared at Jim, and if looks could kill . . . I think at first he couldn't find the words, but finally he began.

" 'Sarah, your father's been very generous to me.'

" 'What!' said Sarah.

" 'Wait, Sarah, please. Yes, it's true. He's done me some real favors in my career.'

"Well, I was just as surprised as Sarah. I mean I could hardly believe it.

" 'And I owe him something. I mean I owe you too, Sarah. Well, the point is . . . Sarah, you've always been rich. But the thing is, coming from a world of prestige and privilege, you don't know how things are on the other side. I mean about money.'

" 'Paul, please! Please don't say another word. Let's just get out of here!'

" 'Sarah, the truth is I was seeing another girl when I met you. She's a model, Astrid Norden. I might have mentioned her name. I felt obliged to see her right along because— well—she's a really nice girl you see, and she'd gotten—well, she'd gotten really serious about me (this was all before I met you, Sarah) and somehow she'd gotten this fixed idea in her head that I was going to marry her. And Astrid's sort of a high-strung girl. I mean she was always making these suicide threats. . . . And I didn't want to let her down too hard.'

"Jim looked up then. 'Mr. Donovan,' he said, 'I think these personal matters are best left between you and Sarah. Our dealings concern business. Could you stick to that, please?'

"Sarah was staring at Jim by then. I couldn't bear to look at her face.

"Paul stammered around a bit and said something about the opportunities and the responsibilities and the future and so on.

" 'What in God's name are you saying?' said Sarah. 'My father gave you *money?*'

"Paul mumbled some more garbage, and Sarah said, 'I don't believe it, Paul! Don't let him make you say this! How did he make you say this?'

"Paul just kept shaking his head, and then finally Sarah turned to her father, and she said, and her voice was deadly calm then: 'Tell me what he's saying, Daddy.'

"And Jim said, 'Sarah, I told Mr. Donovan that if he and I were to do any business together, he must first divest himself of any personal entanglements which might confuse the issue. I named a price, and he accepted it. I think he's trying to tell you we have a deal.'

"And Sarah said: 'Paul?'

"Paul didn't say a word.

"Sarah jumped to her feet. Tears were just spouting out of her eyes. 'Paul!' she said. 'Paul! Why did you do this to me? Why are you telling me all this? Why are you telling me this here, of all places?'

"Paul said, 'I'm sorry, Sarah. I'm afraid your father— Well, anyway, they're your folks, after all. There's no getting around that, really. This is your home.'

"Then Sarah turned and ran out of the apartment. She didn't even take her coat and there we were left with Paul Donovan. Jim never glanced at him. He just went back to his desk and sat down and began looking over his papers.

"Paul wanted to slink out just as fast as he could, but just as he left he muttered, 'I hope he fries in hell, Mrs. Melmore.' (But too low for Jim to hear.) That was Sarah's mountain of honor and integrity. Plus Jim told me there was lots and lots more, if Sarah had let him go on.

"It was amazing all the stuff Jim found out about Paul. I was only sorry it had to happen quite that way. But it had to, you know. Jim could never have trusted Paul to tell Sarah the truth, and she was so crazy about him, he could have weaseled out of anything.

"The next thing was, of course, I was terribly worried about Sarah. Naturally. And Jim said, 'Don't worry about the girl, Sis. Sarah's a survivor.' I wasn't so sure.

"Anyway, after about twenty minutes, I started calling her apartment. No answer.

" 'Don't bother,' said Jim. 'She's not there.'

" 'She's probably not picking up,' I said. 'What should we do?'

" 'Sis, I know where Sarah will be. Just relax,' he said.

"I wanted to tell Jim and his famous intuition to go take a flying jump. I was worried about my daughter. And I was remembering how, in her way, Sarah was as fragile as an eggshell.

" 'What time did I tell you to have dinner, Sis?'

"He'd said dinner at eight-thirty, and of course, it was just about that, on the nose.

"Jim said, 'Sarah's going to go out to the country. So give Nanny a call, sometime after dinner. About ten. You don't want to worry Nanny.'

"Well, I did what he said, except I kept calling the apartment too. And he was right.

" 'I know Sarah,' he said.

"Nanny said she'd come in looking very tired and said she just wanted to sleep. I asked her to check, and she came back and said Sarah was lying in her room in the dark. She must be asleep.

"Jim said, 'You see?' But I was worried. And I was right to be worried. That was the beginning of the end. Sarah just lay around. She didn't speak. She hardly ate. Her eyes were always all swollen up, though I never saw her crying. She didn't want to leave her room. You had to take her arm and pull her up to bring her down. She wouldn't resist, but she was just like her Raggedy Ann doll.

"You can imagine how horrible that was. But I just had to have faith that like the other time she'd pull herself together eventually.

"Jim wasn't quite as upset as I was. First of all, he had a lot more hope. He told me it was all going to work out all right in the end. He said he thought he understood the phase Sarah was going through—she was testing her own power, and the power of other men and so on. But this time when she came out of it, she'd be all right, he said. And she'd accept her fate.

"Jim wouldn't talk about what he meant by her fate, but he did say to me, 'Sis, I promise you she'll be all right.' One funny thing was, Jim wouldn't go to see Sarah, in all that time. I mean it was a couple of months or more that Sarah was in that state. And Jim absolutely refused to go to the country, which was a sacrifice for him. He thought it wouldn't be good for Sarah. But I know he found it painful that she never mentioned him. He didn't understand she just wasn't sane.

"Of course all the doctors kept saying, put her in the hospital, put her away, and so forth. Jim said no, to wait. And then, after about three months, he said, 'I'm going to see Sarah now.'

"I guess I've told you the total confidence I had in Jim. He could always do the impossible. I asked if I could come along, and he said, 'Of course.'

"There wasn't any particular ritual or mumbo-jumbo, that wasn't Jim's way. He just walked into Sarah's room and closed the door behind him. I was nervous as a cat. I couldn't help it. But, on the other hand, Jim was really magic. I believed he could raise the dead.

"But about ten minutes later this horrible screaming started. It was coming from Sarah's room, and it was the most terrifying sound I ever heard. More like an animal, really. As if she was being tortured to death.

"And Nanny went in, and Jim came out. I heard him

walk down the stairs. He knew I was sitting out on the porch, but he just walked out the other side of the house and down into the garden. I didn't know what to do, but I followed him out. I had to. He was just standing there, staring out over the gardens. It was such a beautiful day, that day. No haze at all. He was very quiet.

"And then he said, 'Did you ever think of selling the place, Sis?'

" 'Our place!' I said. 'My God, no. Never. I plan to be buried here. With the dogs. And Mogh Ruith.'

" 'Did you?' said Jim. 'So did I. And we never told each other. But I don't know. Something about all this gives me a bad taste. Do you know at all what I mean?'

" 'Jim, you'll feel different.'

" 'You don't feel it?' he said.

" 'No,' I said. 'Please don't talk about selling our farm.'

" 'Well, Sis, let's face it. You and I, we're not getting any younger. There's the taxes and maintenance here, and, after Uncle Sam takes his bite, well by then—you see it's going to be a whole different world. I'm not sure you'll want to go on living here after I'm dead. It could be a real mess, Sis,' he said. 'It was never my intention to leave you with a mess on your hands.'

"I was so upset. 'Please, please don't talk about dying,' I said. And naturally I started to cry.

" 'Sis,' he said. 'Don't cry. I'm not going to die on you tomorrow. I'm just thinking in terms of the future.'

" 'I don't care about the future,' I said.

" 'Sis, don't be ridiculous. Listen, Sis. I've broken my word to you. I thought I'd never do that.'

" 'Sarah?' I said. But of course I knew the answer.

" 'Yes,' he said, 'Sis, I'm licked.' We were both quiet for a long time.

"Then he said, 'But, Sis, that's not even a human being, that thing up there. I didn't understand. I think you should do what the doctors say, Sis.'

" 'Let them take her to the hospital?'

" 'Yes, I think that's best.'

"After that, Sarah never stopped screaming except when she was sedated, so we had no choice. She had to be put in the hospital. That was really it."

"Well," said Harriet. "I'm glad I stayed single. No woman born could act the way those two men did. It's a wonder Sarah survived at all."

"But Jim only did what he had to," said Sis. "Don't you see? He had to save her from that rat."

There was a long silence between the two women.

Then Harriet said, "What happened to Paul Donovan?"

"Paul Donovan? Frankly, I wasn't much concerned with Paul Donovan, after that. Actually, something strange did happen. About a year later, I got the weirdest phone call. I didn't recognize the voice at first. But, it was Paul Donovan, sounding awfully funny. And what he seemed to be saying was that Jim had been plotting against him or something, from the very beginning, and now Jim had ruined him the way he'd ruined Sarah. And that he'd go to hell for it, and so on. I just hung up. I did ask Jim about it, and Jim said Paul just hadn't been able to make a go of the deals Jim had set up for him. And Jim said he'd make goddamn sure he didn't get any more deals or make any more phone calls. Anyway, that was the last I heard."

"Hmmm," said Harriet, "but then what about Sarah?"

"I told you we put her in the hospital. There was really no choice."

"But she got out."

"Yes."

"And then you let her come over here?"

"Yes."

"So she must have gotten much better."

"Yes. Yes. Harriet, you can't imagine how exhausted I feel. It's all these awful memories, as well as the time. Look how wistful poor Williams looks over there! Drooping over his wheel. I bet he's actually asleep. Let's creep up on him and give him a scare. . . . Won't you let me drop you?"

"Sis, you know I like to walk, and my place is practically next door to here anyway."

"Oh, all right."

Mrs. Melmore held up her hand in a gesture that she and her friends made to each other—a hand curled as if holding a telephone. "Tomorrow?" she said.

Harriet probably didn't understand.

"Telephone you, tomorrow," she explained. "Well, at least I've told you everything there is to know about Sarah."

Part Five

VIE DE BOHÈME

1

Sarah Melmore
Has a Lesson in Art

As SARAH BEGAN to feel better, she spent more and more time
in the living room. Usually, she sat on the sofa, with her feet
up. She still felt strangely weak. Jack wanted her to rest most
of the day, and he said it might be quite a while before she
should use the stairs, or go out on the street. Jack didn't
spend much of the day at home, but when he did, it was nice.
It could be nice, just sitting in the big room with Jack.

Jack would be working. He would make drawings of an
object from many different angles; that came first. Later, he
would make constructions from craft paper. Eventually, he
would choose one that he liked, and begin to make it over
in wax, on a sort of wire armature. But mostly, in the end, he
took it all apart and began again. While Jack worked, neither
of them talked.

"Your work now, Sarah, is getting well," Jack had said. "The best way I know is to be very quiet. Let the dreams just come. The dreams will show you the way. That's your work time, Sarah. Your dream time is your work time."

She believed him. She was feeling stronger. And her dreams were very important to her. She felt she was on the verge of discovering something truly enormous. Jack was so peaceful to be with. He was very confident, never anxious, so she didn't feel hurried. She didn't feel the need to force anything. It would all come clear.

Maurice was much more of a problem. He was around the house most of the time, and it made him restless. Maurice was very moody. Sometimes he was surly and didn't speak to Sarah all day, except to snarl at her when meals were ready. The food was always very good. No matter how angry Maurice was, it never affected his cooking.

Other days, Maurice would be very wild and high-spirited. He couldn't keep still for a minute. He'd run around doing gymnastics, exercises, dance steps. He'd whistle and sing.

Sometimes he told Sarah stories. Maurice's stories were very strange. Sarah could never decide how much was true.

"Let me tell you what happened to a pal of mine, Sarah," he'd say. All the stories that began that way were very gruesome and gory. They were sort of like kung fu movies, except that they were set in the streets of Paris. Maurice got very involved in these stories, and sometimes he acted them out.

"Then these two guys came up behind him, and then he turned and went POW!" And Maurice would wheel and kick or slash at something, and sometimes he'd even roll over and over on the floor. Sarah thought it was probably all stuff he'd seen on television, or maybe at the movies. Maurice wanted to be a movie star.

Maurice told other stories about himself, boasting stories about very grand places he'd been and all the people who'd fallen for him. Sarah didn't think he could have been to all the places he talked about. It didn't sound real. But she supposed a lot of people might fall for Maurice, because he was so very good-looking. There was never any special girl in his stories. Maurice said he never liked girls for more than one night.

The stories Sarah liked were the sad ones. They were about the time when Maurice was very young, too young to fend for himself. When Maurice was little, he was always traveling, but one place was always just as bad as the last. She didn't even know where he really came from. She asked him once, but questions made Maurice cold and cagey. "Why do you ask that, Sarah? Why do you want to know?" and his eyes got very hard. She hardly ever felt like asking him questions anyway.

Maurice's childhood sounded so squalid and brutal, she didn't see how anyone could make it up. But he talked about it quite cheerfully. He joked about the cold and the hunger and the filth and the stink. "It made me what I am, Sarah," he'd say. Usually the things that made him burst into laughter were things that were sad—like the old janitor who had lain drunk in the cellar for three days, so drunk his nose was chewed off by rats.

The only people who seemed to have treated Maurice well were the girls in the whorehouse where he'd lived for a while. Sometimes they slapped and pinched him, but mostly they spoiled him and fed him and dressed him up. But he hated them worse than anyone, worse than the men who'd beaten him or the older boys who'd stolen from him.

"They knew what they were doing, Sarah. They were filth. You wouldn't understand," he said.

Listening to these stories reminded Sarah of parts of Dickens her mother used to read her. She was a little ashamed of how interested she was in the cruel world he described.

The trouble was, Maurice wanted to make all the rules. Sarah didn't mind Maurice's bad moods, but he showed no respect for her desire for privacy. Sarah needed to be alone a lot of the time, but Maurice interrupted her whenever he felt like it.

Sarah had been told once, long ago, that since poor people

had no privacy, they couldn't understand the concept. Jack sounded as if he had been poor, but he had a great feeling for privacy. When Sarah's door was shut, he knew she wanted to be left alone. When her door was open a little bit, that meant something else—that she was willing to talk, if necessary. Still, even when the door was ajar, Jack always knocked, and if she didn't answer right away, he would go off somewhere.

But a closed door meant nothing to Maurice. If he wanted to talk, he'd just give the door a bang, and walk in. Of course, Maurice had been very much poorer than Jack. She tried to explain to him that she would rather talk in the living room. Her bedroom was private. But finally she ended up screaming and cursing at him, and actually pushing him out of her room.

Sarah didn't like the bad side of her nature that came out with Maurice, but Maurice's nature was so much worse, she stopped feeling guilty. And he didn't mind being yelled at. In fact, he stopped bullying her and asking her so many of the sort of questions she didn't like. But he never really learned how she felt about privacy, and he never paid much attention unless she screamed. Jack asked her once in a while if Maurice was bothering her. She always said no.

Unlike most of the artists she had known, Jack seldom talked about his work. He worked from architectural models. He worked with all kinds of different materials, some of them very expensive and hard to get. It was easier here in Europe, he said. He told her he had only one big piece he was working on now, and sometime, when she was better, he would take her to see it. But he had no photographs of what he had done. He had lots of pictures and clippings he looked at, but they were mostly of people. He had told her, once, he made films, but then he'd never mentioned it again. She supposed the photographs must have to do with that, but he didn't say. The various pieces he worked on had no meaning for her. She had no idea what they would look like, in the end.

One morning, when she and Maurice were having coffee together, Maurice brought the subject up by himself.

"Did you ever hear of this family from Argentina, Sarah? I think they're supposed to be the richest family in the world."

"No, I guess not."

"And they're Jews?"

"Uh-uh."

"They have one of Jacques's most fantastic pieces. They put it up on this island they have in Greece—I saw it there myself last year. It's huge. It's like the skeleton of a fantastic palace, with stairways and towers—incredible! You can see what they are, once you figure out what it is. And it's all made out of different colors of gold. You never saw such gold. And rubies! Big incredible rubies! Some of them are as big as my hand, Sarah! Anyway, they're like rubies. But they're made to look soft, so it looks like the palace is dripping blood. Man, it's beautiful!

"It's standing there. A lot of space around it. God, it's beautiful at night, too! It really makes you out of breath. Guess how much it cost, Sarah?"

"I've got no idea. A couple of hundred thousand, I guess."

"You mean dollars, Sarah?"

"I guess."

"Hmmm. You're not that crazy." Maurice was disappointed. "But, Sarah, it was almost five hundred thousand francs. Imagine! Except the materials were all so expensive there wasn't so much profit as you might think."

"Yeah. A good ruby ring would cost that today."

"Then I must have the numbers wrong. It must be *much* more that that, because you better understand, this piece is fantastic."

"Yeah."

"It's got machinery to it. But the machinery to it, it's never been attached. And somehow I don't think it ever will be attached. Not by that particular family, anyhow. Guess why those people won't attach the machinery, Sarah?"

Maurice had begun to smile. Now he burst out laughing. "Because they don't have any electricity?"

"Come on, Sarah, I told you these were the richest people in the world."

"Okay. They didn't pay their electric bill."

"Sarah, I'm telling you something real."

"Yeah, but you're laughing. I thought it must be some funny reason."

"Oh, yes. It's funny, the reason. See, Sarah, if they plug it in, guess what happens?"

"No idea."

"The whole thing explodes, Sarah! It goes up in flames! Could you ever imagine such a thing?"

She had never imagined Maurice could laugh so much.

"Well—um—do they know that, these people?"

"Oh, sure, Sarah. Of course. But that would be just as funny, if they didn't know. Just imagine, they have a big party to show off, and then—" He was convulsed again.

"Um—well—why do they want it like that?"

Maurice's face was crimson. "They're art lovers, the stupid cunts! Don't you understand? Sarah, that's what happens with all Jacques's pieces. His art—it's called *Destructionisme*. They all do the same, the cheaper ones too. But none of them are too cheap, because Jacques doesn't operate that way.

"Jacques has about a dozen big pieces. All a hundred thousand dollars and more. Some of them belong to museums. The rest, mostly to Jews. No reflection on Jews, Sarah. I really got nothing against Jews."

"Are you Jewish, Maurice?"

"What, are you crazy? Why? Why do you ask me that? You think I look Jewish?"

"No. Um. No, it's just that people that talk that much about Jews, that way, usually have some Jewish blood."

"Not the people I know. Not a bit. Anyway, I don't know any Jews."

Sarah didn't say anything.

"You're in a strange mood today, Sarah. But listen, don't

you think that's fantastic? Don't you think that's incredible, about Jacques's work?"

"Mmm. Yeah. I guess if it were that beautiful, you could take out the part that was explosive."

"Sarah, look, you and me, we're not great artists, so let's face it, we can't understand. You see the whole thing—that's Jacques's concept. He wouldn't ever do one without the other. It's all one part. That's one reason he's the greatest artist. How many people could imagine that idea, or even understand it, once someone else imagined it? To spend all that money and time, and craft, with the idea of making it all vanish? In a second? You see!

"But why I think it's so funny, all those people paying the big money for it, I don't think they understand, either. I think they're just assholes.

"Guess what, Sarah? I'm Jacques's executor. You know what that means? If Jacques dies before me, I got to promise to carry out his wish. Guess what it is?"

"Why don't you tell me."

"Well, the minute Jacques dies, I got to go where those very big pieces are, and throw the switch. Imagine."

Maurice laughed some more.

At the end of long conversations like this, Sarah felt exhausted. Just listening to stories was so much easier. It took so much concentration to respond, and after a little while she always longed to get back to her dream-time.

Sarah thought over what Maurice had said about Jack's work. It certainly sounded like weird art. She wondered if it was true, and if so, if Jack really got that kind of money for it. But it fitted, in a way, with a few things Jack had said to her. He was fascinated with fire and explosives. Once Jack had told her that when she was better, later on, they would go down to the river together late at night, and launch some fireboats.

"You'd love it, Sarah. I make them really beautiful, and then when you see them burst into flames on the water—well, it's just gorgeous!"

And he promised her he would make her the most beautiful fireworks she had ever seen. Later on. And he told her
how, when he first came to Paris he had had a whole lot of
trouble with landlords. He used to like to go up on the roof
of his building with these paper flying machines he had
built, set them alight, and pitch them as far as he could out
into the dark night air. Sometimes, he put little explosives
into them—"nothing big," he said, "like firecrackers, sort
of." It was beautiful he told her. But people always seemed
to get very mad and he kept being asked to move, so finally,
he'd stopped. So Jack could be pretty childish, too.

Sarah found herself thinking more and more of Jimbo. It
was Maurice who reminded her the most of Jimbo, but
Jimbo had loved fire and firecrackers too. It was funny. She
wondered if she had been given Maurice and Jack to replace
Jimbo, and if so, what her duties to them were. This was
another subject she thought about when she was by herself.

She almost never spent any time with Jack and Maurice
together. When one of them was in, the other was usually
out. But when they were together, all three of them, Sarah
usually found it very uncomfortable. Jack was silent, Maurice
was sulky or aggressive. She was very surprised when Maurice
told her how well he thought they all got along together.

2

Sarah Melmore
Receives a Proposal

ONE DAY, Maurice banged on Sarah's door and slammed
into her room, and she could tell he was really angry. "Sarah,
I've finally caught on to your little game. What a lousy bitch

you are! I thought you were a sincere truthful person. But
I'm glad I found out different before it was too late!"

"I don't know what you're talking about."

"You know what I'm talking about, you putrid whore!"

"I don't, Maurice."

"You're trying to ditch me. Have Jacques all for yourself."

"What?"

"Don't act so innocent with me, Sarah! You tried to fuck
me up with Jacques. You made up a lot of things I said to
make him mad at me. Well, your plan is not going to work,
Sarah. *I'm* the necessary person to Jacques, not you.

"You think Jacques is crazy about you, huh? It's you that's
crazy. Let me tell you something, just as a kindness—Jacques
feels nothing for you. He's only interested in you because
you're so weird."

Sarah was silent. Maurice seemed to become even more
enraged.

"Look, Sarah. See this?" He thrust his watch under her
nose. "You know who gave me this? Jacques. Now I'd like
to see something Jacques ever gave you. Come on, Sarah.
Show me something!"

He reached down and plucked at her cotton night gown.
"Maybe this old shirt? Big deal, huh!"

Sarah pulled the covers up to her neck.

"Never mind, Sarah, you got nothing to hide."

Maurice leaned against the wall and glared at her. "I suppose you'll go squeal to Jacques. Tell him I'm treating you
mean again," he said.

"Look, Maurice, I don't ever talk about you to Jack. Why
would I? Now, come on, leave me alone."

"Sarah, just because you're the favorite now, you got big
ideas. But they're not smart ideas, because you're not smart.
When Jacques gets tired of you, you're going to go out with
the garbage. Because, Sarah, you may have a good-looking
face, but you got no brain. With Jacques, pretty faces, they
just go out with the garbage, and very quick, too." Maurice
made a spitting noise.

"Leave me alone, Maurice."

"You're not playing games with some little piss-pot school-boy, Sarah. Remember, I come right out of the gutter, and I'm not a bit ashamed. It made me what I am.

"Listen, Sarah, when I was sick like you, and Jacques was helping me out, you know what? Even while I was half dead with the pain, I was figuring out a hundred things I could do for Jacques that nobody else could do but me. See, I learned to be tough, but also I learned to be smart. So I watched and I listened and I learned what Jacques likes, Sarah, because I'm smart. By the time I got well, Jacques couldn't get by without me. I'm no pretty face, Sarah, or I'd be long under the ground.

"So I'd like to know, what can *you* do to be useful for Jacques? What can you do, anyway? With your mentality, let's see if you could figure out maybe one single thing."

"I don't think about it," said Sarah.

"Correct, Sarah, you don't think. You know all you do? Lie around and whine. You don't try to improve your body. You don't try to improve your mind. You don't help out in any way, and I don't even believe you're sick anymore. Let me tell you, kid, when Jacques gets tired of you, you're dead."

Sarah sat up in bed. "Get out, Maurice. Get out this minute and don't come back!"

Maurice gave a nasty smile. "You know what, Sarah? There's just you and me here, all alone. No Jacques to squeal to. I think you ought to watch your manners and look out how you behave with me. I got a very bad temper which you never really seen."

Maurice began to whistle through his teeth.

"Get the hell out! I mean it," said Sarah.

Maurice took out his switchblade, flicked it open and began making grooves on the little table, next to her bed.

Sarah was quite angry, too. At the same time, Maurice reminded her so much of Jimbo, playing one of his tough-guy gangster roles, it was sort of funny.

"Okay, Maurice," she said "you want to cut me up or something? Go right ahead. But why mark up the furniture?"

Maurice laid the blade right against her throat. Sarah stared up at him. Then she couldn't help it, she started to laugh. She couldn't stop laughing. She screamed with laughter.

Maurice was talking to her. He looked worried. "Hey, stop it, Sarah. Stop it. Please. Come on, Sarah. Look, I'll get you a cup of tea. Look Sarah, you wait right there."

His head was bobbing around for a minute, then he turned and ran out of the room. As soon as Maurice left the room, Sarah stopped laughing and thought about Jimbo. Time stopped, and then ran backwards. She was waiting for Jimmy. She was startled when Maurice came in with the tea. She had almost forgotten about Maurice.

"Tea is good for you, Sarah," he said. He seemed very solicitous. "Come on, Sarah. Take a little, please." He kept holding it out to her. "Please." Finally he put it down on the table next to her bed.

"Sarah," he said, "I'm sorry for the mistake I made. I believe you didn't say anything to Jacques. Okay?"

Sarah decided she might like some tea after all. She sat up on one elbow and took a sip.

"I don't know why I doubted you," said Maurice. "It's true. I think you're a sincere person. It's just I've had more evil experiences in the world than you."

"That's okay, Maurice," said Sarah.

"I never had much reason to respect women, Sarah."

"I said it's okay, Maurice."

"Sarah, you're not listening. I think in fact you could be a real pal to me."

"Okay," said Sarah. "Yes. Okay." She was beginning to feel nervous again. She wanted to go back to her daydreams. But Maurice sat down on her bed. "You're a strange one, Sarah. I don't understand what it is about you."

Sarah scrunched herself up so that no part of herself was touching any part of Maurice.

"But the things I said when I was mad," Maurice went on. "You should pay some attention. They're for your benefit."

"Mmm." Sarah made herself even smaller. She had no idea what Maurice had said.

"You see, you're never going to make it with Jacques, Sarah. You got no chance at all. Jacques would never make love with you. Never."

"Um. Okay, Maurice. That's fine. That's fine with me," she said. She had finished her tea and now she held out the cup to Maurice. She hoped he would get off her bed, take it back to the kitchen, and leave her alone.

He just put it down on the table. "What a laugh! Everybody else, he'd probably ball them once. But not you. You know why? Because he began by nursing you. He won't mix those two—healing and balling, never. You know, I even got sympathy for you. You and me are in the same boat. Since Jacques began by nursing me, too. For Jacques, that means he'll never touch me any other way. Even as a friend."

Maurice laughed, then leaned over and ran his fingers over Sarah's hair. "God, Sarah, I wish your hair would grow, don't you? I can't wait. What a difference that will make. You'll look so good."

Sarah lay very still. She thought Maurice's hand was infected. She didn't want it to touch her flesh. Maurice's hand weighed half a million pounds. She tried to erase him from her mind. Maurice wasn't like Jimbo really. Jimbo had gone away.

"What's the matter, Sarah?"

"Nothing. Look, you know I don't like to be—um—touched."

"Unless it's Jacques."

"Oh God. No. Please go away."

"You don't find Jacques sexy?"

"Oh God."

"Huh! Everyone finds Jacques sexy. Man, woman, and child. But especially rich old cunts. But I'm the only one who knows what he really likes."

"Well don't tell me about it, because I don't care, and please get off my bed." Sarah's voice sounded funny in her ears. Something was beginning to well up in her. She was afraid if Maurice didn't move she was going to start screaming.

"Were you thinking I'm a faggot, Sarah?"

"What? No, but I don't care and please get off my bed."

"I'm the last thing from a faggot, Sarah. I'm the opposite extreme. Even when I was a kid, I didn't have a sou, I always acted the part of the man. I hate faggots. Me and my pals, we all hate faggots."

"Okay, Maurice. I said okay. Now please get off my bed." But Maurice had began to fool around, straightening the collar of her night shirt. "God, I'm tired of seeing those same old shirts, Sarah," he said "Should I look to get you something nice to wear?"

"Stop it, Maurice," she cried. "Take your goddamn hands off me!"

Maurice jumped to his feet and stuck his hands in his pockets. "Rat-shit bitch," he said. "I don't know why I'm nice to you. You're too stupid to see I'm trying to give you good advice how to survive. Okay. Go ahead and die."

Sarah was afraid now she was going to start hearing the other voices, voices of people who weren't really in the room. This hadn't happened to her for a very long time. She had to get Maurice out of the room. There would be trouble.

"Die!" she cried suddenly. "How can I die if I'm not even alive. Can't you see I'm dead!"

"Don't get so excited, Sarah," said Maurice. "It's true you're hardly alive, but maybe I could help you out and then we wouldn't get so bored here."

Sarah had begun to tremble. She turned her head away and stared at the wall.

"What are you thinking?" Maurice said. "I said what are you thinking, Sarah, that's so important?"

"Nothing. No," said Sarah. "Nothing." But maybe it would be better if she said it out loud. "Um—well—actually I was thinking about my—um—brother."

"Where is your brother anyway?"

"He's dead."

"You killed him, too?"

"No, God, no. He overdosed on drugs."

"Man! You don't come from too lucky a family."

"No."

Sarah was counting to herself. She was starting from a million and counting backwards. It helped a little.

"Sarah, you want me to teach you some gymnastics?"

"No."

"It makes your body better."

"I don't care."

"Sarah, it's strange. You say 'no, no, no' to me all the time, but still I got the strange impression you really like me, right?"

Sarah had lost count. She'd have to begin all over again. "Could you get me a—glass of water, Maurice? I feel sick," she said.

"You don't feel sick, Sarah. You just don't want to tell me you like me."

Sarah turned and looked at Maurice. "Okay, Maurice. It's strange but I really do like you. Can I have a glass of water?"

"I knew you did! So why do you like me? I know it's got to be some droll reason with you."

"If I tell you," she said, "will you go away?"

"Okay."

Sarah stared at him. "Mmm." She paused a long time. "Well, probably because in certain ways you remind me of my brother."

"The drug dealer?"

"The drug user. My brother who—died."

"Hmm. So you really liked your brother?"

"I liked him the most."

"Huh. So him and me, how are we alike?"

"Well, you both make up all these truly bizarre fantasies. They're right out of some really weird comic book, and half the time you think it's real. You can both act about six years old—"

"God, what a bitch you are, Sarah! Okay. What do I care? You're crazy."

"No, wait a minute. I know you're a tough guy. You've had a tough life, all that. But—okay, I'll tell you the whole truth. I mean, with you, Maurice, maybe I worry about you because of my brother. All those drugs. And then, the way he died . . ."

"Are you kidding, Sarah? I don't use drugs all that much. Only when I feel like it. You're not talking about a little grass? That doesn't count. And Sarah, I want to live!"

"Honestly, Maurice, you use an awful lot of drugs. You use much too much. You just think I can't tell. But look here, Maurice, you keep doing that, you're going to forget these weird things are—well, you'll start thinking they're real. That's what happened to Jimmy. That's what happened to me, too. Truly." Sweat was beginning to pour down Sarah's face now. "And someday you might get carried away, and something horrible could happen. So if you really want to live, Maurice, please bear that in mind. I'm only telling you that because actually I do like you." Sarah took a big breath. "Anyway, now I'm really—can't you see I'm sick, Maurice? You promised me you'd go."

Maurice walked as far as the door.

"We really have the longest conversations, Sarah."

"Uh-huh." Sarah put her face in the pillow.

"You know what I was thinking? It was almost like we were married. That's something I never could visualize before. I had no reason. But you know what I was thinking, Sarah? I was thinking even if we were married, you probably still wouldn't go to bed with me."

"Probably not."

"I don't know. In a way, I respect you for it, Sarah. I think it would be right to have a wife you could respect. Women are sluts, but you, Sarah, nobody could say you were an easy lay."

"Mmm."

"Anyway, we could do a lot of talking."

"Mmmmm."

"Sarah," Maurice said, "I don't mind your dictating to me. In fact I appreciate what you say. Because, like you say, it may be very strange, but I really like you, too. But Sarah, since you don't dig Jacques, what if we just fooled around a little? Who knows?"

Sarah sat up. "Oh, for Christ's sake, get out of here!" she screamed. "Get the hell out of here, you rotten creep! You liar! Get out! Get out!"

"Okay, Sarah, I'm sorry. Don't scream, Sarah. I'm going. But do you still feel the same?"

"Just get out of here! That's all I want. Do what you promised! Leave me alone and I want that door shut!"

"I'm going, Sarah. But do you still like me?"

"Oh my God! Maurice, if you get out right now, shut the door, and don't come back, and don't bother me ever again. *Never,* I mean *never.* Then, if you keep all those rules, then, oh God, who knows? Okay?"

"Okay, Sarah."

3

A Curious Friendship

THE NEXT DAY, Maurice was gone. Sarah was relieved. She'd felt scared the bad times might come back. She wondered if somehow Jack had found out how much Maurice really did bother her. Jack said, "Sometimes M'reez goes away. He gets so nervous." Instead of Maurice, there was the other man she had remembered from the time she was sick. He wasn't wearing black leather now—maybe he never had; it would have been awfully hot. He wore a black T-shirt and jeans, his head was shaved, and his face was pitted with acne. His name was Willy. He seemed to be there to feed Sarah. She didn't like him. She kept feeling he looked dirty, and he might be diseased. He didn't like her, either. Even when he brought her a tray of food, he kept his eyes averted.

The day Maurice left, a big color television set had arrived. Sarah was glad, though not for herself. Willy sat in front of it day and night. He never paid any attention to her, except for preparing her food. Sarah didn't say anything. She just threw her food down the toilet, when he wasn't watching, except for things like fruit, that she could peel.

It was too bad the television hadn't come before—that was one thing Maurice had complained about all the time. He and Jack had had a television and a stereo, but they had been stolen, right before Sarah arrived. If the television had been there, Maurice could have watched it most of the time. He wouldn't have bothered her so much and she would have been nicer to him.

After four or five days, Maurice turned up again. He had a tan and he seemed much happier. He was friendly, but impersonal. He did a lot of exercises. He was always doing dance steps. And just as Sarah had imagined, he kept the television on, all the time. Sarah felt relaxed with him now and nothing bad happened. She felt calm again.

One day, Maurice told Sarah the history of all his scars. All except the one on his forehead. He had a lot of scars. The one on his stomach was from a knife wound. That was how he'd met Jack. Jack had found him lying on the street. He'd brought him home and taken care of him.

One afternoon, he brought up the scar on his forehead, but not to explain it. "Sarah, you think this," he meant the scar on his forehead, "do you think it'll keep me from being a movie star?"

"No, I wouldn't think so."

"Huh. They have all kinds of things they can do today. Makeup. Or plastic surgery."

"Yeah. I imagine."

"So if they liked me, they'd take care of it."

"I guess."

"I had a friend was going to take care of it, but I wouldn't do it. If anyone touches me, it's got to be the best."

"Uh-huh. I think you're right."

"What do you think, I'll make it in the movies, Sarah?"

"Well, I suppose you have to work hard at it, Maurice."

"Hmmm. It's true. And I got no leisure time, that's the problem."

That same evening he showed up with a huge carton.

"Guess what's in here, Sarah?"

"What?"

"You probably wouldn't guess. These are all my records. I just picked them up from a friend who was keeping them. I got some rock and disco, but they're nearly all Frankie. Frank Sinatra."

"Oh."

"Don't you like Frankie, Sarah?"

"My father was crazy about him. They were friends, sort of."

"No kidding. I'd give anything to know Frank Sinatra. Do you know what my dream role is? Playing Frankie in *The Frank Sinatra Story*. It's horrible. Time going by and I might get too old. I want to play him young. Your father's a movie producer?"

"No."

"What is he then?"

"Nothing. A businessman."

"God. I wish we had the stereo. This way, what's the use? Never mind. I'll get my old record player tomorrow. Look, Sarah, I'll show you something."

Maurice jumped out into the middle of the room. He stretched his arms out wide, and crooned: "I gets weary and sick of tryin'. I'm tired of living but feared of dyin'." He sang the song almost through to the end, then stopped suddenly.

"You know that one, Sarah? That's my favorite. Frankie, standing there in that white suit, singing 'Ol' Man River.' "

Then he sat down beside her and brushed the hair out of his eyes. His face was covered with sweat.

"Did you notice anything about my eyes, Sarah?"

She had. While Maurice was singing, he kept rolling his eyes around in his head. He looked so funny she wanted to laugh, but she was pretty sure that wasn't what he intended.

"Um," she said. "Um. Well—were you trying to look—uh—"

"Come on, Sarah. Be serious. I mean, were my eyes sparkling?"

"What?"

"Listen, I know that word is right. I've repeated it about a hundred times. It means shiny. Sarah, you must have heard of sparkling eyes."

"Oh," she said. "Yes, I did notice your eyes."

"Okay, then. That's very important. You know, one time I was up for a movie role. The type I would've played was a real pisser, but it would have been a break for me. There was an American director, Alan Long, do you know him?

"Well, all the time I'd been fucking this lousy old cow, the assistant casting director, and I still didn't get that role. It was all for nothing.

"But anyway she told me Alan Long had said my eyes were too cold. So I said, 'What's to do about that, man? These eyes have seen a lot.' So she said they took this cunt instead of me, 'cause he had 'sparkling' eyes.

"So then I had to find out what was that. I've been working on that for months, Sarah, making my eyes shine. It doesn't come by nature."

"Umm," said Sarah. She didn't know what to say. She knew she should say he had a good voice, at least, but he didn't. He was just very good-looking.

"Well," she said. "Why don't you—uh—ask Jack? I mean he makes movies."

"*Jacques's* movies. He doesn't know about the real kind

of movies, Sarah. Jacques's movies—I wasn't made for Jacques's movies, I tell you."

Maurice's mood seemed to have changed again. All at once, he was somber. He didn't talk about his career any more that night.

4

A Question of Taste

ONE AFTERNOON Jack came back early. He seemed to pay more attention to Maurice than usual. He told Maurice that the next night he'd be going out to a party; he said if Maurice wanted to go out, he'd get in touch with Willy. Sarah didn't understand why someone had to baby-sit her, but she'd said something to Jack about it before and it just hadn't made any impression. Maurice said no, he'd stay in tomorrow. Sarah knew he disliked Willy even more than she did. But right now, this afternoon, Maurice said, he'd go out. He had something to do.

After Maurice left, Jack stood looking out the window for the longest time. Once, he asked Sarah to come over and look at a man down in the street. He was playing the guitar. The man was wearing a broad-brimmed hat—Spanish maybe. Jack asked Sarah if she'd seen him before. Sarah watched the man. She didn't think she'd seen him. Of course, there were lots of street performers all over Paris—it was an established way of begging. But this was a funny street to try to shake people down on. There was a little café on the corner, but the people who sat there were mostly students.

"Here," said Jack. He handed her his pair of binoculars. She supposed Jack thought the man was good, or he wouldn't have asked her to come and watch. It seemed rude not to watch the man awhile. The man had olive skin and a very long upturned nose, like the portrait of Lorenzo de Medici. She told Jack she hadn't seen him before. There was a man sitting at a table at the little café who looked like a guy who stopped by Per and Anna's sometimes. But she wasn't sure, and anyway, Jack hadn't been interested in him.

Jack asked her if she wanted to sit in the kitchen with him. She said sure, so she and Jack went to sit in the kitchen. He got each of them a pear and some cheese.

He asked her how she was coming. She told him she was doing well. He asked her if she was happy. Then he said that was a stupid thing to say, and he took it back, but was she really feeling okay with them, here. She said she was; she felt very comfortable with Jack and Maurice. She felt it was her home now. At first, different things had worried her. She had worried about how much time she had lost, but she was embarrassed to ask about it. They never had recent newspapers around the house, only old ones. One day, she had learned it was almost the end of August. She had been very surprised—she felt she had been living there much longer. She had almost forgotten her other life in Paris.

Sarah believed that she had finally discovered the secret of living in the world without too much fear or anger. The secret was to be able to discard the past. When she was able to do that, she could get by. When pictures from the past flickered alive in her mind, she was frightened. But for the most part, ever since she had come to live in Paris, she had been able to forget the girl she had been in New York. She had simply been Sarah, who lived with Wanda, a difficult and demanding and jealous woman, but someone who needed her terribly. The girl Sarah had also been needed by Manu and Marie Christine and Per and Anna and the others, who very much needed her help for their political thinking. She was able to give them a great many important and practical ideas, and they all valued her. It was important to be needed. It was a better position than being loved.

But, since she had been living with Jack and Maurice, she had scarcely thought of her friends at Advent. They could

get along without her, now. And she had scarcely thought
of politics at all. That was strange, because since she had
been living in Paris, it seemed as if she had talked and
thought of almost nothing but politics, even with Wanda.

It was not as easy to put Wanda out of her mind. Wanda
had personal feelings for her. Wanda would miss her. Wanda
might start drinking again. As dreadful as Wanda might be,
she did represent a responsibility of sorts. Wanda stayed on
as a dark shape somewhere on the edge of Sarah's mind. But
the way to stay alive in this world was to erase those figures.
There were so many people from the past who seemed to
feel she had some sort of responsibility toward them; she
felt she must go to any lengths to avoid them.

Jack was so much easier than Wanda—all he seemed to
want was to let her be herself and when she was with Jack
she felt she was a good person. So Sarah refused to think
about Wanda directly. That way, she felt calm. That way,
she could be very contented living here with Jack and
Maurice. Time did seem very different, here with Maurice
and Jack. But it wasn't alarming, it didn't run the wrong
way, it was all okay.

Jack seemed in a mood to talk. Sarah almost never asked
him questions, but she was curious about his work. "I was
wondering about your work, Jack," she said.

"Mmm-hmm."

She looked at him.

"Well, you've sort of seen what I do, Sarah. Some of it. I
start with these buildings, in the paper, and then I do the
wax. It starts out very geometric in the paper, and then, on
the armature, it sort of gets more organic, you know?"

This wasn't what she meant. "Maurice was telling me a
little bit about it." She stopped, remembering that she must
be careful not to get Maurice in trouble.

"M'reez helps me, sometimes."

Sarah decided to go on. "Maurice said your things are in
a lot of museums. I just thought— Well, I felt stupid, because I didn't know your name or anything."

Jack laughed. "Well, then don't feel stupid. I think M'reez sort of boasts about me. Probably he made it sound like I was world-famous, or something. You got to be a little careful with M'reez. He can be awfully romantic or dramatic or something. I never think there's that many people know my work or my name or anything else. I got sort of lucky when I was real young. I had a friend who was a curator, in New York, and he helped me a lot. He never managed to buy a thing from me himself, but he got other people interested, so I was lucky. Of course, museums don't pay the top dollar, but I sure was lucky to sell my things at all. The museums, they helped a lot. Most people would have thought what I was doing was just too crazy."

"Jack, about your things—um—what is it like? I mean when it's—uh—finished?"

Jack laughed. "Oh, Sarah, that's too hard. Well, I tell you, did you ever go to this museum they have here? The Arts Décoratifs? They've got those eggs there. They're called the Fabergé eggs."

"Yes," Sarah said. "Mummy has a couple."

"Those Fabergé eggs? Well, once I saw them, and I thought the things I do, they're sort of like the yolk in those Fabergé eggs. Do you know at all what I mean?"

"Oh. Well. Um. But, Jack, your things—do they really blow up?"

Jack laughed. "Well, if you throw the switch. No one has yet."

"But they're supposed to?"

Jack laughed and shrugged. "That's not in my hands." He paused. "Well, I'll tell you, Sarah, it's funny. The last part of the time I'm working on them, they're wired. It's funny. It's sort of funny. I never know for sure what's going to happen. You know you can't be real sure with those things—there's always the chance. I suppose it's sort of a thrill, you know? Do you think that's awfully strange? I sort of like the idea. You make things just as perfect as you can—then you set 'em free."

Sarah couldn't really think about it, it made her feel too anxious. "Um. Do you have anything like that here?" she asked. (But she really didn't care.)

"Oh no. I just do this sort of homework here. My real work—it's got to be someplace different. I sort of have to separate the two things in my mind."

"Oh. So you go to work someplace else."

"Uh-huh. I thought I'd told you. I've been working on this one particular thing for more than a year now. This one really big piece. It kind of takes up all my time. It's sort of like a huge environment—architectural or something. It's built kind of like a cathedral and if you stand at the end, it's like you're at the bottom of a V. All the lines go out from there. And you see, all of it, well, it's like the inside of the egg. Like a cathedral inside an egg, waiting to— D'you know what I mean at all?

"I think it's going to be my one extraordinary thing. I'm actually pretty near the end now. It's all wired and everything. That's more fancy, too, but you can work it all from this one place.

"Something happened—they gave me this show in Amsterdam. Well, a lot of my pieces can't be moved, so it was almost all just the littlest ones—ones that weren't so interesting, and some models. To tell the truth, the whole show was a mess. But anyway, it worked out well, and I sold three pieces. That's the only way I could afford to do this."

"Oh," said Sarah.

"I'll take you there to see it, when you feel like going out. I'm just terrible at explaining things. I'd rather show you."

Then Jack changed the subject and talked about Sarah. The most important thing, he said, was for her to get really well. She said she was feeling pretty well.

Jack said one thing she might try doing, it was a good exercise, was to go through her life, in a special way. For instance, everybody had very painful parts in their lives. The first thing was to just label those painful parts, and push them to one side, so they'd be completely out of the way and wouldn't infect the rest. She just listened, trying to remember.

After that she could begin to work on the second part. That would be harder, but maybe she should start thinking about it a little bit. Next thing, she'd choose herself someone to help her, like a guide. It could be anyone. Real, or in books, or like Jesus Christ, or anyone. "Summon them," Jack said. "A person's summoned that way, he's got to come."

She could go over the easy part of her life with this person again, just so it'd be real crystal clear, and then she'd get on to the hard part. The real painful things she'd put to the side. When she got to the bad parts, he was going to help her too. And they'd do some work, and after a little while, all the bad parts would just be burned away. She'd be living right here in the present—no bad dreams or horrible memories. Some people got so far they got all sorts of powers. Jack thought Sarah might be one of those people.

Sarah felt very excited, but sort of scared. She wondered if she was too hard a case for Jack's ideas to work. But some of what he said sounded like what she was already doing, and actually she had even sort of chosen a guide. Her grandfather. She told Jack this.

Jack was very, very pleased. He told Sarah how very special she was—he said she would probably end up teaching him. He really was terribly pleased. She had never seen Jack smile so much; he used to laugh, sometimes, but he almost never smiled. Sarah was afraid she'd been boasting. She explained she wasn't all that far along. She said that most of the really bad things she couldn't remember—they were shut off someplace in her mind. What she didn't say was that she wanted them to stay that way. But Jack was still very pleased, and said not to worry about it. This made her very happy. After Maurice came back, she went to her room. Everyone was in such a good mood, she thought, maybe they'd want to talk. She didn't want to get in their way.

The next day was really strange. Maurice was in very high spirits, running around the apartment, doing handsprings and rollovers. He told Sarah a fantastic surprise was coming that day. She'd never be able to guess what it was. She could guess, but he wouldn't tell her, even if she was right. The surprise was for Jacques, but it would be for her too.

Sarah's heart sank. She hated surprises. In her experience, all surprises were bad surprises. She had gotten used to her life here, she liked it, and she couldn't imagine any surprise Maurice could produce that she wouldn't find unpleasant. Maurice told her she must stay in her room all afternoon, not to spoil the surprise. That suited Sarah, except for her worries about what the surprise might be.

That afternoon there was a terrific amount of noise in the other room. Banging and thumping. The voices of several men. It sounded like very heavy things were being dragged about. There was a lot of cursing, and the sound of Maurice's laughter. Finally, it all died down, except for the loud sound of disco music. A little while later, Maurice came into her room.

"Sarah," he said, "we really should wait for Jacques to come. Both be surprised at once. But I bet you can't wait! So come on, Sarah! I'll show you the surprise. I'll give you one more guess, before you see it. Okay? What do you think it is?"

Sarah shook her head and hoped it wouldn't be anything too bad.

He led Sarah out of her bedroom. The living room had been completely transformed. It had been turned into something—well, Sarah could only think of the sitting room of a French provincial hotel. The room, once sparse and severe, was crammed with heavy oak furniture, covered with crimson damask. There were lamps with fringes, a Turkish carpet with a deep pile, the reds running into fuchsia and magenta. Jack's models had been put on a carved secretary.

"What do you think, Sarah? How beautiful! Jacques will be so surprised! He'll never believe his eyes. Jacques said to me, this time, get what I like. But I didn't say a word about it! All I couldn't get done in time was the air conditioning. How expensive, would you guess? He's going to drop dead from surprise, don't you think?"

It was hard for Sarah to say a word.

"No one would believe I got this done so fast and so cheap, Sarah. Of course, it's very expensive, it's true, but cheap for what I got. Most people would pay for this *fauteuil* only what I paid for all! How expensive? Come on, Sarah! Guess!"

The furniture and appurtenances were all in the style Sarah's father used to call "Louis the Terrible." And Jack was so particular about the way things looked. She was sure he wouldn't like it one bit. How could there be such a complete misunderstanding?

Maurice's enthusiasm seemed more than enough for two. "Try the sofa, Sarah! Look at this! Want to open the drawers? And see? A real place to hang our clothes!"

He ran back and forth, disclosing each new wonder. Sarah sat on the edge of the deep new sofa. She felt very nervous. Maurice was showing her the new stereo, built into the wardrobe, when Jack walked in. The noise of the music had drowned his steps.

It seemed to Sarah for a moment that everything froze. Jack froze. She froze. Even Maurice froze, squatting in front of the stereo, watching Jack's face.

Jack's face hadn't changed, but somehow it seemed drained of color. It made his hair seem very bright. Somehow Sarah felt guilty herself. Jack would probably blame her, too.

Jack made a motion with one hand for Maurice to turn off the music. Maurice switched off the music. He didn't say a word.

"Well, M'reez," Jack said. Sarah wondered how Maurice could bear the tension in his voice. "Well, that was real quick work. I had no idea."

Maurice began to explain, but Jack interrupted him. "Fine, fine," he said. "But, Sarah, why don't you go back to your room? You'll be more comfortable."

Sarah knew she was a coward, but she felt enormous relief

at being spared. She shut her door and covered her ears, but she didn't hear any screaming.

About an hour later, Jack knocked on her door.

"Come in," she said in a low voice.

Jack came in and sat on the side of her bed. It was hard to see his face in the failing light. But he looked very calm, very controlled. He took her hand and clasped it. She could feel a tiny twitching in his hand, as if there were a muscle jumping. They sat that way for a long time.

Jack said, "I feel better being here with you, Sarah."

She had stopped being frightened for herself, but she was worried about Maurice. She had had the sudden feeling, when Jack had entered the room, that Jack might do something terrible to Maurice. Maurice carried on a lot, but in a way, Jack could be more scary.

"Well," Jack said, "it's really not his fault. It's mine. But wouldn't you think— M'reez has been with me for a while. He's worked with me, he knows how I am. It's not as if he's stupid. Well, if that's what he still likes—well, we'll see. We'll just see what we can do. I'm sorry about all this, Sarah. Try not to pay too much attention. You're okay in here?"

"Yeah."

"Well, okay then."

5

An Invitation to Dance

LATER THAT NIGHT, Jack asked Sarah if he could come in and see her for a minute. She said, "Sure." It was dark. She could tell he was in a hurry, and this was unusual, because he never gave the impression of being in a hurry.

"Sarah, I have to ask you something. It's a little weird. Would it hurt your eyes if I turned the lights on?"

"No."

He turned on the lights. He was wearing evening clothes but he had on black lipstick and funny eye makeup, and his hair was all slicked down and dyed black.

"Lord, Sarah, you don't have to tell me what a fool I look. I had to do this by myself and it's so chintzy. It's this costume thing, or something, tonight, and I thought maybe I wouldn't have to wear one, but I do. Then I thought maybe I wouldn't have to go. But I do. Now take a good look."

He took the little lamp by her bed and held it under his face. "If we saw each other at a costume party and I looked like this, now I want you to be real truthful—would you think I looked too weird? Because if you think so, well— that's it." And he made a swift chopping motion with his left hand. "Then I'm just not going to go."

She tried to think. "I never went to many costume parties, Jack, but just from what I see, you look very handsome. Very beautiful. It's more as if you're showing your real face, and the rest of the time you're hiding it. I don't think it's weird at all, maybe it's what you don't like. Is that okay?"

"Yes, that's fine, child." He leaned over and kissed her, stood in front of the little mirror over the sink, smoothed his hair down some more, said, "Lord, I feel like a fool," and started to leave. When his finger was on the light switch, he said suddenly, "Maybe you'd like the light on. . . ."

"It doesn't matter. I'm thinking."

"Well, okay. See you."

After he left, she heard a good deal of banging about. She was glad Jack had turned the light off because all that noise meant that Maurice, who was ordinarily as quiet as a cat, was in a really bad mood. She didn't want to think about it. She was totally engrossed in a sort of dream she was having. Her grandfather was leading her by the hand. He had a beautiful high forehead and a long, white beard, like Merlin, the old lab coat and baggy trousers and slippers that he wore in her photograph. And he called her by name.

"My little Sarah," he said. "I am going to show you all

the wonders and treasures inside the earth, and all the dazzling dangers and evils of the world above, and you will know and remember. Those that would be harmful to you I will mark with a freezing dagger, and those that would be beneficial to you I will place on them a shining cross. But only you and I will see the marks I make. And you must trust me and obey me, because I want only your good."

"Grandfather," she said, "I trust you and obey you. Is my father dead?"

"Yes, my daughter and child of my daughter. Your husband and father is well and truly dead."

"Is he marked with a freezing dagger?"

"He was a danger to you, but he is well and truly dead. He can no longer harm you."

"Hey, Sarah!"

"Oh, for Christ's sake! Shut up!" she yelled at the top of her lungs. Next minute she said, "I'm sorry," and then she began to cry. She had realized that she was also her mother.

"What's wrong?" said Maurice. He came all the way into her room and turned on the light. "You sick?"

"Maurice, please go away. Just for a while. Just for a little while. Oh, shit! It's gone." She pulled the sheet up to her chin and sat up.

Maurice had obviously come to pick a fight with her. He was disconcerted.

"I've got a little coke, Sarah. Want some?"

"No. I don't even like to drink now."

"Do you know where Jacques went?"

"No."

"I've a way of finding out if you're lying."

"I'm not lying."

"He thinks I'm not good enough for his fancy parties."

"Does he?"

"I suppose you do too."

"I don't know anything about his parties."

"Well, listen. Why does he come in here, all of a sudden?

Why does he ask *you* how he should look? I know how he should look. Why the hell does Jacques think all of a sudden *you* know more about fucking society parties and shit than I do?"

"I guess because I've been to more."

Maurice snatched her little mirror off the wall and threw it across the room. There was a splintering sound.

"But he's wrong, Maurice. I don't know."

"Fuck you all," he said. "You know what that broken mirror means? Bad luck to the one who isn't true. Bad for him, if it's him. Bad for you, if it's you. Lying to me. Bad luck! I know! I'm the child of the gypsy."

"I'm not lying."

Maurice frowned. He messed his hair over his forehead. He looked awfully young. She had never asked him how old he was—not much more than twenty, probably.

"Okay, okay," Maurice said. Suddenly he smiled. "Sarah, would you like to dance?"

"Dance?"

"Yeah. That's one of the things I don't really enjoy doing by myself for some reason. Come on, let's dance."

"How about if we just listen to the records?"

"Come on anyway." He drew her out of bed and into the living room, which looked so funny now. It was blazing with light.

Maurice put a record on. It was Frank Sinatra singing "Strangers in the Night."

"Come on, Sarah."

"Oh, Maurice. Do I have to?"

"Yes. Come on." In a little while, he said, "You know what, Sarah? You're a very good dancer."

"Not so good. It was one of the things I had to do," she said. "Dancing, sailing, riding, playing tennis, making conversation—before I stopped. Let's stop now. You're a marvelous dancer yourself, Maurice, but I don't like being—cuddled. It brings the bad memories."

"Okay, let's just sit and talk a little. Want a drink?"

"No."

"I'm getting very nervous," he said, "very nervous."

"It's probably the coke."

"How do you know that?"

"I think you told me."

"Sarah—you sure you don't want to ball? I've got nothing special to do. . . ."

"Yes."

"Yes, you do?"

"Yes, I'm sure I don't want to. I like you a lot, Maurice, but I keep telling you I'm kind of dead that way."

"Could be what's wrong with you, Sarah. You know that can't be good—it's not normal for a woman. And I feel real groovy toward you now. And I know I'm one fabulous lover. I make love so well, everybody says so. It might make you more alive."

"Please, Maurice, just don't ask me again. That's not for me. Not anymore."

"Okay, Sarah. I like you anyway. No harm asking?"

"I suppose."

"I guess maybe you like girls, though."

"*No.*"

"Well, how about a game of cards then?"

"Oh, Maurice, I don't play cards. There's a reason."

"Okay. Okay."

They sat on the stiff maroon sofa. They just sat there. Frank Sinatra was singing "My Way," the one of all his songs Sarah hated the most.

"Sarah," Maurice said, "don't you ever get the idea this might not be a good place for you to be? Not a healthy place?"

"You mean like a murderer's den?"

"Maybe."

"Could I leave if I wanted?"

"Sarah, you've got to try and concentrate, and be very smart. You see, Jacques's one very funny guy. Very strange. And I've never seen him just this way. I don't know what he's going to do this time. Jacques, he doesn't see life and death the same way real people do, Sarah."

"Thanks, Maurice. I know you're being really nice. But I've been living in murderers' dens all my life. It's home."

"You should wake up, Sarah."

"And, Maurice, I don't see life and death too clearly either. Maybe I'm more like Jack. And Jack's been very nice to me."

Maurice stared at her. "Sarah, you ever think of that woman—that red-haired woman you used to live with?"

"Wanda. How do you know Wanda?"

"That's right. Wanda. Do you ever miss Wanda?"

Sarah was silent. She didn't want to think about Wanda.

"Wanda seemed like one real macho broad to me."

"Did Wanda come here while I was sick?"

He shook his head. "No, she didn't. But I guess she must have liked you more than you liked her, right?"

"What about Wanda, anyway?"

Maurice just shrugged.

"Okay," said Sarah. "Never mind—forget it."

"Uh-huh. Let's forget it."

Maurice sat down near Sarah. He picked up a flat purple stone and tapped some cocaine out of a little silver flask onto it. He chopped it up with his knife, divided it into six little lines, and offered some to Sarah. She shook her head. Maurice took out a silver straw and sniffed some up. He sighed.

"Did Jacques ever tell you about this place, Sarah, this fabulous place we've been working on together?" Maurice said. "You'd never believe it. It's just huge. It's a real dump on the outside, but on the inside it's like a city, a temple. The most beautiful thing you ever saw. It's Jacques's latest art work. His most tremendous, too. And I did a lot of the work."

"And it's all going to blow up?"

Maurice shot her a nasty look. "Why, Sarah? Why do you say that? What makes you think that?"

"You said all Jack's art work explodes."

He was silent for a long time, chopping up the cocaine, laying out lines, and sniffing it up through the straw.

"Anyway, Jacques's using it right now. He uses it different ways. He's going to use it for these ceremonies he has. It's useful. This time it's not going to be for sale." He paused. "Jacques never mentioned this to you, Sarah, you're sure?"

"Oh, yeah," said Sarah. "I guess he did."

"God, I hope you get to see it! The money we spent, Sarah! What a folly! But now Jacques's driving me crazy. He's telling me nothing—it's got all this silver and gold and crystal in it. Things are getting so funny. I don't like it. I've got to get some of that stuff out, I don't care what Jacques says."

"Mmm."

"Jacques never told you about the ceremonies, Sarah?"

"Uh—no."

"Part of it was my idea. I've got these really terrific pals, Sarah. Jacques doesn't like them to come around here, so you never got to meet them. There's six of us, Sarah, my five pals and me, and they're all tough like me. Remember how I told you I hated faggots? My pals feel the same. Particularly those rich soft fruity faggots. All of us feel the same. We beat them up and take all their money. We'd kill them, if it weren't more good for business to leave them alive." He began to laugh. "The joke is they love it. That's how they get their rocks off. Oh well. What are you thinking about, Sarah?"

"Um—nothing."

"God, you ought to see what we do to some of those creeps Jacques brings to the ceremonies. You have to have no pity. Then it's a lark. I don't know what Jacques would do without me now. We got a few more guys to help out, but me and my pals, the six of us, what we say goes."

"That's an awful lot of coke, Maurice," said Sarah.

"I know what I'm doing, Sarah. I'm the boss of this all now. Before me, Jacques had creeps like Willy to help him.

What a change, huh! You know what, Sarah? When Jacques has the ceremonies, you know what the bottom price is?"

Sarah shook her head.

"Five thousand francs. And that's just the entrance tax. You see, Jacques and I suit so well because we believe very different things, do things very different ways, and end up the same place.

"Jacques really does believe in these very spiritual things. Black magic, too. Jacques is a sincere person, so what he's doing is always sincere. And sometimes very strange things can happen from it. I don't deny it. But me, I think there's some natural explanation for it. I had too hard a life to believe in ghosts and saints and devils. All that shit.

"It's me who had the thought how to organize things for the most money. Before that, it was a real mess. It's all so very simple. But it's all so good, because everybody gets what they really want in the end.

"See, Jacques doesn't like to pay any attention to anything going on. Jacques doesn't think about the rest of it, not even for one minute. He's a million miles away, with the things he's doing, talking to ghosts and spirits. Jacques doesn't like to worry about a thing. But I'll tell you one thing. When the long dark night is over, Jacques is very, very happy to get that money at the end."

Sarah was silent.

"And by the way, Sarah, you'd be surprised the people that come there. The richest, most powerful persons in France. They think no one knows who they are, because everyone's dressed up, uses secret names. What a laugh! Me and my pals know who every one of them really is. So you see, Sarah, if Jacques ever winds up this religious business, then I got a real nest egg anyway. Then I cash in on every one of these marks. I've figured it out. Just exactly how much I can make off each one."

Sarah shook her head.

"What's the matter? You don't believe me?" Maurice laughed. "You're right. I'm just joking. None of that's true."

Sarah was silent.

"Sarah, what are you thinking that's so important?"

Sarah wished she could help Maurice, but he was a lot crazier than she had thought. "Look, Maurice," she said, "maybe you ought to have more faith." This was something she had been meaning to say. It was terribly hard for her, but still she owed it to him.

"Maurice," Sarah said, "do you think—do you know Jack's an angel?"

"What are you talking about, Sarah? You mean that? *Comme un ange? Je te comprends?*"

"Yes," said Sarah.

Maurice laughed. "No, Sarah. I really don't see Jacques that way."

"Maurice, you've got to try," said Sarah urgently. "He says he is if you think he is. You see, that's the key."

"Okay, so I don't think he is."

"Maurice, don't you have any hope or faith?"

Maurice was silent for a moment. Then he said, "Sarah, I got no hope and no faith. But I'm very, very good with a knife."

Sarah felt sad. If Maurice were only able to believe, Jack could hold him in his hand and he would be safe. But, without faith, Maurice would just fall and fall, like a big black stone, out of Jack's hands, right down through the ages into hell.

"Look, Sarah. Okay. Maybe it's all okay. Maybe Jacques just likes taking care of you. He does like taking care of people, it's true. That was always the truth. I know. The people who think Jacques's just about money, they're just cunts. Jacques needs all that money for these things he does. Money's just shit to him, otherwise.

"They think Jacques really likes all those rich whores he goes out with. Well, Jacques hates rich people, people with money. Sarah, I'm not jealous, that's the truth.

"But time's going by. Jacques's not telling me anything.

And he's acting so funny with me, Sarah. Sometimes I'm getting really worried. It could be dangerous."

They sat on the maroon fringed sofa. Maurice was drinking scotch and taking cocaine. He had brought out a big glass bottle of it.

She concentrated. "Maybe you really should go away if you feel that way, Maurice. You can always come back."

Maurice shook his head. "Oh, no, I belong to him, Sarah. It's the thing I can be most proud of in my life. To have been Jacques's pal. Such a great artist! Anyway, I just fixed up this place nice, so for the first time we got a home.

"But you know what? Sometimes I have this dream we'll just wind up all this art business. Just slam the books on all this art shit. Just say the hell with it—the hell with it all. Say goodbye to all this filth in Europe. Start somewhere new. Maybe we'll go someplace way out in the West—like Arizona. Start life all over again, in the state of nature." He was silent.

"What a laugh that is, huh, Sarah? Jacques can't even ride a horse. They make him sneeze."

People's lives were all so sad, she didn't want to hear about them. She knew it would be nice if she could stay up and let Maurice talk, but she was getting so tired. In fact, she must have gone to sleep while he was talking, because the last thing she remembered was Maurice picking her up and carrying her back to her bed.

He'd looked down at her. "You're not going to remember anything tomorrow," he said.

Then he leaned over and kissed her cheek. "Adiós, Kid. I think I'm going out dancing after all."

6

Sarah Melmore
Is Asked Some Questions

THE NEXT DAY WAS BAD from the very beginning.

Jack had knocked on Sarah's door quite early.

"Sarah?"

"Yes, Jack."

"I'm sorry to bother you, but what happened with M'reez, anyway? Do you know?"

"He's not there? I guess he went out dancing."

"He's not supposed to go out."

"I don't know."

Maurice came in around lunchtime. He and Jack hardly spoke. Maurice put out some cold chicken and mayonnaise. Jack didn't eat. He spent a lot of time looking out the window.

Sarah decided to go back to her room.

After a little while, she heard loud voices. Then silence. Then disco music. So Jack had gone out.

About an hour later, Maurice actually knocked on her door.

"What is it?" she said.

"Sarah, would you please mind coming out here a minute, please?"

Maurice was being awfully polite. She came out. Maurice was standing over by the window. "Look here, Sarah."

Sarah came and stood beside him.

"See that type down there." There was a dark-haired man in jeans and a T-shirt. He was sitting at the corner café, reading. "Could you take a good look at him?"

"Looks like a student."

"I don't think he's a student. He's been there three days."

Sarah took Jack's glasses. The T-shirt said University of the South. It could have been the man with the guitar. He had the same sort of funny-looking nose.

"Well, is that the same guy—he was around with a guitar, a couple of days ago? Jack asked me, but I never saw him before. Who do you think he is?"

"I'd like to know. So Jacques already asked you. You know what? He told me not to bother you about it. Huh."

"Why?"

"I was going to ask you that question, Sarah. Have you got any idea why that might be?"

"No. Why do you think?"

"I wish I knew."

"Well," she said, "I don't know him. You don't. Jack doesn't. If he wants to sit there, that's his problem."

"Unless it turns out to be our problem."

"But why? You think that guy's a *flic* or something?"

"Don't try to talk French, Sarah, it gives me a headache. No, that's no cop. That I know. But how are you so sure Jacques doesn't know him?"

"Don't you believe Jack? Don't you believe he tells the truth?"

"Hmm. I suppose what Jacques says may be the truth, Sarah, but Jacques doesn't say everything he knows. He's not very confiding."

"Well, I'm going to lie down."

"Okay, go ahead, but why?"

"Well, Jack told me to."

"Do you still feel bad? I believe you're better. I think you'd get better quicker doing some exercise."

"I think I'll do what Jack said."

It wasn't long before Maurice gave a bang and walked into her room.

"Listen, Sarah," said Maurice. "You're getting more and more sensible all the time. I think we should have a serious talk."

"I was trying to sleep."

"Sarah, I know Jacques's the greatest authority, but that doesn't mean you believe everything he says."

"Well, what is it?"

"First of all, I don't think you're so sick anymore, not at all. To me, you're not that crazy. In fact, you're smart. I bet your father's a lawyer, right?"

"Mmmm."

"See, I knew it. Lawyers are smart. I knew a lawyer, once. He was very smart, but very mean."

"Mmm. Sounds like my father."

"Listen, Sarah, there's one very serious subject we've never talked about."

"Uh-uh. No. No, Maurice. Just get out."

"Listen, Sarah, I said 'serious,' right?"

"You always say 'serious.' "

"This time I mean it. You know a subject we never really talked about, Sarah? Money."

"Mmmm."

"Did we?"

"I don't know."

"I know we didn't. Now everybody thinks about money, and everybody needs it, right? . . . Sarah, what's the matter now?"

"I don't like to think about it. I don't want to talk about it."

"I didn't say anything about 'like,' Sarah. I said, about 'need.' So how about when you need to?"

"I don't."

"You don't ever need to talk about money?"

"No."

"Sarah, you're one very lucky girl. I wish you'd tell me your secret. I never knew one person in my whole life didn't need to talk about money. Could you tell me how you do it, Sarah?"

"No. Uh—I told you I don't like to talk about it."

"Okay. I'll start again. I can see with my eyes you're not

the most rich girl yourself, Sarah. You're educated though, and you been taken care of somehow, because you don't know much about the world, but you always expect to get your own way, and though you don't know a thing, you're not timid. Okay.

"So let's say without wanting to talk about money, you just need some, someday. What would you do?"

"Maurice, I said I didn't want to talk about it. I want to go back to sleep."

"Okay, Sarah. But look—here's the situation I see right now. Some guy's out in the street, he's watching this apartment. Okay? Now I know for sure he's watching this apartment because Jacques figures it out, right away. And Jacques never pays attention to things like that, unless there's a reason. And Jacques isn't a little bit pleased, but he's not all that surprised. And he tells me not to talk to you about it. You see, Sarah? You see how this situation is beginning to involve me? I'm right in the middle.

"Okay, I'll go on. Jacques picks you up and brings you home. You're sick. Okay—so far, so good. Maybe. Jacques always does nurse people. Okay. But now you're not so sick anymore. And still Jacques wants you to stay in bed, stay quiet, not see anybody. I'm not even supposed to talk to you, right?

"Well. Now things are getting a little unusual here. Now you come here looking like a tramp, but it turns out you come from some life that's very good society where you never even had to talk about money. See?

"Okay, now I bet you, Sarah, Jacques knows everything about you. You know nothing about him, right?"

"No. Jack's told me a lot about himself. I never told him much about myself."

"Oh, really. Well, I'm very sorry about that, Sarah, but I don't believe you. Sarah, I *know* Jacques knows a whole lot more about you than you think he does. He didn't tell me, because, like I said to you, Jacques's not necessarily very confiding. But he *does*, Sarah, because he always does.

"And it happens Jacques got me in a little trouble concerning you, which I'll be like you and say I don't want to talk about, but right now, from what I know, I can't see the reason. And there's nothing at all I like about how the rest of this looks. Okay?

"Okay. Well, Sarah, that's why I'm breaking Jacques's orders about not talking to you about certain things.

"Now it's just possible it may be because you're very delicate, in spite of the way you seem to me, and he doesn't trust much my social graces. Forgive me, Sarah, but I don't think so. I don't think you're sick anymore. I don't think he needs to nurse you anymore. You've been here a long time, and to me there's no indication you're going away. Well, fine. I said I like you, Sarah, and I think you got plenty of strength, and you just say, 'Go fuck yourself,' to me, if you don't like my social graces.

"Although, all the same, when I was in England, I was fifteen that year, I saw more social graces than Jacques in his whole life. I saw nothing but university professors and noblemen, and I didn't offend them a bit. And, besides that, I know enough to know that Jacques uses bad grammar himself, most of the time, and, I want you to understand, I talk that way, Sarah, it's because it amuses me, not because I don't know the difference. But Jacques can't even spell. And I read more books, know more poetry, in fact it's making me more and more furious the more I think about it!

"You feel like talking to me yet, Sarah?"

"No."

"Well, okay. Move your feet, Sarah. I'm not comfortable, pig woman."

"Go to hell, Maurice."

"I just wish Jacques could hear you, how delicate. It's like I said. I don't especially have to watch my manners with you.

"Well, okay, Sarah. I'm going to return good for evil in your case, and be a little confiding. Right before you came home with Jacques, one fine day, we were just about flat broke. That's the truth, Sarah, okay? We were talking about different things we could do about that little thing, though I'm quite tactless and right to the point in my speech, and Jacques less so.

"The situation of Jacques—you've got a right to wonder, Sarah. There's such a number of ways Jacques has he could make big money.

"Now, everyone knows Jacques is the best doctor—it's a talent he has. With that, Jacques does what he has to. But he won't ever take money for that. God! What that talent is worth! People would pay everything for their health, Sarah. They'd pay the moon, right? But that Jacques won't do, Sarah. That he never will do.

"I respect some principles, Sarah, but when it comes to a question between breaking a few scruples and no dinner, I'm not always sympathetic.

"Did you ever have a job, Sarah?"

"You mean a paying job?"

"What's the other kind?"

"Um—I worked for Legal Aid."

"Uh-huh. That's some kind of law?"

"Yes."

"The kind you don't get paid for?"

"Uh-huh."

"Okay. That's not a job. That's interesting, though. What would you do if you just had to get a job? Don't tell me, like most girls do, don't tell me, be a hooker, since you couldn't be a hooker."

"All right, why don't you tell me?"

"Okay. I say you don't know. I say you never thought about it. God, I'm stupid. Okay, Sarah. Money from home, Sarah—that's what you do. Just write the family for money from home. Your father, the rich lawyer."

"Actually he's—he wasn't exactly a lawyer."

"Okay. He isn't quite a lawyer, and he probably isn't even alive, but I get the point. Somehow or other he's got money coming out his nostrils. Am I right?

"Never mind. I know I'm right. So anyway, I suppose your mother, she's alive?"

"Yes."

"Okay. Okay, am I right? You don't talk about it, don't think about it, just write your mother for money from home. I know I'm correct."

"You're not absolutely correct, Maurice—but okay, that's close enough. Are you satisfied? Can you leave me alone a while?"

"Sarah. You don't know how fascinating this is for me. How I wish we'd had this talk before. I could talk about it forever. But you're so tired, and for me too I see it's late. But we got to go back to Jacques one minute.

"Hmmm. Let's see. I said Jacques had more talents than a barrel of monkeys, no? I said, didn't I, Jacques has a talent he can just smell money? Also Jacques got this talent—more like a genius. . . . People just decide they want to make Jacques these very big loans. What a talent that is!

"You didn't ever notice that, Sarah? You didn't make Jacques a very big loan quite recently? Out of thin air? Just like friends, I mean, since you got these big sums of money, without even asking for it?"

Sarah stared at him.

"Am I at all warm, Sarah? You know that game, hot, warm, cold?"

"Yes, I know it."

"Okay. You're not so confiding. Wonder what that means? Sarah, don't you really see we got to make a deal? I've been totally honest with you, Sarah.

"You don't believe me?

"Okay, Jacques and I, the first of August, we couldn't leave town, we were so broke, see? No money from healing, no rich new friends making loans, no new money from art —Jacques got some commission, but he'd spent his advances, he's got no money to begin anything new. How about a little religious ceremony? No, no. He's not in the mood. You see?

"Sarah. I'm not going to ask you do you wonder what I

do. I'll do what I can to get money. I'd rather it's pleasant than unpleasant, like anyone. I don't wish anybody bad, except one or two I'll take care of myself. I'm willing to put up with some unpleasantness and risk. Truly, I like a little risk, but not to the point of suicide. There's a few things in sex I won't do, no matter what the money, but nobody's dared ask me for a long time.

"But it's true, I'm maybe a little spoiled. Jacques thinks so. I like nice clothes, pretty things, good food, good drugs, good sex, which luckily doesn't cost me. . . .

"Back in the beginning of August, Jacques indicated to me he had a problem—a problem that involved a small risk, not too unpleasant, not against my scruples, for certain reasons. If I took care of the problem, he was pretty sure there was enough money I'd stop complaining.

" 'Okay,' I said, 'okay.' I did what I said, took care of that problem. And Jacques was correct. There was a good deal of money. Now I'd like to know how *much* money. You see, Sarah, nothing like this ever happened between Jacques and me before. I told you he did things his way, I did mine —he never paid much attention. We each got something, nothing crossed up. But this time I was stupid. I didn't think about it enough. I didn't know Jacques was giving me one single glass of milk while he went off with the cow. And that's not all. Excuse me, Sarah. I must be getting less and less full of good manners. I'm sorry, Sarah. I'm getting a little too furious to be polite. So just tell me, or okay, let me tell you.

"Okay, Sarah, no matter what you look like, you're one very, very rich girl. All on your own. And Jacques knows all about that. And this is *it*. This is the situation Jacques always knew would happen, one fine day. Okay, Jacques gets to take care of you, so everything's fine, right?

"Well, no, Sarah. Because what do I get? You know what I get? Mr. University of the South. I think he's waiting out there to get my ass. Am I right? Am I right, Sarah? What do you think, Sarah?''

Sarah didn't say anything. Maurice chewed on his finger. "Okay, Sarah. I don't blame you. Look, I believe you don't know a thing about it. I believe you and me are in the same boat in that respect only. Sarah, how much money did you give Jacques?"

"I didn't, Maurice. I didn't give Jack a thing. It's not true."

Maurice stared at Sarah. "Okay. I believe you, Sarah," he said. "Okay. Okay."

Maurice took a big gold coin out of his pocket. It looked old—maybe Spanish. He flipped it up in the air, caught it, slapped it over onto the back of his left hand, and stared at it. "God, Sarah, you're a lucky person," he said. "You don't imagine how lucky. Your life is one big present. The whole time I'm talking to you, it's in my mind, before I leave this place I'm going to take my knife and cut your throat. Leave you right here to fuck Jacques up the way he deserves. No kidding! I was seventy-five percent decided. But no. I'm not going to touch you. I believe you, Sarah. I believe you don't know a thing. You can't help it about Jacques. It's not your fault.

"God, what a joke! You can't imagine how close! What a surprise for Jacques. Are you mad at me? In any case, believe me, I like you, Sarah. In fact, I'll tell you just what I'm doing.

"See, I'm leaving now. I'm going to the house of my best pal, and I'm telling him everything he ought to know. He gives good advice. That's insurance—you can tell Jacques that. But I'll come back. I'll come back when I'm satisfied. I'm a gypsy, Sarah, did you know? I got nine lives. Maybe I owe Jacques one life. We'll see.

"But, Sarah, meanwhile, you can probably walk right down those stairs right now. Maybe you could go somewhere. Your rich family got any friends nearby? By the way, you got any money around here I don't know about?"

Sarah shook her head.

"It's true, I can't imagine where. You're going to stay right here, Sarah? That's it? You still trust Jacques, huh? Maybe so. Maybe it's my bad heart. I get such evil ideas.

"All the same, I'm going up and out, Sarah, over the roof. Just in case. Just in case I don't know how much is really going on. Your college friend got other friends."

Maurice was smiling, and his eyes were shining. "Well, Sarah, so long. The good chances are, we'll meet again. You know, I always did have this weakness for you. Anyway, we have a sincere friendship, no?"

The apartment seemed so very quiet after Maurice left. Sarah tried not to listen to how quiet it was. She had to resist the impulse to go to the window, to look for the man in the T-shirt. Doing that would mean that she believed Maurice. She didn't believe Maurice. She didn't ever want to see him again. But for once she didn't like the quiet.

7

Sarah Melmore
Is Given Some Answers

WHEN JACK CAME HOME, he walked all around the apartment before he came to Sarah's door. She had left it ajar.

"Sarah?"

"Yes," she said.

"Did M'reez just take off?"

"Yes," she said.

"D'you know where he went?"

"He just said he was going away."

"Oh, well. Okay. I guess he won't be back for a while, then."

"I guess."

"Sarah, do you ever feel like going away for a while?"

"No."

"Because you could."

"I don't want to."

"Not even take a walk or something?"

"Would you let me?"

"Good Lord, child, of course. How in the world would I stop you, anyway?"

"I don't really want to. Maybe in a little while. But I was thinking about Wanda. When you stopped by for my things, did you let Wanda know I was all right?"

"She knows now."

"Well, okay. She always used to worry about me."

"I know she's not worried."

"Jack, I don't care what you do. I trust you."

"I know you do, sweet."

"Jack, you're not an angel, really," she said.

Jack sat down at the foot of her bed. "You were the one said that, Sarah."

"But I don't think you are, really."

Jack was silent.

"That was all just shit. You should have told me I was just talking a lot of crazy shit."

"I like it. I liked the time you thought I was an angel."

Sarah shook her head.

Jack gave a long sigh. Then he got up and went over to Sarah's little window. He gazed out over the dark courtyard.

"Sarah," he said. "There's maybe a lot of questions you might want to ask me."

"Mmm," said Sarah.

"M'reez thinks I'm a kind of person—well I keep a whole lot of secrets. That's what he always says. You see, I don't know. I don't watch myself, and I never can figure out what it is people want to know. And, by the time I figure it out, they've mostly lost interest, especially M'reez."

"Oh."

"So maybe you just have to tell me what you want to know."

"Jack, I don't like asking questions."

"Me either. I like being told, though."

"Yes. I guess me too."

"That's why you're so easy to talk to, Sarah."

"Well . . ."

"I don't know. You'd better ask, Sarah. Otherwise it might get in between us. You'd wonder . . ."

"I don't know, Jack."

"Well, I was thinking maybe you might wonder what's going on here, in the first place, especially because M'reez can have a very—uh—dramatic imagination. Especially when there's not much going on."

"Yeah."

"Well, you see, I thought maybe M'reez might have gotten you a little worried."

"Mmm."

"He can have a way of acting like gangbusters or something."

"Mmm."

"Okay. Well, maybe here's the place to begin—with a secret. You see, I wouldn't call this a secret, but it is something I didn't tell M'reez. And M'reez for sure would consider that a secret.

"The thing is, I always intended to be real honest about this, Sarah. To be real truthful, it's your money we're living on now. It just seemed—well, you were sick. And it just seemed the best way to do things, for the time being. I've been trying to make you well. Trying to see what you really wanted. And, at the same time, it's been so difficult with M'reez. He can be a real handful, and I couldn't tell him much, in case he took advantage. Maybe he was getting a little jealous of you or something. I thought I'd get him a nice bike, like he's been wanting, take his mind off things. But you know he just turned me down. That's not like M'reez. So I finally ended up giving him a stack of bills."

Jack measured off about a foot in the air. "Well, for a while he was all revved up—and then—oh, Lordy." He rocked with laughter.

"Lord knows, I didn't dream he'd do *that* with it. All that godawful crap in the living room? You know what he said to me? He said, 'Jack, now we've got a home. We don't have to be gypsies anymore.' Lord, I'd die laughing, if it wasn't so sad.

"I can't hardly walk through that room with my eyes open. I just had to get all my stuff out of there, someplace else. Well, it's not a total mess-up. I'd been thinking about it before. Awhile back, I got another place, just to work. And today I moved my things on over. It's just all—it's just happening a little faster than I'd figured.

"But I guess the point is, you might be pretty mad at me. Taking your money without asking."

"No, that doesn't make me mad, Jack. Money's always been a problem with me. Look, I don't care, just arrange it with Wanda, that's all."

"Wanda—that girl you lived with? I guess maybe it's all okay, then. At least, she went away, after you left. Is it really okay with you? You got a right to be really mad at me."

"I'm not. But Wanda—why did she go away?"

"I think M'reez must have scared her or something. He does that sometimes. I never got to meet Wanda, the way things worked out."

"Oh."

"Did you want to see her or something? It's just you never mentioned her name."

"No. No. It's okay, I guess."

"Sarah, you might have to help me with the questions. But I think that one was about the worst. Well, okay. You didn't ask me this question, Sarah: How come I borrowed your money? Because truthfully, I can make a lot of money myself."

"Um—I don't care all that much about money. Anyway, Maurice did tell me something about that."

"Did he? I'm not sure he understands too well. But then, who am I to say? I don't understand it too well myself. M'reez was always trying to make me do all these things for money that I couldn't charge money for—

"Lord, it's hard to explain. Look, Sarah, I can talk to you so easy, so I'm going to try and say it to you. But remember, I'm not good at explaining, and if it's too stupid, you just say so."

Jack looked at Sarah. "Sarah, you already know—you know a whole lot more about me than most anybody. Well, I might have skipped a little, or something. But about old Emmie, and all?"

Sarah nodded.

"I hardly ever tell people this, Sarah. Truthfully, I don't tell anyone. Old Emmie, she helped me along all right. But in a way, it all would have happened anyway.

"You see—I was born with a whole lot of powers, Sarah. Powers you just have that other people don't. So everything was maybe a little more complicated than I might have said.

"But it's hard. You see, you're born with these powers, you don't know if they're good or bad. I guess it's up to you.

"I have a power, I can get people, like very important people, to do just what I want 'em to. They won't even know what's happened.

"Love powers—now that's a real sad thing for me, Sarah. I try not to think about that, I think it's bad for me. Maybe sometime I'll tell you. But you see, all the powers, I could put them all together and have the whole world right in my hands.

"Except here's where you got to be real careful. You see, you use the powers to get worldly power—it just spoils so fast, so bad.

"You're just the servant, you're not the master of these powers. And so certain things, they're just required. It's not like 'what do I want?' Sarah. It's 'what's required of me?'

"Now, the power to heal. You see, that was directed for me very early, and also it's a whole lot more interesting to me

than most anything. But it's not simple. You see—healing—
it's no carnival trick. It's like you really go right down there
into hell—the hell you believe in, Sarah. You have to go way
down in a person's mind or heart, find out what they're so
angry or sad or cast down about. Sometimes you have to fight
real demons.

"But a lot of times, too, real deep down, there's just nothing. There's people just really tired of living. They just want
to die, but they feel scared or guilty. Those folks—you sure
don't have to use arsenic on them. It's like, deep down inside, you've got to give them permission. Just set them free.
I used to feel that's how I was obliged to use my powers.
That's after I came out of the hospital myself.

"You know, I used to believe in Jesus. We'd have to sing
this song 'Jesus Is My Brother.' Do you know it? Well, I had
this real clear fantasy—Jesus was my brother. Uh, that's
when I was younger. And I thought maybe that was my call
—to spend my life as a healer."

Sarah nodded.

"But things weren't meant to turn out that way. And that
was for the best. It looks like I might've just ended up whor-
ing my talents. It would've gotten out of hand, probably
turned bad. You know?

"You see, there was this thing in my life, Sarah. I was trying to be real quiet about it, but somehow or other, people
would always find me out. And they'd come to me.

"Now you see, Sarah, it's not possible to turn folks away.
Like I told you, I'm the servant, not the master. All I could
do is try and be real quiet, so they wouldn't come.

"But they did come, and then generally I'd make 'em
well. And you've no idea how hard it is to keep that quiet.
But sometimes I'd help them with the other, too.

"But here's how things are. If I'd just charged money,
Sarah, everybody would've stayed real calm. Everybody would
have been easy in their minds. It being free, people all around
would start to wondering. They'd start getting all sorts of

funny ideas. Some of 'em even started this talk about putting me in jail." He laughed.

"You know what? Some of the people talked the loudest was the folks of people I'd *healed*.

"Okay, Sarah. You can see where it had to stop. I just had to move along. I was spending all my life there, down in the dark, in between life and death, and all the time I was knowing more and more clear I had to do something else. Something more important. So that was about it with the healing. I just tried to wind it all up.

"Nowadays, I just say, 'Oh, Lord, don't let it show. Don't send me anybody more to be healed.' And things work pretty good. Course, every once in a while, someone's put in my hands, like you, Sarah. Or M'reez. And I don't have a choice. But most of the time, I don't do it. See, with healing, it's hard to say it right, but I'm not necessarily doing anyone any favor. Like those people wanted to put me in jail.

"I know I've done just a terrible job with M'reez. M'reez, he's learned just enough to make him unhappy, just enough to want a whole lot more. And he can't ever really learn some things. But anyway, mostly the things I don't tell M'reez, that's why. It's not that M'reez isn't smart, but he's just smart enough to know nothing."

Jack came over and sat on her bed. "Did you have any supper, Sarah?"

"No," she said.

"Can I bring you something to eat?" he said.

"Well, I'm feeling better. Why not let me get something? I can cook."

He looked at her. "I like doing things for you, Sarah. You should have somebody to take care of you."

"That's not good when I'm well," she said.

He sighed. "That's another thing I've been thinking about, too," he said. "It does seem now like you're getting well. A lot better for sure. Maybe you might want to go away somewhere."

"Somewhere . . . where?"

"Oh, I don't know. Someplace you'd like. The beach . . . the mountains . . . I don't know."

"Who with?"

"I'd take you if you like, anyplace you'd like. Maybe North Africa."

She stared at him. "I don't know," she said. "I'm used to it here. I like it here."

"The thing is," Jack said, "I think we ought to leave this place for a while. I don't like things to change, either, and I don't like to do things fast, but if you are better, Sarah, and I guess you are, I think we ought to go."

"Oh. Why?"

"Well," he said. "There's different things. I guess you know M'reez is just so keyed up. It might be he's into the coke a little too much. I guess that's his business, but anyway, he's got it in his head there's watchers. Did he tell you he thinks there's people outside, spying on us?

"Remember the other day I asked you about that man with the banjo or something? To tell you the truth, I can't even tell if it's the same guy M'reez keeps spotting. The thing is, what's the difference? We can't do anything about it. Might as well forget it, I say. He likes things to be just like the Foreign Legion or something. I guess that's okay, but sometimes, thinking like that, M'reez gets too excitable. He'll sometimes just do something, just on impulse. It makes trouble.

"Truthfully, Sarah, I just haven't got the patience to go through all this stuff with M'reez right now. See, it's very important to be real honest with you, Sarah, because of how you are. Because—well, this personal stuff is real embarrassing for me, Sarah. I guess it is for you, too. But you are real important to me, Sarah. And I got to concentrate on you a whole lot now. And, at the same time, I got a whole new big piece coming real clear in my head.

"So I'd really like to get out of here, Sarah. Just you and me. Go somewhere nobody knows where we are, so we can just work. I just couldn't figure out what to do about M'reez, but he's kind of worked that out for himself. See, that's the thing. I always believe don't move too fast. Things'll take care of themselves. They'll take care of themselves for the best.

"You know something, Sarah? You never did ask me any questions. Maybe you should."

"Um—you said you found something that was more important than—um—death, Jack?"

"Well, actually, there's lots more important, Sarah. Its just people get so clenched up about death. About dying. They work so hard, just running away. When it's more— well, truthfully, you should just relax right into it. Of course, if you want, it can be a—fulfillment. Like, well, Sarah, I was always able to make it the most gorgeous experience anyone on earth could ever imagine.

"You see, there's like this one moment—it's just perfect— like a split second. It's just the most beautiful thing, Sarah. Just that one moment when someone—well, everything's dropping away. Everything that's ugly and coarse and clumsy and human. It's just dropping away, dropping away, and that person, just that instant, looks so beautiful—so bare. There's this one second of perfect . . . and right then you see the whole idea—the whole idea—so pure . . . it's perfect beauty, like it always should have been, and then, the next second they've vanished into . . . you know?"

Jack gave a long sigh. Then his eyes changed.

"Sarah, I don't want to scare you, but I can see the spirits flocking around you like a swarm of bees. You sure have a lot of family. I could try talking to them, but maybe it wouldn't be right. I know you've been scared for a long time, child, but don't be scared now 'cause everything's going to be all right. It seems like everything's going to be over soon."

"Yes," she said, very low.

He took both her hands and stared into her eyes. She could hardly return his gaze. His eyes were like fire. Brass feet. Would he have brass feet?

"You want to talk to anyone that's here, Sarah?"

"No, no, no!" she screamed.

"All right, all right. Don't worry, it's just you and me. All right, Sarah, all right. Come on, Sarah, open your eyes. You see, it's just you and me.

"You know something, Sarah? You never blink. Doll's eyes." He put a finger gently on her eyelid. "Look, don't get upset now. Sometimes, just once in a while, I can talk sort of funny. It's like I get carried away, and I don't like to do that, not if it's not intended. Okay, Sarah? Maybe if I just finish up, even if I say it so dumb, maybe you'll understand. You see, good or bad, a man's life is just like a blink in time. Not like the stars or the mountains. They say a man's body is trash, Sarah. There's just one part of his life that's not trash, just one part that's pure."

"You mean the soul, Jack?"

Jack looked surprised. "Why, no, Sarah. It's Art. That's the only important thing. Real Art. Art requires everything from you, absolutely everything. Never mind about life and death, or who's used up. Or laid upon the altar. Kingdom come, its will be done.

"And a man has to do the Art that's revealed to him, Sarah. Not whore around. I've been shown a different way, so what I have to do is different, and sometimes people think it's wrong. But it's required.

"You see, my Art, Sarah—well—there's the art I sell. Now that's not as interesting to me, in all honesty. Although I know I can do things sort of right. Better than most people anyway.

"But what's interesting to me, my real Art, Sarah, it can't be bought or sold. It has to be what people call 'real.'

"I've got no education. Anyone can tell that. Never read any of the great books. Ordinarily, I can't hardly tie a shoestring. But it's shown to me and I can do it all. My hands— they can make everything I need. I can build anything. I know all the properties, all the proportions. I can work with any materials. I can put everything together. It's given to me. It sounds real vain, but I can't trust anyone else. I'm the only one who can make everything perfect. Everything's mine. Except the people.

"For the pieces I do, the people, they have to be real. I can't show them how to do. I wouldn't know how. They have to grow up perfect all their own way. If they were like actors, if you had to show them, it wouldn't be right, it would spoil things. But there are all kinds of people, all over, they're just perfect and nobody understands. I mean mostly they're not gorgeous like you, Sarah. They can be these bent-up old men, everybody thinks they've lost their wits. They can be the most stupid-seeming servant woman, never done a thing but slave all their life . . . mostly children, they're perfect, all right. But it's not right. They haven't taken that final form. Kids aren't right. But mostly they can be anybody. Mostly nobody else sees it, that certain quality, how these people they're just right. Just the essence of what they're meant to be.

"And it's funny—I don't really look for them. They come to me. Somehow they sort of understand. They sort of understand if they're right. They understand how sometimes— sometimes it's required. It can be—it's like a perfect—maybe —sacrifice? No, transfor—transfiguration? There's a word begins with an *A* . . ."

Sarah was sitting bolt upright now. "Do you think I want to die?"

"I never try to do the thinking, Sarah. I wait to be shown. I know you're not like any other person. I know you're way, way off somewhere. Near the edge. Soon you'll show me."

"Are you getting ready to help me die?"

"Oh Sarah, to me there's no difference. Healing people, releasing them—it's all the same. It's always up to them. But I would miss you so very much, Sarah. I feel so close to you, like we're growing into one person, you know? For all I said, I'd hate for you to decide that way, on a selfish level." He laughed. "On top of that, you're worth a whole lot more to me alive. See, I really am being honest. But that's a very small part. . . . You know that, Sarah. And you know, too, it's not in my hands. It's up to you."

"Well, just get this straight, Jack. I don't want to die. And I don't want you to help me die. I want to live, so you'd be just plain killing me—understand?"

"Child, you're all upset now. I'm afraid M'reez must have been telling you . . ."

"Maurice didn't tell me a thing."

"Well, I probably explained myself wrong or something. When you're feeling better, I'll show you some of the things I've done. Then you'll understand. Don't worry. You'll understand. And I promise nothing will happen you don't want. Everything will be just the way you want it."

He held her hands again. "Sarah, I've never said this before to anyone, anyone in my whole life, but, Sarah, I need you. I need you to stay with me. I need you to trust me. I need you to understand."

Sarah looked at him a long, long time. Then she said, "I trust you, Jack."

Part Six

TRANSAMERICAN BLUES/B SIDE

1

Mrs. Melmore Becomes Impatient

DAY AFTER DAY, Mrs. Melmore waited for news. There was no news. No news, that is, except the bad news from home. When she had left Locust Valley for Paris, her lawn was already burned and brown, her wildflower garden decimated.

The drought seemed to have settled over the East Coast with the authority and permanence of a new era. Even though they had their own wells, the regulations on water use had become impossibly stringent. Well, she didn't mind washing in a bucket, but her lawn and the shrubs!

As early as June, she had been forced to bring those tank trucks full of water from the Adirondacks, at crippling expense, and even so, MacKenzie, her head gardener, feared they would lose many of their trees. MacKenzie, a dour Scot, had taken to sending her twice-weekly letters, prophesying doom. This man of few words had become almost eloquent in his anguish. He wrote of his despair at losing "The Dexters" and "The Carolinas," as if they were relatives. Of course, there was no mention of any human being.

Actually, she felt the same sorrow. She was trying to resign herself to the loss of at least half her rhododendrons, unless the rains came, "proper" rain, that is.

All she could really count on was her hothouse orchids, trembling always in their own unnatural environment, adjusted always to their own unwavering demands.

"Her" orchids, which she didn't much like; Jim's orchids, really. Visitors always loved them. MacKenzie seemed to distrust them, too—perhaps they were too effeminate?—and left them to that crazy Finn to look after.

MacKenzie never mentioned the orchids. All his letters ended the same way: "Madam, in God's truth, you should come home." But what more could she do? She had authorized the man to take whatever steps he considered necessary!

Two or three times a week, Mrs. Melmore talked to Juliet Sands. Juliet Sands, Mrs. Melmore thought, was the irreplaceable figure in her life. Juliet was for Mrs. Melmore what Miss McMillan had been for Jim—a great deal more than a secretary, more necessary than a friend.

Juliet coordinated every part of her life. Juliet always remembered every tiny detail Mrs. Melmore might have forgotten. Juliet kept in constant touch with her different households and took full responsibility for seeing that everything was in perfect order, including the hiring and firing of servants when necessary.

Juliet had a sixth sense which told her if someone was being careless or slipshod. More often than not, she ended up making the trip to Florida or Canada, smoothing the situation out and doing all the work herself, when she believed things were not up to the standards Mrs. Melmore required. Moreover, she was so calm and soft-spoken and sensible that the servants actually liked her—except, of course, for the few who didn't fit in. Perhaps it was because Juliet looked so cozy. She was a small plump person, with a frizz of gray hair and the remains of a lovely Scottish complexion. Her low sweet voice had just the trace of a burr.

Mrs. Melmore suspected that Juliet had had a brief fling with Jim, years back; very brief, since Juliet was no beauty, and awfully dowdy. Still, any woman had interested Jim once, on an experimental basis. But it was all so unimportant, and so long ago, that Mrs. Melmore bore her no grudge—if anything, she felt it was a bond between them. In any case, Juliet was definitely "her" person, as opposed to Jim's. Juliet had been with her for nineteen years now.

Juliet Sands gave the impression of being friendly and open, but Mrs. Melmore had learned that this was only an illusion. She knew that Juliet was married, but it seemed such an unobtrusive marriage, one Juliet barely acknowledged, occasionally, when alluding to other things. It was only after four or five years that Mrs. Melmore had learned, circuitously, that Hugh Sands was an invalid, wasting away with one of those dreadful paralytic diseases. All Mrs. Melmore's efforts to do something for the poor man had been politely, but firmly, repelled. All she had been able to find out about Mr. Sands (besides the name of his disease, which she always forgot) was that he loved music and crossword puzzles, didn't like television, and was fussy about food. What a nightmare! Mrs. Melmore regularly sent him records and books of crossword puzzles and double acrostics. But what a burden for poor Juliet! And what happened when Juliet took one of her trips? She had tried to probe into the matter with Juliet, very gently, of course, but to no avail. In any case, Juliet was unremittingly cheerful and interested in life. Since Jim's death, she had refused to take a vacation. And Juliet and Sis had begun going to a movie or a matinée together, occasionally.

Juliet was enough of a confidante to know why Mrs. Melmore was in Paris, but not close enough to be told anything but the most highly edited accounts of her progress in the search for Sarah. Instead, they usually ended up talking about the garden.

"Juliet, MacKenzie is such a bully! What can I do anyway? Can't you talk to him, and calm him down a bit?"

Juliet laughed. "Oh, Mrs. Melmore, that's a thing I can never do. He feels about me the way some people feel about the female clergy. MacKenzie doesn't believe in intercession. It does his soul good to write to you. It doesn't matter whether you answer.

"And, of course, no doubt there's a bit of exaggeration. The gardens still look lovely to me. I was there the day before yesterday. The dahlias look beautiful—I stole a bunch to take home. Of course, I read that if it continues this way much longer, they'll seed the clouds."

Mrs. Melmore always felt better after a talk with Juliet.

She began to leave MacKenzie's letters unopened. Still, they rose in a stack, shedding gloom.

She had stopped reading the newspapers over here. All the headlines seemed to concern the drought and the heat wave. If she could only put it all out of her mind!

She couldn't bring herself to care about the French vineyards. They were all screaming about their wine! What did it really matter if they had one bad year? They'd charge more to make up the difference. Meanwhile, the fruit and vegetables in Paris were as beautiful and delicate as ever—and they didn't all come from Israel or North Africa.

It was infuriating, all this fuss, when she knew that her own verdant world, her last refuge, was more imperiled by each day that passed; that it was turning more and more swiftly into a desert, the topsoil crumbling away into the sand beneath it. She'd never have the heart to build another garden.

It was true that the heat in Paris seemed peculiarly relentless. Still, she was often impelled by nervous energy to leave her air-conditioned rooms, her air-conditioned car, and walk about the streets. Unexpected thoughts came to her mind during these walks.

She remembered a young reporter, back from Vietnam, telling her that the refugees he interviewed would describe how their villages had been razed, their wives raped and disemboweled, their children massacred, and then, in the same tone, complain about the monotony of the camp's diet. Apparently, devastating catastrophes and minor irritations became of equal importance after a certain point. She thought she understood that now.

Her husband and her son were dead. Her daughter was mad and had disappeared in what must be considered a most disquieting fashion. And here she was, grieving for her lost gardens.

She needed someone she could talk to, someone she could trust, but there was no one she could trust with everything now; no one who wouldn't say in the end that Sarah should be handed back to the doctors. Even Juliet. Juliet, well, she might not say it, but she would think it.

At first, Sis had had a certain confidence in Anna. Anna, after all, had a very strong motive for finding Sarah herself, and Sis was determined to keep up the pressure.

Her first shock came with the trip to Sarah's apartment. What a chilling experience that had been! A horrid modern building near a Métro stop on the way to the airport.

"Who chose this apartment, Anna?"

"That I do not know."

And once inside—well, it had nothing of Sarah about it. Awful imitation Danish modern furniture. A bulletin board ran the length of one wall. Pinned to it, in intricate geometric relationships, were perhaps a dozen photographs of what at first appeared to be moonscapes, or desert scenes, but on closer examination revealed themselves to be the crook of an elbow, the curve of a breast, the angle of a knee, voluptuous and mysterious. Mrs. Melmore, on examining them, was relieved to note that none of the nudes could possibly be Sarah.

And the books—*The Wretched of the Earth* and a lot of feminist tracts. In the closet: peasant blouses, broom-stick skirts, ponchos, flung on the floor. A few drab garments were hung up. Those were Sarah's, of course; she hadn't become a total slattern. In the bathroom, nothing but a big box of henna. Really, there was nothing of Sarah's here, nothing at all.

"Did it always look like this, Anna?"

"I do not know. I never visited here."

"Is this what you call living 'like an empress'?"

Anna simply shrugged. "That's how young people choose to live today," she said.

Twice every day she called Anna.

"Madame Melmore, we're doing everything possible. It cannot be long now."

"You keep saying that."

"It is very, very unusual. Perhaps it is that Wanda knows you are still in Paris. Perhaps if you were to leave Paris."

"I'm staying here till Sarah is with me."

"And, as I told you, there is a limit to the time. Sarah's check."

Mrs. Melmore said, "I'm losing my patience. I really must have some news before then."

Anna said, "It's not such a long time now, as such things go."

"Well, it's much much too long for me. The fact is, Anna, I really may *have* to call the police. You're not getting anywhere."

"We are working night and day. There are many trails."

"That's not good enough. I want results."

"But you *must not* call the police, Madame Melmore. That you must not do. I told you. The police, they would bring the greatest danger!"

"How do I know this isn't more dangerous? Stop making excuses, Anna, just find her, fast."

Sis had begun to feel that she had lost control of everything when Anna stepped into her life—this girl she had no reason to trust, who kept promising to lead her to a figure who seemed ever more illusory. Was it Sarah she was trailing, or some other anonymous girl from New York? Nothing suggested to her that it was Sarah. "Hi from Sarah." Maybe Wanda had written those cards.

As Sis became more peremptory, Anna grew increasingly sullen. Of course, Sis wouldn't have cared a hang about that if everyone else wasn't letting her down. Cecil and her morbid curiosity didn't count. But Williams, even Williams, her old friend and ally, was becoming stiff and aloof. Of course, the worst was Harriet. Harriet had suddenly seemed to withdraw all her affection and approval, just when she needed her the most. She tried to deal with them one by one.

"Would you like to take two weeks' vacation, Cecil? Take a little tour? Go on a visit?"

"Oh, madam, thank you, madam, but really Europe's not the same these days, is it? Even Paris. I don't like the things I hear. I was just wondering, madam, if you'd decided how long we'll be staying this time?"

Of course, Cecil was dying to know what had happened to Sarah. Obviously, she knew something had gone wrong, since Sarah had never appeared at her mother's hotel. She suspected another catastrophe. She wanted to be in at the kill.

And Williams, she didn't know quite what had happened with Williams. Their coziness had evaporated. Harriet thought Cecil was a prune and she thought Williams was insufferable. No, actually she thought Sis behaved inappropriately with Williams. And instinctively Mrs. Melmore's manner with Williams became more and more remote and impersonal.

Once, she had gone out just to sit in the car and talk to him, and try to reestablish some of their old rapport.

"Williams, there's the most awful mess going on about Miss Sarah. You can just imagine, from what you saw that first day. I can't tell you about it now, but it's making me a wreck."

"Madam."

"It's all so screwy and I can't tell anyone in the world. Even my sister. And I really miss you, Williams. You're my rock of ages. You don't even care how much I'm smoking anymore."

"Madam."

"Maybe you'd like some time off. All this waiting around. You must be stir crazy."

"Any time you wish me to go away, madam."

"Oh, Williams, how can you? I never want you to go away. It's you I'm thinking of. I promise I'll tell you all when I can."

"Madam."

Oh, God, Williams was implacable. She seldom took the car now. She had completely altered her routines. Strolling around, shaded by her pink parasol, she had discovered another and different Paris. She had begun exploring neighborhoods where she had never been: Les Halles, Montmartre, places which held no memories for her. She liked finding funny little cafés with a few chairs outside, where she could sit by herself and have a Vichy; poking around shops she'd never heard of, full of such odd things. She never bought anything.

Naturally Williams didn't care for that at all. He preferred to follow her in the car. Williams was becoming querulous— bitchy, almost. All of a sudden, she wondered if he was a fairy. He must be well over sixty. Never married. What a weird life for a man, just driving her around. Funny that she had never thought about it before.

But worst of all, ever since the evening she had told Harriet that endless story about Sarah, Harriet had changed. She kept looking at Sis in a critical way. Often, she was very sarcastic. She didn't even deign to mention the girl who was "Sarah's friend," as if she were some figment of Sis's imagination. Sis hadn't wanted to talk about it, of course, but she thought it was unfeeling of Harriet not to ask. Every once in a while, Harriet would say, "How long do you propose to wait before calling this lawyer you mentioned?" Meanwhile she seemed determined to make this waiting time as grim as possible. Before, they had had some good times, but now!

"How about playing some cards, Harriet?"

"I loathe cards."

"You used to play cards with Mama."

"Russian bank. It dulls the brain."

Harriet did escort her around the museums—not just the Louvre and the Jeu de Paume and the Cluny, but what seemed like a dozen more that Sis had never heard of.

Sis was sure that Harriet was purposely making it all as tedious as possible. Harriet would stand in front of one picture and stare at it through her thick spectacles for eons. Sometimes, she jotted down a few scribbles in a notebook she carried. Apparently Harriet used to spend four hours, or so, in each museum. Sis liked to drift through, glancing left and right, picking up many ideas and impressions, then return to whatever had taken her fancy. More than an hour in a museum was torture for her.

"I just get exhausted," Sis said.

"I'm sorry," said Harriet. "I thought you said you liked art."

Sis was relieved to find that most of the galleries were closed. She had very little interest in contemporary painters, anyhow. When they were married, Jim had given her a Matisse and, every year, for the next ten years, on their anniversary, he gave her another. Then, suddenly, he had decided the prices were intolerable, and on their twelfth anniversary he had given her a Hans Hofmann. He had sensed her disappointment, and told her he thought she'd find it was one of the best investments he'd ever made. But he never repeated the experiment, and, on their next anniversary, to her delight, he bought her a little Flemish landscape. By now, in her bedroom in town, she had almost twenty of these tiny glowing pictures. Although Jim did not share her enthusiasm, he had been very generous whenever one of her curator friends discovered that something to her taste was coming on the market. This little collection of her own was what she loved.

Jim was amused. "I can tell you're in cahoots with the art

thieves, Sis. They can put the whole shebang in a pizza box and send it all back to Napoli."

Of course, Jim continued collecting Hofmann and Rothko and de Kooning and Albers. Sis found Jim's pictures overbearing. It seemed to her they soaked up all the energy in the room, and she would not be sorry when they went to the museum as Jim had planned.

But she had come to love Jim's Hubert Roberts, and the Morisots, the Forains, and the Corots she had disliked so much when they were first married. Of course, they had really been Marcia's.

Sis had no real taste for collecting. Now that Jim was dead, she preferred window-shopping. Harriet had apparently never heard of window-shopping. She liked to stump along at a fast clip and stop only if she needed to buy something.

Well, if Harriet was disillusioned by Sis's approach to art, Sis certainly felt disappointed by Harriet's so-called interest in flowers. She had tried to talk to Harriet about flowers. She had tried to describe how it felt getting up very early in the morning, and running out to her garden while the dew was still on the leaves. To make sure that the stalks of the newly planted clematis hadn't withered. Or to look at the layers on the rhododendrons, to see if they had begun to sprout. Or to see if the mermaid roses were budding.

She had told Harriet about the excitement she felt in the springtime, waiting for the first crocus, the first snowdrop; the fall, with the viburnum turning purple, and the iceberg roses blooming right up until the frost. She'd talked about her plans for planting mertensia all over the distant hillside. Harriet had looked frankly bored; once or twice, she'd stifled a yawn. Then she'd asked Sis again about her horses. Sis knew Harriet disliked horses.

Why on earth was Harriet proposing to write a book about flowers when she couldn't tell a tulip from a snapdragon? There were no flowers in Harriet's apartment, though flowers certainly would have helped, and the standard fuchsias Sis

sent her would have drowned if Sis hadn't forbidden her to
keep pouring water onto them that way. It would have been
nice to talk about gardening with someone who cared.

The friend Sis missed the most was Melanie Wharton, who
had died that spring. Of course, Melanie had been seventy-
eight—all Sis's "best friends" seemed to be much older than
she. Melanie was the most energetic and intrepid of her old
lady friends, the ones Jim used to call "the flower bugs":
"Worse pests than the Japanese beetle."

She and Melanie and Alison James used to go exploring
in Melanie's old rattletrap prewar station wagon. They used
to root up columbine, and may apple, and, if they were
lucky, bloodroot. Jimmy had gone along when he was little.
"Going thieving," Jimmy had always called it, and Sis used
to think it was funny. Of course, it wasn't exactly stealing.
They used to drive up into the hills of Connecticut and
search the streambeds. Sometimes they would trespass into
unknown woods, and once in a while they had had to run like
hell—well, they hadn't had to, they'd just been carried away.

One of the cruelest things, after Jimmy's last expulsion,
was when Jim had looked at her and said, "Of course, I keep
forgetting it was his mother who taught him to steal."

That was so totally untrue and unkind, and anyway Sis
never believed Jimmy had taken that money from the athletic
fund. There was no real proof, and he always denied it.

Oh, God. Anyway, Jimmy had always loved flowers. Especially wild flowers. One thing they used to talk about for
hours was the trips they would take someday, walking tours
through the foothills of the Himalayas, following the spring.
Jimmy would write, she would take photographs. And the
Alps. All the trips they'd planned.

Melanie had had an odd lot of friendships from those
horticultural correspondences of hers, which had grown more
and more intimate over the years. There was the engineer in
Nebraska who walked the railroad tracks in his spare time,
looking for gentian, the schoolteacher in Oklahoma who

hybridized Madonna lilies, the accountant in Burlington who collected dwarf hemlock. And, of course, there were the sheepherder in Australia, the soft-drink executive in Singapore, the duke in Scotland, whom Melanie had jilted when she found his gardener wrote more interesting letters. She and Jimmy had loved following these stories, and they'd always planned, once Jimmy was out of school, to visit these friends together, and forage.

After Melanie's death, Sis had wondered if she could fill the void by keeping up some of this correspondence herself, but the letters she drafted sounded false and pompous to her. She lacked Melanie's reckless informality and limitless expertise. It would have been so nice if Harriet had had a genuine interest in gardening, instead of this quaint interest in etymology, or whatever it was.

And Harriet had no imagination or humor. She wasn't fun. Sometimes, they would sit and have a *citron pressé* in one of the little cafés along the way. Sis liked to speculate about the people around her.

"Look, Harriet. That man and woman there. Do you think they're married?"

Harriet would shrug.

"Well, but you're not looking, Harriet. See, the man has on a wedding ring, but she doesn't, or if she does, it's awfully weird looking. But they do seem to have an awfully funny relationship. He's so big and strong and really quite good-looking, but I think he's terribly involved—well, actually afraid of her. Not the other way around. What do you think?"

"That it's none of my business."

"You know I'm sure they're not married. There's too much fear and tension. And I'm sure some of it's not habitual. Maybe she's blackmailing him. But you know I really don't think it's that. So maybe it's an affair—but an awfully strange one. He must be fifty, and I really believe she's a lot older. And her clothes—I mean where could you buy such a hat? But obviously he's dazzled. Maybe he's found what he's always wanted. A slave of love. What do you think, Harriet?"

"Sis, I don't know what you mean. But if you're all that curious, why don't you just go over and ask them?"

But Sis kept trying.

"Let's spend a day the way you would spend it if I weren't here," Sis had said.

"Oh, don't be ridiculous, Sis."

"No, I mean it. Come on. Let's pretend I'm not here and just go through your day. It would be such fun for me. It would take my mind off things, Harriet. Well, look—you get up, and then what?"

"Sis, I think it's highly inappropriate to try to play a game like that at a time like this."

"But it's not a game. Your friends, for instance. Are they American, English, French? Your work. How'd you meet this Bill Sparrow? And what's he like? Where do you work? Where do you eat? Which of the streets do you like to walk along? Don't you see, Harriet, it's a whole new world for me. I'd love to meet your friends."

"My friends are all away at this time of year. Bill Sparrow's in Michigan till the middle of September. I was going to go to Greece with Artemis Chase—do you remember her? Probably not. Anyway, she had a stroke, and I was feeling poor this year with the dollar drop, and that's why I'm here."

"Artemis Chase. I do too remember her. She used to be called Bunny. Wasn't she the one—didn't she, after the war —she organized the cities of America with Greek names or something to help out Greek cities with the same names? 'Sister cities' or whatever it was called? I'd love to see her."

"I just told you she had a stroke."

"I mean in the hospital."

"Then go ahead and see her when you get home. She's in New York Hospital. She'd certainly be surprised."

Harriet could be very difficult.

In fact, they had all become less a support than a burden. Why should she cater to them? And just when she was beginning to be really frightened about Sarah! She began to imagine a package tour which involved Williams driving Harriet and Cecil far, far away—the Dordogne, the Haute-Savoie. She'd seen the posters. Or Brittany. God knows, maybe they'd even find Sarah. But she doubted it, unless they ran over her. Harriet might be intellectual, but she was not "bright."

No, Mrs. Melmore was beginning to feel she would have to find Sarah herself. She had almost decided Anna's references to large networks of friends, her claims for the efficiency of her "surveillance" system, were nothing but moonshine.

And too much time had gone by. It was almost the end of August. Sis had set herself a deadline: the thirty-first of August. She was not going to wait on and on into September, for the arrival of Sarah's check. But what course should she take? Not a private detective. Certainly not the police. Maybe a lawyer, but her own lawyer, one who would accept the absolute necessity for discretion.

She thought she knew the man she wanted. She had heard him recommended once by old Mr. Woodruff, and later she had met him briefly in the office of her law firm in New York. Charles Wright. He was younger than she, but not too young, and had seemed as if he might be both tough and sympathetic. She had called Juliet to run a check on him, and what she heard was reassuring. He should be back in his Paris office by now. But she didn't feel like calling him quite yet. Because, of course, Sarah might have gone off on a trip—just vanished, telling no one, as she had done in the past. And Wanda's disappearance would seem to bear that out. Maybe Sarah really wanted to ditch Anna; Sis could certainly sympathize with that. But at the end of August, she must act, in any case. It simply wasn't safe to let it go longer.

One morning, when Mrs. Melmore returned to the hotel after one of her long walks, she was given a message to call Anna, and at a different number, too. This was most unusual, and as she dialed the number, she found herself almost more frightened than hopeful.

"Madame Melmore, I'm glad we connected so fast. We have some news at last. We have traced Wanda to Marseilles."

"With Sarah?"

"We are sure that Sarah is with her."

"She called you?"

Anna hesitated. "We have some friends in Marseilles. They let us know."

"How can I reach Sarah?"

"She is not staying with these friends, Mrs. Melmore. I think she wishes to be very quiet."

"But how can I reach Sarah most quickly?" Mrs. Melmore's heart was beating very loudly.

"Madame Melmore, I think the most efficient and discreet method would be if we go to Marseilles ourselves and discover exactly where they are staying."

"I'll come with you."

"Quite honestly, I can't advise that. We believe it is you that Wanda fears."

Mrs. Melmore digested this. "What if—if they don't want —if Sarah doesn't want to come back to Paris?"

"Of course, we will inform you immediately of the situation, but we don't want to precipitate another flight and another search."

"No, but . . . You're sure they're still there?"

"Without a doubt. They have no reason to be alarmed as things stand."

"Yes, but you'll go immediately?"

"Of course."

"You're going yourself?"

"No, I must stay in Paris. Two of my friends will go."

"If I went—"

"It might attract attention," said Anna.

Mrs. Melmore thought it over. "Listen, Anna, you must give me all the news. You, or whoever goes to Marseilles. You must check with me all the time. You can't imagine how this waiting drives me crazy."

The tension had changed her. She no longer feared a plot to lure her out of Paris. In a way, she would prefer to go to

Marseilles herself, leaving everyone here, not tell a living soul, then scour the city. But she supposed that Anna was being sensible.

"Why on earth Marseilles?" she asked, but Anna had already hung up.

From a period of boredom, she entered a period of terror. She could not bear to see anyone now. She claimed she had a touch of the flu, but declined to see Harriet's Scottish doctor; all she needed was rest and aspirin, she said. She lay in bed and stared at the phone.

Morning and evening she talked to Anna. No, there was no news, but Marseilles was a large city. They knew Wanda and Sarah's patterns of life. Soon they would find them.

Then one afternoon, as she was lying in bed, flipping the pages of a book, the telephone rang.

"Madame Melmore." It was Anna.

"Yes, yes."

"I'm calling you immediately, as you requested. We have for you some news, both good and bad."

"What! What's happened!"

"Sarah and Wanda are no longer in Marseilles."

"But it's been almost a week! Do you know where they are? What's happened?"

"It appears, Madame Melmore, that Sarah and Wanda have parted company."

"Look, I don't give a damn about Wanda. Where's Sarah?"

"Madame Melmore, our surveillance system has investigated every trail. We have been working tirelessly to try and find Sarah—not only through our friends in Marseilles, but our friends here. We have continued to work. To take precautions. Now, the matter of Wanda."

"Look, I told you I don't give a damn about Wanda."

A pause.

"Very well, Madame Melmore. As you like. Although—"

"Sarah."

"It's not absolutely certain that Sarah ever went to Marseilles."

"Oh, for God's sake! How much of this nonsense—"

"Madame Melmore, please, about Sarah, we do have some news, of a sort. This has all been very difficult, very complicated. Please realize how hard we have been working. With no one to help. We have almost exhausted our money supplies."

"Their" money supplies! Boy, that ought to be quite a supply of money. They could buy up a lot of Marseilles with that. She supposed Anna was going to ask her for more.

"Yes," said Mrs. Melmore, grinding her teeth. "Go on."

"I will not burden you, then, with the trail of Wanda, which you might—"

"No, please, don't."

"But through ceaseless vigilance we came upon a series of clues which may lead us to your daughter. I do not want to raise your hopes too high, Madame Melmore. This is not a case of dealing with people whom we can respect or trust."

"What are you talking about? Gangsters?"

"Please, Madame Melmore. Don't go so fast. It is a case which requires a great deal of subtlety."

"Well, what is it?"

"It's a very strange situation. Naturally, we have had Sarah and Wanda's apartment under surveillance, that goes without saying. They have not returned. It is not possible to stand guard outside their very door—it would defeat our purpose —but we have had someone watching their building at all times. Twice we have observed a man going into the building, a man whom we know of, who seemed to us out of place there. The third time he was followed. It appears he has a key to Sarah's apartment."

"Who is this man?"

"His name is Jack Straw, or that is what he calls himself. He is supposed to be an artist of the avant-garde school. We have always dismissed him as apolitical, Madame Melmore. His 'art,' which is bourgeois decadent, is naturally of no interest to us. Nor is the bizarre nature of the events with which he is associated. But, Madame Melmore, he has strong

connections with people of an even stranger and more re-
pellent reputation. We have never been involved with people
of that sort. We do not wish to be."

"Please get on with it, Anna. So you think Sarah is with
this man?"

"We believe that this man, Jack Straw, knows where Sarah
is."

"Well, why can't you find out?"

"That's why I say it's very complicated, Madame Melmore.
Our group, our friends, our interests are antithetical to those
of Jack Straw's. We have watched his flat discreetly, but we
have never seen Sarah going in or going out, or anything
unusual to indicate that she is staying there. He lives with a
young man named Maurice Monaco—not his real name, I
believe. He is not French."

"Couldn't you just—well, break in and look?"

"Of course we have discussed breaking into his lodgings.
But there is always someone there—this boy Monaco, or another. We must face the facts. There is this possibility that
it could be very disagreeable. It must always involve this
small risk, you understand?"

"Small risk? You mean Sarah?"

"Exactly, Madame Melmore."

"You mean Sarah—"

"Madame Melmore, I certainly could not guarantee Sarah's
safety if she is there. These people's reputations are not good.
But we have had a tremendous stroke of fortune."

"What? What is it?"

"In our searches, we have had to go into the sewers where
the rats live. It is only those sewer rats who can help us now.
One of our friends managed to handle this repugnant task
with success. She approached one of these creatures, known
to be in the orbit of this Jack Straw, on another pretext.

"Now this is a very undisciplined young man, and our
friend soon decided that, if she provided enough drinks for
him, he was likely to be quite indiscreet. She paid for them

all, a total of two hundred francs, enormous! But she thought it was necessary."

"Yes."

"She led the conversation around to Jack Straw. Then, with great skill, to Sarah."

"Please go on."

"The results were very negative at first. He pretended total ignorance. But then—forgive me, Madame Melmore—but your name was mentioned. An indiscretion, yes, but it bore fruit. This boy—Johno, he is called—claimed immediately that he knew of Sarah, but had not known that she was your daughter. I had not realized you were a sort of celebrity in your country. Like the Rockefellers? Is that correct?

"In any case, he changed his mind and said he would do this one thing, though it was difficult. He said he was convinced that your daughter was in Jack Straw's care. He said that he would be going Wednesday night to a place where Jack Straw would be. He said that he would take you there, and see that you met. The rest would be up to you.

"What was unspoken but obvious, Madame Melmore, is that this man, Straw, would want a great deal of money. You see, there is something very puzzling here. Jack Straw is known to track down people with money—that is his particular skill. What he does with the money he collects I do not know, but that is his reputation in this world. It cannot be that he does not know what Sarah represents. So in the end it will come down to money. The bargaining, naturally, must be in your hands. But you might need our assistance and advice."

"Dear God. You're sure Sarah's with him?"

"Circumstantial evidence points to that. The testimony of this boy alone, that would mean nothing; we would not spit upon him. But in conjunction with what we have observed and deduced, I think this information may be reliable. Our friend, who is most astute, believed him to be telling the truth."

"You're presenting a pretty god-awful—"

"Madame Melmore, you keep saying you want results. Immediately. Immediately. Very well. This is what we have been able to arrange. If you are patient, we will wait and perhaps we can find out something more, from someone more trustworthy. Of course, it may be expensive. But perhaps we can intercept a letter. Even, we will enter the apartment—with the clear understanding, Madame Melmore, that whatever happens after that, the responsibility will be yours. The blood will be on your hands."

"Oh, my God, no! I'll do it. Wednesday night, you said? When and where are we supposed to be going?"

"This man said that, if you were willing, he would pick you up at your hotel at ten-thirty. He did not seem to want to give any further details until that time."

"Will he call me, or what? What's his name again?"

"His first name is Johno. I do not know his last name. But he will be calling our friend to see if you are willing."

"Yes," said Mrs. Melmore slowly. "Tell him I am willing, but that I would like to take my own car and chauffeur and that I am leaving an entire account of these proceedings to date with a reliable person, in case this rendezvous goes on too long."

"Madame Melmore, I do not think it is fair to include any mention of our group in this document you speak of. I am only telling you what we suspect. I am advising nothing."

"Well, Anna, I'm sorry you seem to have so little confidence in my return. But look here, I'm writing everything down, day by day, and I can't really justify destroying it at this point, on your account. No one will see it unless—well, what I think, Anna, is that we both should remain optimistic about my safety. In fact, I think it's a good thing that we have some mutual interests. Anyway, Anna, please let him know the conditions, and do call me back if he changes his mind."

Part Seven

SPECIFIC REMEDIES

1

A Change of Address

AFTER THEIR CONVERSATION, Jack treated Sarah differently. He was preoccupied, and seemed to have forgotten all about dinner. Late that night he brought a knapsack into her room, full of old clothes. He told her to pick out something to wear. After a while he came in again and, when he found her still in bed staring at the wall, he told her to do what he said this minute and his voice was not so low. He asked her if she could get dressed by herself. She said of course she could. Putting on her old jeans and T-shirt was funny. That girl was a person she didn't really remember. She put the photograph of Jimbo in her pocket. That made it seem more real. Jack gave her a kerchief and asked her to put it over her head. He was wearing a cap and wire spectacles. She hadn't been out for so long. She really didn't know where they were or where they were going. Jack took her arm and helped her along. A car was waiting. Willy was at the wheel. She and

Jack climbed in back. They hardly exchanged a word, just sat in the back, holding hands. Still, she had a feeling that there was an intense conversation going on between them. It was more important than anything that could have been said out loud. She gave a tremendous jump when the car stopped, and Jack spoke.

"All right. Here we are." It was a nondescript street in a quarter she didn't know. Jack said goodnight to Willy, and he drove away. The apartment was on the fourth floor. Jack's old apartment was so different—that huge living room and rooftop vistas. This one was much smaller and more ordinary. The heat wrapped around it like cotton wadding. Jack had his pieces set up in the main room.

"Well, it's not much," said Jack, "but we've got work to do. Not much space in the bedrooms, either. That one's a little bigger. That's yours. My stuff's in the other already."

Sarah nodded. She went and looked at her room. It was very small, but that was fine. She didn't have anything to put in it, anyway.

"Sarah, you oughta sleep now 'cause we're going to start working tomorrow. I'm going to give you a kind of juice I made myself. It'll make things easier. But right now just go to sleep, Sarah. That's the best. Get a good night's sleep."

The next day, Jack was in the apartment nearly the whole time. He seemed busy, sometimes in the kitchen, sometimes working at his drafting board. She spent most of the day lying down. What he gave her to drink tasted so horrible she thought she was going to throw up, but she didn't. It made her drowsy, though. When it got dark, Jack came into her bedroom.

"All right, Sarah," he said, "we're going to have to do some work now. And it's going to be hard, maybe sort of painful, but I'll be right there with you. I'll be feeling everything with you, Sarah. We're going to have to do this together if you're going to get well. Just trust me."

He left the room and brought in two candles, which he lit.

He turned off all the other lights in the apartment. Their street was very quiet, hot and quiet.

He sat down beside her and held her hands. "This comes first, Sarah, before we make any decisions. Your spirit—it's still down there with those demons, so you're not free. Sarah, we've got to deal with those demons now. Don't get scared. I've got the power to deal with demons. You've just got to keep looking into my eyes. If things get too bad, you can trust me to stop. But they won't get that bad, Sarah, if you keep looking in my eyes. Remember, I'll be with you every minute, Sarah, feeling what you're feeling. I'll be your sword and I'll be your armor. I'll be with you all the while.

"Just keep looking at me, Sarah. You've got to go back."

2

Sarah Melmore's Ordeal

SARAH DIDN'T KNOW if there was such a thing as heaven and the angels, which were so real to Nanny. But she knew there was a hell with demons. Whenever she made a mistake, they put Sarah back in hell and began torturing her again. They killed her with electricity, then they brought her back to life, and tortured her some more. It was the same group of demons that had done the same terrible things before. Demons dressed as doctors and nurses, of course, so if the police came, they could fool them. But she wouldn't give in.

Torturing her body and mind. Removing her insides and threatening that she would never get them back. But she wouldn't give in. She was stronger than they were. She would never, never give in. She would always tell the truth about her father, no matter how great the pain, and after she was dead, she would go on telling the truth in hell for ever and ever, amen. All through eternity she would tell the truth about her father. They couldn't stop her. She was too strong.

The worst torture turned out to be not the pain but the thirst—a thirst so great that she would bite her lips till they bled and lick the blood.

"Would you like a little water now, Sarah?"

Of course the water was poisoned, so she couldn't drink it. She would never give in. Like Jimmy. He hadn't given in. And finally they had had to kill him, hadn't they? Was he somewhere in hell with her?

"Jimmy, Jimmy, Jimmy, Jimmy!"

"Please don't scream, Sarah. You're all right. You're getting well."

This was one of the principal demons who said this.

"I know who you are," she said coldly.

"Of course you do, Sarah. You and I have been working together a long time."

She tried to think of something withering to say, but she couldn't.

"I'm wondering if you'd like a little treat this afternoon. How would you feel about a little ice cream?"

"Do they really have ice cream in hell?"

The demon gave a false laugh. "Well, after all, why not? Let's hope they do have ice cream down there once in a while. How would you feel about a little of this, Sarah? Your favorite kind. Rocky fudge. A little bird told me that was your favorite kind."

She looked at the cup he was holding.

"You take a bite first."

"But I don't like ice cream, Sarah, and unfortunately, unlike you, I'm too fat and I'm on a diet. My wife would be very cross with me."

Naturally. Naturally. It was poison, and anyway demons didn't eat.

"No." She turned her head away from him.

"Please try, Sarah."

"No."

"Sarah, you know if you don't try to eat we'll have to go back to the other feeding, which you don't like and we don't like, either."

Sarah said nothing. She supposed it didn't matter one way or the other—they'd just put the tubes into her body and pump the poison through that way. Whenever they weren't looking, she ripped all the tubes out. Then they would strap her down. After a while, she was so uncomfortable she would decide to eat the poison, but she would never, never pretend it wasn't poison. Or agree that they were doctors.

"Listen," she said suddenly, "I'll eat some ice cream, if you let me see a priest."

The demon was naturally very surprised. "Yes, yes, have a bite of ice cream, Sarah. It will do you good. You said—a priest?"

"Yes. A Catholic priest."

"Yes. Just another bite. A Catholic priest. But—your family? A minister?"

"No, a Catholic priest." Who was Nanny's priest? Father Brogan. "I want to see Father Brogan, as soon as possible, and I'll eat what I can."

"Father Brogan. Does your family know him?"

"My old nurse knows him. He's the only one I want."

She ate. It was nauseating. It didn't even taste like ice cream. If they were so clever, why did their poison still taste like poison? Because they didn't care; they enjoyed the mockery.

When Father Brogan came, he was not wearing his robes, as she'd imagined. Only a clerical collar under a blazer. She was disappointed.

"Miss Melmore, I was told you wanted to see me?" He seemed uncertain, not at all authoritative, as she'd hoped.

"I'm Sarah, Father Brogan. You remember me. I used to come to church with Miss O'Donnell."

"I've known Miss O'Donnell for many years. Yes, Sarah, how can I be of help?"

"Do you have any holy water, Father?"

"Holy water." He looked at her and frowned. "I didn't bring holy water with me, but holy water isn't miraculous water, Sarah. It is only water blessed by a priest, a priest like me."

"Please, Father Brogan, make the holy water quickly and sprinkle it on me and all around me."

"My child, you sound as if you think the Catholic church is dealing in magic. In fact, it's concerned with—"

"Father, please, please! Just put some holy water on me and get me out of here. These people are all demons. They're only pretending they're doctors, they're only pretending this is a hospital. This place is really hell. I know they've fooled you. But, if you put the holy water in your eyes, you'll see! Father Brogan, you've got to help me escape!"

"Yes. Yes, Sarah. I see you're very upset. Just a minute. I will be back in a minute." The priest stood up and went to the door, looked back at her for a moment, then left.

She waited. Listened. Instead of the father, a "nurse" came in and gave her a shot. It was one of the sleeping shots. She never knew where she would be when she woke up. What a fool she was! Of course the demons could produce their own Father Brogan. Of course that would be what they would do, so they could learn her plans. But a demon couldn't touch holy water, so she'd caught him out at least. If only, if only they hadn't given her this shot, she would have been able to plan what she should do next.

Sometimes, she was put on the sun porch under blankets. There were other people under blankets, too. She knew she was heavily sedated, but always she fought the sedatives so that she could think and scheme.

They were confusing, all those other so-called patients. Since they were all being punished too, she knew they must have annoyed her father or gotten in his way at some time in his life. Some of them were awfully old. But then her father had a very long memory and kept track of all the people who had done him dirt. Mostly something bad had happened to them eventually. Then he was always very pleased.

Maybe that old woman was the teacher in third grade who had given him a B instead of the A he deserved. And that skeleton there, he must be seventy, with the yellow face; maybe he was the one her father held responsible for black-balling him from that fishing club on Key Largo.

Mostly she didn't feel like speaking, but sometimes she would say to one of those bodies, "Do you remember James Melmore?" Most of the people just stared at her or shook their heads, but once she'd seen a man strapped down on a stretcher; his eyes were wild but his face looked familiar. As she was wheeled past him by a demon nurse, she broke one of her rules and spoke in front of one of them.

"Do you know James Melmore?" she said.

"James Melmore!" the man screamed. "James Melmore stole my inventions! He ruined my life! Everything he has belongs to me!" They were pulled swiftly in different directions, as if they were dogs in a dog fight.

"Sarah, you shouldn't have done that," said the demon nurse, slamming the door behind her. "That poor man is very sick." Sarah just smiled to herself. She knew.

Sarah had read a great deal about concentration camps and she had also been interested in how they tortured resistance fighters to extract information. She knew that, after a period of torture, there would often be a period of remission, so that the victim would begin to feel human for a while, just before the torture began again. It was supposed to be more effective that way.

They gave her these pain-free periods, she realized, but they had come and gone and she had not made the proper use of them. In the past, she had used these times of respite for dreaming. She didn't ever want to mention Jimbo's name, or Paul's, because somehow they might have escaped and, if she said their names, the demons might catch them. But she thought about them a lot, and if she didn't use the dreaming time, she was afraid she would speak about them and the demons would hear. Jimbo was the one she liked to dream about the most, up to the bad part, and maybe, just maybe, that bad part could be changed. Maybe her father had been tampering with her brain all along, to make her think those terrible things had happened. She shut her eyes. "Jimbo."

Jimbo. It was funny. Mostly she called Jimmy Jimbo and that was because he had called her Sambo long, long ago. He called her Sambo, he said, because that was her name—after Little Black Sambo, because she was little and black.

"But I'm not little and black."

"Well, you might grow a little but you really are black," he said. "People just don't want to hurt your feelings."

"I'm not black," she cried. "Look," and she'd shown him in the mirror. He'd just laughed.

"Don't you know they can change the mirrors in this house?" he said.

Of course, she hadn't really believed him—but in a way she had. Whenever his friends came over, they all told her the same thing. So she'd been sort of scared—too scared to say anything to anybody. She got older, and then she'd laughed and started calling him Jimbo. And now she called him Jimbo, but he hardly ever called her Sambo. Only when something important was going on.

Like today. He called her at school, which was against the rules, anyway.

"Sambo," he said, "I really need a hundred."

"Oh, God, Jimmy."

"Can you get it from home?"

She didn't need to ask if it was important. It was always important.

"When?"

"It's got to be by five o'clock. Can you do it?"

"I'll try."

A hundred dollars—that might be more than she could handle. Well, she had managed. Jimbo always counted on the fact that Sarah could manage. She had gotten most of it from poor Nanny; Nanny always had cash around for her missionaries.

Everything about her brother had changed so much over the last two years. Jimbo never came home now. He never called, except on her phone. And those conversations were short; he believed her phone was tapped. He didn't seem to work and he had no permanent place to live, but still they would meet and talk and joke from time to time. She always paid the bills. He used to apologize for this, but she knew he had no money.

But the last six months things had gotten worse, much worse. He had begun regularly asking her for small sums of money—it could be as little as five dollars, it could be as much as twenty-five. Sarah's allowance just didn't cover it. Sarah had tried to talk to her father about Jimmy. They had been sitting alone in the library.

"Sarah," he said, "I know you love Jimmy, and it's hard for you to accept and understand, but by now Jimmy's not the boy we knew and loved. The Jimmy we knew was a sweet and generous boy. The boy today—he's a virtual criminal. I've looked into it, Sarah. I wanted to make sure your brother was safe. But after a while I stopped, Sarah, because I thought if I followed his trail any further it would be necessary for me, as a responsible citizen, to turn him—my son, the son I once had—over to the police. Now do you understand why I don't want his name mentioned in this house?"

"I don't care. If he were a murderer, he'd still be my brother and I'd still love him."

"Sarah, I'm not sure you can even imagine the price you would have to pay for what you're saying." He stood up.

"Oh, Dad, how can you? Family is family. Jimmy's Jimmy. He's the prodigal son, Dad." She knew she was making him angrier.

"I don't happen to have any use for prodigal sons or any other kind of prodigal. That boy broke your mother's heart. She'll never be the same. Just remember that. I wouldn't want you to be a traitor to your family, Sarah."

"What do you mean, Dad? About Jimmy? Seeing my own brother? Talking to him?"

"That's exactly what I mean."

"But I can't accept that. I love Jimmy and I always will."

Her father looked at her in a way she'd never seen before. She used to love watching her father's eyes, because they were always changing color. Usually, when he was with her they were bluish gray and sparkling. When he was serious they became green-gray, and when he was furious, gray. Now his eyes were gray and cold as the rocks in Maine. The look he gave Sarah actually scared her, and then he turned and left the room.

Her father had never mentioned the matter again. He exacted no promises, so she wasn't breaking her word. She went on talking to Jimmy and seeing him when she could, but she was growing more and more disturbed and impatient.

"Jimbo, why can't you get a job? Any kind of job?"

He always told her the same thing, or a variation of it. There was a very important man who was letting him in on a perfectly fantastic deal. He could end up with half a million bucks if things went right. He'd pay her back then, and more.

Sarah didn't believe any part of this story. Jimbo didn't even have an address or telephone number. Who would ever employ him? She was beginning to be very downhearted. It was his lack of dignity that made her feel so bereaved. Anyone could get some sort of job—a night watchman, or something. Jimbo shouldn't be living off borrowed crumbs.

Sometimes he said it was urgent for her to meet him at a certain place at a certain time. Then she would go and sit and sit, and he never came. Or he came very late and drunk. She hated seeing him drunk. When he was drunk, he just ranted on and on about their father. She wouldn't reply. Still, she always met him when he asked.

They were sitting in a dark corner of a dark bar. It was early enough so no one else was there. Just one man in a far corner. Dark light. She could hardly see Jimmy.

"Well, Sambo," he said, "looks like we're both black now."

"I'd just as soon," she said.

"I'd rather. So how are the old folks at home?"

"Oh, the same, I guess." It would have been really nice to talk to someone about her family, but things were so bad she couldn't.

He was holding her hands. That was funny; he wasn't usually very affectionate. When she was very little, he used to beat her up a lot. She'd never told on him. Everyone was always on her side, anyway.

"I called you because I think I'm going away pretty soon. Pretty far. And really—you're the only one who's going to miss me. At least, I think you'll miss me."

Sarah studied him. "Jimmy, honestly now, come on. What's this money for? Come on, what's it for? One hundred dollars—you've got to know that's just about impossible for me to get hold of. But it's way too little to take you very far."

"I know, I know. But I know a way. Wanna come?"

"What's the money for, Jimmy?"

"Okay, Sarah, I'll tell you the truth. I owe a guy some money and he's a bad guy to owe money to."

That sounded like it might be true, unlike some of his other stories.

"Is this exactly what you owe him, or there's more?"

"Oh, there's always more, you know. But this will keep things cool a bit. So I can go away."

Sarah took the envelope with the money in it out of her bag. She put it on the table. Then she put her hand over the envelope.

"D'you really like that school you go to, Sarah?"

She shrugged. "Oh, it's school. You know, you get through."

"Not me, Sarah," he said. "Remember you're talking to one of the ones that didn't get through. Not for one goddamn minute."

He moved her fingers off the envelope. She put them back.

"Well, Sammy," he said, "you're still a good little soldier. How long you going to be a good little soldier? Dad tells you to march one way, and off you go, into the Valley of Death. I ask you to march the other and here you come into the

Gates of Hell. Are you ever going to stop marching? You're going to end up one good little schizophrenic soldier, you know?"

Sarah pulled the envelope back toward her. "Do you mean when am I going to get fed up with all your shit, Jimmy? I'm glad you brought that up because I didn't want to. I'm already fed up."

"Well, I'm not going to be robbing you anymore, Sarah. This is the last time. I promise."

They looked at each other in silence.

"Well, Sarah, if you like school that much—"

"I have to finish, Jimmy."

"Well, anyway, you've got to start planning right now. You've got to go away to one of those boarding schools. I feel like a clown telling you what to do about school, but it's something you've got to do. You'd like it probably, and you've got to get away from Dad. Now listen, you think I'm smashed, but really I'm not, and you've got to remember what I've said."

She nodded.

"Sarah, I can see you just think this is some sort of drunken bullshit. But you're wrong. You're still real, Sarah. If you want to stay real, you've got to get away."

She nodded.

He sighed. "Pilot to co-pilot," he said. "We lost one wing and the other's about to go."

Then he picked her hand off the envelope and stuck the envelope in his back pocket.

"Sarah, you remember what I said. I want you to remember what I said when I'm not here."

"Do you really think you're going away somewhere?"

"Oh, yeah, this yearning for more temperate climes, I suppose, but all the same, if I were going away, you'd be the only one I'd say goodbye to, because you're real, Sarah. Don't let them mess you up."

Sarah didn't know what to do. She thought Jimmy was drunk, but not that drunk. She was beginning to feel scared.

"Jimmy, why don't you spend the night at one of my friends' houses?" Sarah said. "I'll call and fix it up. I'd stay there, too, and then we could really talk."

"No, no. I'm meeting someone in a little while. I'm already late."

"Jimmy, you're drunk."

"No, Sarah, I'm not drunk. But I think you oughta leave me now. I'm going to remember you just as you are. I can't remember you if you're here."

"Jimmy, I can't leave you like this."

"Then I'll have to leave you and that'll make me feel really crummy."

Suddenly it seemed serious. Sarah's eyes filled with tears. "No, I won't leave you. I'm going to stay with you, no matter what."

Jimmy leaned over and stroked her hair.

"Come on, Sambo," he said. "There's nothing to cry about. There hasn't been for years."

"Okay, Jimmy. I'll do what you say, if you just let me stay with you. You asked me to go with you, remember?"

"Daydreams," he said, "just daydreams. You know what I'd really like? I'd like you to give me this."

It was a little ring, a baby ring. She always wore it on a chain around her neck.

"Why? Why do you want that?"

"Well, I always associate that with you. I'd like to have it."

"Why? You said you weren't going away. Why do you want to have it? Here—it's yours. But I'm going with you, wherever you're going." Her tears were falling on his hand.

"Okay, okay, Sambo. But look, my friends today aren't the sort— I mean, I don't even like them all that much myself. And then there are the people—Well, they're not friends at all. But they find out who I am somehow and figure I must be loaded for bear. They can't understand it when I'm not, and it makes trouble."

"Well, I don't care about your friends. I'm staying with you."

"Okay, okay, Sambo. But now I'm going to the gents. Wanna come?"

"I'll wait."

She had waited and waited. Finally she asked the waiter; maybe Jimbo had passed out in the john. But no, he had just slipped out a door in the back. She'd given Jimmy everything except what she needed to get home; she hadn't enough left to pay Jimmy's bar bill. The waiter was a young man with a big mustache. He'd been friendly to Jimmy. Now he went and talked to a man sitting at a table by himself. The man jumped to his feet, banging his head on the overhanging beam, and swore loudly. He disappeared, but a minute later emerged from the back with a sheaf of papers.

"You know that kid?"

Sarah nodded.

"You his girlfriend, or what?"

"I'm his sister."

"His sister. What's your name?"

"Why?"

"I said, what's your name?"

"And I said, why?"

"You see this? Five months old!" He waved the papers at her. "These are all bills that crumbum your brother piled up on us. Five months old. He sure stuck us good. Gave us a bum address. How old are you, anyway?"

"Eighteen," said Sarah immediately.

"The hell you are. You shouldn't even be in a place like this. You know damn well we don't serve minors."

"I wasn't drinking, anyway."

He looked at her school bag. "Look, sister, I'm doing you a favor. You give me your name and address and telephone number, and where you go to school. That's right. And I'm going to check it before you leave. And then you sign your name down there." He pointed. "And then someone just better get ahold of that money real fast."

Sarah looked through the stack of bills. It came to about one hundred and twenty some dollars.

"Or," he snatched her school bag from her, "or I'm going to call your school and your home. Tell them what their little darlings are up to."

Sarah was livid. "Do that," she said. "Call my house. Call the police. I'll tell them you've been pushing booze to under-age kids. You'll lose your license. Plus trying to mess around with me. My father's name is James Melmore." She wrote it down. "Here's his office number. Here's his number at home. Please call him, right now. My father would really love to step on a lousy cockroach like you. My brother's underage, too, you know. So all those pieces of paper—they're just nothing."

"Why, you little whore!" he said.

"Either call my father or give me back my bag."

The man's face was scarlet. Maybe he was going to have a stroke.

"All right! Get out! he yelled. "Get out before I have you arrested. And don't you dare come in here again. Or that fuckin' no good brother of yours. I'll break his neck."

Sarah took her school bag, and walked deliberately to the door. The man with the red face had rushed over to the waiter. He was waving his arms. Probably he was so sore he was going to fire the waiter. Sarah was sorry about that; still, there wasn't anything she could do about it.

She walked down the street. She couldn't go home. And suddenly she knew she was going to be sick. There was a hamburger joint across the street. She ran straight into the ladies' room and locked herself in. It was filthy, but she just knelt on the floor and threw up, over and over. Even after there was nothing left. . . .

What was all this light in her face? It was still light outside.

"Try to relax, Sarah. You're all right, Sarah."

Oh, God, she was in the hospital. She was back in the hospital, but it wasn't false light. It was sunlight.

"I have no brother," she said. This is what she said when she was asked. It was just possible that Jimbo had really gotten away.

"I have no brother. I was always the only child."

"Yes, Sarah."

All roads led back to the hospital. All dreams led back to the hospital. This so-called hospital, her demon home. Whenever she tried to think about the good times with Jimmy, all that happened was that same old scene over and over, the very last time she'd seen him. That man in the bar—he was one of the ones who was torturing her. She knew him by his red face. One reason he was torturing her was because he couldn't find Jimmy. Jimmy must have fooled them. He'd gotten away!

"He's not here," she said.

"That's right, Sarah. It's all right. Just try to relax."

3

A Matter of Interpretation

THE DEMON NURSE had come late, so Sarah was late for her time with Dr. Frisch. She never liked that.

"I'm a little disappointed, Sarah," Dr. Frisch was saying. "I thought we'd made a little more progress here. I thought we'd at least agreed on the reality of your brother Jim."

"Yes," she said.

"But now you're denying it, Sarah."

"No. I told you he was real. He was my real brother. But he ran away."

"Yes, he did run away, Sarah. That's real. But after that he came home. He lived at home with you, remember?"

"Jimmy never came home."

"Someone came home."

"Jimmy never came home. They never found him."

"Let's see. You admit you remember your brother in those

early years. Ummm. Why don't you tell me a story about yourself and your brother from those early years?"

"What sort of story?"

"Well, a true story. You and your brother must have played games together, when you were young. You've told me about some of them. Children's games," said Dr. Frisch. "Maybe cards."

"Oh, cards," said Sarah. "Yes, we played cards. We played for money."

"You played cards for money when you were young children?"

"Sure. Jimmy was a fabulous card player."

"Suppose you tell me about it."

Jimmy and Sarah had started playing cards when she was very young. Jimmy was going to school, but Sarah was too young.

"You're too young. You're a baby." That's all Jimmy said to her anymore. The only time he paid any attention to her was when he wanted something. His way of getting it was always the same. He would teach her a game, usually a card game, and then he would say: "Let's bet." He always won. In a way, Sarah didn't mind. Even though she lost, at least he was paying attention to her.

One time her father gave her a ten-dollar bill. She didn't remember why. She put it up on the mantelpiece. Jimmy couldn't take his eyes off it. He had a great many suggestions about what they could do with it but for once Sarah was firm.

She liked to look at it, she said; she didn't want to change it, ever. Then Jimmy had talked about a game, almost like poker, he said. Her father played poker. This game was a whole lot of fun, he said, but it was just for grownups. Maybe he would teach her when she started school, but probably not. Maybe when she was in third grade.

Sarah had begged and begged. Jimmy hadn't paid attention. "You're too little, Sarah. This is a betting game."

Then he'd been nice and decided he'd teach her anyway.

The only thing was she didn't have any real money. Sarah was indignant. She'd pointed to the ten-dollar bill.

"But you said you didn't want to break it."

They played. Sarah didn't understand the game very well. She lost every hand. Finally, she had lost not only the ten dollars but her green glass animals and her gerbil and her alpenstock, and had promised to be Jimmy's slave for life.

Then Jimmy had stopped. "We can't play anymore, Sarah. Don't you see? You've got nothing left to lose."

That evening she'd spent trotting up and down the stairs and in and out of the house, while Jimmy lay, languid and capricious, in his room, ordering first one thing, then another.

Finally, he told her to get him a left-handed baseball bat. She couldn't find a baseball bat at all, and was rummaging in the downstairs playroom, when her father came in.

"What're you up to, Puss?"

Sarah explained.

"Slave for life, eh? Well, that sounds like a pretty high-powered game to me."

"Daddy, what about the bat? I've got to get it, or Jimmy can kill me."

"C'mon, baby. Jimmy's just fooling. It'll be all right, I promise you."

He had taken her hand and led her up to Jimmy's room. Jimmy sprang to his feet when he saw his father. "Good evening, Son. I hear from Sarah you've found a brand-new game to play."

"Oh, not really, Dad. It's just a kid's game, really."

Jimmy was looking at his shoes.

"Liar!" cried Sarah, indignant.

"Tattletale," he replied, out of the corner of his mouth.

"Don't talk to your sister that way, Jimmy. Well, suppose you show me how to play this game? It sounds like hot stuff."

"You wouldn't like it, Dad."

"Jimmy, do you hear me? I want to learn this game now! Deal those cards! Don't make me ask you twice! Sit down, baby. Okay, fella, now I'd like you to explain this game to me."

Jimmy sat down at his table, and dealt two hands.

"Well, you see, Dad, look, I told you it's just a kid's game. Well, okay, the high cards count."

"What about suits?"

"No."

"So it's more like rummy. Right?"

"Mmm."

"Play the hand."

Jimmy and Sarah played a hand. Sarah still lost, but not as badly as before.

"Hmmm," said her father. "Looks like fun to me. Suppose you deal another hand and I play along with Sarah."

"Dad, that's not fair."

"Why not, Son?"

"Well, you're much older, and you're grown up and—"

"You're much older than Sarah, fella. I'll deal."

When her father dealt the cards, it seemed that Sarah got nothing but aces. After two hands, Jimmy flung down his cards and said he was tired.

"No, Jimmy. Those hands weren't for real, they were just to teach Sarah how to play. Now it seems you're a gambling man. What have you got to bet?"

"I don't want to play," Jimmy mumbled.

"I didn't ask what you wanted. I asked what you had to bet."

"Nothing," said Jimmy.

"That's not what I hear. I know a few things you have to bet with, but I'm curious to know if you've got anything more. How much is left from your last allowance?"

"Nothing."

"Nothing at all?"

"No."

"Hmmm. Well, that leaves two things I know you have. A ten-dollar bill. And your little sister's freedom. I understand you count that as a marketable commodity, Son."

Jimmy shot Sarah a black look, and muttered something.

"What?"

"Nothing. Look, Dad, okay, I agree you can beat me at this game as often as you want. We don't have to play. I'll just accept that. Okay? Just take what you want."

"No son of mine is going to be a quitter. Play the hand."

Jimmy picked up the cards reluctantly, then threw them down again.

"What kind of bad sport are you, boy? Play the cards."

Jimmy lost the ten dollars, Sarah's servitude, and a large portion of his future allowance.

"I'm not going to make you anyone's slave, Jimmy, though you deserve it. That's a despicable idea. Your ancestors all came here to America because they wanted freedom. Freedom. That's what this country is about. And next time you learn a new game, fella, you show it to me as well as Sarah.

"And, Puss, I'd like to give you back that ten spot, but I think instead I'll keep it for you till you get a little older. There's a lesson in this for you, baby. Don't trust anybody at cards, even your old man. And don't wager more than you're prepared to pay. Well, goodnight, Jimmy. Come along, honey bun."

It was a long time before Sarah and Jimmy played cards again.

Sarah's father liked games. He played poker and backgammon for high stakes, and he always won. The only person he ever lost to was Sarah. Sarah was delighted by this, until Jimmy said: "What a moron! Don't you really know Dad cheats with you? He makes you win. Because you're the pet."

When Sarah realized this was true she felt scared and upset. She had thought she was smart, and good at playing grownup games, but it was all a fake; her father just arranged things to make her look smart. It scared her about school, too. Maybe she was as dumb as Jimbo—somehow, everyone in the house seemed to know what bad marks Jimmy got in school. He said he did it on purpose, but Sarah wasn't sure. She had thought school was easy and she had always gotten good marks, but maybe that was all a fake, too; maybe her father just made the teachers give her good marks. It was too scary to think about. Jimbo was the only person she could trust, but he didn't always tell the truth. After that, when her father asked her if she wanted to play a hand of cards, or a game of backgammon, she always said no.

Sarah tried to tell this story, though there were some parts she changed. Like having her father cheat against Jimmy. Probably he did. She didn't know.

Dr. Frisch said, "Hmmm. Hmmm." And seemed quite interested. Then he said, "Well, Sarah, I don't know that you see that story quite as I do. I see a very affectionate, caring father. It seems, from that story, that your father was very supportive to you."

"Yes, Satan was very supportive to me." But she mumbled it.

"You know, Sarah, your constant theme is how much you loved your brother and hated your father. Yet the reality of the situation, from what you have told me, the reality seems to be that your brother exploited you and your father protected you. I sense some sort of riddle here. I think you must be altering your original feelings to suit a story you tell yourself. You'll find we all do that. I do it myself."

"Mmmm."

"What are you thinking about, Sarah?"

"Um. Nothing."

"You know we've said many times that what you may consider 'nothing' is important here. . . . Very well, Sarah. Then let me talk a little more about what your story says to me. You always seem to be very concerned about intelligence. You seem to feel your brother's tragedy was caused by his failure in intelligence. You are overawed by your father's intelligence and have great fears that you may not measure up to him intelligence-wise."

"No. No. That's not true. None of that's true. Look, of course I know my father is more intelligent than I am. That's why I'm in this place instead of him."

"Because you failed in this intellectual competition."

"Um. Sort of. But there were other reasons."

"Mmm. What were they?"

"To punish me. Just like Jimmy."

"But you also tell me in your stories how much he loved you, how much he valued you." He flipped through his note-book. "Every one of these stories speaks of a father who places an unbelievably high value on his daughter."

"Okay. Okay. Sure, I guess he thought I had value. But look, I've tried to explain this before. I mean if he thinks someone can be useful, then he'll keep them in his grip, and just drain them of every drop."

"Drop?"

"Yes. Drop of blood, drop of meaning, drop of use. Then he just throws away the body. On the other hand—"

"Yes, Sarah?"

"If he feels someone has value (and God knows what that means to him), if he thinks someone has value, well, he'll still keep them in his grip, and he'll still drain every drop they have, but he'll keep the body. That's the difference. That's my case, doctor. Unfortunately, he thinks I have value. He's drained me of any usefulness I could ever have had, but he wants the body. I'm trying to make myself clear and easy to understand! Do you understand me?"

Oh, God, she was screaming, wasn't she? She just couldn't control herself. Maybe she was crazy as hell after all.

"Sarah, I understand you. I understand you are a very angry young woman. I don't mind your being angry, Sarah, anger is nothing to be ashamed of. No one here is going to punish you. Anger can be a healthy emotion. Let's just make a guess that some of your problems may come from this anger toward your father that you were too frightened to express."

Sarah was silent. Something had happened with her father —she only wished she knew if it was a memory or a dream.

It was all very blurred—could she have been full of dope? And some of the details didn't make sense.

She seemed to remember a time when she was lying in a high, cold place. The wind was whistling through her ears. And it was dark. She was wrapped up tight in some sort of swaddling clothes, and could move nothing but her eyes.

But after a little while, as she had known she would, she had heard footsteps. Her father was approaching her, coming from afar. He looked small and old to her now—a little old man wearing a vest with a heavy gold chain across it. Although he looked so frail and old, she knew she would need all her strength and power in this battle, and she feared she had nothing left. She must use a serpent for a tongue. Her father crossed the ring of fire and reached the place where she was lying, and looked down into her face.

And he said, "Sarah, listen to me, this can't go on. I can't take it."

Those were not the words her father was meant to speak. But she was wrapped up like a mummy. There was nothing she could do.

"You're a world beater, punkin. All you need to do is get up and fight."

He was leaning over her, looking into her face. If he kissed her on the mouth, the serpent would sting him.

"Baby, I need you. I want you. Remember—we were always partners, the two of us. Partners. It was a partnership. Together we could always take on the world."

Sarah slowly shook her head.

"Sarah, I guarantee you, it can happen again. Just use your will power. There's nothing can stand in your way."

Again she shook her head.

"Sarah, you've always been Daddy's girl. Don't you have faith in me anymore?"

The time was now. The serpent was ready. She would only have this power once.

"No," she said loudly. "No. No. And I never did. I always thought just what everybody else thought."

"What everybody else thought?"

"I always thought you were nothing but a cheap old kike!"

The wind was screaming. Her father must have been blown away by the wind. Sarah had to sing hymns at the top of her lungs. The night was endless. But, wrapped up in her winding sheet, Sarah was warm.

"What are you thinking about now?"

"Oh, um, I'm sorry I screamed at you. Um. I didn't mean to. Um. It's so frustrating though. All these drugs you give me make me lose my memory. I think I'd be better off, uh, if I didn't have to have them."

"Your medication. Let's see. Very well, Sarah, suppose we see what a change in medication will do. Actually, I'm very pleased with our session today. I think we accomplished a lot. We've finally admitted our anger and fear in this intellectual competition with your father. I think this is a very positive step, Sarah."

As Sarah walked back to her room, she realized that she was beginning to feel very frightened indeed.

It had been so different long ago. She had had the power. She had had the upper hand. In a way, she had enjoyed frustrating and exposing those quacks. If she didn't speak, if she didn't eat, it was because she didn't want to, not because it was beyond her control. And, whenever one of those crummy doctors was on the verge of making a diagnosis, she would begin to speak perfectly lucidly, ask for some breakfast, and make fools of them. Then, suddenly, it was like that awful thing the servants used to say: "Don't frown like that, Miss Sarah, or the wind will change, and your face will stay like that forever."

Her silence had been in her control, but suddenly one day it was no longer in her control. And the screaming—she couldn't control that. Then other terrible things began to happen that were not in her control in any way. And finally they had put her away in this place they called a hospital.

She had chosen Dr. Frisch as a kind of desperate ploy in one of her "better" phases. She had watched him lumbering

along on his rounds—fat, ungainly, insecure, always knocking things over, almost a slapstick comedian. She wondered
what he was doing here. They all smirked at him behind his
back. He couldn't be a demon. All the demons despised him.

"You're sure you want to be treated by Dr. Frisch, Sarah?"

"Absolutely sure."

"We have doctors more experienced in the particular treat-
ment you are receiving."

"I'm sure Dr. Frisch is the one who can help me."

She had gotten her way. Dr. Frisch, obviously more frightened than flattered, had been summoned. Their first hours
together, he had stuttered and sweated, and agreed with
everything she said, when she spoke. Well, that was all right
—a good deal more than all right, really, because in the
meantime, they had stopped taking her down into the cellar
to torture her. And they had let up on those drugs which she
knew were ruining her brain. So they waited. Waited for
Dr. Frisch to perform his magical cure. Which was? Well, to
make her curse God. To turn her into a demon too. To make
her recant all her heresies about her father.

Sarah had tried to help him out. She told him little bits
about her life that they would like. She tried not to show
her hatred and contempt for the "nurses" and "technicians"
on her floor. She agreed to see her mother once in a while,
though of course there was nothing much to say.

But they were losing patience. And Dr. Frisch was changing; he must have been taking lessons from the demon
doctors. He didn't listen to her. He told her what she
thought. And he contradicted everything she said about her
father. She still felt sort of sorry for Dr. Frisch, she still
didn't think he knew the score, but she no longer trusted
him. And she was beginning to be very frightened. Too much
time had gone by. Too much time for her father. She was
beginning to think it was really ominous he hadn't shown
up here himself.

She was just boasting when she told Dr. Frisch her father
thought she had value. Once, he'd thought she had value,

but all this had gone on too long. She'd been mad or bad or whatever he might call it too long; she was damaged goods now. She was a liability. It would be easier for him now if she were dead—easier to accept, easier to explain. Another tragedy. It would be so easy in this so-called hospital.

She was sure her father wanted her dead. And in spite of what she said sometimes, she didn't believe she *was* really dead. She didn't want to be really dead. If only she could trust Dr. Frisch—after all, she was the one who had given him his new uncomfortable eminence. He owed her something. If only she could trust him. If only she dared tell him about the demons, and the danger they were both in, for she was sure he wouldn't long survive her.

She was positive the room they talked in was bugged— naturally it would be bugged. She had thought about writing him a letter and slipping it to him, in such a way that even if they were being watched by a hidden camera, no one would see. But she had decided that unfortunately Dr. Frisch was too cowardly and too stupid to handle it. He wouldn't help her, even if she told him it would save his own skin. She would just have to do it on her own. Figure out what lies she must tell to get out of here. And then . . .

4

Sarah Melmore's Strategy

"WELL, SARAH, you look more cheerful, today." Dr. Frisch was smiling.

"Do I? Well, maybe I am."

"Do you want to talk about it?"

"Well, maybe yesterday. Maybe something happened. Maybe something helpful."

"Yes. I felt good too, Sarah. See, I feel good about the same things you do. I feel good you discharged some of the anger you feel—even though it was on me."

"Uh-huh. Well, like you said, it really was my father I was mad at. And I couldn't say so because I'm afraid of him, and he's more intelligent than I am, just like you said. And I get scared I'll—disappear like my brother. But—um—I know that's silly, because my father does love me and wants to protect me. So he would never hurt me. And so I realized —I—um—I shouldn't be so angry and frightened, and that's why I feel much better.

"Wow," said Dr. Frisch. He was writing like crazy. "That's quite a speech, Sarah. Maybe you're coming along too fast for me. That's a heck of a lot of insight from a few humble suggestions."

Sarah saw he was beginning to sweat a good deal. With gratification, she hoped.

"Sarah, I don't want to give you the feeling I'm pushing you along too fast."

Sarah thought this over. She knew she could fool him, but could he fool them? She had better be a little more careful.

"Well. Maybe," she said. "Let's talk about something else."

She noticed how bored and fidgety he became as she told him about her dancing class. It was sort of interesting, if he'd bother to pay attention.

Finally he said, "Sarah, I find you're much more free today. Much freer about all your emotions."

"Oh, sure," she said. "I mean if you think someone wants to kill you because—um—because you've failed, and then suddenly you discover your fear is irrational—I mean, silly— well, I see it's ridiculous, what I was thinking. You're right. My father always treated me wonderfully, much better than I deserved, even though I really acted—badly. So why on earth would I think he'd change? Right? I guess it was all just the guilt I felt."

"What was this guilt, Sarah?"

"Oh—um—guilt, you know. Jimmy, you know. Jimmy

was dead and I was alive, you know. And—um—I was frightened I could never live up to what my father expected, um, and he sort of—treated me better than my mother. Um. And he had this idea I could—he and I could work together one day. But I knew I'd never be any good at it. You see? You can see why I felt so guilty."

"Of course, I can see that you felt it. But, Sarah, I hope you can see you were being too hard on yourself."

"Mmm. Well, maybe. Although actually I believe I can do a lot better than I have. The more I think about it all, the better I feel. I owe you a whole lot, Dr. Frisch."

When she left that morning, Dr. Frisch gave her a sort of hug.

"Well, Sarah," he said, "you're really quite a girl. You ought to feel like you ran the mile in about thirty seconds. I'm really proud of you."

All that week, her sessions were just as "productive." Sarah was not entirely confident about what was happening. She was sure they were taping these sessions and she could feel that her timing was off. Dr. Frisch had reduced her medication; that helped, but still she knew she told too much, too fast. She couldn't help it. She was so anxious to get it all over with. Dr. Frisch was elated. But she wondered what the demons would think.

Then, one morning, at the appointed time, the nurse did not come to fetch her to Dr. Frisch. After waiting for a bit she went and spoke to the head nurse, an evil creature she detested, one of her principal tormenters from the days in the torture chambers.

"Miss Clamm" (what a name), "aren't I going to see Dr. Frisch today?" she asked.

Miss Clamm deliberately took her time. She glanced at her watch, verified it with the big clock overhead, slowly looked down at the book in front of her and slowly around her desk.

"Well, it doesn't look like it, does it, dear?"

"Well, am I or aren't I?"

"There's a note here that says that Dr. Frisch will not be here today."

Somehow Sarah managed to control her anger. "Why? Is something the matter with him?"

"I don't know any more than you do." Miss Clamm made a pretense of being busy by picking up two pencils at once, as if prepared to write with both hands.

"Will he be here tomorrow?"

"Why, Sarah, I do believe you have a crush on Dr. Frisch."

Sarah turned her back. Thank God these demons couldn't read her mind, that was one blessing. Thank God she'd found that out early. But she felt very, very angry. Angry, upset, and most of all, frightened. Had they found out? Well, she'd always known they might. Oh God, if only Dr. Frisch hadn't been such a total moron. And now what? But she had to stay calm. Remember they can't read your mind, only your words and actions.

But Dr. Frisch was not there the next day, or the next. On the other hand, nothing unusual happened. She got no new medication and no new doctors.

It was near the end of the week when Miss Clamm came into her room.

"Well, Sarah, you're off to see the doctor. But don't bother to pretty yourself up. I'm afraid it's not Dr. Frisch."

"Who is it?" She knew Miss Clamm would love to keep her in the dark, but she didn't dare.

"You're a lucky girl, Sarah," she said. "It's the chief himself. It's Dr. Simon."

Sarah said nothing more and followed Miss Clamm. She had not seen Dr. Simon for a long, long time, maybe even since she had entered this place. She tried to remember. She was sure she had been uncooperative, and insulting to him. She believed he was the chief demon doctor, and she had a few vague memories that he had been standing around while she was being tortured in the cellar. But they can't read your mind.

She was led into a big light office, like an office in the real world. Photographs and all that. Simon was sort of nice-looking, tall and gray-haired with glasses. A dark suit with a lab coat over it. He stood up and shook her hand.

"Well, Miss Melmore, we haven't talked for a long time."

Sarah was almost shocked by the use of her last name. The demons always called their victims by their first names no matter how old they were, addressing them like children or inferiors. The victims were supposed to call them "Miss" or "Nurse" or something. It was one of the techniques of humiliation.

"Please sit down."

She sat down.

"So how are you feeling now, Miss Melmore?"

Careful, careful. "Feeling? Oh, um, well, ever so little, um, like the slightest hair's breadth better."

"Uh-huh. Well, that's wonderful news. Even if it's a hair's breadth. Even a hair's breadth makes us very happy, Miss Melmore."

Dr. Simon had a number of folders on his desk, and four or five books. The book he must have been reading was subtitled: "A Doctor's Account of the Leningrad Trials." Oh, God! That was Kamenev and Zinoviev denouncing themselves! That meant she was in for it! Her hands began to shake. She held them together on her lap.

"I see you're looking at my book, Miss Melmore. Have you ever read it?"

"No. No."

"It's very interesting, especially if you're a student of history, which I believe you were."

"No, really I wasn't. Not at all."

"And of course for people in my profession. But you've read of the Leningrad trials in the thirties? The so-called show trials?"

"Um—no. I never did."

"Well, in any case, I do recommend this book to you, Miss Melmore. I'm pretty sure you'd find it interesting."

"Oh, sure. Okay. The thing is, I haven't been able to concentrate on reading. Maybe later on."

"Well, later on. Now, I have been wondering, has everyone been treating you well here, Miss Melmore? Seeing to your needs and so forth? Can I be of help to you in any way?"

So it was just a coincidence, that book? It must be just an unlucky coincidence, and she must stop shaking.

"Hmmm. No. Uh—I really can't think. Oh. Except I was wondering what had happened to Dr. Frisch."

Dr. Simon had been looking at a folder in his hands, but at her question he immediately put it down with a little slap on the table in front of him. "Dr. Frisch. Dr. Frisch."

He stared at her hard. She returned his gaze as well as she could.

"I'm going to be perfectly frank with you, Miss Melmore. Whatever your problems may be, you are a highly intelligent girl. Now, I'm telling you, not asking you, Miss Melmore, telling you that you have been playing games with Dr. Frisch for your own amusement, leading him, as we used to say, around Robin Hood's barn. You've been mocking him."

She continued to stare at him, but she slowly, slowly shook her head.

"Look here, I've read all these notes. Ridiculous. Outrageous," he said. She continued to shake her head.

"Oh, very well then. First of all, could you tell me why, out of all the doctors here, you chose Dr. Frisch? How did you happen to gravitate to Dr. Frisch? I understand you had never exchanged a word with him before. Did you just like the way he looked? Or was it because after talking to him you considered him the most intelligent or the most perceptive of all the multitude of doctors you've seen?"

Sarah considered a long time. Then she said slowly, "No, no. Dr. Frisch is not the most intelligent doctor here. But—um, well; Dr. Simon, you say I'm intelligent. Maybe I am. Or maybe it's—um—all gone. But, at any rate, I grew up among very intelligent people."

She paused while Dr. Simon stared at her and nodded. She twisted her hands in her lap. "Well, you see, I didn't, um, lack intelligent people in my life, I, um, lacked—lacked kindness. I lacked—um—decency. And you see, you see, Dr. Frisch is a kind man. He's a decent man. That's why I wanted him."

And she burst into tears. The tears were real. Although she was terribly frightened, she was carried away by what she was saying, the image of her childhood that it evoked. It was true, too. She sobbed and sobbed.

Dr. Simon looked extremely disconcerted.

"Now, Sarah, please," he said. ("Sarah" he'd called her!) "Nothing bad is going to happen. You're quite right, Dr. Frisch is a decent man. Yes, he is a very decent man, and perhaps, well, perhaps he has done more . . . Well . . ."

He handed her a box of Kleenex, and she mopped her face, although her eyes continued to fill.

"Now look here, Sarah, let me tell you something. I was going to do exactly the same thing in your case either way. I mean to say, if you're competent enough to play all those games with Frisch, you're competent enough to learn to live in the outside world, with help. If you've really been sincere, your cooperation suggests the same conclusion." He gave her another searching glance. She kept using more Kleenex.

"Now, Sarah, you've always been a special case. One about which, I admit, I've been unable to reach any satisfactory conclusion. Even now. In some ways, to be brutally frank— Sarah, I'm talking to you now as an intellectual equal—I have felt you were simply a spoiled rich girl, playing at psychosis. I know how cruel that sounds, considering what you've gone through, but there has always seemed to be an exceptional element of control in that psychosis.

"Believe me, I don't underestimate the very real pain you've gone through in indulging it." He paused. "And, naturally, not all your most paranoid fantasies are without basis in fact."

She stared at him.

"Your life has been full of frightening experiences, no doubt about it, but let us stick to the present for a moment. For instance, at the times when you thought that everyone who was trying to help you (and believe me, everyone here was trying to help you, Sarah), when you thought we were all demons or vampires hired by your father to torment you—"

Sarah could not help uttering a cry of surprise and fear. My God, when had she said that? And to whom? When had they gotten that out of her? And what else had she said?

"You can't remember saying that? There may be a great deal you will not remember, but that was a recurrent theme. Sarah, I will tell you frankly, you sensed quite correctly a great deal of hostility around you, particularly among the nurses, I daresay. That hostility, I'm sure, was quite real, although your interpretation of it was psychotic.

"That hostility—well, it's easy to understand. You're a young girl who seems unbelievably rich, privileged, and endowed, already a 'difficult' patient to deal with.

"But, Sarah, from the moment you came to us here, you treated everyone who dealt with you with the most unspeakable contempt and abuse. You used language that they particularly resented, coming from a girl of your class. And, when you were given the chance, you were physically abusive.

"My staff is all entirely professional, I'm happy to say. They did exactly what was their duty in your case, but I daresay often grudgingly, and certainly with some hostility. As time goes by, I know you'll be better able to put this in perspective and judge your experiences here more fairly. I believe you will end up not thinking so badly of the people who had you in their care."

Sarah said nothing.

"You're going to need medical and therapeutic maintenance for a long time, Sarah. I sound as if I'm discharging you, which I'm not, but in a certain sense I'm considering you— oh well, let's say on probation. You can try going home this weekend—with medication, of course—and if that is successful, you can return here Monday at" (he looked at a book) "three-thirty and we can make further plans at that time."

Sarah had almost stopped breathing. Dr. Simon tipped his chair back on two legs.

"Well, Sarah, now what are you going to do about this difficult relationship with your father? I don't think you and Dr. Frisch have solved that problem."

"No. It's not solved," said Sarah. "Of course I'd rather not see my father."

"Well, he's not going to be at home this weekend. We all thought it was best."

"Oh. Oh, really."

"Yes."

"Oh, well then, oh, well, of course I'd rather not see him at all."

"Obviously I can't help you there. As you know, your father is a man who does just what he likes."

"Yes."

"The best solution in my opinion, Sarah, would be, once you get your bearings, once you feel stable, to start thinking about a place to live and work far, far away."

She nodded.

"Good luck, Sarah. I really mean it. Till Monday, then."

"Thank you, Dr. Simon."

5

Mother and Daughter

THE DAY SARAH WAS RELEASED from the hospital, her mother came to pick her up. Her mother looked the same as ever, but had she always had so much silver in her hair? Sarah didn't know how much time had gone by—maybe years. Was time different in the real world, she wondered.

Her mother took her hand, as if she were a little child, and someone else took her suitcase. All the demon nurses were leering at her and fussing over her now, and making up to her mother, pretending they were such great friends. But of course her mother, like Dr. Frisch, really didn't know. Sarah knew she must be careful, but still she wouldn't look at any of them, wouldn't talk to them, wouldn't even say goodbye. She just turned her head the other way. Her mother punished her for this by being endlessly effusive and full of gratitude.

"Please, let's go, Mother," said Sarah very low. And immediately her mother stopped doing it and they left. Sarah was pleased to see that her mother had brought the station wagon and that she was driving it herself. When they were inside the car, her mother suddenly flung her arms around her and hugged her and hugged her.

"Oh, Sarah! Oh, baby! I'm so happy! Oh, I'm so happy to get the hell out of that hell-hole!"

Hell-hole. "So you knew it was a hell-hole, Mother?"

She felt her mother's body get tense all over.

"Did you know that, Mother?"

Her mother had stopped hugging her and was looking at her, frowning a little.

"All hospitals are, aren't they, Sarah? If it were up to me, no one would go to any hospital, ever."

"Mmm."

Then her mother hugged her again and kissed her and told her how much she had missed her. Then she took her compact out of her bag and fluffed up her hair.

"God, I look like a witch," she said.

A witch. Oh, well. Sarah remembered her mother always used words like that, it didn't necessarily mean anything. Her mother didn't seem to be able to start the car—she was being very clumsy with the keys. Suddenly, Sarah realized her mother's hands were shaking badly. Why, she was scared of her.

"Don't worry, Mother, I'm not going to hurt *you*, anyway." Sarah felt like saying it, but didn't. After all, how could she tell for sure? She didn't know yet what was ordained.

Finally her mother got the car started and they began the drive home. It was an overcast day. Her mother began apologizing for the weather. When her mother was nervous, she would start apologizing to everyone about everything she could think of. Now it was the garden—it didn't look its best right now. She let her thoughts drift. Her mother hadn't said a word about her father—that was unusual. It was almost always "Your father and I" whenever she spoke.

"How's Nanny?" said Sarah suddenly.

"Nanny. Oh, Sarah, oh, darling! I just didn't know how to tell you. Darling Nanny. Well, she died. Quite suddenly. In January. I think I must feel just as heartbroken as you do. She was really one of us, wasn't she? I loved her too, you know. I didn't have them tell you in the hospital—I should have, I suppose, but I was afraid it would upset you and, well, honestly, I was scared you'd never come home."

She took one hand off the steering wheel as if to embrace Sarah, but Sarah moved away and looked out the window.

"Did she die in a place like the one I was in, or at home?" she said.

"What? Oh, at home, of course. Sitting bolt upright, reading her Catholic paper. A perfect way to die, if it has to be. No fear, no pain. Darling Nanny. I really miss her. She was longing so much . . .

"Would you like to see where she's buried, Sarah? I think you'd like the way it looks. And there are always flowers there. She loved flowers, you know, though she could never remember their names."

Sarah kept looking out the window at the country. She was seeing it, but not seeing it.

"Is Toddy dead, too?"

"Toddy? Of course not, darling. Though he's gotten awfully sad. Not so big on slaying the rabbits anymore. Just sitting around the house, moping and waiting for you to come home."

"Oh."

After a while, Sarah asked, "Has anyone else died?"

Her mother frowned. "Of us, you mean? Well, your Aunt Anne, of course, but I told you that in the hospital, remember?"

Sarah didn't remember, but she didn't care. She had hated Aunt Anne, who looked like the angel on top of the Christmas tree. She had come to live with them one summer when she was getting one of her divorces or something, and at first Sarah had been almost speechless with awe. It was her first real crush, she supposed. Aune Anne was so beautiful— much more beautiful than Mummy, she had thought, with all that golden hair and those rosy cheeks and black, black eyelashes. Aunt Anne had seemed so cozy and sympathetic, and she smelled so wonderful. Sarah liked to visit her in her room. Aunt Anne would invite her to climb in bed with her, or else to watch her making up. She would make up Sarah, too. And they would talk and talk. Aunt Anne would ask her about her boyfriends. Then she would tell Sarah about her boyfriend, and she would giggle and giggle. She had a nice giggle.

Then one day Sarah told her about something very special and unusual she had seen, and Aunt Anne was very, very interested and giggled a lot, although it wasn't funny. But that afternoon, when her parents had friends over for drinks, and Sarah had been brought in to make her curtsies, Aunt Anne said, "Listen, you all! This is just too divine. Sarah, come on, honey, tell us who you saw on the beach this morning?"

Sarah glared at her. Didn't Aunt Anne understand that it was private? She found herself getting red and hot, but she was silent. Aunt Anne didn't take the hint.

"Well, Sarah was on the beach this morning, and guess who she saw? She saw Mrs. God on the beach, walking along with Mrs. Noah! And then, honey—tell us how you knew which one was Mrs. God."

Sarah looked at her feet.

"I asked her how she knew which one was Mrs. God, and Sarah said because she was better dressed than Mrs. Noah! Now, isn't that her mother's daughter!" Everyone howled with derision. Everyone was laughing at her and making fun.

"You ugly old witch!" Sarah screamed and ran out of the room.

Once she'd found Aunt Anne out, that she couldn't be trusted, she began to notice a lot of other bad things about her. She was prying and mean, always making fun, or trying to get the servants in trouble, or telling secrets.

"Daddy, I hate Aunt Anne."

"Same here, Puss. Painted old tart. But she is your mother's sister."

"How long does she have to stay with us?"

"It does seem as if she's stayed just long enough. Maybe a little too long, eh, sugar?"

Sarah nodded. A few days later, Aunt Anne left. She was making no pretense of being best friends with Sarah anymore.

She hadn't liked Aunt Louisa either. Aunt Louisa wasn't beautiful like Aunt Anne, even though they were twins. Her hair was just plain brown and she didn't have such pink cheeks. Just as much as Aunt Anne giggled, Aunt Louisa cried. She held people's hands a lot when she pretended to cry. Sarah couldn't imagine why Jimbo liked her. Aunt Louisa called him "Big Boy," and was always hanging on to him. She called Sarah "Little Sister" and ignored her. Sometimes when Aunt Louisa was carrying on, Sarah's father would wink at her.

But then, one night, a couple of months after Aunt Louisa had married Uncle Fletcher, she had gone into her father's room—she never used to knock—and there were her father and Aunt Louisa, hugging and kissing. She'd been terribly scared and run out. And she didn't dare say anything to her father about Aunt Louisa, because if he loved her so much, of course that meant divorce. She'd heard all about it from her friends. Things like that meant divorce.

She'd have to live with Aunt Louisa, who'd be crying all day, and Jimmy would be "Big Boy" and get spoiled rotten, but "Little Sister" would be sweeping up the ashes or something. That's what would happen.

But, strangely enough, Aunt Louisa left the next day, and Sarah had hardly ever seen her again. A few years later, Aunt Louisa and Uncle Fletcher were in an automobile crash. Uncle Fletcher was the one who was driving, but Aunt Louisa was the one who died. Sarah was glad but terrified, too. She watched her father carefully, but he didn't act a bit sad. Uncle Fletcher kept on coming to their house for a while, but then he didn't come anymore.

"Here we are," said her mother. "We're home."

Home. Home without Nanny. Where was her father, anyway? What was he up to? Suddenly she felt so tired all she wanted to do was go to bed. All she wanted was her room and Nanny. Oh, no. No Nanny now. And Toddy.

"Can I go right to bed? I'm so tired." She didn't want to talk to any of the other servants. There was Toddy, darling Toddy, covering her with kisses. But he was old, old. His muzzle was gray. He ran up to her room with her. She knew he expected at least a walk after all this time, a long walk with her in the deep woods they both loved.

"I'm sorry, Toddy."

Her mother was in the doorway. "Darling, let me get Cecil. Your bed's not even turned down."

"Oh, please, Mummy, please. I don't want to see anybody. Please. I just want to sleep." Her mother turned down her bed. And she had slept. It must have been nearly twenty-four hours, with Toddy beside her, hardly moving.

The days passed. Most of the days she slept. One day was

just like the next. She took her pills and checked back with
Simon. Yes. Everything was all right. Yes, she wanted to stay
at home.

Actually, it was very strange at home. Everything was different. Her mother's day, both in town and in the country,
used to be run with Prussian precision. During her mother's
telephone hour, Cecil would be doing her nails and massag-
ing her feet. During her language lessons, she would be
doing needlepoint. There were always the hours spent with
Paulette, and of course a big chunk of time with Mrs. Sands.
Sometimes, while she was dictating to Mrs. Sands, she would
be projecting slides on the screen showing table settings and
flower arrangements and architectural effects. Part of this
was in preparation for Bathie.

Bathie was her mother's librarian and consultant. She was
a little mouse of a woman, not even five feet tall, who never
shaved her legs. She had a very slight hump on her back.
Bathie was never there when her father was home—her
father couldn't stand cripples. Bathie never talked to the children. At first Sarah thought she hated children; then she
decided Bathie hated everyone who wasn't a cripple, except
her mother.

Bathie did all sorts of research for her mother. She read
things like social chronicles from many countries, covering
many centuries, to see if there might be something "amusing" her mother might adapt for her dinners. Then her
mother would bring out the files, and she and Bathie would
look at slides of her china and silver and glass, and discuss
what arrangements had been particularly successful. Then
they would plot out new and unusual effects and put them
in a file, for future use.

Of course, her mother spent an hour a day doing her yoga,
and Nicolo came to the house to do exercises with her four
days a week. "At least, I'll have a firm corpse," her mother
would say. While she did her exercises, she played music.
Except for Verdi, she didn't like any composers later than
Beethoven. And all the time a steady stream of people came

to the house: museum curators, art dealers, people from the UN—all people her mother felt she could learn from. She never saw her "social" friends during the day. Of course, in the country her mother spent at least an hour or two, sometimes the whole afternoon, going over the garden.

But now it was so quiet. Her mother scarcely left the house. Of course, she talked to Paulette and MacKenzie and Mrs. Sands, and did her yoga exercises, but Bathie didn't come. And there were no guests at all.

In the old days, Sarah used to mock her mother's routine, and sometimes her mother would smile too, and say, "Oh, I know, Sarah, but it's the only way. If I were ever to stop, even for an instant . . ." She always left the sentence unfinished, and she would laugh.

Sarah had not laughed, but now she felt uncomfortable. Her mother had always been the constant in the life they had led. Sarah had always known how her mother would feel, and how her mother would react; she had always known where her mother would be at any moment of the day or night. She was surprised at how disturbed she felt by the changes.

Most of the time now her mother listened to music and did needlepoint (it was her father who always wanted television on), or just sat around and read. She wasn't even redecorating anything. Her mother had always been in the process of redecorating. She'd done the "little room" over. (It was called the little room because it was the smallest of the sitting rooms.) Sarah used to like the little room. It was more cozy than the library.

"Do you like it?" her mother had asked.

"Mmmm," said Sarah. She didn't like it. It wasn't so cozy anymore and she didn't like things to change all the time.

"Daddy just hated it! I'm afraid I'll have to work out something else."

Her mother was awfully stupid about things like that. She never really figured out what her father was up to—that how her father felt about the way things looked was completely dependent on his mood. If he said he hated something or was bored with it or whatever, it just meant something had happened that day that put him in a lousy mood.

In fact, her mother's taste pleased her father. Their houses always had a style of their own that was original but comfortable, never anything too fashionable, too arty, or too far-out. Her mother didn't want places to look "decorated"; she wanted a feeling of comfort and use, luxury and pleasure. Her father liked to make his own contribution to detail, and he usually decided about the paintings.

But actually the opinions he expressed were mostly capricious, and didn't mean a thing. Once, her father was away for three weeks, and her mother had managed to redo his library, as a surprise. She had managed the impossible, and was awaiting, expectantly, her father's reaction.

Her father had glanced into the room, and said: "Well, Sis, I don't know whether to offer you my congratulations or my condolences."

"What—what do you mean?"

"I presume one of your relatives must have kicked the bucket and left you a small fortune. I'm pleasantly surprised. I thought they were all a bunch of deadbeats."

"Jim—"

"How much did this set you back?"

"Well—"

"Was it the fat lady or the half pint?"

"But—"

"Tell Miss McMillan to let me see the figures. Oh, and if you can afford it, I'd like my armchair back the way it was. That was the only comfortable chair in the house."

Her father had gone upstairs. Sarah saw that her mother's eyes were full of tears.

But a few weeks later her mother had been radiant. "Sarah, Daddy says he's gotten used to his room now. He likes it after all."

Sarah supposed she could have saved her mother a lot of

anguish by explaining that such scenes were totally unimportant—they were just games for her father. But she wouldn't have known where to begin. Her mother would never understand.

But her mother no longer seemed anxious about changing the house around. Her mother seemed very different these days. She always wanted to have Sarah near her now, but she didn't press her. When she and Sarah were together, even if they weren't saying a word, if one of the servants came in to say there was a phone call, her mother always said, "Oh, tell her I'm out," or "Say I'll call back later." But they never said her father was on the phone. It was strange.

The very first day that Sarah was up and around, she had taken care of what she had to. The pistol was still in the place she had hidden it in the attic ages ago. And, of course, there were shells. She was afraid she wouldn't be able to shoot anymore, that the pistol would have rusted and would misfire, but everything was all right. She managed to make some time every day to go down deep in the woods with Toddy and practice, where nobody could hear her up at the house, and it was all right. She was getting good again. Of course it would have to be a silver bullet. She knew that. And it was a real problem. How the hell could she get hold of a silver bullet? They made it sound so easy. But how? And without her father finding out?

She went back to the lab work she'd been interested in once. Her mother actually seemed pleased. Melting down her silver nursery spoon was no joke. At first, it seemed impossible. Her equipment was inadequate. All the time she could see it wasn't going to make anything like a bullet—it would just mess up her gun. There was no one she could ask about it who wouldn't tell. And she still didn't know how soon her father was coming home. She didn't want to ask, either. Still, it weighed on her terribly, not knowing, not knowing how much time she had.

One day, she couldn't stand it anymore. "Where's Daniel?"

she asked Cecil. She loathed Cecil, who was a sneak, but so many of the other servants were new, and at least Cecil would know.

Daniel was her father's black valet. He was almost the same age as her father and had been with him ever since he was a bachelor.

"My best friend is a Negro," her father used to say, showing off to his friends how liberal he was. He meant Daniel, of course. Daniel probably was her father's best friend, though he didn't know it. She liked Daniel herself, respected him, too. He wasn't like a servant. He joked around a lot, but he could be strict. He had even spanked her, one time. "I'll tell my father on you!" she had shrieked.

"Go right ahead, missy, and he'll give you another spanking himself." She had been afraid he was right and never told anyone.

"Daniel? He's with your father, of course," said Cecil.

"I want to ask him about something."

"Well, he'll be back soon. But I should imagine I could help you more than Daniel."

"No," said Sarah. "It was about something else."

She wandered away. But all the time she watched for signs. Every night she lay awake and wondered. The worst thing was she didn't know whether her father could read her mind. She knew the rest of them couldn't, because she could fool them, but her father was different, of course. And sometimes he *was* able to read her mind, that she knew. But always? She wasn't sure. Not at a distance, anyway, she thought. Maybe he had to be looking into her eyes, and maybe if she always kept her eyes on the ground and kept her crucifix on ("Pray for me, Nanny") . . .

Then one morning her mother said to her in quite a normal voice, "Oh, there's good news, Sarah. Your father will be home tonight. It may be pretty late. Do you feel like waiting up?"

"These pills I'm taking make me so sleepy all the time," said Sarah immediately.

"Well, anyway, you'll see him in the morning. I'm very excited."

She wasn't ready. She wasn't ready for him. What if the bullets were just dipped in silver? Would that count?

She stayed awake worrying. It was after midnight when she heard the car. She would know it anywhere, the sound of a car with her father in it. Any car. And the car noises, the slamming, the door noises. And, very faintly, her father's voice. Not what he was saying, just his voice. She could have eavesdropped, she often had, but now she didn't want to know. It might scare her too much. And she had to concentrate now. Now there was no more time.

6

Sarah Melmore
Surprises Her Father

SARAH HAD DECIDED to stay in bed the next day; she would just wait until her father had gone out somewhere. At about nine-thirty, there was a knock on her door. Her mother. She didn't answer. But her mother walked on into her room. "Sarah, are you asleep?"

"Um—yes, I guess so."

"You're usually up so early. Well, never mind. Please come on down and have breakfast."

"Um—I'm not feeling too well or something."

"Really, darling. Well, look, just come on down for a few minutes. It's been so long since Daddy's seen you and you know—"

"I'm not dressed."

"Honestly, Sarah, what difference does that make? Put on your wrapper and slippers. Come on."

So she made Sarah go downstairs with her. "I can't bear to touch my father," Sarah thought. "And I can't look at him or he'll know. And he's going to want to kiss me and hug me."

She dragged along. When they reached the dining room, she took a very quick glance out of the corner of her eye. Yes, there was her father, sitting over the remains of a huge breakfast, reading the *Times*.

"Jim," cried her mother, "here's Sarah!" as if she were an impresario presenting the star turn. Her father never looked up. He just kept on reading the paper.

"What's that, Sis?"

"Jim! Here's Sarah!" He just kept on reading.

"She wanted to come down to have breakfast with you," pleaded her mother.

"Sis, as you can see, I've finished my breakfast, and I'm late already."

"You're not going to the office today?"

Her father put down the paper and walked right past Sarah without giving her a glance.

"I'll be spending tonight in town, Sis," he said in the hall. Her mother ran after him.

"But Jim—Jim, I thought—" More conversation. Mutter, mutter. Then her father got in the car. Slam. He was driven away.

Sarah was stunned. What was her father up to now? She wished she were more skillful at reading his mind. The only thing she was sure of was that he would have his revenge. And it would be slow and horrible.

Life became even stranger. She could tell that her mother was terribly upset. Often now she would hug Sarah or kiss her for no reason. Her father stayed in town. He never seemed to call, but she knew her mother called him a lot. She could hear that emotional note in her voice right through the walls, but she couldn't hear the words. She felt sorry for her mother—her father was torturing her mother just as he had tortured her. It was just that he always managed to fool her mother with his games.

The next weekend, she expected her father would come out, but he didn't. And her mother got more distraught all the time.

"Would you like it if I read you one of the books we used to like?" her mother asked her one night. Sarah really didn't want her to, but she said yes, because she felt sorry for her. But her mother couldn't even concentrate. She chose *David Copperfield*. She read a little, then she stumbled over the words, or her voice broke.

Sarah said, "You know, Mother, I'm getting sleepy. The pills, you know."

What would be the very worst thing her father could do, she wondered? Then it came to her! Make her mother kill her. That way he could punish them both: Sarah for defying him, her mother for giving birth to a child like Sarah. Oh, and Jimmy, too, of course. Two children like that. Then, she supposed, her mother would kill herself. And they would all be in hell, forever.

She really did feel sorry for her mother. Still, she had to watch for the signs. They were out here alone together, so her father couldn't be blamed. He was so good at arranging things that way.

But the next week some things happened that puzzled Sarah. For one thing, one afternoon when she and her mother were sitting in the screened porch, her mother reading, Sarah playing at doing a jigsaw puzzle, the phone rang, and it was her father. Her mother took the call in the little room, and it was so close Sarah couldn't help hearing the conversation.

Her mother sounded happy at first. "Jim—will you be out tonight? It's so lovely right now." Then disappointment.

Then, "Jim, I'm sorry. I just can't. I've told you again and again what I think I should do. I want to stay right here, right where I am. It's the right thing, I know it. Why don't you come out here, then? I'm sorry. I can't agree with you,

Jim, I did not say I'd go. It's just another opening—they don't care who goes. I am not. He would not. He has the hide of a rhinoceros. Anyway, if I'd promised the President, this is more important. Jim? Jim? Hello?"

When she put the phone down, she went straight up to her room.

Sarah puzzled over this. Her mother wanted desperately to please her father, and she would certainly prefer to be with him in town, Sarah knew that. But it sounded as if her mother wasn't totally pliable. Her father had asked her to come to town—ordered her—and her mother was disobeying. It didn't make sense.

The next week passed, and twice her mother had friends for lunch. She asked Sarah if she minded and Sarah said no. Her mother had a good many friends who were much older than she; it was Jimbo who had first pointed out to Sarah that these old ladies were her mother's real friends. Jimmy knew a lot more about her mother than she did.

"How come? She never sees them with Dad."

"That's the point, stupid. Don't you ever notice the people she and Dad see together don't ever last more than about three years? Of course, there's the Yardleys and the Allens and so on—you know, maybe twenty people. But the others—well, Mummy knows Dad is going to get bored, so she doesn't get too attached."

Sarah watched what happened after that, and it seemed true. Simone Villiers and her husband—her mother used to talk to Mrs. Villiers every day and they used to see the Villierses at least once a week, sometimes more. But suddenly her mother stopped calling Mrs. Villiers so much, and if she asked them to do something, it was when her father was away, and when Mrs. Villiers called, she usually made some excuse.

Sarah decided that was a really two-faced way to behave, even though she didn't much like the Villierses herself and she quite liked those funny old ladies. "The old crows," her father called them.

"The funny thing is, I bet those old biddies don't even know they're Mummy's best friends," Jimmy had said. "They probably think she doesn't think they're grand enough for her chic parties, but really she's saving them."

Well, that's what you got if you were such a big hypocrite, Sarah decided. Actually, she had never found her mother that interesting a subject.

It turned out that Sarah quite enjoyed those lunches. The old ladies weren't gossipy or bitchy, and they knew a lot about interesting things, poetry, local lore, natural history. Sarah felt quite comfortable with them, vaguely listening, contributing almost nothing.

Then, Thursday night, her mother came down to dinner more dressed up than usual. When they were alone, she almost always wore pants all day, dressier pants at night. Tonight, she wore a long dress and more jewelry and she seemed pleased and excited. She talked very animatedly all through dinner, as if Sarah were a guest. Her stories were very, very funny, really—about Aunt Cottie, who was the alcoholic; Aunt Harriet, who was sort of a lunatic. No wonder Mother's children had turned out so queer. But after dinner her mother took her hand and said, as if she were giving her a present, "Guess what, darling? Daddy's coming out tomorrow! That means a lot of people around—do you think you can bear it?"

Sarah just gazed at her. "Sarah," her mother said uncertainly, "you do love your father, don't you? In your heart, I mean?" Sarah gazed at her and said nothing. Sarah watched the glitter drain from her mother's face. It was like watching a dolphin's colors fade, once you had landed it on deck. Faster, though.

Careful. Careful. She needed her mother on her side. What would be the right answer? "Always tell as much of the truth as you can afford," her father had told her. "You'd be surprised how that always works best."

"Sarah?"

"It's just that I love you more—Mother."

It worked. Her mother hugged her and kissed her and let her go.

Her father came out. There were a couple of big parties at the house, but even though she had not asked for it (she wouldn't have), all her meals were served in her room. Like the hospital. She was glad about this, but surprised. Only once over that weekend did she even see her father. They were walking along the upstairs hall at the same time, but in different directions. She kept her eyes down, but still she could see he was paying no attention to her at all, no more attention than if she were a ghost. In fact, unless she moved, he was going to walk right into her as if she weren't there. She angled herself to the right a bit. They passed, without a glance or a word. When her father left Sunday night, Sarah began to cry. It was the strain of it all, not knowing.

Her mother stayed on in the country with her, still very upset. She jumped at every noise, fidgeting and smoking constantly. Sarah just wished they could speak frankly.

Once she said, "Mother, you seem awfully nervous. Does it have anything to do with, um, Dad?"

Her mother had cried, "Oh, no, Sarah. Of course not." And then paused. "Well, I suppose I have been jumpy. But it isn't Daddy's fault. It's mine. He thinks I'm being pig-headed about something. He's just not used to it."

"Is it something to do with me?" Bold, but careful.

"Oh, of course not, Sarah. Well, actually, in sort of a way, maybe. Your father likes to be in town this time of year, but I'd rather be out here in the country."

"But you could go to town, Mother. I'm all right here."

"Yes, of course I could, if I wanted. But you like the country better and so do I. And I'd rather stay here with you."

Sarah thought this over. She didn't suspect her mother of subterfuge; she just wondered how her father would manage this double problem. Her mother was being so disobedient—"ungrateful," that was always the euphemism— she would have to be punished, too.

And, if her mother wouldn't come to town, then her

father would feel not only that she was being ungrateful, but that she was losing her value for him, and what's more, making him look bad. That meant he'd have to get rid of both of them, didn't it? A double tragedy. That might be a little more difficult. Still, of course, there were a thousand ways. Naturally, he would prefer what would be the most painful.

The next week, her father stayed in town and her mother bit her lip, chain-smoked and fretted. Sarah made sure her pistol was near her wherever she went. She didn't know when she would need it. Soon, she thought. She dipped two of the bullets in silver, but it didn't really adhere.

The next week, her mother surprised her again by saying that her father would be coming out for a quiet weekend. She didn't seem ecstatic this time—even though she said it would be nice, really nice. "No guests. Just family. Just the three of us. The way it used to be."

Their eyes locked. Then both of them glanced away. "And after that, on Sunday, I guess, almost everyone here will be going into the city. Paulette. All the servants. But we can stay here as long as you can bear it. I'm not a bad cook, you know. Although we could always keep Maggie on. With a little supervision she'd be just fine."

"I can cook, too. We don't need Maggie, Mother. I'd like that," said Sarah.

Her mother gave a sort of quavery smile.

Friday night, Sarah had her gun strapped on under her jacket over her jeans. She didn't see her father until dinner. The three of them sat down at the table. One of her mother's "special effects," Sarah thought, looking at the flowers and the linen. Ginger leaves and heliotrope to match the Victorian china. It was really very pretty.

"Well," said her mother, "I must say this is divine! I'm so happy we're all here together again. Just by ourselves for once."

Sarah hated herself for it, but she couldn't say a word. But then neither did her father. Again, he had not glanced at her or acknowledged her presence in any way. He ate his dinner, slowly and in silence. Her mother babbled on a while, particularly when the servants were passing things, then fell silent, too. Sarah was glad of the weight under her jacket. Dipped in silver—would that do? She couldn't find Bram Stoker's *Dracula* in the house. And, if she tried to get it out of the library, everybody would know.

As her father stood up at the end of dinner, he said to her mother, "Sis, would it be possible to see that the people attending meals in my house are dressed like human beings? I'm not used to it, and it takes away the appetite."

Sarah went up to her room after dinner. She knew her mother was going to have a bad evening, but since her father was still trying to bend her to his will, there might be a little more time. She wondered how she could manage to hide her pistol better. It was bulky.

The next day she was not too surprised to learn that her parents were going out, after all. At least, her father was going out for lunch and golf, and then they were both going out for dinner. She didn't see her father, of course, but she had lunch with her mother, who tried to talk but seemed very sad and preoccupied.

That left Sunday. The servants were leaving for town. Cecil and Daniel had been in town over the weekend. Sunday would be the last day.

Sunday was sunny—one of the last really hot, summer days before it got cool—and her parents would be out to lunch. She wandered out in the woods with Toddy. They walked for miles. She was really broiling in her jacket but she didn't dare take it off. It might happen any minute. How could she tell? She had thought about putting her gun in a bag, but she couldn't draw as fast, and you couldn't take a bag to the table.

She had been watching the sun, and decided it was time to start home. When she got in sight of the house, she saw her father's car. So they were home. She went inside, very quietly, listening. They didn't seem to be around. Nobody was around. She wandered out toward the *allée,* and sud-

denly she heard her mother calling her: "Sarah!" They must
be over at the pool. How weird. She walked over very slowly.
There was a big hedge around the pool—she could see
through it in places. There was a poolhouse at one end of
the pool. Her parents were lying in deck chairs at the other
end—her mother in slacks, her father in bathing trunks and
a T-shirt. He was talking on the telephone. Sarah stood over
by the poolhouse and looked across at her mother.

"Aren't you hot, Sarah?" said her mother. "It's so beautiful today. Why don't you take a swim? Your father decided
he'd take one last swim before going back to the city."

Was her father really going swimming? He liked to swim
naked. Sarah couldn't stand seeing that great bare body. It
was strange. Her mother, who had such a beautiful body,
never showed it off. Her mother's friends had teased her for
years before she would wear a bikini, and even then she
would only wear it in private.

Her father was roaring with laughter. "That must've been
quite a shit!" he said. "Listen, did I ever tell you each time
a Masai tribesman takes a shit it weighs five pounds? All that
fiber! No kidding! That's a fact. Who do you suppose weighs
it, anyway? Listen, I got a lot of influence with Kenyatta.
Maybe I can get you the job." He laughed some more.

That must be one of his toadies. Theo. Theo was a Greek,
raised in England. He never missed a day. And he always
sucked up to her father by talking about the things her father
liked the most. Like shit, literally. Theo actually called her
father every day to tell him every detail of his bowel move-
ments. Those were the calls her father had his people put
through ahead of everyone—Theo and Giles and Philippe.
Her mother really hated them. Sarah used to enjoy it all,
especially when she was little.

Once she had started telling one of her shrinks about this
aspect of her father. At first, he had seemed intrigued, then
frankly disbelieving. "You're saying, Sarah, that a man in
your father's position would interrupt an important meeting
just to have one of these conversations you described?"

She just shrugged and refused to talk about it anymore. Of course, the truth was these shrinks had no conception of what "businessmen" were like. Or, for that matter, what "the real world" they always talked about was like. They only knew about other shrinks.

"Come on, Sarah," her mother was saying. "You haven't been swimming once since you've been home. And I really should take a swim myself. I'm so lazy. If you go, I will too!"

Her father was still talking and laughing. Now Theo—she was sure it was Theo—was telling her father about the extravagant sexual misbehavior of some woman, probably an old girlfriend.

"I don't believe it," he was roaring. Obviously he did believe it, and loved it. "Old man Hardwick couldn't get it up with a derrick! Listen, I have that from an unimpeachable source."

Next to shit, he really liked these tawdry stories. He liked it when his old girlfriends went downhill. He couldn't live without these stories. Sarah remembered how, even when he was watching television, he'd pick up the phone and check in with these people all over the world: "What's new?" "What's the latest gossip?"

"Come on, Sarah. Please. I think your bathing suit is right there in your locker," her mother said.

Sarah went into the cabin. She thought she'd just go in there and sit until they went away.

Her father had hung up. His voice was quite audible.

"Sis, are you mad? Or are you just trying to spoil my last day out of spite? You're pushing me very far, Sis. And I'm not going to be patient much longer. Those doctors have always been full of horseshit, and you know it.

"Well, you've lied to me, you've tricked me, and you've gotten your way so far. But, Sis, I'm telling you, I've been patient with you too long, and you're going to have to make your choice. There's only one reasonable way to behave: write it off. I've done it. That's not Sarah—that thing. It doesn't matter where you lock it up. Just lock it up. And throw away the key. My God, even Jimmy made a more graceful exit."

"Oh, Jim, how can you be so cruel!" She could hear—see—her mother spring up, begin to walk back toward the house. Sarah took off her jacket. She felt the pistol. Held it. Felt the trigger. Then she walked out and faced her father. He was starting to make another call, and didn't look up at her.

"Look, Daddy," she said and fired. God, her hand must have been shaking! She'd meant to hit him right between the eyes, but the shot was too low. Lousy! It was the neck. Oh, God!

Now everything got mixed up. Her mother running back —cradling her father, whispering to him. If only her mother weren't in the way. She wanted another clean shot. Just dipping the bullet in silver, had that been good enough? It was minutes. It was hours. Sarah had never envisioned what would happen after she did this thing. It hadn't seemed important. She started slowly toward them.

Then things happened—if they happened—if her memories were true. Her mother suddenly dropping her father. Her father flopping back like a heavy fish, a heavy dead fish. Dead. Dead. Her mother running over to her and snatching the gun. To kill her. Okay. But, no, wiping the gun over and over on her silk shirt, putting her hands over it herself, not threatening Sarah, not at all, but cold, cold as ice.

"Sarah, go up to your room this instant. Take your clothes off and get in bed. Immediately! Do as I say! This instant! Don't you dare leave your room till I tell you."

And Sarah had done what her mother had told her. Gone to her room, undressed and gotten into bed, Toddy cuddled up beside her. That was nice, but something was missing. Yes. She was not used to sleeping without her gun. That was it. But she wasn't frightened now. It was like being dead again. Much later, her mother had come into her room and said in the same cold voice, "Take these."

She knew what they were. And that was an awful lot.

Maybe her mother wanted to O.D. her on Seconal. Still, she took them. What did it matter? Later, she woke up for a minute, when a nurse came in and gave her a needle. She hardly needed that, did she? Strange tormented faces in the corners of the ceiling, fountains of fire, steam streaming from the cracks in the earth—a sea of glass and of blood. Back to hell again. And through it all, finally, her mother's voice: "Sarah, it's Mummy. Sarah, it's your mother. Sarah, do you know me?" But she wasn't really awake.

One day, she opened her eyes, and her mother was sitting by her bed, holding her hand. There was a bowl of soup on the table.

"Sarah, it's Mummy. Are you awake?"

Sarah looked at her and nodded.

"I wish you would take a little of this soup for me, would you? You've really got to try to eat something."

Was she back in the hospital? No, this was definitely her bedroom. The whole thing was a dream then, but starting from when? How long ago? She was scared to ask. She took a little spoonful of the soup. She was thirsty and she had to go to the bathroom. Her mother gave her a bedpan; she never took her eyes off her.

"Is Nanny here?" Sarah asked tentatively.

"Oh, darling Sarah, poor Nanny died. I know what a blow that was to you. You must have forgotten."

"Toddy?"

"Oh, Toddy's here, of course. He's been waiting outside your door until you got better."

"Is—everyone else—all right?"

Her mother suddenly burst into tears.

"Oh, darling! Oh, baby! You don't remember! I knew you wouldn't remember. It's just so awful. Daddy's dead. Please, Sarah, just listen to me. I have to tell you. Daddy died. He had a heart attack, and just died. Just in an instant. Of course he'd had trouble before, and the doctors had warned him, but you know he never paid any attention to the doctors. Just went right ahead and did all the things he shouldn't have—and then, well—it just happened out of the blue, the way things do. It happened so suddenly—just seconds, really —and he was gone." She continued to cry. "I was with him."

Sarah stared at her. "My father is dead," she said slowly.

"Yes, darling. Daddy's dead."

"He's really dead?"

"I know. It doesn't seem real. I'm sorry to give you such a horrible shock, Sarah, but there didn't seem any other way."

"Can I see his body?"

"Oh, baby, I'm afraid not. Would you really have wanted to? You've been a little bit sick again. You've been sleeping nearly a week. Daddy was cremated, you know. That's what he always wanted. Sarah, are you all right, darling?"

"Yes," said Sarah. "I'm sorry, Mummy. I'm just sleepy."

7

Dinner for Two

BUT SHE WASN'T in her bedroom after all. She was in a little room, a little cell. A jail? No, Jack was there. He was holding her hands and looking into her eyes.

"Sarah," he said, "Sarah."

"Oh, Jack," she said.

"You're okay, Sarah. I was with you the whole time. You feel okay?"

"Oh, my God, I guess—okay. Though— Yeah, okay, I guess."

"You know what day it is? It's been one whole day and two nights. You must be hungry."

"Oh, God. Hungry. Is that what I am? Is that what I am? I guess so. I guess I'm ravenous, actually. What about you?"

"Me too. I've got a steak in the icebox. Why don't I cook it up?"

"Let me do it."

"No, Sarah. You're too weak right now. Just stay in bed. But you were fabulous, Sarah, just fabulous. Just remember, you've lived through something most people, they couldn't even stand a little part of it. You're so strong, Sarah. But look, child, you've lived through that hell of yours and it's all burned away. I could see your body—just clear like crystal. All those rotten human things other people have, just burned away." He shook his head. "You're gorgeous, child, and you're strong. But this whole thing takes so much out of you. Please, just stay where you are. I'm going to bring you some juice. I want a drink. And then we'll eat."

"Jack, what was that? It wasn't a dream. Did it all happen like that? All that stuff? Do you know?"

"Yes, Sarah, it all happened like that. Near enough, anyway. But Sarah, those demons, they've left you once and for all, child. Gone back where they belong. You can be peaceful, child." He brought her something to drink.

"But, Jack—I killed my father! That's a mortal sin! If that's all true, I really did kill my father."

"It's all over now, Sarah."

"But, murder, Jack, *murder!*"

"Oh, Sarah, that's not for you and me."

"Jack, what are you talking about? What do you mean?"

"Sarah, I guess the real true painful things you have to tell yourself."

"No, tell me. You tell me."

"Oh, Lordy. Well, maybe . . . Well, Sarah, did you ever think that maybe we're here all alone? Sarah, for me on this earth, as far as I know, there's just me and God alone. Or sometimes people, well, not even people, just the shadows of people. Maybe they get in the way. That's why sometimes . . .

"But you can think of it just as you like, Sarah. It's your story. Maybe you had a nightmare."

"Jack, I don't like this story."

"Sarah, it's just a story. That's all it is. It's just a possibility in your head, one possibility. Truthfully, all I do is just lead you to the gate. Then you have to look for yourself. So it's what you get is what you pay for. That's what I say to some people—like customers, sort of. But otherwise I say, what you see is what you want to see. Does that apply?"

"No, it doesn't apply, Jack."

"Okay, then. Well, maybe we should go back a bit, try it again."

"How? How on earth?"

"We could go back to when you're walking in the woods. It can turn out different."

"No, Jack. If it's true, I want to know."

"Well, okay. But there's different ways."

"But I want it to be true."

"Little ways, then. How about I say, 'You must be hungry, Sarah'?"

"Jack, look, I can't."

"Yes, you can, Sarah. Now you pay attention to me. Just listen. I say, 'You feel okay, Sarah?' "

"But now I can't forget."

"Yes, you can forget. I say, 'You feel okay, Sarah?' You say—remember?"

"I said, 'Okay.' "

"You said, 'Okay.' I said, 'You must be hungry.' "

"What'd I say?"

"You said, 'Hungry?' "

" 'Hungry?' "

"We're okay, now. 'Hungry,' and then—"

"I said, 'Hungry.' That's right?"

"You said, 'Is that what I am?' "

" 'Is that what I am? Actually, I'm ravenous.' "

"Right."

"Right?"

"And I say, 'Me too. I got a steak in the icebox.' Okay?"

"Okay."

"Just stop right there. There we are. Okay? You see, it's okay."

"Okay, Jack."

"Okay."

"Well, okay then."

"Suppose I blow out this candle, Sarah. But I'll be right here if you need me. Okay, Sarah?"

"Okay, Jack."

"I'm going to cook up that steak. Okay?"

"Okay."

"Okay. I think we're home free."

Part Eight

CHEAP MUSIC

1

Mrs. Melmore
Gratifies Her Servants

ANNA DIDN'T CALL BACK. Mrs. Melmore learned the next day that the engagement had been confirmed. She had had time to think over the situation, and had overcome her original fear of being robbed or kidnaped. Surely someone who had that in mind wouldn't pick her up at the Crillon. Most probably it would all end in nothing, like that wild goose chase to Marseilles. Anna and her friends seemed hopelessly inefficient. Or else they were just stalling. If this led nowhere, it was time to consult Charles Wright. Still, if by any chance they were right—if this Jack Straw did know where Sarah was—suppose he didn't want to tell her? He had made no attempt to get in touch with her so far. Maybe Sarah was there of her own free will. He didn't sound like a kidnaper, somehow.

Oh, well, it would give Cecil and Williams something to do. It was awful to have to make your life interesting in order to entertain your servants. Cecil had been so sulky, and now she was absolutely thrilled to hear that Mrs. Melmore was going out. There had been no social life, no excitement, not even a friend for tea. She didn't count Harriet—even Williams didn't. He thought Harriet had infected her with this mania for walking.

So on Wednesday night she took a great deal of care with her appearance; more for their sake than hers, she felt. God knows where she might be going—the wharfs? some opium den?

"No big jewelry. Too many robberies," she told Cecil, who immediately embarked on a story about a friend who had been mugged on Seventy-third Street and Park Avenue. Mrs. Melmore just listened, while Cecil combed her hair out for her and talked. That was good. Cecil always did the best job on her hair when she was telling a story that interested her. That is, unless Mrs. Melmore told Cecil, which she did only occasionally, that she was going somewhere very grand, or rather, with people who would impress Cecil. Then Cecil did a superlative job.

The people who impressed Cecil were gossip-column socialites, television performers, and royalty, and Mrs. Melmore always felt ashamed to cater to Cecil's nonsense this way. Still, that's what she did, if she wanted Cecil's level best.

She looked surprisingly well, she decided. Not a bit haggard. She'd chosen a white silk dress. Silly—she'd probably be covered with grime by the end of the evening. She didn't care—white looked right. The baroque pearls. The pearl ring. White sandals. Face—not bad. Well, after all this, the man probably wouldn't show up.

She had no expectations from this encounter, if it took place, none at all, yet she found she was actually looking forward to it. It was a novelty to be doing something venturesome, after what had become a routine of waiting, wasting and marking time, and longing for the telephone to ring.

She hoped that wherever they were going would be air-conditioned. Probably not. If it wasn't absolutely filthy—a cave beneath a bar—it would be four flights up, all the windows open, but hot as blazes.

The phone rang. There was a Mister Greeno downstairs, waiting for her. Johno, Anna had said. Johno Greeno. Sounded like a ballad. She gave herself a last look in the mirror, checked her handbag: cigarette case and lighter, Valium, five hundred francs (she certainly wasn't going to deal in big figures tonight), lipstick, compact, eye drops, glasses. Then she went down.

2

Mrs. Melmore Meets a Young Man from the South

MRS. MELMORE TOOK IN the lobby with one glance. A sewer rat, Anna had said. Leather jacket and jeans? Probably swarthy and greasy. On the other hand, Georges's voice on the phone had been completely neutral; he hadn't said the name interrogatively, as he might have. She looked around again quickly, and saw no one who looked appropriate. She went over to the concierge and asked for Mr. Greeno.

He indicated a figure standing by himself in the middle of the room. Well, if she hadn't been looking for the sewer rat, she actually would have observed this young man with the greatest interest. His posture seemed designed to invite attention.

Mr. Greeno was dressed all in white too. Oh, my God—twins! He was young, she decided, maybe twenty-four or five, pretty rather than handsome. But very pretty: beautifully defined cheekbones, straight nose, big dark eyes, white

face, longish dark hair, a lock falling over his forehead. All
that was striking enough—but his attitude! His hands were in
his jacket pockets, his head flung back in a theatrical pose—a
look of pain, almost martyrdom, on his face, as if the flames
were creeping up above his tasseled shoes and he was determined not to utter a cry. Well, that position must be pretty
uncomfortable to maintain for long. Since his eyes were fixed
in troubled rapture on the ceiling, she supposed the burden
of the introduction was on her. She approached him. "Mr.—
Johno?" she said.

The young man gave a tremendous start, as if indeed the
flames he was pretending were there had actually burned
him. Then he turned, taking his hands out of his pockets,
looked at her from under his long eyelashes, seemed to re-
coil, then, rather gracefully, moved forward again and kissed
her hand.

"Madame Melmore," he said.

Mrs. Melmore gave him her public smile.

"She walks in beauty like the night," the young man
intoned, then paused and gazed at her, as if taking her in for
the first time. "How does it feel to be the most beautiful
woman of the century?" he said.

That was it. He'd done it in half a minute. That loathsome question, what *was* one supposed to say? But she went
on smiling. "Oh, don't you think that's too much for anyone
to live up to, particularly in this weather?" she said.

"You're very modest, Mrs. Melmore. You're so gracious to
receive me at all! I can imagine how disgusting you must
think I am!"

Yes, he was quite disgusting. Theatrical, false, intimate,
and a *lunatic!*

"But I don't even know your name," she said.

"Oh, God! I'm so sorry! I thought—John Greenough.
Johno, to my friends."

She stopped smiling and raised her eyebrows.

"I'm an informer, aren't I?" he said. "They say that's the

lowest form of life. Lower than being a whore. Though I've been that too." He paused. "Am I shocking you?"

"No, Mr. Greenough. But please don't embarrass yourself. I don't need to know anything except our plans for this evening."

"My God!" he said, and flung back his head again, though the lock of hair still fell in his eyes. Could it be glued there?

"You seem very disturbed," she said. "Would you like to sit down and order a drink? The only thing I must do is talk to my driver. I'll tell him we'll be a few minutes, unless perhaps you could give me the address? He doesn't know Paris very well."

"Oh, you're kind," he said. "You're being incredibly kind to me. If you only knew who you were offering such hospitality to you wouldn't be so good to me. You'd tell him—" and he nodded his chin at one of the captains—"to throw me out into the street."

"Please, sit down here," said Mrs. Melmore. She firmly indicated the chair she meant, then walked over to the door and asked for Williams.

"Williams," she said, "we may be in for quite a trip. I think you'd better put up the partition between us when we go out. I'd just be too embarrassed. I'll tell you later." Williams bowed. She wasn't at all sure she was up to an evening of this. But on her return the young man was equipped with a drink—so, he was competent to that degree —and seemed altogether more composed.

"The inscrutable smile," he said as she sat down, and laughed.

"Inscrutable," she said, trying to sound cheerful. "I'm baffled. I still don't know where we're going or why!"

"Oh, you know why!" he said. "You do know why! You want me to put the finger on Jack Straw."

"Jack Straw?" she said. "Just exactly who *is* Jack Straw?"

At this, a look of real amazement came over his face— a surprise so real it made a mockery of his previous theatrical expressions. "Jack Straw?" he said. "Jack Straw, the artist?"

"I'm sorry. I've never heard of him. You know I'm not what you'd call in the forefront of the avant-garde. So you're telling me this is an important artist? That I should know his work?"

"But you must have heard of him," he said. "Five years ago? In New York? He was a sensation. Everyone was talking about him. He's the founder of a whole new school. Why, there was a big spread in *Vogue!*"

A Southern drawl kept mingling with his transatlantic tones.

"Well, I'm very sorry I missed the spread. Anyway, I take it you're his friend."

"Friend!" The young man struck his forehead quite hard. Mrs. Melmore decided she would order a drink herself. He asked for another vodka martini.

"I can't believe it," he said, lighting her cigarette before she could do it herself. "I can't believe you never heard of Jack, you're such a famous patroness of the arts. You never heard of destructionism?"

"I wonder if you have me confused with someone else?" said Mrs. Melmore.

"Confused? All right. Now think carefully. My name—John Greenough. Does that bring anything back to you? Eight years ago?"

"We met?" she said hopelessly.

"Met?" (God, she hated that trick, too.) "John Greenough. That's G-r-e-e-n-o-u-g-h."

"Look," she said, "I have a terrible memory. I can't guess. Just tell me."

"I designed two dresses for you," he said.

(Oh, thank God.)

"Oh—maybe I do remember. But it's a long time back for me. Were you working for—oh . . . ?"

"You never wore them," he said.

Damn that idiot Anna! She could not believe this was a

trail that would lead to Sarah, and certainly not to anywhere else she wanted to be. She decided she would finish her drink and say goodnight. "I'm sorry," she said. "But, on the other hand, maybe I did, you know. A lot of my favorite things I only wear at home."

"Well you couldn't have worn these—they were only sketches," he said. (The monster!) "I designed them especially for you. I wanted to make them for you. I got a letter back from your secretary, Mrs. Juliet B. Sands. She said that you liked the dresses, but that you were dressed exclusively by Givenchy at that time. Do you remember now?"

"Two evening dresses, one was sea green, like your eyes, draped over one shoulder, like this, the other was white, cut on the bias. It was a little like a Grès, but not so *drapé*."

Wasn't it typical that with all this blather he didn't even know what color her eyes were? She had almost finished her drink.

"If you'd sent me a word of encouragement, yourself, I'd have come to New York on my knees. I'd have worked like a slave for you, I'd've worked for nothing. You were my idol. My life would have turned out so very differently."

She made a sympathetic noise, and turned a bit, so she could light her own cigarette.

"But you didn't," he said. "You didn't. And I never even knew if your secretary showed you my letters." He looked at her accusingly.

If she said no, he might bring out more sketches right now.

"Of course she would have," said Mrs. Melmore. "But a talent for designing makes itself felt anywhere. Here in Paris you must find enormous inspiration."

"You didn't write me yourself, Mrs. Melmore," he said. "I believed you hated my dresses. If I had gotten just a word from you, yourself—in your handwriting . . . ! That was one of the bitterest moments of my life. Do you know where I come from? Tuscaloosa. Tuscaloosa, Alabama. Can you imagine growing up a great dress designer in Tuscaloosa, Alabama? Can you imagine a seventeen-year-old boy waiting every morning for the mail? For a letter from you? A letter that never came? You had it in your power to make me or break me! You could have made me."

Mrs. Melmore signaled for the bill.

"But I went to New York. Oh, yes, I went to New York. I didn't care what happened to me, really. So what happened? I fell in love with Jack. Jack Straw."

"That's the artist you've been talking about," said Mrs. Melmore, signing the check. "Well, I'm terribly sorry about the dresses. I think from what you say it was my loss. Or rather, I think you must have idealized me much too much. As you see, I'm a total thimble-wit about art, and so forth. You probably should've worked for someone who was truly inspiring. Anyway, it's awful to say, but I'm frightfully tired. It happens, when you get to be my age."

"What, you're not coming to the party?"

"What party is it? I really am quite tired."

"It's at Tony Chappell's. I thought you wanted to meet Jack."

"Tony Chappell?"

She was surprised. She didn't know him, but she had heard of him, seen him having lunch with her friends. He was quite a chic French decorator. Or an English-French decorator. "Kept man" background, she thought. Did a lot of grand houses—still . . .

"What exactly is supposed to happen if I meet Jack Straw?" she said. "Please tell me."

Again he gaped at her. "Your daughter!" he said. "I thought you wanted your daughter."

She had been hot, but suddenly she was cold as ice. "What about my daughter?" she said.

"Well, she's with Jack, isn't she?" (She hadn't believed it.)

"My daughter has been in Paris a year," said Mrs. Melmore carefully. "And she has a great many friends I don't know. You must have gathered I don't know this Jack Straw."

"But isn't your daughter with Jack?" asked the young

man. When he wasn't acting, the southern accent was pronounced.

"What makes you think she is?"

"I—I thought so. I thought someone said so. So you didn't want to meet Jack? You mean I just sold myself out for nothing?"

"Look," she said. "If you haven't done anything, you haven't sold yourself out. Anyway, let's just go ahead and go to your party. Why not? It sounds as if it might be fun. But please don't mind if I leave early. I really am tired."

She got up and moved toward the door. "What's the address?" she asked. Then, entrusting nothing to this young man, she asked the concierge for Tony Chappell's address. They went out into the hot night air. Williams was waiting.

"God, I never thought I'd be sitting in a car like this with you. My life might have been entirely different."

Mrs. Melmore was silent. She was examining a whole new possibility. If Sarah was living with this artist, Jack Straw, that might resolve a good many mysteries; everything would be much easier to understand, and certainly much less sinister. It sounded as if she must be hiding from Anna and her group. Thank God she hadn't called the police after all!

Did this mean that Jack Straw was Sarah's lover? Anna had said he was some sort of horror, hadn't she? Of course there was no reason to take Anna's word for anything at this point. She hadn't been right one single time. The young man with her was pathetic and unbalanced, but he hadn't made the situation sound alarming. But certainly Sarah was in bad shape, so most of all Mrs. Melmore needed to see this man Jack Straw for herself.

She lit a cigarette. "You don't smoke?"

"No. I'm a health nut." He took out a small silver flask and a pill box. "I take these vitamin pills. They're good for my nerves."

He took two large pills, and drank from the flask.

"I'm too high-strung," he said.

Mrs. Melmore couldn't help wondering if the health drink might not be vodka. She was enormously relieved she had made Williams put up the partition; she had known that this would not be the sort of scene she would want him to overhear.

"Tell me about Jack Straw," Mrs. Melmore said, grimly.

"Oh, God, I loved him so! Everyone was in love with him. Oh, God, he was so beautiful when he first came to New York. The 'cowboy,' they called him. And these incredible eyes, like a Burmese cat. God, he's so brilliant! So brilliant! I worshiped him, he was my God. I would have been flayed alive for him. But Jack never loved me. He just used me."

He heaved a terrific sigh, and took another drink from his flask before putting it away.

"I did costumes and décor for a piece he put on. All for nothing, of course. They were these series of film clips, one after another. They got raves."

"Well, that must have been great for you."

"Oh, my costumes went up in flames at the end, and of course I never got the credit, but I still love him. It's in my blood. It's too late for me now. And now—I'm going to turn him in."

"Really," said Mrs. Melmore. "I'm not the sheriff."

"For God's sake, don't tell him anything I've told you," said the young man. "If he were to know, I'd have to cut my throat."

"But you haven't told me anything," said Mrs. Melmore.

"Don't even say you know me."

"Well, we're going to this place together, after all."

"There'll be a lot of people. He won't know."

"But I thought you wanted me to meet him."

"Oh, you'll meet him all right."

"I don't even know what he looks like."

"Well, he knows what you look like."

"How do you know?"

"We used to talk about you in New York, all the time.

And my costumes—he wanted them to look like something you would wear."

The car stopped in front of a very grand house. Yes, really grand, an old *hôtel particulier*. Mr. Chappell must have done very well. And there were a great many people flooding in the door.

"Please try to pull up as close as you can, Williams," Mrs. Melmore said, as she got out. "I don't think I'll be staying very long."

3

Mrs. Melmore Goes to a Party

"Golly!" Mrs. Melmore thought, as she ascended the curving staircase. "This fellow really must have made a packet."

It wasn't often you saw this sort of luxury today. The T'ang vases, marking every fourth step, were filled with white cattleya. There were liveried footmen all along the stairs. And in August! The room she was entering was lined with Coromandel screens, but there were so many people she couldn't really see very much.

Nothing avant-garde about Mr. Chappell's taste, she decided. Just his guest list. The guests seemed to run the gamut—very young people with bizarre makeup; old French dowagers, erect, reserved, bejeweled; tycoons with wives; tycoons with mistresses; actors and directors; agents and producers; editors, couturiers, photographers, and models.

Oh, no! There was that fashion couple she loathed—Marina and Gregory. They were most noted for being the object of a wisecrack she couldn't remember anymore. She never remembered jokes.

She'd felt relieved they were going to the house of someone she'd heard of, but, of course, that was exactly what she *shouldn't* have done. Everything she had gained by keeping so quiet would be lost. And how on earth would she find Jack Straw, if he were here, in this crush?

She had been asked several times if she would like champagne, a drink, or something to eat? She had only shaken her head. Her host hurried over. She remembered him very well now. Maybe they had even met.

"Mrs. Melmore, I'm Tony Chappell. I'm so very happy you could come. Actually, we've met before—at Molly Smith's."

He was an aged beauty—or, maybe not so aged. Perhaps it was his extreme emaciation that made him look like a mummy, even in this light.

"You're very kind to let me come."

"Oh, please . . . They haven't brought you anything to drink? I can recommend the champagne—although, in this weather—" He hesitated, and looked at his glass. "Perrier, I'm afraid," he said. "My misspent youth."

"Perrier for me too, please. I only wish I had misspent my youth. It seems the cheapest time to do it."

Mr. Chappell laughed at this slight remark, and said, "Now how can I make you comfortable? I'm sorry it's such a crush tonight, but it's for Audrey, you know. She's been filming, and now she may be too tired to come, after all."

He shrugged philosophically. A fat bald man with a big black mustache stood beside them.

"Was that Jeanne Moreau?" he asked anxiously. "I think I just missed her. I think she was leaving, just as you came in."

Tony Chappell's very lifted eyebrows rose even higher. "Mr. Appolyon is a great film fan," he said. "Mr. Appolyon, may I introduce you to Mrs. Melmore? But you are really in the most uncomfortable place, Mrs. Melmore, with everyone jostling you this way."

He darted a furious look at Mr. Appolyon. "Through that way we have a little cold supper, and some comfortable places to sit. And there is my little library, also relatively quiet, where one of my men will bring you something hot, if you prefer.

"I'm sure you have many friends here, but perhaps I should take you around a bit? Or would that be a bore?"

Johno, despite his avowed desire for discretion, was sticking to her like a cocklebur.

"Well," she said slowly.

"Johno, be a good fellow and go and talk to Mrs. Segumi. She's all by herself over there in that corner."

"She doesn't speak any English," said Johno sullenly.

"Well, you're so very pretty, you can just recite nursery rhymes and make funny faces. She'll adore you! Now! Quick!" He clapped his hands.

Johno departed, although not quickly, in the direction indicated. Mrs. Melmore began to understand how Mr. Chappell had risen from—well—from wherever he had risen—to this. He had good instincts and efficiency, all you really need, after all.

"Sorry. Was that awful? Now, what can we do. . . . It's a perfect mess here, isn't it? But one can always manage. There are some not uninteresting people here tonight." He looked around the room, considering.

"Really, Mr. Chappell, you're an angel. Why didn't you come into my life before this?" (Oh, God, that sounded like Johno, didn't it? Never mind.) "The thing is, I do know some people here, but they're the same people I see in New York and so . . ."

"Ah, the fabulous Marina," he said, his eyes lingering ironically on the fashion editor she dreaded. "So vivacious, isn't she? I see she's quite firmly ensconced behind our German fabric friends."

He was really a mind-reader, so why beat around the bush?

"There is someone I'd be very curious to meet, if he's here," she said, and suddenly she saw his deepset sapphire eyes begin to sparkle with the excitement of a born pimp.

"Of course, who is it?"

"Jack Straw. Jack Straw, the artist?"

"Oh, Jack, yes, of course. He is absolutely brilliant, isn't he? Absolutely original. A genius, one would say—but one shouldn't say that about the living, do you think?"

He was watching her face now with the prurient anticipation of a man expecting to see a peep show. She wasn't up to a long tease.

"Yes," she agreed. "Is he here tonight?"

"Jack? Oh yes, of course he's here. We're great friends. Let me see where he's wandered off to."

There were huge electric fans in the hall blowing ribbons, like armorial banners.

"It's very hard on the ladies to have it like a wind tunnel in here, but otherwise we'd all be *pommes frites*."

Mrs. Melmore didn't comment, but she was very glad Cecil had put her hair in a chignon.

He took her hand and began to lead her through one room after another, each one dimmer than the last.

The "little supper," as she had imagined, was a huge table on which every sort of dish, seemingly lacquered and untouched by human hands, was arranged. Was it like the windows of those Japanese restaurants she had noticed, just for display, while the real food came out of the kitchen?

She was waylaid and kissed by several people she was positive she had never met before, but always Tony Chappell extricated her, gracefully but firmly. Finally, they came to a little room lighted only by electric bulbs, beneath enormous amethyst crystals, in the fireplace. A tall, fair man in blue jeans was leaning against the mantelpiece, holding a drink. Next to him was a plump dark-skinned woman wearing a black Dior dress and more diamonds and rubies than Mrs. Melmore had ever seen on one body (except in those old photographs of the maharajahs). There was a semicircle of youngish men in front of this couple.

Tony Chappell, delicately but relentlessly, swept the young men apart into two groups.

"Jack, I would like to present you to Mrs. Melmore, a great admirer of your work. Mrs. Melmore, this is Jack Straw."

She smiled and gave the tall man her hand. She expected him to smile back or acknowledge the compliment in some way. But he just took her hand, clasped it lightly, and said, "Hello." The look he gave her seemed cold and severe.

Tony Chappell seemed, for once, at a loss. "And Señora Pérez," he continued after a moment. "Mrs. Melmore."

Señora Pérez was full of enthusiasm at meeting the world-famous Madame Melmore, of whom she had heard so very much.

"Well," said Tony Chappell, "look after the ladies, will you, chaps? I have the feeling my good fellows stop serving once you get past the buffet. I'll be back later."

"Why don't we sit down? It's more nice for us ladies, with our little short legs," said Señora Pérez. Sitting down with Señora Pérez was the last thing Mrs. Melmore wanted to do, but Jack Straw had simply turned and walked away. He was talking to a red-haired man, and they were staring down into the little garden. His back was to her.

What could she do but sit down? Tony Chappell had brought some English comfort into the room. The chair she sat on was luxurious and cozy, but it didn't swallow her up, either. Mrs. Melmore was able to sit erect, as she liked.

"Never let your back touch the back of the chair." "Thank you, Mama." All the books on the head, and the threats of a spinal brace—well, they had worked their wonders. On everyone but Harriet. How had Harriet turned out so round-shouldered? She must have driven Mama crazy, those last years.

Señora Pérez had so much wanted to talk to Madame Melmore. She had heard so much about her famous goo. What was that? The culture. She had always felt that as Madame Melmore was so famous a *protectrice des arts* (What was all this "patron of the arts" business anyway? They had a great many beautiful things, but while Jim's collection was impressive, it was not overwhelming. They had a small foundation and she'd always given substantially to all the museums, but still . . .), Madame Melmore and Señora Pérez would like each the other greatly. (Dear heaven.) Of course in North America, the people had not the culture of Europe. But the people made the forceful efforts, no? While in her country, the people were—what was that word—some kind of animal? They responded only to the wop. (The wop. Paraguay? No, he was German. The whip? Argentina?)

Mrs. Melmore thought she really must make some sort of effort. She'd forgotten all her Spanish. She'd only taken a year of it—that had been stupid and lazy. She gave Señora Pérez a big smile.

"*Señora,*" she said, "*usted es demasiado buena.*"

Lord. She couldn't possibly keep it up. Why try?

Mrs. Melmore felt that Jack Straw had been decidedly rude to her. He didn't need to say much, but he could have acknowledged her presence a little more gracefully. He had literally turned his back on her. Of course, if he was a friend or lover of Sarah's, maybe Sarah had told him terrible things about her. Probably she had—Wanda had apparently expected the worst, and so had Anna. So that would explain it. But he didn't need to be so blatantly rude.

Or maybe it was all some crazy lie of Johno's. (A strong possibility, too. Jack Straw had certainly shown no flicker of recognition at her name or face.) Well, that was just as rude —ruder, really. Maybe he was just tired of middle-aged women gushing over him, and had seen a chance to dump Señora Pérez at the same time. Why had she ever expected him to have any manners? "Little short legs." Señora Pérez should go to charm school!

"But I find you so sympathetic, Madame Melmore. I wish you would now tell me everything about yourself."

Oh no! The *protectrice* of the arts, she had forgotten. "Señora Pérez, my life is just the life of—a woman. But with your knowledge of the arts . . . is Jack—Jack Straw—a friend of yours, Señora?"

Señora Pérez began to giggle. Her face was covered with dimples and she looked much more attractive. Before, she had had the expression of a pupil trying earnestly to follow a conversation class.

"Jack—oh my God—'and how!' as you would say." Suddenly she stopped laughing. "But believe me, Madame Melmore, not in that way—oh no, not at all. Do you think I want for my husband to shoot me? Fernando has a very jealous nature. No, Fernando and I, we adore everything new. Fernando and I have perhaps been the first to show a great admiration for Jack's work. Yes, we commission him to do the first of his big work. It's so amusing for us. Sometimes people tell us that Jack is more famed for his work in our country than in your own. You see, the other people, they follow our example, in our country."

"Oh, how terribly interesting! What was that work?" (And what was that country?)

"The Dynasty series, Madame Melmore. You'd know it without a thought, from the reproductions. We have those that are the originals. Against our landscape—a little wild —that makes such a surprise."

At this moment, Jack Straw turned away from the window and was gazing out the door. He was really very attractive, Mrs. Melmore decided. A mysterious, closed face, and those golden-brown eyes, that cowboy figure, and relaxed graceful posture.

"Oh. Let's see if we can get him to come and sit down with us," she said. "I'm sure he'd do it, just for you." But, just as she said it, he walked straight out of the room, without looking at either of them.

"Oh, that Jack!" Señora Pérez giggled some more. "He's always living in a dream. I tell him he'll get himself run down by an automobile someday, for sure."

Damn and blast! What the hell was she going to do now?

She hadn't quite the nerve to assault the man, when he obviously wanted to avoid her. There was no one here she could bear to talk to. She had better have a stiff drink, make one final effort, and then, if that failed—go home.

A butler appeared. Señora Pérez was holding out her glass for more champagne.

"Avez-vous de la vodka?" asked Mrs. Melmore.

"Yes, madame, we have vodka. Do you prefer Russian or Polish?"

"Oh, Russian."

"With tonic, madame?"

"Well, look, I'd like a glass like this. Please fill it with straight vodka. Nothing else. Is it chilled? Well, it doesn't matter. No ice."

Señora Pérez's eyes had grown very large. Well, what did she care what Señora Pérez thought?

"It's so fatiguing, all this party, party, party," the Señora suggested.

When the vodka came, Mrs. Melmore drank it down as fast as she could. Okay. Now she was going to leave Señora Pérez, go to the bathroom, check her face, take a Valium— yes, in spite of the vodka—and go talk to Jack Straw.

"Do you know where the ladies' room is?" she asked. *"Las Damas?"*

"Ah—the W.C." Señora Pérez directed her, very kindly. She actually looked worried, and asked if she should come with her—if she needed help—a nice woman, probably.

Mrs. Melmore thanked her, but said she had faith in the Señora's directions. In fact, the Señora's directions led her to the pantry, but that was probably her own fault. How could one find anything in this semi-darkness? There seemed to be no women servants, but one of the ubiquitous men in livery led her to a door.

Even the bathroom was dark as a crypt. She peered at herself, desperately adding a little lipstick and rouge. God, she had really better skip that next Valium. She wondered if she was going to be reduced to putting on her glasses.

What she really needed was a flashlight. This place was so dark she was afraid she was literally going to fall over somebody. . . . Or just on her face.

She was too cowardly, and, she was afraid, too drunk, to pull it off; she might as well lock herself in the bathroom until tomorrow morning. Oh, God. Someone was hammering on the door. She sat on the sink, her head between her hands. Maybe she was going to be sick? But it passed. All right, go on out. Do it.

She opened the door. There was a couple outside—a boy and a girl. Apparently they were going to use the bathroom together. How—how weird. Oh, well.

The room directly ahead seemed to be another library, and she walked into it and sat down in the first empty chair she found. There was an indeterminate number of people sitting or lying over a huge sort of sofa bed. This was the darkest room yet. She supposed her eyes would adjust to the darkness, and then she would go and hunt for Jack Straw. And say what? "I'm Sarah's mother."

She put her head between her hands again. She was a wreck, a drunken wreck. She was an idiot, a damned idiot. Funny how one got to count so on something—like—well—beauty. . . . And then didn't even realize it was leaving—till—till something like this. The future seemed to stretch ahead of her, barren and drab. Only fairies would be interested in her now.

She became aware, after a while, that there were many more people in the room than she had realized. They were sitting or lying all around the room. Also there was a lot of smoke. Some people were smoking, and some were passing around what she knew was marijuana. She knew the smell by now. Somebody even tapped her on the hand and silently offered her a cigarette. It was thinner and messier than a regular cigarette.

Well, why not? She inhaled it. It didn't seem to do anything but burn her throat a little. Someone else took it away. The good thing about this room was that it was quiet.

She could hear Tony Chappell's guitarists in the distance playing Scarlatti. Funny. Outside she had seen them, but couldn't hear them. That was nice. They gave her a marijuana cigarette again and she inhaled it again and again nothing happened. Another hand plucked it away. She became aware that someone was sitting very quietly at her feet. It was nice that there was no need to make conversation. She was beginning to see a little better in the gloom. She felt the bottom of her right shoe being touched, very softly—a finger being run along the sole, from the toe to the instep.

"That's so pretty," said the voice below. "How do you get the soles of your shoes to be so beautiful?" And she looked down into the dark. The man sitting on the floor beside her was Jack Straw.

4

Mrs. Melmore Meets an Artist

"MY MAID DOES IT," said Mrs. Melmore. She wasn't frightened now. This was all so unreal. "She has a passionate respect for shoes. Something about rhinoceros horn. But, if you really want to go to the source, talk to Cecil. She's poetic on the subject."

Yes, unreal. His hand on her shoe. That was how she had met Jim. God. Unreal. Well, really met him. She knew who Jim was, of course. He knew her name. But they had been at a dinner party, and after dinner he'd been sitting cross-legged on the floor—he was slim then, and very lithe. She had been wearing high-heeled silver sandals, with fake emerald tassels. Looking back on it now, they sounded horrible—tacky. And Jim had started playing with one of the emerald tassels, and weighing it, and he had said, "I must have given you these, didn't I? When did I give you these? You know, I don't remember giving you these."

And she had laughed. And she had looked into his strange, light eyes—and—oh, my God, it all happened so fast! She shook her head.

"Would you like another joint?" Jack Straw was offering her another cigarette.

"Thanks," she said. She took it. It was marijuana. And gave it back. It was all very strange. He did have eyes like a cat—at least they shone in the dark. There was a long silence and there seemed no need to say anything.

"Do you really know my work?" Jack Straw asked her.

"Ah—no. I'm sorry. I really don't."

"Don't be sorry. I didn't think you did."

More silence. They passed the cigarette back and forth, until it got too small.

"What are you doing later?" he said.

"Later." She was aware it must be very late right now.

"Mmm-hmm. I have to drop Carolina home. The problem is, she really likes to stay up all night."

Mrs. Melmore said nothing. It wasn't real. There was nothing she needed to say.

"She's been very good to me," he said. "I feel responsible."

Mrs. Melmore said nothing. It wasn't real.

"Maybe I could find someone who would feel like taking her on someplace. Will you stay right there, where you are?"

Mrs. Melmore nodded. He got up. He was really very tall. None of it mattered. It was all unreal. A hand from the sofa passed her another marijuana cigarette, and she smoked it, until the same hand took it back. She was enjoying herself in a very weird way. She could never have imagined that any pleasure could be derived from sitting in the dark with a bunch of strangers who were making no effort to entertain her or each other. But the music was very nice. Tony was really very nice. Jack Straw—who had talked to her like Jim—well, he seemed extraordinary.

"A genius," Tony had said. She supposed Carolina was

Señora Pérez. It sounded like an older woman, at least, not a girlfriend. He might be a long time. But that was all right too. If it were a very long time, and she felt tired, she could always go downstairs and Williams would be there. It was all the same. She knew that she and Jack Straw understood each other very deeply, although they had hardly spoken. He would help her with Sarah. He would never hurt Sarah.

But Jack was back. He sat down at her feet again.

"It's all right," he said. "Carolina did want to go on. She's Brazilian, you know. She really loves night clubs. Her husband—he's South American, too—they both like to stay up all night. But it's all okay. I found someone for her."

They sat for a long time in silence, Mrs. Melmore thinking of nothing but feeling serene and contented. It would all turn out all right.

"Are you any good at this? I'm so clumsy," Jack said. He seemed to be offering her a piece of paper. She didn't know what it was. She just shook her head. He worked on it for a while, tapped something into it, and finally lit it. It was another marijuana cigarette. He gave it to her. She drew on it, and gave it back.

"I feel very peaceful with you," Jack Straw said to her.

"Me too," she said.

"Would you like to stay here, or go someplace else?"

That question seemed unimaginably difficult to answer.

"I like it here, too," he said.

"Where is there to go, anyway?" she said dreamily.

"Well—that depends, I guess. . . . Where are you staying?"

"Oh—well—I'm staying in a hotel," she said.

"A hotel," he repeated. "Would that be a problem?"

"A problem?"

"Could I come back with you?"

Something told her she had better wake up. Go back with her? To the Crillon? Why? It was perfect here. And there, what would they do? Here it was so dark and sweet and timeless. At the Crillon, they could have a drink downstairs in the lobby, she supposed, but that wouldn't really be very nice. Not as nice as it was here. And she didn't know how late it was, either.

At this moment of indecision, there was a noise, a disruption of the sense of harmony. She looked around. A figure in a white suit, framed in the doorway, the face distorted. It looked like a madman. Why, it was Johno!

"Bitch! Bitch! Bitch!" he shrieked. Mrs. Melmore thought he was screaming at her, and recoiled. But he took the drink in his hand, and threw it in Jack Straw's face. The liquid splashed on her legs. "How could you do it, you bitch?"

Jack quickly got up, wiped off his face, and took Johno by the shoulders. First, he gave him a shake all over, as if it were Johno, not he, who had been drenched and needed to be dried off. Then he held him in place with one hand, while with the other he gave Johno a very hard slap across the face.

"John," he said. He had a very low voice, Mrs. Melmore had noticed. He didn't raise it even now. "John, when are you going to learn that you are the one who has to pay for what you do?"

Then he turned his back on Johno, and came back to Mrs. Melmore.

"I'm so terribly sorry," he said. "Is your dress ruined?" Jack began to mop her skirt and legs with a big napkin.

"No, not at all. It couldn't matter less."

There was a whining, keening sound. Was it coming from Johno? It was horrid. Mrs. Melmore shuddered.

"Are you sure? Maybe we should go."

"Yes," said Mrs. Melmore.

She rose to her feet. Jack took her arm, walking a little ahead of her. The noise had stopped and Johno seemed to have disappeared altogether. Thank God! They were at the stairs.

"Mr. Chappell?" she asked.

"Oh, that's all right. Tony knows. He understands."

They went downstairs together. Yes, Williams was outside, parked quite close, and he was asleep.

"I wonder what we should do," she said slowly. She knew she needed to talk to him. Maybe they could just drive around—but Williams . . .

"Don't worry. It'll be all right. Do you have any of this at home?" He meant marijuana. She shook her head.

"Well, that's all right. I've really got plenty."

"God, it must be late."

"I don't really know. I keep such funny hours. I usually work at night, you see."

She knocked on the glass to wake Williams.

"Oh, hi!—hi there, Williams! Sorry it's so awfully late. What should we do?" she said, looking helplessly at Jack Straw.

"Why not go back to the Crillon?" he said. Had she said the Crillon? She was foggy.

"Oh, then, back to the Crillon please, Williams."

Jack Straw's shirt was very clean, but he wasn't wearing a jacket. Williams would really be shocked. Oh, well, he'd think he was a friend of Sarah's. Sarah!

Jack Straw and Mrs. Melmore climbed in back. Jack began to roll another cigarette, but Mrs. Melmore pointed at Williams and shook her head.

"You know Sarah," she said, not dreamily now.

"Sarah, yes. Johno told you that?"

She nodded. Jack began to laugh. He had a nice laugh.

"That's really very funny," he said. "I'm sorry. It's not funny to you, and you don't know why it's funny to me. Johno, of all people. Yes, I know Sarah. But almost nobody knows that. Certainly not Johno. Sarah used to be living with some very stupid people— Well, who am I to say that? Probably they're not stupid at all. Anyway, they're very political.

"And Johno, well, I haven't seen Johno for years. But one of Sarah's friends got hold of him, because for some insane reason they thought he could find out where Sarah was. It's all so ridiculous. Johno and I haven't spoken for years.

"But Johno had always wanted to meet you, he's very interested in fashion and so on, so he pretended he knew where she was. So he could meet you." He doubled up with laughter. "I guess he said Sarah was staying with me."

"Oh, but look, please—you know Sarah—could you tell me about her, please? Please tell me where she really is? I'm really very . . ."

He stopped laughing. "I'm terribly sorry, Mrs. Melmore. I'm so sorry. I must seem so unfeeling. You're worried about Sarah. Of course. Please don't be. There's no reason to worry, none at all. She's perfectly okay."

"But—you know where she is?"

"Well—yes. But almost nobody else in the world knows that— And then you see Johno—a really confirmed liar—that's why it struck me as so funny."

"But—is she with you? Where is she?"

"I've been sort of helping to take care of Sarah," he said. "She wasn't feeling well for a while, but she's really all right now." He paused. "The thing is, I know how you must feel, and I really do sympathize—but after all, she has to decide, doesn't she? About what comes next?"

Mrs. Melmore stared at him. "Will you let me come and see her?"

He gave a long sigh. "I don't have anything to do with people's choices," he said. "Sarah has to choose. Doesn't she? It's up to her, isn't it?"

They had reached the hotel.

"Maybe it would be better if I went along, now," he said.

"No, please." She grabbed his sleeve. Williams was trying to help her out of the car at the same time.

"Please come back, and—have a—a—drink with me."

God, how late was it? Could they get drinks served in the lobby at this hour?

"Well . . . okay," he said.

"Williams," she said, "I'm so terribly sorry to keep you up so late. It's brutal, I know. Please go and get a good night's sleep. At least I won't need you in the morning.

"Oh, wait a minute. Mr. Straw—you'll need Williams to drop you home. It's death getting a taxi at this hour—even when they call, you have to wait and wait. . . . And we probably won't be more than—oh—twenty minutes?"

He shook his head. "No, thanks. I can always get home."

"You're sure?"

"Mm-hmm."

"Really? Oh, well then. Goodnight, Williams."

"Well," she said briskly, as they entered the hotel, "it does look like the red death here. Really tragic. It must be terrifically late. Do you think they'll still serve us? Maybe we could just sit over there and talk."

"Do you have anything to drink in your room?"

She hesitated. "Well," she said slowly, "yes—just vodka and brandy."

"Those are the things I drink."

5

Mrs. Melmore Is Imprudent

Mrs. Melmore had never seen the young man who gave her her key. She felt perhaps that was just as well.

They rode silently up in the elevator. She was feeling stranger and stranger. Why was she bringing this man up to her room? Of course, of course. He knew Sarah. And he knew where Sarah was. And he said she was all right. It didn't sound sinister. It wasn't that she was frightened of him, but —it all seemed out of control, somehow.

"Your dress got stained," he said.

"Oh, that doesn't matter. That's nothing."

"It was something very stupid and ugly," he said.

She turned the key in her door. What had she left out? Money? Jewelry? Well, Cecil would have taken care of everything. She had all that cash still, locked in the desk drawer. That was stupid, she'd kept meaning to take it back to the bank or at least put it in the vault. Why on earth hadn't she? Oh, well—what a silly thing to think about now.

There was the room on the place de la Concorde, and the sitting room on the rue St. Florentin. Mrs. Melmore noticed a few dead flowers. For God's sake. The less Cecil has to do, the sloppier she gets, she thought.

"Let's sit in here," said Jack, indicating the room over the place de la Concorde.

"Okay, sure," she said. "What would you like? Vodka? Anything in it?"

"Just straight. Do you have any ice?"

"Yes—oh well, it's mostly slush, now." She brought him a drink and went into her bedroom. Then her bathroom. God! Three-thirty! She combed her hair and put some eyedrops in her eyes. A couple of Bufferin and a Valium. Sarah! He knew Sarah! He knew where Sarah was!

When she came out, Jack had turned his chair around so that he could stare out the window. He had rolled another marijuana cigarette and he began to smoke as he sipped his drink. He got up when she came in, and drew up a chair for her beside him.

"Do you mind if I turn the lights off?"

"Why?"

"They're too bright. They're ugly. And you can't see outside." But he had already done it. "Here." He offered her the cigarette.

"Gosh, I don't think I'd better. You know I've never had any of this stuff before this evening."

"Go ahead, anyway. It makes you so beautiful."

She didn't want to. "Could you just tell me all you really know about Sarah? I mean just really everything. Everything."

He handed her the cigarette. She inhaled it automatically. After a little while, she had actually gotten to like that burning sensation.

"Look at those teeny little lights, way off there. That's where I live. Sure, I'll tell you whatever you like about Sarah, Mrs. Melmore. She's okay, now I'm taking care of her. Please trust me. There's nothing we can do tonight. And the rest is up to her. Maybe you should just relax and look at how pretty it is from here. You're so tense. I feel like I need to take care of you more than I do Sarah."

"Mr. Straw—is that your real name? Jack Straw. It's a children's game."

"Um-hmm. Please don't call me Mr. Straw, though. I don't like it when you do. I knew your husband too, Mrs. Melmore."

"Jim? How did you know him?"

This man was unbelievable. He seemed to know all about her. But she did trust him. He was so quiet and simple—like Gary Cooper in one of those cowboy films.

"Oh, I didn't know him well. But I'd heard a lot about him. I knew how smart he was supposed to be. I knew he'd made a whole lot of money, and everybody came to him for advice. He was almost like the President, wasn't he? I knew he had—" he paused a moment—"you. So I thought he must be a very extraordinary man."

"Oh, yes. He was extraordinary."

"He wasn't what I expected."

"How did you get to know each other?"

"Oh, I decided to get to know him. I was just a kid and I needed a whole lot of money and help at that time, so I thought I'd go and see him, and talk to him. I thought since he was such a smart man, and so rich, he'd understand what I was trying to do, and he'd help me."

"Did he? I'm amazingly ignorant, it seems, about a lot of things Jim has done."

"May I have another vodka? Let me bring you one. Do you like it—with something?"

"No, nothing at all for me," she said. Then changed her mind. "Well—okay. Just one—like yours. Straight, with a little—slush." He knew where Sarah was. He was taking care of her. She was all right.

He handed her her drink and sat down beside her.

"Oh, no, he didn't help me. It was all sort of funny. First

of all, he was terrifically surprised when he saw me there—
in his office, I mean. Really surprised. As if I'd come there
to strangle him or something."

"Why? You mean you didn't have an appointment with
him or anything? How'd you get in? Who let you?"

"Well, I guess that's why he was so surprised and all. But
I'll say this. He let me say everything I'd come to say, once
I was there. After a little while he started laughing. He
thought my ideas were terrifically funny. Weird, I mean.
Lordy, he must have laughed for half an hour. But I kept
right on. And then at the end I asked him if he was going
to help me.

"Well, he got up and came over and shook my hand, and
he slapped me on the back and he said, 'Jack Straw, you've
got the craziest ideas of any guy I've ever listened to. Well,
I'll tell you something. I wasn't bored, and I get bored very
easily, but on the other hand, I wouldn't dream of giving
you a nickel. You're too goddamn interesting,' he said. 'I'll
give you your carfare home,' he said, 'because you didn't
bore me. But I'll tell you something else. If you got into my
office without getting shot down by my boys, you may go a
long way. Tenacity and enterprise—that's something I know
something about. Originality—believe me, it's not commer-
cial. But if you ever get your head screwed on right and get
interested in business, you might get somewhere. And then
we might have a real talk.'"

Mrs. Melmore laughed. That certainly sounded like Jim.

"It wasn't that funny to me at the time. Actually, I didn't
even have carfare home. But that was one of my first experiences with rich people. I thought I might as well begin at
the top. Your husband—he was my first failure."

"What does this do to you?" asked Mrs. Melmore, as they
passed the cigarette back and forth.

"This stuff? Oh, nothing. Nothing at all. It's very, very
mild."

"I don't really feel anything. Why do they make such a
fuss?"

Jack didn't answer. He took her hand and held it. It was funny holding hands with a man. Had she ever? Even as a girl? Except with her children? His hand felt nice.

"You get such wild fantasies about things when you come from a little town," he said, "way out in the middle of nowhere. No one anywhere near you anything like you."

"Yes," she said.

He kept on holding her hand. He only put it down to roll another cigarette.

"The ideas I used to have about New York," he said and laughed. "Rich people, grand people, people who cared fantastically about the arts . . . I thought there was this whole world out there, living this sort of wonderful, secret, glamorous life. We all think like that, you know? Kids like me from the middle of nowhere. Can you understand that at all?"

"I think so. I wasn't born rich, you know."

"No? Well, I don't think it's the same. You must have been, I mean you always were—beautiful and glamorous. I've seen pictures of you before you were married. I used to study them. All your pictures. I mean all along the way.

"I thought one time I might have to be an actor to make a living, so I used to look at a lot of different pictures and study a lot of different things. Like what is 'beauty'? I would mostly look at you for that. Of course, with you, it came naturally, but with me I had to study it, in case I'd need it. It's something to do with the way you carry the head, it's the carriage, it's partly the regard, and partly it's a kind of giving, but holding back. . . . The holding back is more interesting —it makes everything more mysterious. I'm not really explaining it right, but I can do it. Not now. It's not a parlor trick. I don't like to use it unless I need to."

Mrs. Melmore laughed again. "Yes, I do know what you mean. Actually it *is* a sort of parlor trick. I've never heard anyone explain it to me before. I'm glad, because if I'd had to think about it, I'd be plain."

Jack got up and poured himself another vodka. "Would you like a little more?"

"Oh, gosh, no. I'd be out cold. I haven't been up so late or drunk so much or I don't know what since—gosh, I don't know when."

"It makes you look beautiful," said Jack, "but beautiful in a different way. You always looked sad to me. I mean you were always smiling, but you always looked sad. I never saw a picture of you laughing."

"Probably that's because the times I would have been photographed there was nothing to laugh at."

"Really? When I was living in New York, for all those years, I used to see you a lot. We liked the opera and the ballet and I used to see you at the openings. Sometimes we couldn't afford to go to the openings, but we'd just go and stand. Watch people like you going in . . .

"Do you think that's creepy? With me, I always went to look at you. I can remember every time I saw you. What you wore, how you held your head and moved your hands. . . . The expression you had when they took your photograph. Mr. Melmore didn't go with you much. I guess he didn't like those things so much."

"No, he liked Broadway—but the old Broadway. When it was sort of—oh—fun, and had—glamour. But then he lost interest, really. Anyway, he didn't have the time."

"The time? We'd be up at four in the morning to get into line for standing-room tickets, then work all day, then go and stand all night. That's what I mean. It seemed to me like he didn't take care of you," he said.

He leaned over and kissed her. It was a very chaste kiss—like a child, she thought again.

"Funny," he said, "fantasizing about those sort of magical people living perfect lives in a style you can't even conceive. . . . And if they only wanted to, if they only knew you—well, they'd make these marvelous things happen for you. . . . The way they did for—oh—Diaghilev or Richard Wagner."

Mrs. Melmore put her arms around him and kissed him the same way he had kissed her.

"I'm sorry," she said. "I'm sorry it isn't like that. I'm sorry we aren't like that. I know how shallow it all must seem. It must be terribly disillusioning."

"Don't be sorry," he said. "It's a gorgeous thing to have illusions. They keep you going till you see it's all in your head anyway. Everything important is really right there in your head. In your imagination."

"But you have to eat and so forth."

"Yes. And so forth," he said slowly. "Yes, that's the price you people have to pay. For what you do."

She didn't really understand this. It was poor people who had to pay, surely.

"Not you," he said. "I don't mean you. You're special. But very, very few people are special. I've only met a few in my life."

"You're special," she said.

"I'm different."

They sat and smoked.

"Do you want to go to bed?" he said.

"I suppose I should. It's horribly late. But we haven't really talked about Sarah."

"Let's talk about Sarah in the morning."

"But . . ."

"Can I stay here with you?"

"You mean . . ."

"I just can't sleep alone tonight."

They looked at each other.

She stood up. "Look," she said, "are you Sarah's lover?"

"No," he said. "I'm not any woman's lover."

He took her hand and they went into her bedroom.

Part Nine

TRANSAMERICAN BLUES/B SIDE TAKE 3

1

Mrs. Melmore Sleeps Late

MRS. MELMORE WOKE UP ALONE. She lay very still, hardly breathing. She looked around, scarcely moving her head. Her bed? The sheets . . . The pillow! My God! She sat bolt upright. What time was it? Where was her nightgown? She automatically drew the sheets up to her chin. Three-thirty? It had been three-thirty last night. The clocks had all gone mad. My God! She was going crazy like Sarah. And what about Cecil? Oh, my God!

But the next moment she slipped down under the covers again. After all, what did it matter? There was no one to punish her, was there? And if Cecil was bitchy, she could just replace her. It would be hard to find someone with

Cecil's competence, but even the hangman's daughter would have to be more fun.

God, it had been heavenly. . . . Heavenly! She hadn't really been aware of how much she had missed sex. She knew she wasn't highly sexed—certainly not like most of her women friends (Cottie and Anne, for that matter), who looked every man over speculatively, who couldn't live without a lover, any lover. She had lived like a nun for so very long. She and Jim hadn't slept together for years. She didn't mind for herself exactly, but it had made her tense and nervous. Of course she would have felt so much more secure if Jim had wanted her in that way.

Last night was so totally different. A revelation! My God, the luxury of it! The luxury. Jim had the reputation for being such a great lover—well, she knew now he had had a lot to learn. Things might have been so much better between them if she had really loved it, the way he had, instead of having to pretend. She went over as much as she could remember of the night. Things she hadn't even heard of before. She should be mortified. Actually, she felt terrific. No hangover or anything.

One thing she had really missed in Paris was her quiet, healthy life at home. Most people never believed how quiet her life really was—early to bed and early to rise, sensible food, and lots of exercise. But here in Paris, all this terrible tension and too many pills and more than she was used to drinking, and no matter how carefully she ordered, the food was still too rich. She'd felt terrible, really; her body was complaining, it was going to hell. She was really just a country girl, after all.

But this morning—this afternoon—she felt glorious! She felt eighteen years old. Her body felt so young, so fresh. She stretched and yawned. She felt as if she'd crawled out from years underground. She wished Jack were still in bed with her. Jack. She had so much to tell him. She felt so open, and she wouldn't mind . . . Where was Jack, anyway?

Oh, there was her nightgown on the floor. She put it on.

She had never liked walking around naked, though she still had a very okay body. And nothing done to it. She looked around. A letter. There was a letter lying on the little table near the door. Hotel stationery. The envelope said "Mrs. Melmore." Pretty formal.

She seized it and tore it open, reading through it very fast, to see if it was bad news. The handwriting was a little disappointing for a genius, round and even and legible, like a child's.

She read quickly: "I thogt I ought to go. I didn't want to wake you. You looked so beautifull. I saw your servant. I hope you don't mind, I said I was a freind of your daughter. And I kept you up talking all night. I said I slep on the sofa. I hope that's alright. I asked her about the shoes. She sure does know a lot. I said not to disturb you. Hope that's alright with you. I thogt you ought to sleep.

"I guess I got so fasinated with you I never talked about Sarah. Sarah wasn't well but she's getting better every day. She's really coming along fine. I'm doing everything I can for her. Please trust me. I don't have a telephone so I thogt I'd better call you maybe around six. I hope you don't feel bad about anything. It's all my fault whatever hapened. I always wanted you so much. It was gorgus for me and re- member what I said about fantassys. Well it was just as good. Please don't you feel bad because I'm not going to impose on you. I just want to say thank you. Love Jack."

No one had said he was a literary genius. But it said every- thing she wanted to hear. She read it over and over. Who cared about spelling anyway? Of course she trusted him. How extraordinary! It was all so extraordinary. She felt so strange —something had been touched, deep inside her, as if a string had been plucked and the sound of it was still vibrating, un- believably sweet—part of a long-forgotten melody that moved her almost to tears. And something else, not sentimental— urgent too. Oh God! Was she in love? In love! Come on, Sis. What would the age difference be? Fifteen years? Maybe twenty?

She called the operator and picked up her calls. Harriet. Anna, three times. That was unusual, and at yet another number. Marina Stillman. Damn and blast. Well, she'd better get Cecil. Clean up a little first. Call Anna, just in case.

Anna answered her phone on the first ring.

"Madame Melmore, I was terribly concerned about you." Anna's voice was very tense.

"Well, I'm quite all right."

"I hadn't wanted to frighten you, before you went out last night, but I know those people you were seeing would stop at nothing."

(Wasn't that like Anna? "I was terribly worried about the blind date I arranged for you with Monsieur Landru. Hope you got home okay?")

"Obviously, for once you were misinformed, Anna."

"Are you trying to joke with me, Madame Melmore? Sometimes I'm not very humorous. Were you able to find out anything of significance about your daughter?"

Now that was difficult. Mrs. Melmore wanted Anna and her friends out of the way, but not off the hook.

"Uh—I gathered your informant was, as you suspected, unreliable. But he took me to a large gathering, where I met—" (What was all that jargon of Anna's?) "Well, Anna, I am unable to divulge my source. You understand. But I've come in contact with a person who can perhaps—be very helpful." She paused. "You know, Anna, that as I respect your desire for secrecy in this matter, I respect it in others who may be of help."

"Madame Melmore, I think you have no right to keep us in the dark in this matter. Only we would be able to gauge the authenticity of this source. Frankly, Madame Melmore, you are venturing into quite unfamiliar territory, no? Without a compass. You can have no possible understanding of the situation here. I believe I told you we have many enemies."

"Often."

"You cannot understand these things, and may, by your ignorance—you may, inadvertently, involve us. Madame Melmore, I have not said this to you before, but there may be some things worse for us than the police."

"Look," said Mrs. Melmore, "I've played fair with you so far, haven't I? I haven't mentioned your name to a soul. Not a soul. Now this is a different thing entirely."

"It is imperative that we know your plans. The situation is grave. I have found out more about the sort of people you are dealing with. They are fiends."

Mrs. Melmore thought of Tony Chappell and Señora Pérez. She supposed Anna might consider them fiends.

"Paris seems full of fiends," said Mrs. Melmore.

"You are being sadly frivolous about a serious matter, Madame Melmore."

"Look, Anna, I've been at your mercy for weeks now. Any sensible person would have called the police long ago. Come on. You began with forty-eight hours. Then you just kept stringing me along and stringing me along. . . . There was that snark hunt in Marseilles. Frankly I don't know why I've continued to rely on you at all! I've kept my bargain and I've kept giving you more time.

"Almost everything you told me about last night was nonsense. What I did find out I did on my own. And now I want to see if it leads anywhere. I'm not going to get you in any trouble in any way with anyone. This does not involve you, Anna. Please get that through your head! It's not your business! Let's just keep in touch as before and see how things work out. And if Sarah's all right, you're home free, no questions asked. Okay?"

Anna obviously thought it was not okay. She said: "Madame Melmore, for us this is totally unsatisfactory. You do not want to be frank. I can press you no further. But one thing I must ask you. It is important. Was there any question of money, regarding the return of Sarah?"

"Absolutely not." Mrs. Melmore felt rather smug about that.

But apparently this made Anna unhappy. Obviously, she was longing for her to pay through the nose.

"But you must see, Madame Melmore, how strange that is?"

Mrs. Melmore said, "I'm sorry, Anna. I'll just have to hope that all Sarah's friends are not so mercenary. Anyway, I must go now. Of course, we will keep in touch in the same way, please."

She hung up. A little cleaning up . . . Those cigarette butts down the toilet. All the rest didn't matter. She rang for Cecil. Gosh, how cross Cecil would be, waiting around till this hour!

2

A Sentimental Interlude

BUT, WHEN CECIL ARRIVED, she did not seem dour; in fact, she was almost cheerful.

"Some tea, madam?"

"Um . . . Tea . . . Yes. But, Cecil, I'm really ravenous. More like a club sandwich or something. But tea first," she said.

"Should I draw your bath, madam?"

"Oh, please."

When Cecil returned, she broke all the rules of protocol established between them over the years. Cecil was allowed to address her about her clothes, her shoes, her jewelry, the weather, her food, the cleaners (Cecil didn't believe in cleaners), another servant who had done something wrong, arrangements for guests—but never, never to initiate a personal conversation.

"I would say Miss Sarah's a lucky young lady, madam."

Mrs. Melmore gaped at her.

"The young man. He's a real gentleman, isn't he?"

"Oh . . . oh yes."

"Not like so many young men today. Beautiful manners, hasn't he?"

Good God. "Oh, yes. Yes. Very nice."

Cecil was bustling about the bathroom, drawing a bath, putting things away. Mrs. Melmore could tell she was absolutely dying to chat—about Sarah's "engagement," or the probability of it.

Now, let's see. Mrs. Melmore put on her dressing gown. She put Jack's letter in her pocket and followed Cecil to the bathroom.

"You know, Cecil, I feel like a total wreck upon the sand. Miss Sarah's friend, well, we stayed up very late and I'm not used to it."

Cecil nodded. She still looked cheerful, a ghost of a smile —as if she liked Mrs. Melmore doing this sort of thing, staying up all night with a stranger. Good God, Cecil was very immoral.

"Cecil, I get so many calls from people I don't want to talk to. Even Miss Milbanke," she said treacherously. "She does talk so much. Could you just guard the telephone for me? There's really no one I want to talk to. Just take the messages. Except of course if Miss Sarah calls, or—her young man. His name is Mr. Straw. Jack Straw. Oh, and I would like that club sandwich."

"You'll be going out this evening, madam?"

"Not till seven or so."

She washed her face and rinsed it, and cleaned her teeth, then stepped into the bath. Mrs. Melmore always used her bath as a period of reflection; it had become a habit. She couldn't put it off any longer. She had to face it. What was she up to anyway? Was she here to find her daughter, to pay any price to bring her home? Yes, she was. But last night. Oh God, hadn't she acted just like one of those rich bored middle-aged women she despised? If she'd heard the same story about one of her friends, she'd have thought it was pretty sordid.

But she must be dispassionate too. She hadn't chosen this way—this was where the road had led. And, since she hadn't chosen the road, it was as if fate had arranged it. All those coincidences. The road that would lead her to Sarah, well— it had turned out to be this one, and in the end, she and Sarah had trusted—gotten involved with—the same man. After all, they were mother and daughter, it wasn't so strange really. It even made a sort of sense. Of course, Mrs. Melmore had believed Jack when he said he wasn't Sarah's lover or she'd have never . . .

Anyway, Sarah—the Sarah she'd seen on the rue de Rivoli —you'd have to be a necrophile! She looked down at her body, elongated in the water. She was pretty thin herself, but in good shape. Although without her exercise class and massage, even in this short time, even though she did her yoga religiously, she could tell the difference.

Okay. Back to the point. Face it. What did she want? To have Sarah back safely. And—to have Jack. Sarah—and Jack. But Jack—how? Just an affair? No, she had never been interested in that. She frowned, then remembered that it was bad for her face and automatically raised her eyebrows to compensate. Marriage? Good grief! But, what then? Well, something intensely serious. Something lasting. How did people manage that without looking ridiculous? She lifted one long leg and looked at her toes.

Suppose there was a scandal? She had led a very quiet life; she could afford it. And after all, what did she care? She could even live over here, particularly if that suited Sarah. Who would punish her now? She kept coming back to that thought. Who was there to punish her now? That fear was so deeply ingrained in her. How had Anne and Louisa dared—with Mama alive too! Of course, Cottie—but, Cottie never cared about anything. . . .

But now she could do what she liked at last, couldn't she? Mend things with Sarah. Have Jack. She stepped out of the bathtub, wrapped herself up in a towel, and stared at her face.

The trouble with getting older was that it happened so slowly you hardly noticed. One day, in a strange mirror, you thought, who was that older woman in gray, with the sweet expression? Why, she has a pin exactly like mine! And then . . . And the whole time you were just a girl inside.

But naturally not to other people. She looked hard at herself. "The cruel looking glass." And no makeup, of course. Well, she certainly looked like a woman of fifty—a "good" fifty. She hated that super-lifted look that so many of her friends had, or the "Italian" look, silicone cheekbones and cats' eyes. It was the same old face, just older. She had never really believed in this "cult" people had for her; all that extravagant admiration and attention had never seemed real to her, it seemed almost an affectation. Of course, one finally got used to it, as an actress would, she supposed. Just another familiar face. But now, all of a sudden, she desperately wanted to believe in those things. Johno had certainly sounded sincere, if deranged. Jack had seemed to confirm it— he certainly had seemed to admire her looks; he had been attracted to her. And Jack after all was an artist, and a good one, they said. Not some little tango dancer.

"Sis, you've got to be careful all the time," Jim had told her. "The visible rich are natural victims. Cultivate a little healthy skepticism." The children too, he told them the same thing. God, he had turned out to be right too, hadn't he?

"Healthy skepticism." Well, it didn't grow very well in her garden. Maybe with Jack, maybe she and Señora Pérez and God knows who were all just standing in line. He hadn't asked her for anything, but then he was smart. Maybe he'd wait.

She put on her nightgown, dressing gown, and mules. Of course she could call Tony Chappell—he would give her a rundown on Jack in a minute. No, that would be too ig-nominious. Even for Sarah she wouldn't do that. She would send Tony Chappell flowers and a note. There was that nice flower store practically around the corner, she'd forgotten the name. Cecil was sitting tensely by the telephone as if it were a grenade and she were prepared to throw herself upon it, the moment it threatened to go off.

At least she'd ordered some food. "Thank you, Cecil," she said, and went to the desk to write a note to Tony Chappell.

"Look, Cecil—there's not that much time. Could you take this around to that flower shop, the one I like, and choose a really pretty bouquet for Mr. Chappell? That's where I was last night. The name and address are on the envelope. I'd like it basically white and black—you know, those dark, sort of mahogany-colored tulips they have over here? Or ask them what he'd like. They'll probably know."

"But the telephone," said Cecil in anguish. Gosh, what was this drama? What was up? Cecil was longing to stay.

"It hasn't rung," said Cecil reproachfully.

"Well, maybe it won't. All the better. Anyway I can take over now."

"Hmm." She thought a minute, then gave Cecil the five hundred francs she had taken with her last night.

"Probably it will be a lot less, but I want it to be very nice."

Cecil seemed not at all obliging about this errand—actually recalcitrant. "Madam, what would you be wearing tonight?"

"Oh, gosh, Cecil, I'm just going to stay in my nightgown all afternoon. I can't make up my mind right now about tonight. Now please don't worry, Cecil. But the flowers are important. If you'd just get that done for me."

Cecil stood where she was. "I wonder if you noticed what was spilled on your dress last night, madam?" she said. The rat.

"Oh, it was a huge party. Wine or liquor, I guess. Can't you tell?"

"I thought madam might have noticed."

"Look, Cecil, the French cleaners are the best in the world. If you can't cope with it, take it to Starisky."

Frozen silence. Cecil took the note and the money, and made a dramatic turn of her back.

"I'll let you know if I need you, Cecil," Mrs. Melmore called after her. That did it. Cecil snapped the door to with as much of a slam as she dared.

She ate her club sandwich, devoured it really. Nobody was watching, but Mrs. Melmore always did everything just as gracefully when she was by herself. It was an important part of her discipline. But, my goodness, that sandwich! It looked as if it had been gnawed by a wild dog.

She called Harriet. Harriet sounded quite peremptory, anxious to get off the phone.

"Are you busy?" Sis was rather curious.

"Well, actually I'm having dinner with some people tonight."

"Oh. I hope it's fun."

"So do I."

Harriet certainly didn't seem very forthcoming. Probably Harriet's real friends were coming back from their vacations now. Maybe it was just as well. She really had been selfish—making claims on Harriet's time and telling her almost nothing.

The phone rang. She rushed to lift it off its cradle.

"Darling, I've been trying to get you all day." (Oh, damn, Marina.) "Darling, you ruined the party last night. You were so beautiful! You made every other woman there feel like a gorilla!" (Oh, my God!) "Darling, we were so furious not to see you today."

Marina was capable of going on like that for hours. But glory be to God! Marina was leaving for Deauville any minute.

"Do say yes! Gregory will strangle me if I tell him we won't see you before the end of September!"

Mrs. Melmore said yes to whatever it was. It was far enough away, anyway. Then she gave a huge sigh, and went back to her bedroom. She kicked her slippers off and read Jack's letter again. She had to have him.

．　．　．

She had to have him. All her life she had been trying to please someone else, and when it came time to tot it all up, unsuccessfully, at that.

Had she been a good daughter? A good wife? A good mother? She'd tried, God knows, she'd tried. What was the evidence? No, no, and no.

She thought about it. Was she to blame? With Mama? No, no. Mama really was perverse. That failure was painful but she wasn't to blame. Jim? God knows she'd done her best— she'd have gone through fire to please Jim. God damn it, no. There, she wasn't to blame.

Her children. Yes, her children. That was the part that hurt so much. Jimmy. Jimmy. Her heart's blood. Dear God, yes. Her fault, her fault. Sarah? She lit a cigarette. Heavens, it was her first of the day, and it was after five o'clock! Well, she had done what she could, hadn't she? Maybe she'd begun too late. Jim was already there. So what did she owe now? Whom did she owe—what?

She thought about Jack. It had all been so strange—strange but sweet. For someone from the sticks, he sure knew his way around.

Six o'clock. She stared at the phone. It didn't ring. And now, who could help her? The only person she could think of was Tony Chappell. She could have rung him up, instead of sending flowers; it would have been natural, really. But now—well, why not? She could begin by asking him for some sort of professional advice—about lacquer or Boulle. She could even ask him for lunch, then— Dear heaven—she was becoming demented. She got up and sat in a chair looking over the place de la Concorde. It was prettier at night— you saw the lights and not the traffic. Though now they were entering that impossibly long sloping French twilight.

What time was it? Six thirty-five. Gee, what the hell could she do? She didn't even have Jack's address. And now she couldn't telephone Tony Chappell. She would just have to wait.

Maybe she should get dressed anyway. Good luck or bad? What would she wear on an ordinary evening? Black, and a few jewels. God knows, she couldn't compete with Señora Pérez, even if she cleaned out the whole vault. She would get dressed herself. She didn't want Cecil.

At nine-thirty she was still sitting by the window. Cecil had knocked on the door and entered in prim silence. She had arranged Mrs. Melmore's bed, and her things for the night. Silently. She had taken things out, put things away in drawers, taking her time. Rubbing it in, Mrs. Melmore thought.

"You won't be needing me after all." She didn't say "madam."

"No, thank you, Cecil. Why don't you just tell Williams to go to bed early tonight, too?"

"Williams? Madam hasn't spoken to Williams all day?"

"No. But I'll call downstairs myself. Never mind. Good night, Cecil."

She sat and stared out at the soft night and the lights.

Part Ten

OVERDRAFT

1

Sarah Melmore Receives a Shock

SARAH WAS SITTING at the table writing. Jack had a huge stack of letters which had been piling up. They were sent to him at another address, but every day or so he brought more home. Some were personal, some enclosed photographs of people, but a lot of them were about business.

Finally, Jack had begged her to help him with the business ones. She told him she didn't know a thing about business letters, but he told her she could do it a whole lot better than he, and at least she knew how to spell.

So Sarah had begun. She wrote the letters out in longhand. Jack thought they were masterful. When he came back, he would read them, shaking his head with admiration at her acumen, then type them up very fast and send them out.

The new apartment was much smaller than the other: two tiny bedrooms, a kitchen-bath, and this room she was sitting in. Not big, like the room in the last apartment—

but it was light. Sarah and Jack had been living in the new apartment such a short time, but already it seemed permanent to her.

Jack's blueprints were pinned all over the walls. His models were on the floor and the window sill. He liked having Sarah here, it seemed—just sitting there, hardly speaking. Sometimes he would stay up all night working, and when she went to bed he would always say, "Tired?" as if he were really disappointed. Sometimes he would ask her advice about something he had done. He took her opinion very seriously.

They each had their own part of the room. She had a table near her door. He had a desk in front of the window. It was covered with newspaper and magazine pictures and glossy photographs. Jack's desk was private. Sarah never went near it if she could help it, but she couldn't help seeing the photographs on top. Some were of people she had seen before. But often they were very weird. There was a photograph (it looked like a very old one) of a man, Chinese maybe, tied onto a sort of cross. There were some swords sticking into his arms and legs. Someone up close was apparently in the process of disemboweling him. It looked real. Maybe it was a photograph of an execution. The thing that haunted her was the man's expression. He was smiling. His eyes and his smile were indescribable. She kept thinking about that smile. Maybe they drugged people before they executed them in China or wherever it was. She never felt like asking Jack about it. In general, she didn't like asking him questions.

Jack let her cook now. He never seemed to care what he ate, but he always told her what a good cook she was. He still didn't like her to go out during the day to do the shopping. "Wait just a little while longer," he said. He brought her whatever she asked for.

What was occupying Sarah's mind most of the time now was something Jack had promised her was going to happen. He was going to use his powers so that she could see her grandfather. She *had* to see her grandfather now—he was the one chosen to show her the way. It would be like a vision, but they could really talk, Jack said. He had promised her. But those things took time, he told her. There were different things he had to do. She never asked what.

The frightening part was that she couldn't help thinking that, if her grandfather could appear, then so could her father. He was so strong. Jack promised her not, but she wondered if Jack could really stop him. It was very exciting, but scary.

She was used to Jack being gone all night. Last night, he hadn't come home. No one ever called, because there wasn't any phone, but it didn't bother her, because she was never lonely. Jack never said anything about Maurice, and she hadn't asked. Anyway, she had always liked being alone.

Sometimes, early in the morning, Jack would come and get into bed with her. She knew he had a hard time going to sleep. That was all right—except often he had horrible nightmares that woke her up. When he slept alone, he slept with the pillow over his head. She didn't want to know what he was dreaming.

She never mentioned Wanda, but sometimes she would dream about her. Wanda had become linked in her mind with her mother. Sometimes she dreamed they were wandering over Paris together, looking for her. She never spoke of her dreams to Jack.

She wondered about the next letter. "Mr. Alexander Plinska." Apparently, he had commissioned, but not paid for, a series of Jack's elevations. It seemed Jack hadn't done the drawings, actually, but he had told this man he needed all the money right away, cash up front.

"He's that kind of person," Jack had said. "Make it just as tough as you can, Sarah. Don't mention the drawings. Just say I need that money right now." He gave her another address where he should send the money.

"Dear Mr. Plinska," she began. "You have not acted in good faith . . ." Was that strong enough?

She heard Jack's footsteps on the stairs. She wasn't supposed to open the door for anyone else, but no one else ever came. Jack usually ran all the way upstairs, but he wasn't running. He'd been out all night, but that didn't make any difference, usually. She knew something had happened before he opened the door. She'd gotten like a dog, she thought. She could sense people's moods from their steps. Like poor Toddy.

Yes, when Jack came in, he looked very grave.

"Hi, Sarah." He kissed her on the top of the head.

Then he went and stared out the window. That was something he always did when something was wrong.

"Sarah," he said. "I've just done something bad. Something really terrible."

Sarah put down her pen. But she didn't ask Jack any questions.

"It's so bad I don't know how I did it. Or if you'll ever forgive me."

Sarah tried to think what that could be. Forgive? She had never ever heard Jack call anything "bad." People did what they had to, Jack always said.

"Sarah, I went to bed with your mother last night."

"Liar!"

"Oh, my Lord—I know—I know. But it's true."

"You? My mother? She's not like that. What are you talking about, Jack?"

"Oh, Lord, I know. I sure didn't plan it that way. I don't mean it was her fault—Lord, no. It was all my fault. It never entered her head. Your mother's not very sophisticated, Sarah. I didn't know. She really needs someone to look after her. Anyone could take advantage of her.

"Well, we got talking. She was at this big party. She really wanted to find out about you—that's why she talked to me. Otherwise, she wouldn't have seen me for the dust."

"I don't understand."

"Oh, it was all my fault. I was the one. I was the one to take advantage of her. She wasn't used to any of the stuff she was taking."

"Drugs? You mean my mother was taking drugs?"

"Sarah, she didn't even know what they were. And you

know, sometimes—most times—I know clear as day what's right. And I know what I have to do. And that's easy. Other times, I realize I'm in a situation for some reason, and I don't know the reason, but I know it's going to be revealed, so I just drift with it, you know, and I wait to see the reason.

"Well, with your mother— I certainly never— you know, she used to be a fantasy to me, a long time ago. Sometimes still. I use her when I need to conjure up how certain sorts of things should be. Your mother, Sarah—she's got a certain kind of perfection. You can't go any further in that particular direction."

"You gave my mother drugs?"

"It was funny. She was actually taking them. Oh, not drugs, I mean, smoking grass—and I had some pretty strong hash, too. And we started talking. I hadn't planned it, Sarah. And everything happened as if—well—as if it sort of had to happen that particular way. By the way, I really liked her, Sarah."

"Yes."

"And she was looking so beautiful and so sad. And she was so unhappy about you. Well, it got late. And I guess we were both high or something, and then we went back to her hotel and talked some more, and then—it just—happened. It was all my fault. She hadn't a clue what was going on."

Sarah stared at him. "Jack, my mother never takes drugs. She never ever had any lovers I ever heard of." She thought. "What did you say to her? What did you do? Was she passed out or something? I mean did you actually . . ."

"Yes, Sarah. I mean no, she wasn't passed out. We spent the whole night together, and it was wonderful. The only thing is she's going to feel just horrible today. I mean horrible about herself when she wakes up. I left her. I figured she'd sleep a long time."

"But Jack—why? Why did you do it?"

"Sarah, I don't know. That's why I'm feeling so rotten. I kept thinking every step of the way—well, to be honest, I don't even think about certain things, you know, I just do them automatically. Because I know—this step follows that

one, and so on. But with your mother I didn't have that in
mind. I kept thinking, next minute it's all going to be revealed, and I'll know what the whole picture is. I'll be shown.
But it wasn't that way. So I just kept on, Sarah, sort of waiting. You've got to believe me. I never planned it. However
bad I was, that's all I can say."

"What are you going to do now?"

"Sarah, I don't know. Your mother seems so fragile to me.
In a way, more than you."

"Oh, yes. She is."

"I would like terribly not to hurt her. What am I going to
do?"

"Do you—care for her?"

"Oh, my Lord, Sarah, you know me. Sure I care for her.
She's so beautiful. She's so vulnerable. I love the way she
holds her head, and the way she moves her hand like this,"
he turned his wrist and moved it toward his face, "when
she's smoking. And the way she smiles, so sad. . . . Last night,
she was laughing. It was beautiful. And she has all this sort
of warm, womanly love she's never really given any man. I
could tell. But, Sarah, God knows, that's not for me. She
should have a man who loves her right. She needs someone
to take care of her."

"What are you going to do about her? Jack, you shouldn't
have done that. Jack, I know my mother."

"Lord, I know. I know. What should I do, Sarah? What
would hurt her the least? I'm no good at things like that. I
left her a letter. I said not to feel bad. I said I would call her.
But maybe she's really mad at me now, anyway. That would
be the best, really. I'm just so afraid she'll be so mad at herself. And she only talked to me to find out about you."

"What did you tell her?"

"That you're okay."

"Good. Did you tell her . . ." Sarah thought it over. She
always believed Jack, but this situation— Maybe she didn't
really know her mother. She went back in her mind. No, she

was sure her mother had never had a secret life. It was all for her father. Everything to please or appease her father.

"I don't know, Jack. Oh, Christ, this is perfectly god-awful! Maybe you should just write her a long letter and try to explain. Tell her I'll write, too. I was thinking about it even, myself."

"Could you write it for me, Sarah? Then I could copy it. I'm so stupid about those things. I already wrote her one dumb letter."

"No!" Sarah almost felt like laughing, but God damn it, it wasn't funny. Her mother, unless she'd changed a lot, was going to be totally wrecked. "Dear Mrs. Melmore," she thought, "I have not acted in good faith."

Well, there was nothing to laugh about. It was perfectly terrible. She was so goddamned angry! How dare Jack mess around with her family, mess up her private life that way?

"You've got to help."

"Well," she said, slowly and coolly, "maybe you should introduce her to Maurice."

"M'reez? What on earth are you talking about, Sarah? Why, M'reez—he couldn't ever in a million years understand what your mother was. What she represents. All he ever cares about is movie actresses and rock stars. My Lord! I wouldn't know the words to explain a woman like your mother to M'reez. And then if he found out where she lives, well, she has all of this stuff lying around—money and jewels. He'd probably cut her throat and rob her or something.

"Well, no, not M'reez. That's not fair. But the kids he hangs out with, they'd do it. They only think real short-term, Sarah. They're street kids. You shouldn't say things like that."

Sarah was glad he was so upset. He should be.

"I don't know," she said. "From what you say, my mother must have changed quite a bit. Taking hash and asking you home. You see, I would never have thought you were her type."

Now she knew Jack was angry too, but she was glad. How could he do this to her mother, her mother whom, in spite of everything, *because* of everything, she loved! It was unforgivable. Her mother! Her mother might have been weak, but she had never been cheap, like most of those women.

"Type? Do you think your father was her type? Do you think he ever did her much good?"

"How dare you talk about my father," said Sarah. "My father was a great man. He was the smartest man I ever knew. My father could be more fun than anyone I've ever known in my life." She paused. "He was just way too strong for my mother." She sighed. "Too strong for me, too."

Jack walked into his little room and riffled through some papers. He took a shower and put on some clean clothes, then came out and sat down.

"What are you doing, Sarah?"

"Finishing these letters."

"Who are you writing to?"

"Mr. Plinska."

"The bastard. Listen, Sarah, I know you're mad at me. Maybe you'll never trust me again. Maybe you have a right. Your mother's a valuable person. But I'll show you I know how to mend things too.

"Lord knows, it's going to be hard, but I can do it. I know I can make your mother feel all right again. I know it, Sarah. Not by being—well, you and I know that's ridiculous. But I'll do it somehow. I promise you.

"If I do, Sarah—will you trust me again? I know it's hard, but if I do, and I think I can—will it be all right?

"My Lord, I'm so sorry I had to tell you that thing. I'm so sorry I had to tell you, but I couldn't be here with you, and not. I have to be completely honest with you, Sarah. But I am sorry. I'm so sorry I did this to you."

"I'm not the one to be sorry for," said Sarah, and looked back at the page. "Dear Mr. Plinska," she wrote, "rats like you should be exterminated."

2

Mrs. Melmore
Is Crossed in Love

WHEN THE PHONE FINALLY RANG, Mrs. Melmore refused to
hurry. She walked very slowly over to it. She didn't expect
anything now. Maybe Harriet had finished her dinner and
wanted to chat.

"Mrs. Melmore?"

It was Jack.

She was frozen. "Yes?" She sounded brusque and cold.

"It's Jack. Jack Straw."

She knew she couldn't say anything she had meant to say.

"Did I call at a bad time?"

"No. No."

"I'm sorry if I'm a little late, but I got caught up with some
stuff. Business."

"Yes," said Mrs. Melmore.

"Are you okay?" he said.

"Yes," she said.

"I thought maybe we could arrange to see each other sometime. . . . I guess you're pretty busy, though, and . . . Tomorrow's kind of bad," he said. "What about the day after? I
have to get this show done now, and I'm terrifically busy.
That might be better."

"But . . ." she said. There was a silence. "What are you
doing tonight?" she said. There was a very long pause. She
looked at her watch. Ten to ten.

"Tonight," he said. "I was going to—I ought to work tonight."

"Well, I've never seen any of your work," said Mrs. Melmore boldly. "I'd love to."

"But nothing's really finished now. It's a real mess."

"Then, why don't you come over and have a drink first—or we could have a quick dinner, if you haven't eaten, before you go to work. I'm absolutely starving."

Gee, she was really pushing. She had never done that before, never. There was a long, long pause.

"Well . . . Okay. If you don't mind having a steak? Over here? I'm in a sort of funny part of town. Do you have your driver?"

"Yes."

"All right." He gave her an address in a quarter she didn't know. In about half an hour, he said. God, she was shameless, shameless. But it was for Sarah, too. She called downstairs. There was a problem. They couldn't reach Williams. Oh, damn—Cecil had probably gone right ahead and told him to take the night off. Well, she could get along without Williams too. The desk got her a limousine.

She wondered about her dress. Would it be better if she put on a silk skirt and sweater? Less jewelry? No. This was not the time to be appropriate. This was the time for more rouge and more scent. She ought to start soon. It sounded pretty far.

This place of Jack's really was a bistro. Or a dive. It was dark, everything seemed dark here, a couple of tables upstairs with young people sitting at them, and circular iron stairs going down. A man pointed her way down the stairs. She didn't see Jack. She asked a man who was wearing a sort of butcher's apron. He shrugged and spread his hands. There were several tables free, he indicated. She went and sat at one. She had brought her watch tonight. She was a little late. Jack was even later. A surly young man came over and asked her what she wanted. She asked about the house wine. It was Italian. Oh well, white wine was all the same to her, as long as it was cold.

Dante's—an Italian steakhouse in Paris! How odd! She hadn't wanted to sit and wait. She hadn't wanted the doubts and depression to set in.

At that moment, she saw Jack. He was running down the stairs. He came over and kissed her. He held both her hands. It was all right. It was all right. Nothing else mattered. She almost burst into tears.

"Have you been waiting long? Lord, I'm so sorry. I just got caught up. Couldn't get away. Did you order?"

The surly man came back and handed her a glass of white wine.

"Vodka," said Jack, *"une grande vodka,"* and then, "I picked this place because it was sort of near where I was, but I see it's horrible—really horrible. Shall we go someplace else?"

"No, this is fine."

"Can you get something you'd like to eat here?"

"Oh, sure."

He leaned over and kissed her again.

"I was scared to call you," he said. "I thought you'd be awfully mad at me."

"How could I be mad at you?"

"Well, I think I did something wrong. Anyway, things don't usually work out for two people, you know."

"It worked out for me," she said.

"Well." He kissed her hands. "It sure worked out for me, too. Is that wine awful? Don't you want a vodka?"

"No, it's fine. What do you have to do tonight?"

"Well, I really do have to work. I'm putting together a show for Caracas, or anyway I'm supposed to be. It should be ready now, but I've hardly started. But it's all right. Once I start working, I work all night.

"Oh, and I saw Sarah, too. I talked things over with her. She said she'd like to think about it. About seeing you. But she was very friendly. Something will work out, soon. She said she'd write you a letter, maybe."

"Really? Really? Oh, please, do get her to. Or call. Anything. If I could only see her for a minute—really, I wouldn't be demanding, I wouldn't try to make her do anything. Tell her that. Maybe I should give you a letter for her. You know I saw her on the street for just a few minutes. But it was so awful. She seemed just as 'strange' as back in her worst days. I'm afraid she's not taking her pills."

"No. She's not taking any pills. But I think she's much better now, anyhow."

"But Dr. Simon said they were essential. Maybe for the rest of her life, he said."

"Well, Sarah's trying to get well on her own. She's got a lot of strength. She's not taking pills or booze or well— anything. *Une autre vodka.* What about you?"

"No, I really can't drink too much; I haven't got the head for it. What about this woman Wanda? What's happened to her? She sounded most forbidding."

"Wanda?" he said. "Wanda? Oh, that dyke, you mean. I guess she went away. She probably went home or something."

"Really? I thought she was Polish or Eastern European. I got the impression she couldn't go home and was just living off Sarah."

"I don't know," he said. "She hasn't been around, anyway. Maybe she's with those other people—those ones—which ones did you meet, anyway?"

"Just one. A girl." She decided belatedly that she wouldn't say any more than that. And he knew that much himself.

"Well, they're almost all girls, aren't they? Let's see. There's Per and Anna Josefson."

"Per and Anna! They're married?"

"I always thought they were brother and sister. Aren't they? Then there's that dark guy, and the Russian one, I guess—"

Mrs. Melmore examined this new idea. Brother and sister! Some brother and sister! Well, she'd thought they looked alike, hadn't she? And all this talk about sexual propriety! If ever there were a clear-cut case of incest—

"Maybe I'm wrong," Jack was saying. "Are there more? I really don't know them at all, though."

"They think you're very dangerous." Mrs. Melmore had a faint smile on her face. She couldn't wait for her next conversation with Anna.

"Dangerous? I wonder why? It's always funny how other people think about you, isn't it? I never knew much about them, except they were real political.

"It seems like they used to take care of all Sarah's money. I don't know what they did with it, but maybe that was 'political,' too. Or maybe they used it for her good."

Mrs. Melmore decided she was being very honorable not to comment on this.

"I did kind of wonder why Sarah had all that money of her own, to do just what she liked with. I mean, when I met Sarah, she wasn't in too good shape to handle money. Usually families like yours—well—"

"Oh, God. I know. Her father left her that money—it's all hers. In trust, of course, Sarah just gets the income, but you're right. Something probably needs to be done."

"Would you like to order something?"

The menu was short. She looked it over—mostly different kinds of steak. She wondered if he would let her pick up the check.

"I'll just have another white wine," she said. "I'm really too excited to order."

"Really? I'm excited, too, but I'm going to have a steak. *Sanglant*," he said to the waiter in joke French. "And *un autre vin blanc*. Shall we get a bottle?"

"No," she said, "not for me. Listen, what are we going to do, anyway?"

"Do? . . . Now?"

"Do about anything," she said.

"Well, it's really nice being here with you. You're looking so beautiful. Your skin—it looks as if a lamp is shining from right inside it. How do you do that? I guess maybe it just must be the way your skin is made. I just wish I could get that light on film."

Sis was used to being praised for her luminous skin. She didn't say anything. She just watched him, wondering how she would say it.

"I wish I didn't have to work, but I've put things off for

such a long time. I just put everything off and then it all piles
up, and then I have to do it all at once. So that's why I can't
see anyone for a while. I mean even now—I was about an
hour late before I even came through that door."

"But," Sis said, "but." She said it very low. "I love you."

"I love you," she said, more loudly.

Quickly Jack leaned forward and put his fingers over her
lips. He shook his head. "No," he said. "Please don't say it.
Please."

She had hoped he would tell her he loved her too, or at
least kiss her again. But instead he ordered another vodka.

"Look," she said. "You probably think I go around falling
in love with everyone. Getting in bed with everyone."

"Lord, no," he said, "that's the last thing I was thinking.
But please—please don't go on. Please. Forget you ever said
that. You'll just be sorry. It's not right."

"Not right? I'm much older."

"Of course that's not what I mean. You know that. Lord,
I wouldn't even know where to begin. You don't know me."

"I know we just met, I know that part. It must seem ridiculous. But I've only been in love about three times in my
life and I've always known right away. I know I should wait,
but—but I've spent my whole life waiting."

He simply shook his head, not looking at her.

"Is there someone—in your life?"

"Not the way you mean."

"And then, well—I could help you."

"You don't even know what I do," he said.

"I know you're an artist. I know people admire your work.
I could help."

"Help? How?"

"Well, uh . . . well . . . I'm quite rich."

He sat very quietly and stared at her with those strange
yellow eyes. She felt miserably crass, utterly humiliated. "We
have this foundation," she added. "We help artists." That
didn't sound much better.

"Mm-hm," he said. "Well, I still don't know what you really mean. You mean you'd give me a lot of money, or commission a lot of work that you've never seen? Something like that? Is that it?"

"I—I guess whatever you needed for your—art."

"And you don't even know what I do."

"I don't care. I believe in you."

He began to sketch on the tablecloth. "But what do you think you'd be getting?" he said. "I mean for all that money?"

"Well, I just said, it would be for you."

"Mmm-hm. But you don't know anything about me. And I'm telling you I could never be to you what you would want me to be."

"Do you really know what I want you to be?"

"Well, I really do sort of know what women want. I'm sorry if that sounds crummy. I mean you're special—you're the *most* special—I've watched them all and I know. But you are a woman."

"You mean you don't really—like women?"

"Oh, I love women. But there's problems. And the people I hang out with—well, some of them don't like women at all. So you'd be uncomfortable. Of course Sarah, she's different. . . . She can go anywhere, do anything. She's so spacy."

Mrs. Melmore felt terribly confused. He certainly wasn't a fairy. So what on earth did he mean? Then she felt her first real pangs of jealousy. Jealousy of Sarah. "I thought you said that you and Sarah weren't—"

"Lovers? Oh, no. Sarah's not in love with me. Love? I think that part of her is dead. Maybe that's why she's not like a woman, maybe that's what I mean. Maybe that's why we sort of understand each other—why we get along so well."

Mrs. Melmore gazed at him. "You're saying—" she hesitated. "Is what you're saying, Jack, that you aren't—I mean—can't—well, ever be in love?"

"Love. In love. With another human being. Mmmm. No. No. I guess not, Mrs. Melmore."

"Oh, for Christ's sake, stop calling me Mrs. Melmore!"

"Well—Sis—do you have another name? That name never seemed proper to me."

"How about Maud—after my father's favorite poem?"

"Maud. Hm. Oh, well. Okay, Sis."

"You've never been in love, Jack?"

"Um—no. At first I used to think I could be, but later on I found out it was different from what other people mean. But I feel a lot of other things. Pity, curiosity, desire, compassion—a whole lot of compassion, honestly."

"Last night. That was—compassion?"

"Oh, Lordy, last night was gorgeous. It was wonderful for me. In all kinds of ways. You see, I'd always wondered . . . Well, anyway . . . It was very wrong, too. A big mistake. I broke a promise. . . ."

"A promise? You mean someone—"

"No, no. To myself. That I wasn't going to get involved on that kind of basis with anyone ever again. Anyone who cared. I've just made too much trouble that way all my life."

"So last night—it didn't have anything to do with—love—for you?"

"Love—oh, Lord. It was very good sex for me. I felt so close to you. I felt like I could please you. I really like that. Is that love?"

Mrs. Melmore was silent.

"Listen. I got up when you were sleeping. You look beautiful sleeping too, you know? And you had all this stuff around, I mean really valuable stuff. And you know what I did? I took twenty francs from you. For carfare. It always made me mad, that thing about your husband. But of course I didn't use it. I just walked. Gave it away to some old man in a doorway.

"Taking twenty francs. Is that love? Maybe only taking twenty francs? And leaving the rest? Maybe that's love?"

Mrs. Melmore felt like crying, but she'd be damned if she'd let herself. The waiter brought Jack a steak. Jack took a bite, then cut off a tiny piece.

"Here. Try it. It's okay. You ought to eat something, please."

She shook her head. "But I guess I will have a vodka," she said.

"I don't understand what you're saying," she added; her voice was shaking, she knew. "But I know I love you."

"Well, but that's what I mean exactly. I mean you don't understand what I'm like, and if you did, you wouldn't like it. And you certainly wouldn't love me.

"Excuse me, it sounds so conceited, but I felt—I feel like I do understand, a little, what you're like. It isn't any accident. I told you all that stuff—about your pictures. Watching you. Remembering every little way you moved. So I could feel almost like I could get inside your skin, if I wanted.

"When I was about twenty-four years old, I had such a strong fantasy about you. About how it would be to be with you—be your friend, be your lover, I don't know. And I used to think, if I had been born—well—if I had been you—how would I do those things you did so well? Could I do them? Or would I do them different? It used to be so strong, that fantasy, I guess it never really went away.

"So last night, like I wrote you—that was all my fault. Just never believe anything else for a minute. I really do get these very powerful fantasies—so powerful people usually go along with them, sort of. It's always my fault. But this time it hurt you. And so I'm very, very sorry."

"Don't be sorry for me. But listen—don't think I'm an absolute idiot. It's not fair. It's true I don't know your work. I don't know anything about it. And I know that what I said —it came out as if I was just coming over here to buy you. I'm sorry about that. I've never done anything like that. I was just so nervous. But please believe me, I do have a feeling for quality. That's why I don't have to see anything you've done. I believe in you.

"And I do have very strong intuitions, and I believe in them. Maybe you don't feel anything for me. All right. Forget about it. But, Jack, you may not love me, you may not feel anything much for me, or anything at all—but I have a strong, strong feeling that it was always meant that we should be friends."

He had pushed his plate aside. He was staring straight at her with his golden eyes.

"Friends," he said, "well, look—just to be my friend, you'd have to go so far down. . . . You see those stairs?" He pointed. "Let's say that below those stairs there's another flight of stairs. Let's say it goes right down under the streets, down to the sewers. And even then, there'd be more stairs. And you'd have to keep going down and down. Further and further." He was sketching on the table again.

What was he drawing? Flights of stairs?

"It wouldn't be right for you. You wouldn't like it."

She was silent.

"Don't look so sad," he said, "you can have the saddest look."

"There's nothing much to laugh about."

"Actually, I'm letting you off easy. Really."

"You mean about money?"

"No, I mean about everything. Don't think what you've been saying doesn't—well, it hits me real hard. But anyway, I really—I really do have to work."

"All right," she said. She signaled for the check.

"No," he said. "I'll pay this one."

But he was looking at her in a different sort of way.

"Sis," he said, "I said I've watched you, but I see in a way I don't know you that well. I'm not really sure how far you'd be willing to go with me."

"I don't know what you mean," she said. "Pretty far, I guess."

"You do—trust me?" He began to sketch on the table again.

"Yes."

"Let me think about it. Things have gotten so messed up and I haven't helped at all, involving you. I know it seems like I'm taking these very serious things you're saying very unseriously and that's not my way. It's just—so much is happening, I can't concentrate."

When the waiter brought the bill, Jack didn't pick it up. "Listen," he said. He started to say something, then stopped. "Excuse me," he said and went to the men's room. It seemed a long time. When he came back, he pushed the check under his plate, and ordered another vodka. "You too?" She nodded.

"I really am late. I wish I had more time. You know, in a way, certain things might work out," he said.

The waiter came over with the drinks. "We could forget about last night? Like it was—just a dream? Just all be close? Sarah's getting so much better. You see, I think I can take care of Sarah better than anyone. If you saw her now, you'd understand.

"But of course the best would be if we all three— You see, that kind of love—mother love—that's the most real there is. Believe me. It's more of a love than a man can feel. I know.

"And then, well, you see, Sarah's interested in my work. She could help me, and—I need that, and if that suited you, well, in a way, it might be a sort of an answer?"

He paused and looked at her. She didn't really see at all.

"Jack—do you—would you—want to marry Sarah?"

"Marry Sarah? Oh, Lord, no. It never entered my mind. Only if she—no, that's too ridiculous. She never would. You see, Sarah is just completely out of this world. It's like she's not made of flesh anymore. Like—like a madonna. It's just totally completely different with us. I thought I'd told you."

He wasn't making much sense to her. In a way, it sounded as if he were in love with Sarah—even if the Sarah he seemed to be talking about bore no resemblance to the girl she had known.

"Please, have a drink. I think what I'm saying is all mixed up. Or it's coming out wrong, or something."

She automatically took a swallow of her vodka.

"You know, there was something I really wanted to ask

you, though. It's sort of personal. Would you just tell me, if I'm being too personal?"

"Anything," she said.

"What did you do with Mr. Melmore, anyway?"

"What?" She took a great swallow of her drink, and almost choked. "What do you mean?"

"With his body."

Sis thought she was going to faint. She put her drink down and her hands over her face.

"Sarah says she shot him. She's sure she did. I believe her. I've listened to her stories a lot now. And I just couldn't figure out what you did with his body."

Jesus. Jesus. Now she knew what she was being punished for and how. She began to shake. It was buried so deep.

"Sarah imagines things."

"I don't think she imagined this. So I just wondered."

"You shouldn't—you shouldn't."

"Okay. I'm sorry, I'm really sorry. Let's not talk about it. There's no reason you should trust me, and I shouldn't have asked you."

She began to cry, quite silently, the tears rolling down her face.

"I do trust you. But—but—I didn't know Sarah remembered. I really had hoped and prayed she didn't. No wonder —well . . . Oh, that's—it's almost the worst thing. Okay, I'll tell you. But you have to understand—you have to believe me. You'll have to promise you'll believe it happened just the way . . . well, I'll tell you exactly how it happened. It was a total accident. You see that's why—

"You see, Sarah had this old gun, no one would ever have believed it could even function, and she did shoot—shoot it off. And it went in the direction of her father. I know she didn't mean to hit him. She just wanted to get his attention or something. Anyway, she was just out of the hospital. Well, my God, he was dead in a minute. I knew it couldn't be the wound.

"Well—I knew what people would think and I just—well —sometimes, it's like something atavistic takes over, you know. I was just so cold-blooded. So cold.

"I called Mac Spofford. He's our doctor in the country— but he's also a good, good friend. And thank God he was home, and the servants were away. And I said, 'Mac, if you ever loved me and Jim, get over here fast. There's been a terrible tragedy. And please don't tell a soul. Not even Cynthia.'

"Mac was there in about a minute. I said I'd been playing around with this pistol. (It wasn't exactly my style, but I couldn't think what else to say.) And I'm not used to guns, you know. And it just went off. And Sarah's just been home for a few weeks. And she's still asleep, I said. And I was afraid now she was really going to go over the edge forever—and so on. Well, he was very quick. He laid Jim down and looked him over and everything. I couldn't watch.

"Then he said, 'Sis—Jim died of a heart attack. You know I've been warning him to cut down on everything for years. But you know how stubborn he is (was, I guess).' And he wanted to take care of me. Comfort me. Give me a sedative or something. I knew I shouldn't take a thing. I wasn't even crying.

"I just said, 'Oh, Mac, please fix it fast. As fast as you can. There just can't be a breath of scandal. Jim always wanted to be cremated, you know. He hated all the other stuff.' We were out by the poolhouse. It was still warm. Well, Mac covered Jim over with something and we both went and had a stiff drink. And then he made those calls. He was the one who signed the death certificate. He took care of everything —the coroner and everything. Of course, Mac's just like God out there. I don't know how he did it. Everything went so fast. And I got him to give Sarah some strong stuff to keep her quiet. And I hoped it would take that memory away. I hoped she wouldn't remember anything. I knew she didn't really mean it. And Jim did die of a heart attack, anyway,

Mac said so, so it had nothing to do with Sarah." She wiped her eyes. "Do you think I'm a terrible person?"

"Terrible? Why on earth? I think you're very smart and very good."

"I think Mac did after a while. After a while. First, he started getting very familiar with me in this creepy way. And then he got very cold and strange. Because it was this—this sort of weird, well, almost crime between us. Because of course he was involved, too, wasn't he? Almost as much as I was. And then I felt so funny. I make a point, well, I hardly see Mac and Cynthia anymore. Just give money to his hospital. The same amount Jim always did."

Jack looked at her. "I think you're very, very smart," he said. He paused. "Well, it's like two ways." He had been drawing again—pyramids, it looked like. First he'd add a little to one. Then to the other. He looked at the clock. "Lord, I'm horribly late. And I can't put it off. Look, I'll be up all night, but if I can come by your place tomorrow— let's say around three—or between three and four. We'll both have time to think. I'll try to get Sarah to write you a note, if I have time."

"Please," said Mrs. Melmore, and took the check. "You go on now. No, go ahead. I'm still a little undone."

"I hate to leave you like this."

"Go on."

"You're sure?"

"Yes. Go on. Hurry."

"Good night then, Sis." He kissed her. "I'll see you tomorrow. You have that guy to take you home?"

"Yes."

He hesitated, gave her a last look, and ran up the stairs.

3

Sarah Melmore
Makes an Engagement

SARAH HAD HAD a difficult time getting to sleep. Bad thoughts about Jack kept coming into her head. This had never happened before. She was very troubled. Jack had certainly screwed things up. How could she trust him with anything important, if he behaved that way with her mother? Saying he wanted to protect her, and then . . . How could she trust any of his promises after that? If he had actually fallen for her mother it would have been a little better. Poor Mummy. Sarah really needed someone to help her think things through. Someone who was hers. Her blood.

Well, everyone was a mess, really. If her life had shown her one thing, it was that. Jack had performed better on his promises than most people. She thought she was awake all night, worrying and wondering, but no, near dawn she sat up with a shock, when she heard Jack's footsteps, running. Running meant good, but what could be good now? She didn't want to see him. She lay down, her face to the wall.

"Sarah," Jack said, "I hate to wake you. You can go right back to sleep. But I just had to tell you. I saw your mother and everything's all right. I sort of explained. I said how it was all my fault and she didn't seem to feel that badly, or anything. See, I want you to know I keep my promises. She'd like to see you sometime. Or have you write. Is that okay?"

Sarah didn't look at him. She felt so angry. It wouldn't be easy to get rid of all that anger.

"And, Sarah, I have some other news for you. Good news. I didn't want to talk to you about it till I'd cleared up this other mess, but look—this thing for you."

For her. She stopped breathing. That meant her grandfather.

"Sarah, it's on for tomorrow night. Tonight, I guess. Is that
okay? Did I just mess up too much, so you don't trust me? Is
that too soon? Do you need some more time?"

Sarah looked away from his eyes.

"Tonight," Sarah repeated. Now she felt unsure. Before
this, she had kept begging Jack, and Jack had seemed reluc-
tant. He'd said, "Maybe," or "Later on," or "Let's wait and
see," or "It'll take time for everything to come together
right."

Now, all of a sudden, it was right away! What would her
grandfather say to her? His child and grandchild . . . murderer, murderer.

"Would it happen here?" Sarah asked.

"No, I'd take you to a different place. If you want the
whole thing, Sarah, the only way is to have the whole ceremony. You want a manifestation, see, and that takes work.
Do you think you'd feel up to it? You'd have to fast the whole
day, too. Just rest and relax. Just drink maybe a little water."

But she needed direction so badly. And Jack—he could do
some things, but he really couldn't help her with that. Jack
really didn't know anything at all about what was right.

"Okay," she said slowly. "Tonight. Yes."

"Oh, that's just fabulous, Sarah. I told you some of this
would be weird, even sort of scary, but nothing's going to
happen that can hurt you. It's like a movie, sort of. You sure
I'm not pushing you too much?"

"No, but are you sure I'll see my grandfather?"

"I can't swear, but I'm pretty sure."

"How can you stop my father from being there?"

"I hate your father, Sarah. He represents everything I hate.
Your father won't be there, Sarah. Over my dead body. I
mean it.

"You're not a virgin, are you, Sarah? You told me not, I
guess."

"No, not. But why?"

"I don't know. There's different ways to do things. I'm going back out. I probably won't be back until tonight. I've gotten you some clothes and stuff. I'll bring everything then. Please, I hope you can go back to sleep. I was just worried you wouldn't sleep because of all this mess about your mother. But now, anyway, everything's okay. Everything's working right. I wanted you to know. So please go back to sleep, and just try and keep quiet. Just rest and relax. Sarah, everything I'm doing now is for you. Just for you."

"Well, okay, Jack."

4

Mrs. Melmore
Balances Her Books

MRS. MELMORE AWOKE in a great drift of sadness. She was aware of it before she actually remembered what it was all about. Jack. She had lost something precious, but what in the name of God had she had in mind, anyway? Making love all night, dancing through Paris like those old Technicolor movies.

It was her fault things had gotten so mixed up. She'd been mad, just insane! Acting like some sort of bacchante. Jack was right. He was strong and he was kind. She couldn't have brought him home, like some exotic specimen from Patagonia. And would she have wanted that, really? Not on your life! "Too old," she said aloud. *"L'amour fou?"* Too old. Too set.

He had his work and a life of his own. And his life, well, she didn't really understand what he'd been saying or suggesting, but—the life all these young people seemed to be living today, unisex, or whatever it was—she loathed the words and ideas. And all those drugs, that boy and girl in the bathroom of Tony Chappell's house. She didn't know why she kept thinking about them. Things seemed so undifferentiated today. She supposed people had found new and frightfully exciting ways of making love. Well, come on —she *knew* they had! Still, what did it all matter, if you didn't care, if you weren't mad about someone?

Jack had seemed so unlike the people around him. Masculine, quiet, old-fashioned, polite. Still, what he'd been trying to explain to her, she thought, was that he too led that kind of life. And with Sarah. What a strange idea! A man and a woman being so close, with no thought of sex between them. It seemed unnatural to her. She really didn't like things today at all. If she were only a little different, she would have loved to spend another night with Jack. But now, knowing he felt nothing for her (and she mustn't fool herself, he really didn't—or maybe just curiosity), that would never happen again. "Never again," she said out loud.

Mrs. Melmore felt cold. The air conditioner was turned on too high, but she felt too cold to get out of bed. But was it the air conditioner, or this sudden feeling of mortality?

Perhaps that was what she felt, and for the first time—the true realization of her mortality. Of course, like everyone else, she had pretended to believe in the possibility of her own death. Children always had to pretend that—it was a sign of being grownup. But here she was, quite grownup, and she had to acknowledge to herself that in her heart she had never believed that she would die. Did anyone, really? she wondered. Yes, she admitted now, the world would go on just as smoothly without her perceptions, without her presence. No god would sweep down from Olympus, ravished by her beauty and charm, to carry her back with him into immortality. No, soon, quite soon, she would be as dead as Jim, as Jimmy, as Anne, Louisa, Cottie, and Mama.

She jumped up and switched off the air conditioner, picking up her cashmere shawl on her way back to bed.

But that wasn't all of it. She realized that there was something else, something important, that she must face. She had never envisioned her life without a great romantic love. Without even thinking about it, she had always assumed that, if Jim were to die (but, of course, Jim wouldn't die), her life would revolve around someone equally compelling.

Naturally, she hadn't thought about this for months after Jim's death. Only recently had it dawned on her how peculiarly difficult her situation was. Jim—well, men of Jim's status (and she knew she wouldn't be satisfied with anything less)—how many were there? Perhaps a dozen, if you counted Western Europe. She had known them all for years, known them too well. Of course, most of them were married. She believed that all these men liked and admired her, but she would have no novelty for them. Beauty was a commodity easy to purchase, and youth, even taste.

She was aware that she had a reputation for having a cool temperament. It sprang from Jim's endless liaisons and from her own discouragement of serious flirtations. "Frigid," people probably thought. Certainly not "sexy."

What if she changed her focus to a different world, to someone completely different—the president of a university, a senator? Where different standards would apply?

Mrs. Melmore had to admit that she had a certain scorn for men who were intellectual, rather than active in the world. Of course, they were her favorite dinner companions, but a real man—well, a real man was earthy, like Jim, not introspective. Of course, politicians weren't intellectual, but then the whole manner of life seemed too demeaning. If she were ten years younger, maybe, but no, she was too old. She could never adjust.

It would have to be a younger man, in any case. She knew all the appropriate men of an appropriate age. An artist? Artists weren't graded in the same way. It wouldn't mean taking such a visible step down.

And Jack—of course, Jack had about him a certain toughness, ruthlessness almost, that she respected. Jack was no pretentious, ineffectual aesthete.

Jack. Well, there it was. Jack had shown her how hopeless

was her quest. Oh, of course she could always buy a man, but that was the last thing she wanted. And she knew, now, that she would always feel, with men like Jack, the terror that she might not be really attractive to them, that they might be dreaming of younger bodies. Mrs. Melmore shivered, and wrapped her shawl more tightly around her.

The triumph of age! The triumph of death! But it was unjust, unfair. She had been fashioned by a beneficent deity to be beautiful and charming—but perhaps, above all, to understand and delight a complicated, exacting man.

She had to the highest degree the specific gift of complementing and pleasing the richest, the most powerful, the most difficult man in the world.

But with Jim dead, what? Some gifted women could exercise their powers forever. But she? What could she do with this talent? She might as well have cast herself on Jim's funeral pyre. There would never be another Jim, never another man with that magnetism, that aura of excitement and danger. She missed all that, missed it like an addict. She had adored playing her role as Scheherazade, knowing that each night she must invent a new and tantalizing distraction, or she might not live to see another morning. It was addictive, yes. If only she could see Jim again, even for half an hour, now that she'd learned so much and understood so many more things!

She must put all this behind her, and stop thinking like such a self-centered idiotic child. She was middle-aged and getting older. She could not expect a great romantic love— or any love, perhaps. She would continue going out in the evening with her usual escorts—"confirmed bachelors," they would have been called in Mama's day. She would grow old. She would die. Like anybody.

But something else was making her cold and fearful. Last night. Last night Jack had made a liar out of her. He had made her say terrible things. He had somehow seduced her into saying things that should never have been said. Certain things should never be said.

Jim had been struck by lightning. He had died of a heart attack. Sarah hadn't killed her father. Jack didn't understand. He had forced her to say those things, and while the words may have been correct, in a literal sense, the meaning was entirely wrong. She could understand it herself and she could deal with it. She was the one who bore the pain. But it was too delicate a thing for anyone else to touch. Jack should never have meddled. She felt an enormous anger, as if Jack had raped and robbed her.

Sis wrapped her shawl round and round her. Her nature simply wasn't made for anger and revenge. And with Jack. It had been her fault, after all. Hers alone. Her foolishness, her infatuation. She had hunted him down. He was discreet and concerned. Everything he said showed it. And he had Sarah.

All that was left in her life was Sarah. Her most intense feelings were for Sarah. Yet Sarah was infinitely mysterious to her. Well then, her single, most urgent need was to solve this enigma.

Maybe Sarah really loved this man. Jack said she didn't, but Sarah liked him enough to trust him more than anyone else. And Jack seemed to care for Sarah very much, in his way—a way Sis didn't understand. Jack thought Sarah was like the madonna! Heaven knows what he meant. But if Sarah cared for him, if he was good to her, she wouldn't interfere.

Of course, she would have to do a great deal of checking in any case. People seemed to know Jack Straw, but still she'd have to find out more, much more. And she must spend time with Sarah. She must try to get close to Sarah and win her trust. Find out about the pills she wasn't taking. Decide something about her money. Maybe Jack, if he really was responsible, was a kind of answer.

Now, let's see. When Jack said he would be by between three and four, that could mean five, six, or seven. She knew that. She should go out. It was hard to leave her room. She didn't feel like seeing anyone. She didn't even want to look in the mirror. She probably looked different—old and debauched.

Cecil knocked.

"This came by hand, madam," said Cecil, looking neutral. Their little feud was over.

Expensive writing paper. She looked at the address on the back. Oh—Tony Chappell—three pages. My goodness! Ornate thanks for the ravishing flowers. Undeserved. Apologies for the ghoulish party. She skipped on. He was going to Deauville for ten days—everyone was going to Deauville it seemed. Only hoped when he got back— What was this? "I don't know if you heard the tragic news about our young friend John Greenough." She went back and reread that sentence. "Jumped or fell, they say. But the window was high, and it seems there can be no doubt he killed himself. As I'm sure you know, suicide was very much on his mind. Poor boy. The sad part is that he had a real talent which he never seemed able to utilize. Such silly things go through one's head. I keep thinking I shouldn't have thrown him into the clutches of Madame Butterfly. Do you think she was the last straw? Morbid. I wasn't quite sure how well you knew John. Of course he was your most extravagant admirer. I know his family comes from the South, but I don't know if they will be coming over. In any case, I'm sure there will be some sort of ceremony. Unfortunately, I will not be here to attend, but if you would like to make any inquiries, the address I have is c/o Ngola Mbandi, 16 rue Verlaine (Tel: 222-33-75). I hate to close on this sad, sad note. But rather on a happier one— the hope of finding you again on my return. I would love you to see my house with no one in it. A dinner for six or eight? May I call you? All my thanks. Tony."

Mrs. Melmore looked at the letter. How horrible. How sordid. That boy probably had jumped out the window, unless someone had pushed him. Naturally she felt sorry for anyone who was so demented. But that young man was really dangerous.

Oh, of course she was sorry, sorry for his family. She would send flowers, if she found out where the service was. But she certainly wouldn't call that other number. Goodness, could it be his boyfriend? She really wasn't involved in it at all. And didn't want to be. No, no flowers. How grim. How grim.

Suddenly, Mrs. Melmore felt she must talk to Harry. Really, she should have done so before. But it was awfully early. Oh, goodness, Harriet got up very early. She went over and dialed her number. It rang and rang. Could she really have gone out at this hour? She put the phone back down again.

Maybe it was just as well. Full disclosure might be a little premature. Jack had sounded quite encouraging about Sarah. She didn't trust Anna, but in spite of everything, she really did trust Jack. Trust him! She was in his pocket! My God, she'd gone to bed with him! Told him about Jim! Everything! He could actually blackmail her if he wanted, couldn't he? Jim had been cremated. Mac had taken care of all the records, hadn't he? Could there have been any sort of slip? My God! Talk about scandal!

But no, that was really unfair. Jack hadn't asked her for a thing. He wasn't interested in Sarah's money; he wanted to protect her. And he wanted to bring them together. She'd wait to talk to Jack this afternoon, collect a little more information first.

And then Harriet. Gee, she'd really behaved badly to Harriet. What had she been up to? She had been "playing" again, hadn't she? Oh, she'd felt something—sentimentality, nostalgia, whatever. After all, except for Sarah, Harriet was her closest living relative. But the fact was, she'd hardly seen Harriet for thirty years, and there were good reasons for things like that, weren't there? What had she been looking for with Harriet, after all? Two old ladies traveling around the world together, taking cruises, doing needlepoint, gardening, exchanging comforting confidences, sharing a cat. . . .

Well, Harriet had never been like that. Prickly—always

so prickly. At least Harriet was straight and honest and she
was honorable, not mean and envious or bitchy like so many
of the women she knew. She should have been more careful
of Harriet's feelings. She supposed it must have seemed
"typical" to Harriet—Sis picking her up and then dropping
her, sort of. That was how Harriet would look at it.

Still, it was funny Harriet hadn't called. Harriet was the
one who usually called her. She moved restlessly over to the
phone, and tried the number again. Still no answer. Well,
she'd call later, and ask Harriet up for dinner. Try to mend
fences, if she could. That would take care of her evening.
Surely Harriet would be free tonight, and maybe Sis would
have seen Jack by then, and found out something definite to
tell her about Sarah. Well, all right, having Harry in the
wings would prevent any backsliding on her part.

Cecil had put out her new silk suit. Suddenly she changed
her mind and asked for an old favorite, a ten-year-old blue
dress from Chanel. That was one thing about being a widow
—she could wear her old clothes. There would be no more
dresses like this now. This dress was a protection.

Her room was beginning to seem musty and evil to her. It
needed a good airing. She told Cecil that she might do a little
shopping. Strange. She hadn't bought a single thing since
she'd come to Paris this time. Strange. She was looking for
omens in everything, wasn't she? Nothing but flowers. Maybe
she'd look for something for Sarah. That might be the right
thing to do.

Sis knew that one thing she might have been doing, actually
should have been doing, was her Christmas shopping. This
would be her third Christmas without Jim, and it was really
necessary to establish the pattern she would follow. Their
Christmas list had been extremely complicated. It was a
double list, business and personal. (Most of his girlfriends
had been on the business list.)

A year in advance, Sis would order their Christmas cards
from Tiffany, with the message printed: "Best wishes from

Jim and Sis Melmore." "It can be simple, but make damn sure it looks expensive," Jim always said.

Jim's Christmas card list included more than seven thousand people in twenty-eight countries. Most of the names on it meant nothing to Sis. The year Jim died, Miss McMillan took care of the whole thing, somehow. The next year, Sis had ordered three hundred cards from the botanical garden, with an illustration of Christmas roses.

She had never paid great attention to Jim's business list. It was done by rote. It ranged from presidents of corporations and government officials—people whose goodwill Jim wanted without making an obvious effort to buy it—down to the newest, most inexperienced girls in the typing pool. Miss McMillan marked everyone by category. The highest price category was a thousand dollars, the lowest, twenty-five dollars—a crystal bowl from Tiffany, or a book of photographs.

Girlfriends usually got the newest color television set. Mostly, Jim's girls were off the list after one Christmas; but Sis took a faint, malicious pleasure, if they lasted through a second Christmas, in sending them the same color television, with "Best wishes from Jim and Sis Melmore."

The bizarre thing about Jim's Christmas list was that, except for girlfriends, once a person was on Jim's list he never got off it. He could only sink in value. All the people who had fought with Jim, or had left him in bitterness, all his old enemies, were still there on the twenty-five-dollar list. Sis couldn't imagine why Jim kept this up. She didn't want to ask Miss McMillan, who probably wouldn't know either.

Sis had no intention of carrying on this tradition, but she had wondered after that first Christmas if she should keep it up for one more year.

The cases of Dom Perignon, the Georgian silver, the tins of fresh caviar, the coffee-table books had already been ordered. Naturally, she would take care of the people at the office and so forth, but perfect strangers?

Harold and Lee Gottsegen were another matter. Harold Gottsegen had been appointed chairman of the board after Jim's death. Sis loathed Harold Gottsegen. Harold was the last of the men Jim had tried grooming as his heir apparent. Most of these men had been bright and a few had been charming—but Harold Gottsegen! Sis had never understood how Jim had been able to abide Harold even for a moment. His flattery of Jim had been so unctuous it made Sis writhe. His wife, Lee, was another serpent. Lee courted Mrs. Melmore as assiduously as Harold courted Jim.

"I wonder if it wouldn't be a good idea if Lee made some friends her own age," Sis had said at last.

Jim had given her a sharp glance. "I realize the girl can be a perfect pain in the ass, Sis, but she means well. Lee wants to do her best for Harold, and she really admires you. Why don't you take her to a matinée? That wouldn't kill you. What about taking the girl shopping sometime? I've heard her dropping hints about that and she could use a little help."

Sis had sighed. Of course, Jim hadn't understood the dimensions of the problem. Lee called her every morning at nine-forty-five sharp to ask what she was doing that day. Her evasions were always followed by a hurt silence. Then Lee would plead in a little-girl voice, "Couldn't I just tag along?"

As a consequence, Sis felt that she saw more of Lee than she did of her closest friends.

Jim had interrupted her reflections. "Give me a break, Sis. Harold is important to me right now, and at least he's loyal. I tell you, that's something I value more every day."

Sis was convinced Harold Gottsegen was far from loyal. She was sure Harold and Lee were both vipers, but there was never any question of expressing her distrust to Jim. Jim was nobody's fool, and he always knew just what he was doing. He was worn out with all the business about Sarah and wanted peace. Jim thought Harold was "safe." He believed that Harold hadn't the wit or the nerve to intrigue against him. Sis was sure that, when Jim was himself again, he would get rid of Harold as swiftly and as painlessly as he had his predecessors. But the tragedy had intervened and Harold Gottsegen had found himself the unlikely heir to Jim's empire. Now he held forth in Jim's office, smoked Jim's cigars, and lately, at meetings of the board and the foundation, she had noticed to her fury that he was even trying to ape Jim's mannerisms.

Still, at Christmas Harold and Lee must get their presents. This was a duty Sis loathed. While she chose presents for the Gottsegens that were obviously extremely expensive, they were quite unlike anything she gave anyone else. She had decided that she could never hope to gauge their real tastes, so she picked things from the first few pages of the Neiman-Marcus catalogue. This year, for their house in Scarsdale, she had chosen a stainless-steel barbecue trolley, the size of a Cadillac.

The presents which Sis took pleasure in selecting were more rewarding. There were nearly seventy-five families whose presents Sis chose with great care. These included, besides her friends, all the people who worked for her, and those people who had been important to Jim. She never liked giving only a check. She prided herself on being able to choose something perfectly suited to each recipient. If they were friends, it might be something they collected, it might be something she felt they should have wanted, even if they hadn't realized it, or some treat they might have considered too expensive. With the people who worked for them, it might be a trip, or a credit at an appropriate department store, or, if it was a woman, some days of beauty at a health spa.

There were perhaps twenty people whose presents Sis shopped for all year long. She found the time and work involved enjoyable. It might be a particular first edition of a favorite writer, an Hermès saddle for a child who hunted, a Russian icon, or a piece of antique jewelry for a younger woman. She looked forward very much to the pleasure she thought these presents would bring.

This year, Sis had done all her specific shopping. She had begun, as usual, immediately after Christmas (and what a Christmas! without Jim, without Jimmy, without Sarah) and she already had everything in order. But this had never prevented her from making additions to her list, or even preparing for the following year. She had a room in the country which was devoted solely to presents, and cards, and wrapping paper.

But something had happened to her will. She simply couldn't make herself buy anything. She felt in a sort of limbo here, waiting, waiting. It was as if no action were possible till things with Sarah were resolved.

It was a little past two-thirty when she returned. Most shops were closed. All she had seen was the sort of junk even the tourists wouldn't touch. She took her key and went up to her room. When she opened the door, she collided with Cecil.

"Oh, madam, you startled me, madam. I was tidying up your things when Mr. Straw called. He said please to apologize to you, madam, but he won't be able to keep his appointment this afternoon. It's his new show, you know, madam. He said he'd call you tomorrow. In the morning."

"What's his number?"

"You don't have his number, madam? I'm sorry. He said Miss Sarah says hello. I'm sure Miss Sarah would have it."

Oh, for Christ's sake! Cecil was becoming a malevolent presence in her life, like one of those ominous, troublemaking nurses out of Sophocles.

"Thank you, Cecil. I'm sure she would."

If Cecil gave her a strange look, then, that was it! But she didn't. She looked demure.

"I think I'll rest a bit, Cecil. I'm sure you've done quite enough in here."

"Your nightgown, madam?"

"No, please don't bother."

She stood in the doorway until Cecil made her exit. Then she went into her bedroom and called Anna. Anna would know Jack's address, although she felt terribly awkward asking her for it.

No answer. Of course it was the wrong time; she'd have to wait until ten. Oh, but she had the other number from the other day! A man's voice answered. "*Ja?*"

"May I speak to Anna?"

"Anna? No Anna here." The man hung up.

God—that left seven hours—and then twelve hours, and then. Mrs. Melmore called Harriet again. The phone rang and rang. Maybe there was some weird problem with the switchboard; she simply couldn't believe Harriet was still out. She called the desk and explained her problem. In a few minutes, a young man called her back to tell her that the number she had requested was out of order. It had been reported to the Post Office.

"Drat," as Harriet would say. Harriet should have called her. She must have known Sis couldn't get through. Harriet was usually so responsible. She wondered how long telephone repairs took in Paris. And with the weekend coming up? She'd probably have to get Williams to drive her over to Harriet's in the morning, but she just wasn't up to it now. And, what's more, she had nothing to tell.

Mrs. Melmore had dinner in her room. She didn't want to read. She played patience. Time passed so slowly. She hadn't even been able to reach Northrop at the bank. It was a long weekend. He was away, and she didn't want to talk to anyone else.

At ten she called Anna. Usually she used one of those gadgets to dial, but now she did it, without thinking, with her long nails. Naturally the polish on her index finger chipped. She waited. Four rings. Eight. Twelve. There was no answer! Maybe she had dialed the wrong number. She tried again. The phone rang and rang. Once more. No, there was really no answer. But Anna had promised! Had they just bolted? Oh, hell! She should have called Anna this morning. Maybe she'd really scared Anna yesterday. A long weekend. Nothing official would be working full force either. Oh, blazes!

Well, she was in a pit of her own digging, wasn't she? She had to get through the night, and trust that tomorrow Jack would call as he had promised.

She went and sat where she always did now, looking out across the Seine toward the Left Bank.

"Way over there—the lights." She shook her head.

Jack. She had been thinking of Jack as a replacement for Jim, really. She got up and made all her preparations for bed.

Of course she had been carried away by that blaze of glamour—the youth, romance, and that marvelous sex, the wonder that all this should suddenly, so unexpectedly, be hers. Glory, yes. But somewhere, in the back of her mind, she realized that she had been looking for someone who would take responsibility for the direction of her life, who would give it meaning. That is to say, someone like Jim. Someone who could use the concentration on detail, the obsession with perfection she tried to bring to every aspect of her life, who would appreciate it, and use it to build on. But only Jim had held those standards, for Jim her best was often not quite good enough. Instead of letting her rest, Jim made her work harder. Mama? God knows Mama was hard to please, but Mama was capricious; she was always changing the rules. Jim was a cruel taskmaster, but a wonderful audience. If she managed to please him, that made it all worthwhile.

There was no one else worth pleasing in that way. She ran over some names in her mind, and almost laughed out loud. Most of those men wouldn't notice the difference, and she would become indifferent herself, indifferent and, maybe, contemptuous.

So here she was with this beautiful empty shell, and what was she going to do with it? Her body, well, the truth was it was still a beautiful body; it would last a long time. Her houses were beautiful houses, though she must make some decisions about them now. She didn't really like Florida, and the fishing camp had always been Jim's—she only went there to redecorate. Put them both on the market. Even the apartment in town—what did she need a huge apartment for? Even if Sarah . . . Really, she spent all her time at the farm. In her garden. Yes, there was her garden.

Her garden. Could a garden give meaning to a life? Could that really be a sufficient occupation and preoccupation for a woman? Was that too ridiculous? She thought about her garden, shutting out all the obtrusive things that cluttered up her mind.

Sis thought about her path through the garden, her special path, the one she always followed. It had enormous significance to her. She had always known that she must walk down that particular path in that particular way. It was no more than three feet wide, but, as long as she kept to it, everything would stay in its proper place, and the wild things did not come out of the woods. It was all hers, her pattern. Beyond the path—well, she was not supposed to look far beyond that path. The woods, the world, were full of strange and horrifying things over which she had no control. . . .

She paused. But what folly! The wild things—the wild things had gone. They had vanished soundlessly, without a trace. She was safe, all too safe. The woods were quiet, decorous, empty. She was alone, all alone.

Begin again. Her garden. She imagined herself standing in the woods near the stream, with the confederate violets blooming and the scent of lily of the valley in the air.

Almost at once, she felt very happy. Her garden. Her garden was infinitely absorbing. And she might get another horse. A tired hunter, or an old polo pony. Not a horse to grip her heart, just one to hack around the place. She'd like that.

She began to think of making a path from the east side of

the house through the oak grove; not really steps, but Belgian blocks. It would be a moss garden, like the ones she had seen in Japan. She wondered if she could engage MacKenzie's interest in an idea so subtle and foreign to his training. Then she wondered how difficult it would be, in the dry, sandy soil of Long Island, with those annual extremes of heat and cold.

She stopped herself. There she was, thinking about her garden again. But, the truth was, she was always thinking about her garden. There was nothing else she needed to think of, now. Nothing except her garden and Sarah. Sarah was the other thing which gave meaning to her life, her intense and troubled love for Sarah, and her responsibility toward her.

She decided suddenly that no matter how things turned out, she could never stay on in Paris. She would stay as long as she was needed, but she could not really live away from her country, the farm, her garden. Over here she would feel uprooted, and somehow foolish. An aimless urban creature. No, in the end she would have to go back to her land, with or without Sarah. She sighed. "In God's truth, madam, you should come home."

She walked over and picked up one of the small volumes of letters she'd brought. Letters were what she liked to read now—Madame de Sévigné, Horace Walpole. Those times, probably the epitome of graceful civilization. The letters told one how sympathetic, witty people had gotten through their daily lives, often externally quite undramatic, dealing with daily events in a sane and sensible fashion. But with feeling. Feelings she understood.

She opened to the letter Madame de Sévigné's daughter had written on her mother's arrival: *"Oui, nous sommes ensemble, nous aimant, nous embrassant de tout notre coeur; moi, ravie de voir ma mère venir courageusement me chercher du bout de l'univers, et du couchant à l'aurore; il n'y a qu'elle au monde capable d'exécuter de pareilles entreprises. . . ."*

She lingered over the paragraph, musing, then closed the

book. She mustn't allow herself to lapse into daydreams and self-pity. She had the rest of her life to get through, and make a good job of it. She couldn't abide weak people.

"Okay, Sis," she said to herself. "No regrets."

No regrets? Well, that was silly. But no regrets anyone ever need know about.

Part Eleven

BEFORE DAYLIGHT

1

Miss Harriet Milbanke at Home

Miss Harriet Milbanke sat over her solitary tea. It was high tea, really—a soft-boiled egg, Westphalian ham, brioche, Tiptree marmalade; she still liked that the best. Tea was a civilized meal, she thought. The most civilized. She always enjoyed it. And today she was feeling a certain self-satisfaction.

Miss Harriet Milbanke wasn't a total fool. The world might have passed her by, the world might have changed more than she had, but human nature, human motives, hadn't changed much.

People always wanted the same things, didn't they? Money and power, that's what they wanted. Love. Ha! From time to time they had that delusion. She had always doubted that Helen's beauty had kindled the Trojan War.

No, people were motivated by money and power, the desire to get it or the desire to hold it. Money in all its forms—dead metal and dead men's goods and dead men's lands.

Power—if you were smart, you got the power, and then you could get the money. If you were smart and had the money, you could get all the power you wanted. Money and power. First getting it, then guarding it. And all the little dogs in town, barking at your heels. Avarice and envy, ambition and fear.

There was no doubt Sis had too much money for her own good. Much too much. It made a person abnormal. Especially a person who didn't have discipline. Sis didn't seem to have much of that, except about her diet. Religion? She supposed Sis had had to give that up when she got married. Anyway, there Sis was, like a child playing with the controls of a powerful machine. Just pulling the switches, not realizing that the machine had a life of its own, that it could hurt people, that it could endanger people she didn't even know. Sis didn't seem interested in power, beyond the power to get a good table at a restaurant.

Money without responsibility. Funny. None of her sisters had seemed to have any sense of responsibility; none of them. Why, they'd never done a useful thing in their lives! The Junior League? My foot! Just tried to amuse themselves. They'd pick something up, a person, a man, for instance—and the minute they got a little bored, they'd drop it (or him) and go on to something else. No sense of responsibility. How could that be? Grandpa had certainly done his best to drum it into their heads. One's direct responsibility to the people and the community around one. She felt it sometimes like a terrible burden, weighing her down. What about the other girls? What had gone wrong? Was it Mama's fault? Mama was so obsessed with the chastity of the beauties. Maybe too obsessed.

"Who in the world would marry Cottie now?" she would say, again and again, shaking her head. "Why would they need to?"

Well, a lot of people had wanted to marry Cottie, it seemed. Four, before she drank herself to death. More than

any of the daughters. Four husbands! Much good it did her—
or them!

"My goodness," thought Harriet. "I'm glad I never married." She thought of the sordid stories Sis had told her.
And Sis had been the best of the lot by a long shot. Sis had
had something.

She had been a fine girl—frank, high-spirited, kind, and
loving. Was it the man or the money? Sis had certainly
changed. She was her blood, yes, but she hardly knew her.
She had listened to Sis attentively. She had tried to be fair.
She had tried her very hardest to understand how things
might look from Sis's point of view. But finally she could
reach only one conclusion: Sis had never been looking for
what was right. Never. Only for what was expedient. She
didn't seem to worry about what happened to the people
along the way. The other people in her stories—they could
have been sacks of manure; she didn't know they were alive.
Sis didn't look left or right, just waited for the strong wind
that would blow her first one way, then another. Things "just
happened" to Sis. She didn't try to control them. She didn't
try to do the right thing. Why, it never occurred to her!

Oh, she believed Sis loved her family. Sis was affectionate
and emotional and sentimental. But love? Could there be
real love without judgment, without standards? What kind
of love? Sis had a passionate desire to please, to do things in
a pretty way, to create harmony out of chaos. If she was in
the middle of an evil situation—what did she do? All she
wanted was to tidy it up, so it would look pretty from the
outside. Nothing Sis said had suggested to Harriet that she
had any conception of the awful things that had been happening around her. Or worse, that she had learned anything
at all from them. It was the insulation created by all that
money. Money without conscience, without a feeling of
responsibility.

Maybe they had the right idea in the Middle Ages. A
woman as rich as Sis had to go into a convent after her hus-

band died. Sis would actually love a convent—a Catholic convent, naturally. She would look so beautiful in that robe and cowl. She wouldn't mind obeying the rules. If she believed she was fulfilling God's commandments, she would obey with tears and ecstasy.

How everyone would adore her! All the young nuns would have crushes on her. And she wouldn't have this burden (Harriet felt it was a burden) of deciding what she would do with the rest of her life.

She would be a legend. Heaven knows, Sis was extraordinary. Sis would probably turn out to be a Catholic saint. Miraculous roses blooming in her room, beautifully arranged and so on. My goodness, what rot! What had brought this on, anyway?

Mother Maria Magdalena, of course. Mother Maria Magdalena had been Harriet's best friend when she was young. Jacqueline Griswold. She made everyone call her Jack. A tomboy, a feminist. And then—it had happened slowly. After the war, she had taken a teaching job in France, and become more and more involved in working with orphans, then the church, and finally she had broken it to Harriet in a letter. She was becoming a nun. A nun! Jack? Harriet had been dumbfounded. Then, when Harriet was allowed to visit her, in the convent at Neuilly, she saw that that round red face, almost as familiar to her as her own, was full of something— well, radiance, really. She wasn't boisterous and she was calm. She was busy—busy and peaceful. She had a calling. And now she was a mother superior.

After Mama had died, Harriet had sold the house in Charlottesville. It was much too big and cumbersome for her, and more than she could afford. But there was Cousin Emma's apartment in Paris. Cousin Emma had left that to Mama. It was all done fair and square and legal back in the dark ages. And a Belgian family had a five-year lease on it, which was up the first of the year. The coincidence seemed a happy one. Harriet really didn't know where she wanted to live. She was American through and through—and not just American: a southerner, and proud of it. Still, somehow she didn't feel like looking for an apartment in Charlottesville. Not just yet.

Ever since Harriet had gone to Paris to stay with Cousin Emma, she had wanted to try living there, and Mama had always thwarted her. Mama had said, "Wait till Papa retires, we'll all go," and then every year something else had come up, and then Papa had died, and later Mama had said, "Maybe next year," and then it had been too late. She'd really been cheated.

Harriet thought of Papa's deathbed. That was just the cruelest moment of her life. Not Papa dying, which he had done beautifully, of course, like a hero in a Victorian novel: lying on that white bed, with his beautiful white face on the white linen pillow, his perfectly cut white beard, his white nightshirt. All the servants crying.

He had taken her hand and said, "Harry, my darling. You know I always hoped you'd go on with your studies. You've such a fine mind, Harriet. I always hoped you'd go on with your studies and be a teacher. That you'd write some fine books one day. I want you to make use of your gifts, my darling."

To her dismay, what Harriet had felt was fury. If only he'd said a word to her before! He'd never encouraged her, never spoken up for her, never taken her side. No, Papa had adored his beautiful, popular, high-spirited daughters. Their horsemanship, that's what he admired—he didn't give a hang for her brains. He didn't care that she had been turned into a drudge.

She sat there beside him. She knew that her face was bright red with anger and guilt.

Papa had always known she wanted to get away. He wasn't just vague and absent-minded—he'd known. And he'd nailed her into that house with Mama—cut off from the whole world, cut off from a life that counted. Oh, she had her books, and her library job, and her museum trips. But looking after Mama, that had been her real job. And Sis had been around long enough to know just what a job that was.

What really made Harriet boil was that, nowadays no one seemed to have the least understanding of her predicament. She'd been doing her duty, and her life hadn't been such a pleasant one. Mostly, it had been hard and bitter. And now here came Sis. With her "Oh, Harry, why didn't you do this? Why didn't you do that?" Sis, of all people!

And young people! It was like explaining something back in the tenth century to them. First a little curiosity, then a lot of contempt, that's what people felt about her devoting her life to Mama. That was what happened when, all of a sudden, they changed all the rules, when she was almost too old to do anything about it.

Of course, she didn't really regret it, giving up her life to Mama. Mama was Mama. It was her duty, and how could she have had any self-respect if she hadn't done the right thing? Even though no one else seemed to understand and respect her for it. But she did see now that maybe, probably, she could have had more than that life. She could have had a formal education and a career and taken care of Mama too. That was the bad thought. Papa had taught her Latin and Greek and physics, but there had been no one to show her how to leave home.

Yes, Harriet felt she had been cheated. After Mama's death, she had decided quite suddenly and firmly to spend a year living in Paris. Just see what happened. She hadn't been altogether displeased when her neighbors shook their heads and said, "Harriet Milbanke, you've always been a dark horse."

She had to admit in the back of her mind had been the thought of Mother Maria Magdalena. Harriet had hoped— almost . . . But it was not to be. Harriet was brusque, she was impatient, she lost her temper all the time, and she didn't like anyone bossing her around. She lacked the vocation to be a nun and the skill to get the sort of job she wanted. Still she tried. She gave her services: she worked at the hospital three days a week, she taught Protestant orphans English. She gave her tithe to the church even though she loathed the new minister who had come when the Reverend March retired. All the changes in the service. Those beautiful words! Made into new-speak! The interruptions, when he would tell everyone to shake hands with total strangers. Piffle.

Still she did her best. When she became discouraged, she trudged around the city.

Beauty might not be useful—but, heavens, this city was beautiful. She saw the museums, the shows, went to the concerts.

But it was curious—after a year, she decided to stay on, for a while anyway. She'd made friends. She enjoyed her life. She liked the children she was teaching.

Then she'd gotten to know Bill Sparrow. And out of the blue he'd talked her into this book.

Bill Sparrow was bossy, too, but they got along. Sis was right, Harriet didn't care that much about flowers. But she enjoyed the work. She read Greek and Latin, and she had always loved the myths. And Bill admired her mind. He relied on her, too. That awful family of his could make him almost hysterical. Bill teased her a lot. He made her feel young. Well, that was when she sent for her things. Expensive, maybe, but so was storage.

But maybe she'd been over here too long now; she was beginning to feel that. She was an American. She didn't really belong here. She belonged back home.

All this trouble about her apartment. They wanted a lot more money. It was getting unpleasant. Well, she'd have to decide where she wanted to live out the rest of her life. Certainly not the convent—it was Sis who would love the convent. Then she wouldn't have to run that huge machine. And she might find peace, and all the goodness and sweetness she had once had. It was still there, Harriet was sure. It was all that money that was making her so blind and feckless.

It was understandable, that was the thing. Hadn't she

felt it, the power of money? When Sis came into her life? It was almost palpable—like a strange scented breeze, wafting around her, confusing her, promising excitements, delights, strange and unknown dramas. And Harriet had been seduced right away, hadn't she? Like the soppiest schoolgirl. And when would she have come to her senses, if Sis hadn't gotten a little bored with her? Harriet shook her head.

Money—it had a life of its own, rules of its own. All the time you thought you possessed it, but it possessed you. All the time it was growing stronger, while you were growing weaker. Some people thought money made you free. No sir. Big money limited your vision and ensured that you would never be told the truth, and in the end it devoured you, before it found another host.

Well, she mustn't criticize Sis too much. "Let him who is without sin . . ." But little Sarah. It seemed as if she had tried to run away from all that money. Sis had made her sound crazy, but not corrupt. Did Sis really understand Sarah? It was certainly hard to get a clear picture of what Sarah was like. Sis's big gray eyes just didn't see much.

The way Sis was "looking for" Sarah, for instance. Staying at the Crillon with her maid and chauffeur, for goodness' sake!

And then, when she was here, what did she do? Why she treated the whole thing like a girls' adventure story—with herself as the heroine, of course. But, even in girls' adventure stories, the heroines won out because of their guts and tenacity. High-spirited, yes, but they were always tenacious. She had the strongest feeling that Sis was counting on her charm. Sis thought her charm could melt people's hearts and open their treasure chests. Well, Harriet knew charm wasn't what made the world go round. It just made people like to have you at parties. Charm without purpose was one of those pretty wasteful things Sis liked.

There were two ways to do things, two ways that worked. The best was to try to live by the cardinal virtues, and respect the work ethic—especially tenacity. That way one could almost always get what one wanted, even without much money, and at the very worst, one kept one's self-respect.

The other way to get things done, she had to admit, was with money. Money, if one was smart, could buy most things. It could make things happen fast—not necessarily for the best, but fast. Yet Harriet was absolutely sure Sis was counting on her charm, not her money, to win Sarah back. A mistake, she felt. Maybe Sarah didn't even belong back with her mother. How could she tell, unless she knew the alternatives?

Sis hadn't fooled Harriet for a minute. She knew from that night she'd taken Sis to dinner that she'd gotten in touch with Advent. Obviously those people wanted something in return for Sarah. And just as obviously it wasn't money. That would have been easy; it would all be over by now. So it must be something difficult. Something against the law. Sis didn't seem to have many scruples, so it was hard to guess how far she'd go. Of course, there was a possibility Sis might be bluffing them, playing some game of her own. Harriet didn't believe that, and she certainly didn't have much confidence in her sister's skill at that kind of combat.

But how could they use Sis, except for her money? That was a puzzle. She couldn't see Sis on the barricades, or planting a bomb in the Chamber of Deputies. As some sort of Mata Hari? Well, it was no use guessing. And since Sis hadn't told her anything, there were no promises to break.

Mama had loved the classics, but when she was really sick, she liked Harriet to read her detective stories. There were only certain detective-story writers Mama had liked. Dorothy Sayers, in particular. Others, that Harriet enjoyed, Mama found "vulgar." Well, Harriet thought, she certainly wouldn't want to be sitting here explaining her predicament to Lord Peter Wimsey, with his monocle and his affected slang. She had secretly found him an awful drip.·

Miss Harriet Milbanke had never aspired to being a de-

tective. And, after all, she had to give Sis a period of grace.
(Sarah might appear. It might still be a fuss about nothing.)
But, after what she considered a reasonable delay, she sent a
pneumatique to Advent, care of Persson at 10 rue Minou.
The message was short. She stated that she was Sarah Melmore's aunt. She had some very important information to
impart. She gave her address and telephone number and
added that the matter was extremely confidential.

The days passed, then a week, two weeks, three, and unlike a detective story, nothing happened. Sis seemed fidgety,
but kept assuring her that Sarah would be back soon. But,
after a while, she began to sense Sis's nerves were fraying.
Things were not going well.

Harriet decided to go back to rue Minou. The slot which
had said "Persson" was blank now, but she rang the bell
again and again. There was no response. Then, out of frus-
tration, she rang the bell marked Charcot. It buzzed back.
Again Madame Charcot was at the door, but a different
Madame Charcot, with *maquillage,* a nice dress and smart
shoes. She was charmed to see her visitor.

"Madame," she said, "if I had only known your name, I
would have written to thank you for your help."

"Yes?"

"Madame, you have all my gratitude. I can be peaceful
again."

"Oh, yes?"

"Everything is solved, madame. They are gone."

"What? The whole bunch?"

"Yes, yes, madame. All of them. Several days ago. Now I
will cease to have those nightmares that I could not control.
I thank you, madame."

Oh, blast!

Harriet Milbanke thought things over. Then she sent a
wire to Sarah Melmore, c/o Advent, using the bank's address. She repeated her former message and added: "Most
urgent to your interests." That night, there were no calls.

Nor the next day. No calls at all. Four days passed. Then in the middle of the afternoon the phone rang. It was a girl's voice, with a slight accent.

"Madame Milbanke?"

"I am Miss Milbanke."

"You are Miss Milbanke who wishes information concerning a certain relative?"

"Yes, my niece. To whom am I speaking?"

"My name is Rosa. But wait, Miss Milbanke, if you please. There is someone else here you would do better to speak to."

Harriet had no idea what rubbish she could invent for these people. At least she could try to frighten them a little.

Another voice came on the phone. "Miss Milbanke, this is Anna. You are the sister of Madame Melmore?"

"Yes. I'm her older sister."

"I am Anna."

"Yes."

"Does my name signify nothing to you, Miss Milbanke?"

"Anna? What do you mean?"

"Your sister has not told you of our conversations?"

"No, she hasn't."

"I see. So you are not in her confidence?"

"Apparently not to that degree."

Anna hesitated. "Then, Miss Milbanke, how much influence can you have with your sister?"

"That depends," said Miss Milbanke. Little or none, she thought.

"Why did you get in touch with us? What is it that is urgent for you to say?"

"I think my sister is in a dangerous situation."

Again there was a silence. Then Anna said, "Miss Milbanke, we think so too. We think your sister is acting very foolishly and it is very dangerous. There is more at stake than she seems to understand. We too wish to find Sarah and restore her to her mother. But your sister is making it most hazardous for us."

Harriet was enormously surprised. Sarah wasn't with these people at Advent? Then where on earth was she?

"Miss Milbanke, I think it is only fair that you tell us what role you play in this situation?"

Harriet hesitated. "Naturally I want to help my niece in any way that I can. Her safety comes first."

"Miss Milbanke," said Anna, "forgive me. I assure you I believe in your good intentions, but we do not see, at this point, any way in which you can be of help to us. We might be able to give you some information which you do not have, but a bargain must work two ways, no? It would help us if you could control your sister, and assure us that she would not indulge herself in these imprudent dramas. But it seems you could give us no such assurance, Miss Milbanke, isn't that so?"

"Well, I consider myself a strong-minded, sensible woman, and I certainly have more influence over my sister than you have."

Anna was silent a minute, then she said, "Miss Milbanke, I need to discuss this matter with my friends."

She must have put the phone down. Harriet could hear the sound of voices murmuring in the background. When Anna returned to the phone she said, "Miss Milbanke, I have talked to my friends. Would you object if I were to ask you some personal questions?"

"Let's hear what they are."

"How old are you?"

"Sixty-four."

"What are your views on marriage?"

"At the moment, negative."

"Have you ever been employed?"

"As a librarian and cataloguer of books."

"Do you believe in the virtue of work?"

"I certainly do."

"And now—you work as a librarian, here in Paris?"

"No. I'm working on a book on an aspect of botany. I'm also involved with various social services."

"What are your political persuasions?"

"Very old-fashioned. Jeffersonian democrat."

"Religious affiliation?"

"Episcopalian."

"Do you have an inherited income, Miss Milbanke?"

"I have a small legacy from my mother."

"Have you a savings account?"

"Yes."

"What are your commitments over the next few days?"

"I have nothing pressing," said Harriet.

There was a long silence. Finally Anna said, "We have no choice. Things have gotten very bad. We can no longer trust your sister."

Harriet said nothing.

"You sound like an honest woman. You will find we are honest and frank too. We would like to meet with you. We have things to discuss. Ordinarily we would ask you to come to us here, but times are unusual, and I don't like that as it is. A café—that's out of the question. Is it possible that we can come this evening and talk to you at the place where you live? I have the address here." She read it off.

"Yes, that's right. Certainly," said Harriet immediately. "I'll give you something to eat and drink if you like. How many people are we talking about?"

Anna hesitated again. "Fifteen. And we are all used to sitting on the floor," she said finally. "But please, Miss Milbanke, I beg you not to trouble yourself about our needs. It's not necessary. We will bring something to drink with us. We do not use alcohol. And we will bring refreshments. We make our bread—much of our own food, too. I think you would find it nourishing."

"Good heavens, no," said Harriet. "I wasn't thinking about that. I just wanted to have enough."

"Please. That's quite unnecessary. Seven-thirty. Would that time suit you? Generally we keep early hours."

"Seven-thirty would be fine."

"Miss Milbanke, I must ask you—that you do not mention this meeting to anyone, particularly your sister. Will you give me your word on that?"

"You can trust me that far," said Miss Milbanke.

It seemed they had been dealing with Sis for quite a while, and they hadn't hurt her. And the girl on the phone had a pleasant voice.

But, good heavens, what on earth was Sis up to? Maybe Harriet would be the one to find Sarah after all. She felt quite excited—not at all frightened, but interested. How many worlds there seemed to be of which she knew nothing.

Well, she deserved her tea. She didn't know how late these young people would be staying. Then, disobeying orders, she went to the nice charcuterie near her and made a number of purchases. When she returned, she told the concierge that she was expecting a group of students at 19:30 that evening. The woman had a wall eye—always difficult. And she was just as unpleasant as she looked. "Even more difficult," thought Harriet.

"Students." She gave a loud snuffle. "Not too much noise, please, miss."

Harriet went upstairs and straightened up a bit. She wasn't going to change, just run a comb through her hair. Why pretend to be something she wasn't? She poured herself a brandy, sat down with a book, and waited.

2

Miss Milbanke Receives

THEY WERE VERY PROMPT. Exactly seven-thirty. Harriet Milbanke felt extremely curious to look at these people. Advent. Who or what was Advent?

They filed in, introducing themselves as they came. Marco. Anna. Renée. Rudy. Nadja. Rosa. Marie Christine . . . fourteen of them she counted. Four boys and ten girls. After a point, she couldn't remember their names. She was amazed by the way they looked. How extraordinarily good-looking they all were! How washed and polished and shining! She was aware of her wrinkled dress, and her shoes, run down at the heels. She had been expecting some sort of hippies. She could have powdered her nose. Well, it wasn't a fashion show. But, my goodness, she hadn't seen such nice-looking young people since she had gone to watch one of Papa's classes at the university when she was a little girl. The students had all looked like Greek gods to her then, she remembered.

"Please sit down," said Harriet. "I'm afraid some of you will have to sit on the floor. I do have some glasses, and things to eat in the other room." Each of them had brought an offering, glass jars full of colored liquid, fruit and vegetable juices, they said. Bread, cheese, and fruit. Two of the girls went and put the food on the table in the other room.

"We have come to talk," said a thin blond boy. "I think maybe we will talk first. There may be much to say. But, if there is not, we must not waste your time."

"Miss Milbanke, would you like to try a glass of our carrot juice? Most people are very pleased by it," said the blond girl, Anna. Anna was the girl on the phone. On the phone she had sounded domineering. Now she seemed almost deferential.

"No, thank you very much," said Harriet. "I'm sure it's good, but I do like alcohol. In fact I'm drinking it now. But please sit down, wherever you can, and help yourselves as you like."

A dark boy with hazel eyes was looking at her books. "You have some very interesting books here, Miss Milbanke. I like your apartment very much. It reminds me of the apartment of my great-grandmother." He paused. "I hope that does not offend you. I was very, very fond of my great-grandmother. This piano—you play yourself?"

"Yes, but not very well."

He ran his fingers over the keys, silently.

"Marco," said Anna, "Sit down, we do not have all that much time." Her voice was sharp again. She turned to the thin blond boy. "Per," she said, "Do you think—"

"Anna, perhaps it is easier if you tell Miss Milbanke very briefly what is necessary," said Per.

"We are assuming, Miss Milbanke," said Anna, "that you know very little about recent events. You know your niece has disappeared. You know she was last seen with us? This was the situation when your sister proceeded on her own? Is that correct?"

"More or less."

"Very well, then," said Anna. "Miss Milbanke, we are a group of friends with similar philosophical convictions. It is not necessary to review those convictions, I think, only to say that we are very sincere, and our beliefs are not destructive to any person in any way."

Harriet looked around at their faces. They looked like a troop of angels to her, but probably they were Communists. All young people seemed to be nowadays.

"If what you say is true, and if you have Sarah's interests at heart, I agree that philosophy is quite irrelevant," she said.

"Very good. Sarah and her friend Wanda were very inter-

ested in our ideas and came often to visit us. Madame Melmore mentioned Wanda to you?"

"She spoke about a girl. I'm not sure of her name," said
Harriet.

"Undoubtedly, it was Wanda—Sarah and Wanda lived
together. In some ways, it would have been difficult for
Sarah to live alone, as you probably realize, Miss Milbanke.
The day after Sarah's disappearance, Wanda vanished. No
one has heard from her since then. We have told all this to
your sister, Miss Milbanke. We decided Wanda and Sarah
must have gone away together—taken a trip. It seemed logical. Wanda was very possessive of Sarah, and she was frightened by Madame Melmore's visit. But Wanda was also very
involved with our group. She used to call us every day. The
days passed and Wanda didn't call. I didn't disguise from
your sister that this was very strange. Perhaps I did not stress
sufficiently how strange it was. You see it was very difficult,
Miss Milbanke. Your sister was continually threatening to
turn the matter over to the police."

"Well, why not? If you have nothing to hide?"

They looked at each other. "It would have put us all in a
very bad position," said a dark-haired girl with a red barrette.
"The police do not like people with strong political convictions."

"Unless they represent powerful economic interests," interrupted another boy.

Harriet looked at the boy who had spoken. He was frowning. He didn't resemble an angel now that she studied him.
Those arms and shoulders! He must be fearfully strong.

"Rudy, it's only necessary to tell the parts which relate
to Sarah," said the blond boy. "Please, let us stick to the
point."

"But, Per, it's important," said Anna. "It's important for
Miss Milbanke to understand. Once the police were involved
—they would detain us all, perhaps. But it would do you no
good. And as for Sarah—for Sarah, it might be a matter of
life and death."

"Life and death? What on earth do you mean?"

"Are you willing to help us? If we were guilty of anything, we would have left Paris, don't you see? It's not
logical that we would remain. You cannot imagine how very
unsafe it is for us here."

"Look, I'm prepared to help you if I can. But I'm puzzled. My sister certainly has the strongest motive of all. She
would do anything to protect Sarah. Why are you here?"

"Your sister," said Anna, "has only the most tenuous grasp
of the reality of the situation. We have concluded that she is
dealing with persons we know to be very dangerous. We can
no longer trust her. She is jeopardizing all of us."

"I see." Miss Milbanke thought this over.

It didn't sound impossible with Sis. Actually she had been
thinking along the same lines herself, hadn't she? They were
talking about great danger. If there was real trouble, naturally she would do what she could to help, and at least she
had common sense.

"Well," she said, "you young men and women belong to
a philosophical organization you don't want to discuss. That's
fine and dandy, as long as you're here to help Sarah, and
you're not contemplating breaking the law in any way. If
that's the case—well, let us continue."

The children were sitting all around, six on chairs, eight
on the floor. There was room on the sofa and the chairs in
the kitchen, so they must like sitting on the floor. As she
spoke, they all turned and looked at each other. Anna to
Per to the others. It was as if they were throwing a ball
slowly from one to the next. All the way around, and back
to Per.

"We have some grave and alarming things to tell you,"
said Per. "We are being forced to do things for pragmatic
reasons which are not in accordance with our ideals. At the
same time we are asking our friends, not our ideological
sympathizers, but our friends, to put themselves at risk."

"If we tell you our story," said Anna, "it's not good enough to shake hands and trust. We must deal with you as you deal in the world of business.

"We feel that we alone have the knowledge and ability to return Sarah to her mother. It is that grave. So tell me, Miss Milbanke, what is the price of this thing I am telling you?"

"My sister loves her daughter very much," Harriet said. "I'm sure she would deal with you very generously. But I'm not her agent. And I must admit it sounds as if you're being a bit melodramatic."

"When you hear our story, you will perhaps not think so. But we must decide now. Otherwise, it is a waste of time, both for you and for us. And the price we are asking, it will be you, not your sister, who will pay."

"Me? I don't understand. I'm not a rich woman. What is this price?"

"One price that you would pay is that you must remain under our supervision. That would last scarcely more than twenty-four hours, but it's necessary. But, once you have committed yourself to us, Miss Milbanke, there can be no turning back."

Harriet Milbanke scowled. "Why do you want to tell me anything at all, then?"

"You will see, Miss Milbanke."

"Humph. And the purpose of this plan is to help Sarah?"

"Yes," said Per. "If it were not for Sarah, then we would not have to take these steps. It is contrary to our policies and beliefs."

Miss Milbanke hesitated. Really, she had no choice, and if she didn't like what she heard, there would always be a way. She didn't believe all that much in scout's honor.

"Very well, then," Miss Milbanke said. "I suppose I brought this on myself. Go ahead."

Per nodded. And again there was the slow glance around the room. But the atmosphere had changed. These children were relaxing now.

Per stood up. "I'm honored that you trust us, Miss Milbanke. Forgive me for being so impolite, but two of our friends—they speak so little English we must explain to them fully. Since it is a matter of the greatest importance to each of us, we, all of us, must understand and agree."

"Oh, certainly," said Harriet Milbanke.

There were two girls sitting on the floor at the back of the room. Per and Rudy went and sat beside them, talking to them very intensely. One girl had a long copper-colored braid. The other was dark with high cheekbones and slanted eyes. Miss Milbanke could only hear them murmuring, but she was quite sure it was a language she had never heard before. Could it be Finnish? Basque?

Anna said in a different tone, "Perhaps it's time to have something to eat and drink now."

Two girls went into the other room and returned with trays. How did they manage it all so quickly and neatly? And they made everything look so attractive. "Fruit juice, Miss Milbanke? Vegetable juice? Try our cheese. It is good."

Miss Milbanke actually tasted some carrot juice. It wasn't bad. But where were the pâtés, the prosciutto, the salami, the sliced beef, the chicken in aspic she had bought?

The girl with the braid was whispering to Rudy, who said, "May Tani use your bathroom, Miss Milbanke?"

"Of course. Shall I show her? It's off my bedroom—that way." She hadn't noticed that the girl had brought a guitar with her. When she left the room, it was lying there—the size of a child.

Marco, who had been sitting closest to Harriet's feet, addressed her.

"Do you know, Miss Milbanke, that my great-grandmother actually heard Liszt play the piano? It was in Lubeck when she was a little girl. She is dead now, of course. Still, doesn't that seem incredible?"

"Marco," said Anna, "would you help Rosa with the plates?"

The conference was over. Per came back and sat beside Miss Milbanke. The young people were all very polite and thoughtful. Some of them took away the plates. Harriet could hear someone washing the dishes.

"They needed to eat," said Per. "We've been through a time of stress. Normally we go to bed early."

"All right. I'd better hear your story. I'm not hungry myself, but I think I'll get a real drink first. You lead me to believe I may need it."

"Can I help you?" asked Per.

"No, thanks." She poured herself a brandy, then returned to her chair.

"Go ahead," she said.

3

Miss Milbanke Rides the Tiger

ANNA BEGAN. "Miss Milbanke, all these things we have told your sister, until very recently. But now there are things we must tell you that she does not know. We prefer dealing with you. We have spoken among ourselves about your character. We trust you. We like you, Miss Milbanke."

She smiled at Miss Milbanke. She was a very pretty girl, she had a pretty smile and pretty teeth, but somehow, Harriet Milbanke did not care for Anna. She preferred Marco. She was sorry everyone seemed to squelch him so. And there were two French girls, who were sitting together. They were not as pretty as Anna, but they looked very spirited. Even that huge brute Rudy seemed more sincere.

"Miss Milbanke," said Anna, "we said that we would not discuss our philosophy, but I would like to make sure you understand that we are people of rectitude and integrity. We believe in democratic and unanimous action. We look to Per for guidance in matters of principle."

Harriet glanced at Per. With his pale coloring and long, thin limbs, he reminded her of a stork. He seemed polite, but she didn't think he looked very intelligent.

"We made an error in regard to your niece," said Anna. "We neglected to consult Per on a most important matter, and it has had grievous consequences. You see, Sarah decided to give us substantial financial support."

Harriet nodded, very alert now.

"Our error: we did not tell Per any of the details."

Per was gazing far, far away. In fact, he looked more like one of those sea birds, Harriet thought. They always looked so lofty and above-it-all. A sea gull or an albatross. What were they thinking about all the time? Fish she supposed, or garbage.

"This was wrong, not only in moral but in practical terms. We did not grasp that there would be terrible consequences: that it would make us the focus of all the malice and envy around us."

"Evil begets evil," said Per tonelessly.

"What are you talking about?" asked Harriet. "What exactly happened to you?"

Anna glanced at Per.

"Per, why draw things out?" she said. "We are sure, quite sure, that Wanda is dead."

"Dead? I thought you were suggesting Sarah might have been kidnaped."

"Sarah, yes. But, you see, Wanda was Sarah's custodian. Wanda was the immediate obstacle to those interested in gaining possession of Sarah and her money.

"Wanda had an exaggerated distrust of banking facilities. She insisted on keeping an enormous cache of bank notes in the apartment they shared. After her strange disappearance, we searched the place exhaustively. All the money was gone, every sou, and Wanda's passport, that too was gone.

But Wanda's clothes and her spectacles—she was unable to read without her spectacles—they are still there. You understand, that was disquieting."

"But if Sarah is being—'held,' why not Wanda?" said Harriet. "Why would you think—?"

"Let us tell you what we have discovered.

"We have friends and correspondents in many parts of the country. We had asked them to be alert for news of Sarah and Wanda. Two weeks ago, we heard from a friend in Marseilles. Something curious had come to her attention. A passport belonging to Wanda had turned up on the unofficial market. There was trouble about that passport. It was not even valid. It would have been dangerous for Wanda to have sold it." Anna sighed. "We were uncomfortable about this business of the passport and we felt it was imperative to investigate it ourselves. I spoke to your sister, but I was perhaps a little evasive with her.

"Two of us went to Marseilles—Manu and Marie Christine. They could find no trace of Wanda or Sarah, none at all, nor could they discover anyone who had seen two women of that description. Sarah, of course is particularly striking.

"They succeeded in tracing Wanda's passport. It was difficult and expensive, but at last they found a man who had been offered not only the passport but also a pair of garnet earrings. When he described the earrings, there could be no doubt. They were in the shape of two hearts, one through the other."

The blonde girl with the ponytail spoke. "The hearts could also be read as initials, you see: those of Wanda's grandparents. They were made for pierced ears. Wanda never took them off. They were all that she brought here with her from her country. She would never have sold them."

"But this man told Manu these things were offered to him not by a woman but by a boy," said Anna. "The description of him was very vivid."

"Yes," said Marie Christine. "Manu and I . . ."

"They felt sure they knew who he was. He is from Paris, Miss Milbanke, and he goes under the name of Maurice Monaco. He is a criminal, the leader of a gang of hoodlums. He is a good-looking boy, but there is one thing impossible for him to disguise—he has a long scar across his forehead.

"Our friends in Marseilles were able to confirm the fact that this boy, Monaco, had been visiting Marseilles. He is well known there. He always seems to have a great deal of money. At least, he spends a great deal on drugs. We immediately believed the worst.

"It's possible that Wanda could be alive. They could have captured her, taken everything she had of value and spared her life, kept her a prisoner. But we don't believe it. These are ruthless people. And there is also Wanda's nature to consider. She is violent and disruptive. And there is no one who would pay ten francs to bring Wanda home. No, Per, it's true. Forgive me, but it's true. Where and how it happened, we don't know, but we're sure, quite sure, that Wanda is dead."

Anna drew a long breath.

"And Sarah?" said Harriet.

"Sarah is a different matter."

"Yes," said Harriet. "How do you know Sarah is alive?"

"We *know* Sarah is alive, Miss Milbanke, I promise you that. The problem is how to keep her alive."

Harriet stood up. "We must call the police immediately."

"No, Miss Milbanke. That, above all, you must not do."

"*Must* not? Are you mad? That's just what I can and will do."

"No, you must listen to us. Sarah is under constant surveillance. If the police were involved, Sarah would survive only by a miracle. As you must know, Miss Milbanke, these French police, they are brutal. They would come in force."

Harriet slumped back on her chair and chewed on her ink-stained thumb. She felt baffled, angry, and afraid.

"This boy—what's his name?" she said finally. "Exactly what is this gang you're talking about?"

"Maurice Monaco and his lot are gutter-scum, cutthroats. Everyone knows them by their ugly reputation. They deal in drugs and every other bestiality money can buy. But I have not made myself clear. These hoodlums, all of them, they're creatures of the man who has Sarah in his power now."

"What? *What* man? Who's this you're talking about?"

"Jack Straw is his name. He is American—a so-called artist. Do you know his name?"

"No, no." It sounded vaguely familiar, but Harriet couldn't place it. Her head was beginning to ache badly.

"It is apparent that Sarah is staying with him. Now, Jack Straw knows very well what Sarah is worth, even if his henchmen do not. Straw controls them. They obey his orders.

"Jack Straw has a disturbing reputation. He is associated in people's minds with bizarre happenings of which there are very strange tales. He appears to preside over a cult which conducts rites of the most vicious sort, appealing to those of morbid and depraved tastes. He pretends to possess powers to raise the dead, and to summon spirits who will respond to questions, and predict the future.

"For three years or more, ever since this man Straw settled in Paris, these ceremonies have been an open secret. A scandal, but one that no one has dared to deal with. Among the people who attend, are many who hold high positions in the eyes of the world."

"I know *nothing* about witchcraft," said Harriet Milbanke. "But you mean Sarah is involved in it, with this man you know?"

"No! We don't *know* him, Miss Milbanke. None of us had the slightest interest in these stories. We are not sensation-seekers. We are not policemen. It goes without saying that this man, Jack Straw, has never been political. It is apparent that he is a parasite, interested only in money."

"Wait," said Harriet. "You believe Sarah has been kidnaped by some sort of sorcerer who's after her money. Well, why haven't they gone to her mother?"

Anna gave a sigh that was more like a groan. "Mrs. Mel-

more no longer tells us what she is doing, and we have concluded she can no longer be trusted. We did everything for
her. We did our utmost. You see, we had managed to make
contact with a young man—a homosexual member of Jack
Straw's coterie. He confirmed that Sarah was staying with
the man, Straw. He promised to arrange a meeting between
Straw and your sister. We hoped that for a sufficient sum
of money . . ."

"That might be very dangerous for my sister, if she were
not protected."

"No, Miss Milbanke. You have talked to your sister today?"

Harriet nodded. She'd been gruff with Sis, lately. She was
sorry about that.

"The meeting took place last night, so you must know
that she is safe, quite safe. But the young man who arranged
the meeting, he is dead."

"What!"

"Last night he fell five stories onto the pavement. It has
been registered as a suicide."

"And my sister? Does she know this?"

Anna glanced at Per. "Your sister has played a very am-
biguous role in this drama. She has refused to be frank with
us. She told us only that she had made contact with someone
who knew where Sarah was. We believe the person she is dealing with is Jack Straw. It seemed dangerous to confide in her
further.

"You see, Miss Milbanke," said Anna, "it is not your sister
who is in danger now. We had been watching both Sarah's
flat and that of Jack Straw. We believed this had been done
discreetly. At the same time it was necessary to take certain
risks. We have had to expose ourselves. We have had to
make these attempts to reach people who might give us
information about Sarah. We believed we were achieving
some success.

"Then it began. Suddenly, every day, every night, there
would be three or four of Monaco's band—not Monaco

himself, but his cohorts. Three or four of those boys, always in black, always waiting. Waiting for us, waiting outside our very door. They had learned the places we work, the places we meet, all the patterns of our life. They never spoke. They made no gesture. But they were always there, no matter what steps we took to evade them. It is we who had become the hunted. Do you see?"

"But nothing has happened yet," said Harriet.

"No, Miss Milbanke," cried Anna. "The worst has happened. We have lost Manu. It is blood of our blood. It is Manu, Manu, the young man who went to Marseilles with Marie Christine."

The girl with the blond pony-tail had begun to cry very softly. The girl with the red barrette put an arm around her, and was whispering in her ear.

"Manu was in certain ways the most able of us all," said Anna. "But he was also the most visible. His flaw lay in his very relentlessness. He became imprudent. He allowed an emotional quality to enter into his approach. He was fond of Sarah, you see. But to treat the matter as a personal vendetta was quite incorrect. It was obvious that the moment Jack Straw and his creatures appeared to be threatened by us, they would have no scruples.

"Manu knew we did not approve of his adventurous tactics, so, most unfortunately, he concealed from us his plans. It seems that two nights ago he had planned an action. He told no one."

"He told me," said Marie Christine.

"Who told no one," said Anna in an icy voice, not glancing at Marie Christine. "He never returned. We became more and more fearful for Manu's safety—even for his life.

"Then this morning, when five of us walked out into the street—for we can no longer travel by ones or twos—we saw them waiting there, those boys in black. Watching us, as always, not speaking, not moving. They were all in black, all but one. He was wearing Manu's jacket. He looked at us.

He turned slowly around like a mannequin. They laughed in our faces. And then they turned their backs on us and walked away. We have not seen them since."

There was a long silence.

"So you think they're holding him," said Harriet. "Do you know where they're holding him?"

"Oh, if we knew that—" muttered Rudy impatiently.

"Don't you see it's not logical to have any such hope that Manu is still alive?" said Anna.

"Dear girl," exclaimed Harriet. "You must see now, that's for the police."

"Oh yes," cried Anna. "Call the police, Miss Milbanke. You will be signing two death warrants—one for Manu, one for Sarah!"

"It is necessary to change our tactics," said Rudy.

"Don't you understand?" said Harriet. "You're not equipped to deal with this! Couldn't you have the police surround the place where this Jack Straw lives? Couldn't they bring Sarah out? And then see about your friend?"

"Yes, perhaps. If we knew where Straw lives now. But it would be taking a great risk. Sarah might be killed. We would lose any chance of rescuing Manu. And for us, every day we stayed in Paris, there would be that little accident. One of us would be missing."

"I see—but you say you don't know where Jack Straw lives now?"

"No, we don't know where he lives now, Miss Milbanke. He has abandoned his home, and our surveillance system—perhaps you understand, it is no longer effective."

"So then?"

"We have only two alternatives, Miss Milbanke," said Anna. "To leave the country and abandon our comrades. Or to act ourselves, and without delay. There is no more time. Our philosophy of nonviolence is no longer appropriate."

"What? How?"

"You see, Miss Milbanke, we don't know where Jack Straw is, but we know where he will be. We had a strange visitor today. He came directly to our door. He knew our hiding-place—he treated it as common knowledge. That shows both the efficiency of our enemies, and the contempt in which they hold us.

"This man was very overwrought. He is the one who informed us of the death of the young man we mentioned, the boy Johno. He was, in fact, the boy's male lover. He is a white man who has assumed the name of an African. But the fact that he is abnormal, even deranged, does not in our minds invalidate his information.

"Now, this man had once been an assiduous attendant at these rites to which I referred. In fact, it is our belief that he would still be a participant if his increasing peculiarities had not led him into financial difficulties. These ceremonies —perhaps I did not make this clear, Miss Milbanke, but they are only for the very rich.

"This man, Wilkins or Ngola Mbandi as he prefers to be called, wishes to believe his friend was murdered. His desire for revenge overcame his fear of this cult. He came to us, and we agreed to supply him with money—enough to ensure his admission to the rites. It was a vast sum, which depleted the last of our funds. He knows meeting-places, the password, the disguises—in short, their most secret proceedings. These people are so hungry for money that he needs only to demonstrate his solvency.

"But there is no time to lose. The next ceremony, Miss Milbanke, the first in many months, we were told, takes place tomorrow night. They are all to be there, Jack Straw and his gangsters and Sarah."

Some of the children had gone into the other room. The girl with the braid had taken her guitar with her. She was playing a wild melody. Four of the girls were dancing, arms linked.

"Quiet," said Per.

"Quiet!" Anna called more loudly. Per shrugged. "Why not give them a few more minutes," he said, "if it doesn't disturb you, Miss Milbanke?"

Miss Milbanke said, "Oh, let them dance."

"Everyone is too excited tonight," Per said. "It's not good. Perhaps this will relieve the tension."

Harriet Milbanke felt like crying. Everyone was saying once again that it was her responsibility—her responsibility to put things right. It was Grandpa. It was Papa. It was Mama. It was Sis. It was Sis's mess. But even these people knew Sis was incompetent. It was Harriet's duty to be the good one again.

All right, you old fool. You're grown up. Pull yourself together! (She hoped she hadn't spoken out loud.)

Harriet wiped her nose. Her headache, and the feeling of nausea it gave her, were passing. She began to concentrate. Some of what they said must be true. God knows, even a little was bad enough.

"But how do you know *Sarah* will be there?" said Harriet Milbanke.

"We believe what we have been told. It is logical."

"But if she is there, I don't see how on earth you can get her out without the most tremendous danger! If I believed you—and let's say I do—even if I cut everything you are telling me in half, well, it still sounds to me as if you expect to be tackling a whole roomful of murderous brutes."

"We have approximated there may be as many as twenty of these boys. The number of members of the 'congregation' undoubtedly varies. But the visitors should present no problem. They are foolish dilettantes."

"I don't see how you can manage this at all without the police! You are only fourteen! And you're mostly women! You say these people are vicious. You said Sarah would be in danger from them. It sounds as if this place, whatever it is—"

"No. These boys have only chains and knives."

"Good Lord! You must be mad!"

"No, Miss Milbanke," said Anna. "They will be taken by surprise. They do not fear us now. They treat us with contempt. No one will be expecting trouble tomorrow night. We are quite sure Sarah will be left unguarded. We can take them completely by surprise. We can surround them and bring Sarah out in safety. And then, if you like, *then*, it might be time for the police. We have made a plan for this as well."

Miss Milbanke thought this over.

"But how? I don't see—"

"You see, there's only one way now. I'll explain." Rudy had come over to Per. Now he bent down and whispered something in his ear. Per frowned and shook his head. Then his face became impassive once more.

"Miss Milbanke," said Per, "I regret that I must tell you something has happened of which I am deeply ashamed. Were you expecting any calls tonight?"

Harriet looked at her watch and shook her head. "Why?"

"Tani" (that seemed to be the girl with the braid) "tends to be overzealous. Since she speaks almost no English or French, this is particularly difficult. She did something on her own initiative for which I can only say I have the deepest regret. I am very deeply sorry, Miss Milbanke. Tani has cut the wires to your telephone. I give you my word we will do our best to repair the damage as soon as possible. Tani has not been with us long enough to assimilate our rules. We demand obedience and unanimity of action. What she did was very wrong."

"It's absolutely outrageous!"

"Miss Milbanke, I can only offer my deepest apologies."

"Dear heaven! Look here, young man, you've told me I'm a prisoner. You've cut my telephone wires. You say all these people are dead or missing! And finally you tell me that tomorrow night something perfectly beastly is going to happen involving my niece. That's quite a lot for an old woman to take in in one evening. All right, I'd much rather know than not know. But there's one thing I don't understand. Since you are not expecting me to lead my sister around on a leash, why are you here at all? Not just for the pleasure of my company, I presume. Just what do you need from me?"

Anna spoke: "Money, Miss Milbanke," she said, "Money for guns."

"Guns!" cried Harriet. "You mean to say you're going to behave like the same sort of vicious hoodlums they are!"

"Miss Milbanke," said Per, "one dies for one's principles, but one fights for one's life."

4

Sarah Melmore Embarks on a Mysterious Journey

SARAH HADN'T HAD a watch for a long time. There was no clock in the apartment. Still she felt she usually knew what time it was. In her solitude, she felt other senses developing. Her sense of hearing was acute now, and she had learned to separate and interpret the noises she heard all day. And her sense of smell—it was very interesting. Everything had a different smell. She was sure that this sense could become so refined that in time she would find that even with minerals, each would have its distinctive odor. But by that time she wouldn't be able to abide the smell of people—even Jack, who was so obsessively clean. She had begun to think she could scent out his emotions. Now she was curious to go out on the street and experience strange people. But maybe that would already be too much; people, one by one, would be easier.

She was glad she was developing these senses. They would

probably be more accurate than listening to the words people used, which seemed to be mostly lies, even when they
tried to be honest.

She hadn't gone back to sleep after Jack had woken her up.
Something was wrong, she was sure something was wrong.
He wasn't lying to her, but at the same time it wasn't the
truth either. How had he fixed things with her mother so
fast? He had probably made another error in judgment. This
was grave. He was talking about her real mother, her own
blood. Her mother had borne her and protected her and
sacrificed herself, even—even if she had not understood very
much. Her mother loved her so much, and she, she had done
her mother nothing but harm, and yet she loved her mother
too. She could never escape from her mother. Her mother
was part of herself. And Jack, who understood everything—
Jack had done this unforgivable thing. Oh, why the hell did
it have to happen that way? Well, no. That was it. Jack had
forced it to happen that way. It was going to be very hard
to rest and relax.

For the first time, she wished there was a telephone in the
apartment. She would have liked to call her mother. Maybe
not to speak to her, but to leave a message. "Sarah called.
She says please don't see Jack again. She'll write and explain."

She trusted Jack, but she didn't trust him altogether with
other people. As Maurice had said, so long ago, he didn't
look at things in the same way. She sighed. She was going
to do her best to empty her mind and think of her grandfather. She needed someone to show her the way. She had
come to believe, through reading his notes, that her grandfather was a sort of an alchemist—a necromancer, a white
wizard. The clues were in his notes, but no one else seemed
to have found that out. There were only a few questions she
needed to ask, but she had to ask somebody she could trust.
Someone who was a magus, but who understood the word
"bad," someone who understood about atonement. Someone
of her blood. She loved Jimbo, but when she tried to think
of him dead, she thought of him angry. Nineteen years old

and angry. No one could ever repay him for his lost youth. Her father—well, she no longer thought of her father as Satan. He was a strong, dangerously destructive man. It was like living with radium. But Jimmy had cooperated in his own destruction. He needn't have gone to pieces.

It was Jimbo who loved to read "The Rime of the Ancient Mariner." But probably just because it was spooky. He had never really understood the point.

> *Like one that on a lonesome road*
> *Doth walk in fear and dread,*
> *And having once turned round, walks on,*
> *And turns no more his head;*
> *Because he knows a frightful fiend*
> *Doth close behind him tread*

That was the heart of it all. That was life. That was the point: not to turn your head. If you never turned your head, it really didn't matter. Jimmy was always looking behind him.

Nanny, darling Nanny, always full of nursery aphorisms. "Well, dearie," she would say, if Sarah asked her opinion. "Circumstances alter cases, broken noses alter faces." That wasn't a lot of help. Or "If you're in doubt, Sarah, always pray to Jesus. He'll help you. Always turn the other cheek. That's what our Lord Jesus did."

Sarah simply hadn't paid any attention to all that when she was young, and it didn't seem a very wise course today, for that matter. She needed something else. She wasn't going to look back, but she wanted to look forward. She knew she had been wicked and she wanted to be good. She had been tormented and she wanted to be peaceful. She wanted no part of her father's life—his passion for controlling people. Nor her mother's life—her passion for pleasing people. She wanted to pay her debts and then live quietly, calmly, classically, in an even line. Her grandfather had been chosen to show her the way.

Of course, Jack was the most peaceful person she had ever known. He made her feel peaceful too; even when she knew he was very angry and very tense and upset about something, he kept it inside himself, and was very calm, and spoke in a very low voice to her. When he did something wrong in his work, he would swear, sometimes slam things around. But then he'd always apologize to her. "I'm sorry, Sarah. It's just I did something stupid."

And he never interfered or asked questions. It was hard to imagine living with anyone but Jack now. Of course, she didn't like some of Jack's ideas. He seemed to believe in some things she was terribly against. He thought some people were more valuable than others. And once he had started talking again about his "real" art.

"I'd really like to show you some of my things, Sarah. You'd understand a lot more, once you saw how beautiful it is. How necessary. I didn't even want to film it for real at first, just keep it like my own film, like a memory in my mind. But I had to, because of the money. And the most terrible part, the people who are really interested in it, the people who pay the big money for it, they don't understand it at all. They just like it for all the very worst reasons—the most horrible disgusting reasons. But I'd like you to see some of my real work, Sarah."

"Jack, I—I just don't want to, right now," she said.

"Well, maybe you're right. Maybe it's better. Not yet. Or maybe I can't expect more than two or three people in the world ever to understand."

He didn't mention it again. But ideas didn't seem to interfere. Usually they hardly talked, or if they did, it was just about prosaic things. She was glad, because she didn't feel like talking about ideas now. She wanted so very badly to find the right way to live. How she should live today. Tomorrow. Next month. Next year.

Jack was helping her in so many ways. She believed in him. He was a "healer." Her mind wasn't racing ahead anymore;

she didn't feel so "crazy" and frightened. She was sure that her father was dead. She believed she had really killed him. But then, then it must have happened somehow that her mother had taken care of everything. Her mother hadn't blamed her or punished her, she had helped her all the way. She would have to stick with her mother against Jack, if it came to that. But why would it come to that? Did it need to come to that?

In the afternoon, Sarah lay down and rested. All the time she kept trying to think of her grandfather, who would show her the way.

She had gone to sleep, and when she awoke, she knew it was very late. How late? Eleven, twelve? Jack wasn't back. Did that mean it wouldn't happen that night after all? She lay very still and tried to see her breath going in and out. She tried to use her animal senses to guess the time. Something to do with light. Something to do with smell. They were in a very quiet part of town. The window was open. She heard the little noises, the tiny rustles, as the houses settled down. There was a smell of leaves, mice, paper, and old bread. Then suddenly she heard Jack's footsteps at the end of the street. He was hurrying. He ran up the steps, opened the door.

"Sarah."

"Yes."

"Oh, you're awake. Fantastic! Okay. Just a minute." He went into his room. Then the bathroom. Then he came into her room.

"You're okay, Sarah?"

"Yes."

"You didn't have anything to eat or drink?"

"No."

"Okay. Great! Just take these." He had two pills. "They might make you a little sleepy. Just a little."

She looked at them. She had seen a lot of pills, but these were unfamiliar.

"It's okay. It just makes things better. Easier."

She took them.

"Okay. Now this stuff is for you to wear."

He had a paper bag under his arm, and he opened it. Black jeans, black T-shirt. Men's sneakers, black too.

"It all ought to fit. And the shoes are your size. Oh, wait. First, you better come into the other room, the light's better."

She went into the other room. He sat her on a stool, turned the strong drawing light on her, and took out a pair of scissors.

"Lord," he said. "I'm probably going to make a real mess of this. Wish we weren't so short on time."

He looked at her a minute, then put a towel around her shoulders and took the scissors. He began cutting her hair. It seemed as if he wanted to clip it right down to the skull.

"Oh, Lord, did I hurt you?"

"No, it's okay."

"Lord, I wish I could do this properly. I don't know what's wrong." He stopped, looked at her, and then cut some more. She must be practically bald. She kept brushing the tiny pieces off. They clung to her neck and made it itch.

"Okay," he said finally. "Now, Sarah, if you'd go put on those clothes. I want to look."

She went into her room and put them on. They seemed to fit. There wasn't a mirror in the room, but she felt without looking that probably Jack had made a mess of her hair. She went out.

"M-m-m," Jack said, looking at her. "There's something about the way you walk, Sarah. You sort of wander along—I do too, I know—but could you sort of look more purposeful?" Then he attacked her hair again. "Okay. I think that's okay now. Now listen, Sarah—this place we're going, you've got to do everything just the way I say. Just exactly, or you might get in trouble. Now could you put this on?" He handed her a long black robe with a big hood. He pulled it over her head.

"See, you're going to want to pull this right over your

head, really over, so it hides your face. But you don't want
to put your hand up to it, or fiddle with it or act anxious or
anything. It should hide your face, but not as if it's on purpose exactly. Do you see? Look." He took her into the bathroom. Sarah looked at the black-hooded figure in the mirror.
It was a monk's robe, sort of. She could hardly see her face.
It looked like a skull.

"Do you see? If you put it on properly, it's not going to
fall back. So just don't worry about it. Forget it. But if by
any chance it should, don't worry about that either. You
look okay anyway. Now, take it off. You're going to put this
over your arm, and don't put it on until I tell you, okay?
Sarah, I'm afraid we ought to go along. We're really short on
time. The Métro's still running. I'll tell you the rest while
we go."

"Okay."

It was strange going out in the night like that, and she
could feel the pills now; they were making her feel quiet
and dreamy. Soft night. Glowing lights. She saw the red and
blue lights of the Métro, so pretty. They ran down the stairs.
They were lucky. A train was just pulling up.

They huddled together in the big empty car.

"When we get there, don't look at anybody or anything.
People may hand you something to drink. Just make pretend.
Okay? Don't really drink or eat anything where we're going.
I want you to stand right up near the front. Try to stand
away by yourself as much as you can. If someone speaks to
you, don't answer. Just put your finger on your lips. I can't
be with you most of the time, I'll be up in front doing this
number. Remember? Don't let anything scare you. It's not
real. Just like a movie. But you'll know when it's time for
you. I'll let you know, Sarah. Everything okay?"

"Yeah. I'm a little spaced out. I haven't had any junk in
a long time."

"Well, that's just to get you relaxed and in a mood to see.
Here—here's where we get off. It's only about four blocks
now."

It didn't even seem like Paris, where they were. They hurried down the forlorn streets. All the buildings were dark. Warehouses, markets.

Suddenly, Jack pulled her into a doorway. "Here," he said, "put it on now." She put on the cape, the hood well over her face.

"Good," he said. "That's great! That's great, Sarah! You're doing fantastically."

He took her hand and they walked along the dark cobblestones.

"Now remember, Sarah, do just what I said, and if anything different is going to happen, I'll let you know somehow. And if for some reason I need to tell you to do something, you do it. Quick. You don't feel too dopey?"

"No . . . no."

"You weigh so light," he said. "Maybe it should have been just one pill. Sure you can pay attention?"

"Yes . . . am I going to speak to my grandfather?"

"I'm pretty sure. I told you I couldn't swear, but I'm pretty sure."

Jack stopped by what appeared to be a blank wall. He let go her hand.

"Sarah, in a minute now I'm going to have to leave you."

He looked up and down the street.

"Lordy, Sarah. There was supposed to be someone here to guide you. I guess they must've gotten tired of waiting."

There was no sound except Jack's breathing.

"Well, okay. It's okay anyway, Sarah."

Sarah saw that Jack was staring at an unmarked door, so much the same color as the wall as to be almost invisible. He had drawn a key which looked like a can opener from his pocket, and after a little fumbling, he opened the door.

Inside there seemed to be only a great gulf of darkness. Sarah didn't want to go in, but obviously that was what Jack expected her to do.

She stepped over the threshold.

"Well, this isn't the way I planned it," said Jack, "but

you'll just have to go down there by yourself. I can't stay with you, Sarah.

"Look, I'll explain. See, this is the back entrance. Everybody else comes in through the other side."

He pointed a little flashlight into the void, and Sarah could see a metal staircase, descending.

"You just go down there, Sarah. You'll find a door at the bottom. That opens into this long waiting room. There'll probably be one or two boys there, maybe with a dog. He looks much worse than he is. They'll be expecting somebody. But not a girl. So don't say anything to them. If they look surprised, or anything, give them this." He handed her a smooth little stick. "They'll know it's okay then. That's a sign."

Sarah stared at what he had given her. It looked like a knucklebone.

"There's two doors. Take the one to the right. It takes you down this long passageway. There's lots of noise, music and stuff, and you just keep following it to the end. There's a door. You can't miss it, and it takes you right out to—well, that's the door takes you closest to the altar. Then you just walk right in. It's kind of dark, but your eyes'll be used to it by then. So then you just stand up real close to the altar, like I told you.

"You better go down now, Sarah. You'll find the door. And you'll see from there it's very easy. Sarah, it's going to be very beautiful. I think it's all going to happen tonight. You'll see."

He guided her to the top of the stairs and turned off the flashlight. After a second or two, Sarah could make out the shape of the stairs descending into the gloom from some dim light below.

"Are you okay, Sarah?"

"Can I have the flashlight, Jack?"

"Oh, Lord, I'm afraid not. I'll need it 'cause I must be real late myself. And it makes people mad. But, Sarah, you won't have any trouble. Just go down the stairs and open the door."

Then, without another word, Jack stepped back and let the door slam behind him.

A feeling of rage and panic pierced the dreamy passivity Jack's pills had induced. She couldn't trust Jack! She should have known she couldn't trust him! As she held the icy bannister, she breathed deeply and closed her eyes. Why should she go down those stairs?

Taking tiny steps, she found the wall, and inched along it until she felt the door.

She ran her hands over it. It must be locked. Certainly there was no knob. There seemed no way to open it. No way to get out.

"Okay," thought Sarah, grimly. "I guess I'll have to go on down."

She found the stairs again and started to fumble her way down. Each time her foot hit the metal tread, there was a clang and an echo. It was damp. She turned on a landing, and gripping the bannister, rough where the paint was flaking, she went down the next set of stairs. At the bottom she could see light coming from under a door.

She remembered the beginning of *Alice in Wonderland*. She had always hated the part down the rabbit hole, and when her mother read it to her, she had made her skip to the caucus race.

Before she opened the door, she could hear a loud roaring sound, like a jet motor, reverberating. She opened the door and stepped through into a chamber almost as dark as the one she had left. What she had thought was just a shadow by the door was a man standing there, his hand out, like a toll keeper. He was all in black, with a black helmet on his head, and dead eyes. She thrust the bone at him. He took it with a sort of grunt, and waved her ahead to the right. The room was lit only by a flickering green torch, and she couldn't see whether that shape in the far corner was another man, crouching, or the dog Jack had referred to. If it was a dog, it was a monster! Sarah had never been frightened of dogs, but she didn't want to look. She could feel her hackles rising, as if she were a dog herself.

When she opened the door into the long passage, the noise was ear-splitting. Was it an electronic organ? Or some kind of Moog synthesizer? It was music, she supposed, but it was an awfully unpleasant sound. God, what was this, anyway? What had Jack pushed her into? She was frightened to go forward and frightened to go back. In back was that horrible man and the dog, and the locked door. Don't look back. Okay, forward.

As she reached the door at the end of the passage, she was overpowered by a nauseating smell: heavy incense and, underlying it, something that was both sweet and rancid. Was it blood? Or could the smell of a crowd be like that?

She opened the door. The noise was an assault. She seemed to be entering a vast underground cathedral. It was crowded with people, stepping in a kind of rhythm. But it was so dark she could hardly see them, though she could feel their excitement.

The only lights seemed to be on the ceiling far above, glowing greenish and metallic, in arches and groins. The sound seemed to be crashing down from there too. There must be speakers of some sort near the ceiling.

What was this? Sarah didn't want to join the throng. But something told her it would be dangerous not to. She wished she were not feeling so high and dizzy now. She put her hand against the wall for a moment. The wall felt cold and faceted. She stared at it, then dropped her hand. Was that piece of the wall made out of a rough-cut crystal? Could that be possible—that it was real? Was this Jack's last "art work"? What did that mean?

To her right, there seemed to be some sort of platform, or perhaps that was the altar. Okay. She knew Jack wanted her to walk right on out, and stand in front of it. Sarah felt that somehow, if only the music were not so deafening, she would be able to see better. Were those niches in the walls? Were those men in black, with silver chains, standing in them?

The music grew shriller. Up on the platform, straight ahead, there was a bit more light. Well, not light, exactly, but sort of a glow. There was some kind of big table up there. On it was something pale, and behind the table a strange figure in some sort of oriental costume, gyrating about.

Could that be Jack? What was he doing? Certainly, the movement of the arms had the quirky grace that she had come to recognize as Jack's. What was that on the table? A statue? Something made of plastic?

No, my God! It twitched a white limb. It was a naked child.

5

Miss Milbanke Travels by Night

HARRIET MILBANKE COULDN'T IMAGINE why she wasn't frightened. Probably because everything seemed so ridiculously gothic. Tripping over this dratted black dress, all muddled up in the middle of nowhere, in the middle of the night, half running, slipping and stumbling, trying to keep up with the two girls who were with her, Anna and Renée. She knew they were trying to make things as easy for her as they could, but they were in a hurry.

Anna and Renée. She hadn't known of their existence before last night, and now she was going with them to confront and entrap these people whom they accused of every imaginable infamy. Everyone said repeatedly that these ruffians had no guns, but why was everyone so sure? How did they know?

She had insisted on being here. They had wanted her to

stay safely at home, but she was having none of that. The power of money. It was her money, and she could dictate the terms.

Humph. She was just an old windbag. She hadn't dictated a thing; she had just paid the price they wanted. Her whole savings account! Her old age. Her future security. And all for what? Guns! She hated guns. Hated them. Guns, like money, had a life of their own. Guns assumed command. They made people their agents. What an argument they had about it, and in the end, in the end she had given in. It was the only safe way for Sarah, they said. They had gone over the tactics again and again. And finally she had given in, given in because she had promised—not because she was convinced. It made sense in theory perhaps, but once someone had a gun in his hand, he didn't think the way he did on paper. So Harriet said. Per and Anna just went on and on about logic. But really, in the end, she said yes because she had promised. Just because she had promised. But on one point she had been inflexible. She must be there herself. No one had liked that. But she had been stubborn.

"I want to bring Sarah home myself."

The one clear picture in Harriet's mind, now, was one of bringing Sarah home. Home with her. Sarah would be tall, like her mother, so she would put Sarah in her bed. She would sleep in the library. She had lots of nursery food—nursery food was what Sarah would need. And someone of her own blood. Sarah wouldn't have to talk to her, or answer any questions. Not if she didn't want to. And of course, Harriet's phone wasn't working. She couldn't really call Sis till the morning. Anyway, one more night wouldn't really make that much difference to Sis, after all this time. Harriet had an instinctive feeling now that she would get along with Sarah. Little Sarah. It made sense. A kind of full circle. That must be the reason for all this.

But there was another motive, too. "I want to be there to make sure there is no violence. That was part of our bargain."

At last it had been Anna who said, "I think we should agree. It means we can all be there."

She did not mean that Harriet Milbanke could be there. She meant that no one would have to stay behind to "look after" her.

Still, once they had the money in their hands, they needn't have kept their bargain. They all knew it. It had even passed through her mind that once they had her money they might put a bullet through her head, or at least tie her up and leave her in the closet. How much could she know about these people after a few hours of talk? But they had played fair. They had played fair.

So here she was in this robe she had been given, much too long and smelling like the elephant house. If it had belonged to a monk, it must be one of those orders that never washed. Anna had told her the robe was a necessary precaution—all the guests wore this disguise. She had told Harriet she would only need it for the last walk—about ten minutes. Thank heavens! And the others, they were all coming from different directions.

"We will be arriving last," Anna said. "So if there is any difficulty with guards or sentries, you will be in no danger, Miss Milbanke."

Harriet felt humiliated. She had not intended to be a burden. For the first time she was almost glad they were using her money. Really, she hadn't much else to offer.

Anna fell behind Renée, keeping pace with Harriet.

"I wish to ask you a favor, Miss Milbanke," said Anna.

"Well, what is it anyway?"

"You don't like me much, Miss Milbanke," Anna said.

Harriet said nothing.

"I have been told that I am lacking in charm. Charm is perhaps insufficiently important to me. However, this is not a question of liking or not liking. It is a question of justice."

"What is it?"

"They say history books are written by the winners, Miss

Milbanke," said Anna. She paused. "While I have no reason to be apprehensive as to the outcome of this encounter, it would be illogical to make no provision for reversals."

"I don't understand you."

"Once we join battle, we will doubtless be separated."

"Join *battle?*"

"It may be that something unforeseen may take place. It may be, Miss Milbanke, that you may be the one who must tell our story."

"Just a minute. What on earth are you talking about?"

"Contingencies, Miss Milbanke. It's prudent. Will you keep this some place safe? It is the address of our archivist. If things do not go well for us, promise me that you will do what you can to see that our records are published. This should principally contain Per's writings, in their entirety.

"I believe you could count upon your sister for financial aid. She will know by then that we have given all to help her daughter."

"I thought you said—I thought—no danger!" Harriet found herself gabbling.

"You could turn back now, Miss Milbanke. It's not too late. Myself, I would very much prefer it—for this reason, no less than any other."

"No, I'll not turn back."

"But will you do what I ask?"

"My dear young woman, if we're heading into a trap, I daresay you've much more of a chance of getting out of it than I. What about *my* archives?"

"I will take on any responsibility you may ask of me, Miss Milbanke."

"Well," Harriet said gruffly, "I only hope the need does not arise."

Anna pointed. "Miss Milbanke," she said. "That is it."

The building they were approaching was just a big, dark shape like the others. Not a light anywhere. There was an alley, a door, some stairs. Harriet slipped on the steps going down, tripping whenever she forgot to hold up that infernal dress.

What rot! What dangerous stagy rot this whole business was. Play-acting, self-indulgent, dangerous rot! At the bottom of the stairs, Renée threw open a door, and then—

She saw the huge animal first. The girls passed it by without looking. A great black dog, but much bigger than a wolf, with a chain around its neck, dead. Obviously it was dead, though it seemed frozen in a crouch, its mask rigid with rage.

But at the end of the oblong room, pale green in the light, stood Rudy, leaning against a wall, pointing a gun at two boys trussed up on the ground. Harriet forced herself to follow the girls.

The boys were dressed up like drugstore cowboys. They were tied up and gagged; very efficiently, Harriet noted. But when she looked down at them—their eyes! Heavens, what eyes! She could believe they were murderers. Eyes like tigers! But Rudy—when she looked up at Rudy, his eyes had exactly the same look. The way he was watching those boys, the gun trained on them . . .

Mercy, Harriet thought. Rudy was going to shoot those boys. She was absolutely sure of it. Whatever happened that night. Were they really planning to turn these criminals over to the police as they had promised? Or was it going to be a massacre?

Anna's eyes lit up. She shouted a word Harriet couldn't understand, opened a door on the right, threw off her robe, and began to run. Renée was close behind. Harriet was sure that she was never going to be able to keep up with the girls.

They were in a long passage. The noise was simply deafening. Anna had opened a door at the end of the corridor. Good Lord, right over that din, she heard it. Three gunshots in rapid succession. And then the sound of one, two shots from behind them. The noise echoed and re-echoed down the corridors. My Lord, my Lord, she had known it! And the next moment, Rudy was racing past her, and then right ahead of her—there was a big hall, where all hell was breaking loose! People shouting and yelling and a whole lot of people milling around fighting! Directly in front of her was a white man dressed in an African robe. He had dyed orange hair and his face was made up like a woman's.

He was shrieking in a high crazed voice. "Jack Straw! Jack Straw! You'll pay for what you've done!"

He was firing off a pistol. But it seemed aimed right at the ceiling. Rudy just kicked him out of the way.

What had gone wrong? How could anyone get Sarah out of this mess? Where was Sarah, anyway? The place was so dark she could hardly see what was going on.

"Sarah! Sarah!" she shouted. "Sarah! Sarah!" Oh, God bless America! Sarah would never be able to hear her, if she *were* here. She could see that there was a sort of stage on her right, with steps going up. The route to it was almost clear. Nobody seemed to be on it. She ran toward it, not caring if she was knifed or clubbed or shot. But she was only pushed and jostled. No one seemed to pay any attention to her. She climbed up on the stage. It looked as though some sort of play had been going on. And then, facing out toward the hall, she began to shout, "Sarah! Sarah! It's your Aunt Harriet. Sarah! Sarah Melmore!"

Nobody cared. Nobody here cared about Sarah. Well, after all, they were fighting for their lives. Was Sarah here? Had she ever been here? Or had they been fooling her right from the start? Maybe this was just some sort of gang warfare. Maybe they had tried the same thing on Sis but she'd been too smart. Harriet noted that she felt very little fear, only the most bitter self-contempt.

Who had been playing girls' adventure stories? Who had gotten caught up in the excitement, and disregarded all common sense? Who had been flattered to death, flattered into giving all her money away for something evil? Not the frivolous sister. No, the frivolous sister was sitting there at the Crillon, smoking cigarettes and doing crossword puzzles.

This nightmare scene of murder and revenge, this was what Harriet had bought and paid for. She only prayed Sarah wasn't here, otherwise, she might be responsible for Sarah's death as well.

If she ever got out of here, she was going to go to Sis and make the most abject apology.

Well, step by step now. That she had been arrogant and stupid enough to pay for all this butchery was no reason to be a part of it.

She was glad she hadn't worn her glasses. Whatever was happening down there below, she'd just as soon not see it. There must be some way out of this place that didn't lead straight back into that slaughterhouse. She turned. And then she saw *it*. The naked body of a little girl, with fine blond hair, lying on a big table. Harriet automatically took her pulse. She was alive. Drugged, she supposed. She looked around. Various objects were strewn about the floor. A huge pig's-head mask, with a hideous leer. The papier-mâché head of a goat.

There was a black silk dress lying in a heap near the table. She used that to cover the child's nakedness.

She squinted down at the little girl. The child's eyes were rolled back in her head, and there was a sort of smile on her face, if you could call that a smile. A grimace! Terrible, really. But this little wax doll with the goblin face—that could have been Sarah!

Suddenly, a boy in black leaped onto the stage. He was holding an axe in his hand.

Well, she'd said her prayers. But he didn't even look at her. He began hacking frantically away at a sort of altar on her right. It was golden, and set with colored stones. He was cursing out loud as he worked, chopping off great pieces and dropping them in a sack he was carrying. He would hesitate for a moment, draw a great sobbing breath, and attack it again.

"Do what lies closest to you." Well, that was this pathetic

little child. She must try to get this little child, this little body, out of here. The chances weren't good. That dark-haired boy was going to turn around any minute and sink that axe in her head.

The child was much heavier than she would have supposed. She might have to drag her.

There was something rushing up the steps toward her—a sort of monster, it was, with two heads. Drat her eyes, anyway! No, it was a big man with light hair, making off with a body.

"No! No!" she screamed, for it was another child! A boy, with a pale face and shaved head. No, a girl. Somehow, she knew it was a girl. Half-dressed, in the same sort of robe she'd been wearing.

"No," she screamed. "Stop!" The man dropped the body on the floor. Then he kicked something aside, threw the figure over his shoulder again, and was gone. He'd seemed to go right through the wall. It must be some sort of backdrop.

"I can go that way too then," thought Harriet.

The young man in black was cursing frightfully. He kept looking over his shoulder, not at Harriet, but somewhere out over that frightful melee.

A girl. A girl, with short shaved hair. Sarah. Sarah Melmore? But was she alive? She mustn't think about it now. Harriet found that if she knelt she could place the drugged child over her shoulders.

Suddenly, inexplicably, the young man in black gave a last frightful curse and threw his axe on the floor. He slung the sack over his shoulder and made off faster than Harriet had ever seen anyone run. He ran straight toward the back of the stage.

Harriet stood up with her burden. Suddenly, something (was it her imagination?) seemed to be helping her. The whole room seemed to be leaning toward her, while at the same time she was being lifted up to meet it. It was melting, crumbling toward her. There was a light, too bright to see.

A noise, too loud to hear, and then she was being swept up—up—up.

Mama. Somehow, she had always expected, at the end of the road, to see Mama. But no, it was Papa. How kind he looked. He was smiling at her, as he lifted her up, up, up to the stars.

Part Twelve

GONE WEST

1

Sarah Melmore and Her Champion

SARAH REALIZED she was lying on the ground. Something had hit her on the head. All the noise. The screaming, the shooting. Was it still part of that horrible nightmare? That ghastly throng, Jack, that little child . . . And then the man with the gun. And suddenly, all those people from Advent. The boys with their chains. . . . That crazy old woman with red hair.

Her head was really throbbing. God. It must be real. Suddenly she was jerked up off the floor and lifted into the air. Someone's arms were holding her tight. Jack. It was Jack. He was running up some stairs. He dropped her on the ground! What the hell! But then he lifted her up again, put her over his shoulder, and kept running.

She didn't know where in God's name they were going. They were at the bottom of another flight of stairs. These stairs were broad and better-lighted, different from the ones she'd come down so hesitantly.

Jack ran up the stairs. He was carrying her slung over his shoulder, her head bobbing, like a pig or something. "Jack." She tried to say his name out loud, but it didn't work. Jack pushed on a big door with a spring. He pushed it open. And they were out in the air. Out in the street. Out in the fresh air.

Jack set Sarah on her feet, his arms under her armpits, holding her up. He'd ripped off her robe. He was wearing his blue jeans. His face was sort of gray. This was no dream.

"Sarah, are you okay?"

"Jack."

"Sarah, are you okay? You're really okay? Sarah, d'you think you can walk? D'you think you can hurry? I mean really hurry. I mean run! We've got to run!"

"Yes," she said.

They ran down the dark streets. She was dizzy and terribly out of shape, and couldn't keep up with him. Every once in a while he would stop, give her half a second, then grab her arm and make her run some more. All of a sudden there was the most horrible, terrifying, horrifying noise. The whole city was falling apart. It must be an earthquake . . . an atom bomb . . . the Apocalypse! Babylon the Great is fallen, is fallen; Sodom and Gomorrah! With flame and the sword. She felt the wind and the heat.

"All right," she said aloud. "All right. Go ahead. Do what you want. I don't care."

But Jack had stopped and seized her shoulder. "Sarah," he said. "Look."

He had turned and was looking back. She looked. The noise was still echoing in her ears. There were fingers of light reaching up into the black, then a whole castle of flames leaping up and up, higher and higher.

"My Lord, my Lord," said Jack, drawing a long breath. "Did you ever see anything like that? I just wish we could stay here and watch. We'll never see that again." He rubbed his face. "Well, we can't, Sarah," he said. "We can't. We've got to run. We'll run as far as you can make it. Then I'll see if I can carry you. Then—we'll see."

He couldn't take his eyes from the flames, just looked at them and shook his head. He gave a huge sigh. "M-m-m," he said. "Kingdom come. Well . . . Oh, Lordy . . . Well . . . Come on, Sarah!"

They ran some more She was really gasping. It felt as if her heart were going to come right out on the sidewalk.

"I can't, Jack," she said.

"Oh, Sarah, you're terrific! Lord, child, you've been so good. You're almost home. Here. Stop here a minute."

"Jack, I can't do it. You've got to go on without me."

"Go on without you, Sarah! Why, I'm here to see you're safe."

"I don't care. I'm all right."

"Sarah, I came back for you. If I'd wanted to be safe— well, that crazy man wanted to kill me. You saw that! All I was thinking about was you. And I couldn't do the stuff to get your grandfather to come."

She sat down on the curb. There was nowhere else to sit. "My grandfather! You mean kill that little girl! You mean you think my grandfather—"

"Sarah, I told you to look at everything like a movie. It was just make-believe. Please come on. I just did it for you." There was a glow in the sky like sunrise and it sounded as if every fire engine and police car in Paris was on its way.

"Jack," Sarah said, "your hands."

Jack's hands and wrists were caked with blood.

"Look—that doesn't matter right now. I can wash 'em when we get home." Suddenly he paused, looked at her, then thrust out his hands to her. "Look, Sarah. That's just pig's blood. Honestly. That's all. You don't pay attention."

She didn't know what to do. Maybe she would just sit here. But Jack pulled her up. She ran some more. When she thought she really didn't care anymore, he just slung her over his back and carried her, walking fast. The streets were always empty where they lived, but tonight there were some people standing around. He put her down. "Okay, Sarah— can you make it up the stairs?"

"Oh, sure."

Jack hurried up the stairs. Sarah walked up very slowly. She felt like an old, old woman. When she reached their apartment, Jack was rummaging around in it, putting things in different piles. When she came in, he stopped and gazed at her.

"Do you want a drink, Sarah? I know you don't ordinarily, but maybe tonight?" He'd poured himself a vodka.

"No, no thanks," she said.

"Something to eat?"

"No."

"You're holding me to blame. You think I failed you, like everyone else."

"I don't understand," she said. "What were Per and Anna and Marco and—and all of them doing there? What on earth was that all about? And then what happened?"

"Honest to God, I don't know. Everything's turning out so wrong. That weird friend of Johno tried to kill me. Honest to God, I don't know. I kept looking for a sign, and everything was telling me wrong. And those maniacs, they were smashing my panels! It was bound to happen. And I'm beginning to think maybe, maybe I'm beginning to push it a little. Maybe I'm beginning to fake it. Sarah, if my powers are failing me, nothing matters anymore. I'm just a piece of trash. It's only the powers give me permission."

Sarah looked at him for a long time. Then slowly she walked over and put his head against her breast. She stroked his cheek. This is what you were supposed to do with men, who were always wrong, who always felt they had permission for all their madness, all their badness.

"Lordy, Sarah," he said. "All the same, wasn't it gorgeous?"

2

Mrs. Melmore
Receives a Command

MRS. MELMORE'S PHONE WAS RINGING. God, she had lived through this all before. Yes, she had lived through this before. Jimmy. Jimmy. She picked up the phone and turned on the light at the same moment. What was she saying? Sarah! It must be about Sarah. Four-thirty in the morning.

"Mrs. Melmore?" It was Jack Straw.

"Yes."

"Were you awake? I'm sorry to disturb you."

"Yes. No. I mean it doesn't matter. What is it?"

"Are you all right?"

"Yes," she said. "What is it?"

"How soon would you be able to leave Paris?"

"What?"

"I know it's a little sudden. But how soon would you be able to take Sarah, and—and your servant, and get a flight out of Paris?"

"What? What is all this? What do you mean?"

"Look, I wouldn't ask you if it weren't very, very important. But I'm telling you I think you should take Sarah home. Right away. Today. There's been a terrific—well—accident. You know Sarah's friends—the ones you met? Well, all of them, well there was just a terrific accident. There was a big mess—maybe an explosion or something. Anyway, I think they're all dead."

"You mean—Anna? Anna's dead?"

"Yes, Anna. Per, too."

"Wanda?"

"Yes, Wanda. All of them, I think."

"My God! What was it? They were making bombs? I always thought they'd blow themselves up!"

"I guess something like that. But I don't want Sarah to find out. It would just upset her. And then I'm afraid, if the police start looking around, they might think she was involved somehow. . . . You know?"

"My God, yes. My God! How perfectly ghastly! How horrible!"

"I think the only way is for you to take Sarah away. Right away. Tomorrow. I mean today. The first plane home. Take her home. You have a place way up in the woods somewhere?"

"Canada. Yes."

"Sarah always liked that place. Take her there. Don't let her see any papers. She doesn't look at them anyway, but just make sure. Maybe they won't even carry that sort of stuff over in the United States. It'll pass. Just take her away for a while. Sarah's a whole lot better. She'll do it."

Mrs. Melmore put her feet on the floor and tried to think. "So—tell me again exactly what you're suggesting," she said.

"I think you should get the first plane you can back to the United States. The Concorde, I guess. I can meet you at the airport with Sarah. I know it's a mess, but I don't see any other way. Oh, and the servants, too."

"My servants don't ordinarily fly on the Concorde."

"Well, whatever then. That maid—she's awfully nosy. And servants, they always read all the most trashy papers. They might upset Sarah."

"I have my driver as well as my maid. I'll have to arrange things with the hotel and book tickets. I haven't got a secretary here."

"Well, okay, you go ahead with Sarah. Make them take care of it. They could take a later flight. But they should leave. Absolutely. As long as it's the same day, it'll be all right."

"But—I haven't even got tickets."

"Well, the Concorde flight's at eleven. You have to be there at ten."

"God, I couldn't make it."

"If you started now?"

She thought. "Yes, okay," she said.

"The servants could come later. They could go through London if they had to."

"I don't see the point about the servants, but—well . . . and Sarah? She doesn't know about any of this?"

"No. I don't want her to know, Mrs. Melmore."

"And she's willing to come home?"

"Yes. But I don't think you should stay in New York. Just go right on. Go right on to someplace else. Someplace very far away."

"Suppose I can't get tickets?"

"You'll know how to do it. I'll meet you at the airport with Sarah."

"Listen, Jack, I'll be out at the airport. You're not giving me much choice. But if Sarah's not there—"

"Sarah will be there."

"I can't even get in touch with you. I'd like to talk to Sarah."

"But I don't have a phone. I'll see you at the airport. Around ten. With Sarah."

"Wait," she said.

"Yeah."

"What does Sarah want?" she said.

"Sarah wants a quiet life," he said. Then he laughed. "Lordy."

3

Mrs. Melmore Crosses
a Palm with Silver

THE IDEA OF CECIL was the worst. But why did she have to have Cecil? She was conditioned, wasn't she? Just as the Marxists said: "Workers of the world, throw off your chains!" Well, she might not be a worker, but Cecil was her chain. She doubted that Anna would think that was funny . . . oh, my God—Anna was dead! Could that really be true? All of them? He had said so. God, that was horrible about Anna, but thank God—thank you, God, for sparing Sarah.

Okay. Don't think about it, Sis. Get to work. The idea of not having to talk to Cecil made getting up at this hour a positive pleasure.

Mrs. Melmore wrote Cecil a note. Illness. Concorde. Tickets for herself and Williams as soon as possible. Essentially: pack, pay, and follow. Well, Cecil was no Isabel Burton, trudging uncomplainingly through unknown lands. All Cecil had to do was leave the Crillon in Paris for the apartment on Beekman Place. However, she decided she would rather not see Cecil for a good long time. But she left her a great wad of bills. Conscience money. Time for a bath, makeup. Her hand was shaking—there were tears in her eyes. Who were they for? Anna? Sarah? Herself? She mustn't cry.

Who would be at their place in New York right now? Helen and her niece. Probably they'd just be spending a few hours a day. Someone must call Juliet Sands. Of course, it would be almost midnight in New York. Still, Juliet might not be asleep yet. She read a lot.

Juliet would make the necessary arrangements with the servants. Have the car waiting at Kennedy. But at this hour!

How cross everyone would be. Well, Juliet would manage somehow. She didn't feel up to talking to Juliet herself; she'd turn that over to the concierge. Oh, and of course he must arrange the seats on the Concorde. And a taxi. She wanted a taxi to take her to the airport, she wasn't quite sure why.

She sat on the bed in her slip and called downstairs. It was an ungodly hour. Five-fifteen in the morning. She'd have to get them started on things. She really ought to leave by eight-thirty. Naturally she didn't know the man on duty. He was very nice, very helpful, concerned.

Harriet. It was too early to call Harriet, and maybe what Jack said wasn't true. She didn't want to call her with a false alarm. She'd call Harriet after she saw Sarah, if there was time. Oh—Harriet's phone was out of order, she'd forgotten. Oh, well, she could always get in touch from New York. Maybe now Harry would come to visit her. Maybe she could even teach her a little something about flowers.

Her telephone rang. It was the concierge. They had reached Mrs. Sands in New York, and she had called back to confirm the arrangements: Goodfellow would meet Mrs. Melmore at the airport; tea would be waiting for them, she knew they would be tired.

Now what should she put in her little bag besides her jewelry? Her makeup, overnight things, pictures? Well, why did she need pictures with her if she was going home, if she would have Sarah? She'd let Cecil pack them. All but the three by her bed.

All right. She looked in her pocketbook. All that cash. She still had most of it—paper clipped into different denominations, her American money. Pills, passport, a book. Well, that was it. What else did she need really?

It was so curious traveling this way. Her pocketbook. Her little bag. So free. She felt like a hippie. She could see why the kids liked it so much.

Downstairs, the exchange of courtesies with the concierge. He told her he had not yet reached the flight office of the Concorde, but they were assured that for Mrs. Melmore seats

would be available. He was sorry about her family. He hoped
it was nothing too grave. She thanked him. "If you would
call my maid, Cecil, at nine o'clock? There is a note for her
in my room, explaining what she should do. She might need
help with tickets home." Of course. If there were any problems at all, Mrs. Sands should be called. She would arrange
things. There was a taxi outside.

Oh, gosh, Williams. She grabbed a sheet of paper and
scribbled a note. "Darling Williams—I'm so sorry to treat
you so scurvily. It's all been very grim and ghastly for you,
but I'll explain in New York. Please forgive me. M. Melmore."

"For John Williams, my chauffeur," she said, sealing the
note. Followed by a stack of bills. "For all of you. For everyone who's been so kind to me."

The concierge bowed and followed her out the door. A
bellboy tried to take her little bag, but she smiled and shook
her head.

Juliet had said, in her message, "them"—the plural. That
meant Sarah. Juliet expected Sarah to come back with her
mother. A good omen. Somehow, it made it all seem more
real.

She wondered how Juliet would accomplish her usual
wonders. How would she have the apartment filled with
flowers and fresh vegetables from the country?

She hoped Juliet knew she didn't expect all these miracles
from her. Still, she would be willing to wager that Juliet
would manage, even if she had to drive to the farm at two
in the morning and pick them herself.

She reflected, not for the first time, that although she
might be accused of leading a luxurious, self-indulgent life,
she really represented something like a cottage industry. Her
demise would leave almost a hundred people unemployed.

Mrs. Melmore decided that, if she were Juliet, she would
prefer driving out to the country and picking flowers in the
moonlight to dealing with the complaints of the gardeners.
Juliet would have to drive back, but by then Helen would
be ready and could arrange everything.

Juliet always kept up to date on her work. So the mail would be in order, new books and magazines arranged, articles which might interest Sis clipped on her desk.

Would Juliet be there when she arrived? Probably not. She knew the precarious situation with Sarah. Juliet would be waiting at home, on call.

The taxi driver was standing outside his cab, rubbing his chin. He had a face like one of those men drinking brandy at five in the morning in those old French movies. Pot belly, blue jaw.

She climbed into the back.

"Goodbye, Madame Melmore. I hope it is good news."

The concierge spoke to the driver.

"Oh, thank you. I hope so, too."

"And we will see you here again soon. With everyone in good health."

"Oh, yes. Thank you so much. Goodbye."

The taxi driver started to talk. He had a grumbling way of talking. Complaining. There were streets shut off or something. They were doing demolitions it seemed.

Well, that was sensible. More so than New York. On the weekend, there would be less traffic.

She stopped paying attention. He turned on the radio. She didn't like French popular music, but if she asked him to turn it off, he would feel he was entitled to some conversation. And she couldn't chat or even pretend to listen. She was too absorbed in her own thoughts. First of all, would there really be seats? The concierge had seemed certain, and with a little time, of course, it was simple to arrange—but those French ticket offices, she had been told, didn't keep real working hours. The first obstacle.

If they didn't have tickets for her, what then? She would wait near the Concorde till Jack and Sarah arrived. And they could take another flight. Charter a plane? No, that would take even more time. And she wasn't really sure she knew the mechanics here. It had been so much simpler with Jim's plane.

All right. Say she got the seats. What were the chances that Jack and Sarah would be there? What if they didn't show up? They were a far from reliable couple. Maybe Jack just wanted her out of the way. But of course she wouldn't leave without Sarah, Jack couldn't believe she would do that. But what would she do? Wait and wait and finally go back to the Crillon—where Cecil—ugh! She could never do that. She'd spend the night at the airport hotel. Wait till Cecil and Williams were gone. Then sneak back to the Crillon. Oh, it was all too confusing.

Or suppose only Jack turned up. With some new game. Or more waiting. Another turn of the screw. She wasn't sure she would be able to deal with Jack. She had a terrible fear she would always end up by doing just what he wanted. Maybe he intended to come back to New York with her—pick her bones dry. Actually, what evidence was there, aside from his quiet, persuasive voice, that he even knew Sarah? Oh, God! Jim's death. She'd forgotten that. Yes, he knew Sarah.

Suppose he turned up with Sarah. Sarah as she had last seen her—crazy, sullen, or screaming "Murderer." Violent, maybe. Would they let someone who acted like that on the plane?

This drive was endless. This man, out of spite, must have driven her twice around Paris, while she was lost in thought, before this long, ugly interminable ride out to De Gaulle. She hated this drive. She couldn't let her mind wander because then she would remember Anna. She mustn't think about Anna. It was all too horrible. But Anna had been lying to her all along. Anna had really brought it on herself. It was just God's grace that Sarah hadn't been hurt! No, she must not think about Anna.

Thank God, here they were at last. She had thought she would have lots of time, but she would barely be there the obligatory hour before departure. The driver was still grumpy. She'd be damned if she would give him a big tip; he didn't deserve a thing, but she gave him all the change in her pocketbook. Appeasing the gods. She went in the door and was approached almost immediately by a man in uniform and a flight cap, wearing a name tag. "Madame Melmore?"

"Yes, yes."

"Monsieur Courtin called us about you. We were very lucky. We have been able to find two seats in the front for you. No luggage, I was told." She nodded. "And the other passenger will be?"

"My daughter, Miss Sarah Melmore. She's tall and thin, very short hair, probably wearing blue jeans. You know children today." She managed to smile.

"We will watch for her." He spoke to another man.

"The passport control and baggage check—well, madame, that should take no time at all."

He walked her through the formalities and accompanied her to the lounge.

"Some champagne? Or perhaps you would prefer coffee."

"Yes, coffee," she said gratefully. "Black."

He brought her a cup.

"My daughter will probably be coming here with a friend. A very tall young man—who—who'll be seeing her off."

"We will make sure. The only problem, madame—they are quite strict about boarding time, you know." He looked at his watch. "Perhaps I should go and try to facilitate matters."

Mrs. Melmore drank the coffee. It was good, but golly, it hit the system like a depth bomb! She decided she probably didn't need all that nervous energy. But she drank the whole cup. These were going to be the dreadful minutes now, when she wouldn't know.

But, when she put her cup down and looked up at the clock, she saw, out of the corner of her eye, that nice young man (What was his name? She hadn't looked) far, far away, herding along, like a good shepherd dog, two people. A man and a woman. The man was definitely Jack. And the woman? Sarah. Sarah.

She put on her glasses. Yes, Jack was wearing blue jeans

and a blazer. He was carrying a briefcase. And Sarah, my word! Sarah had cut off even more of her hair. She was wearing jeans and a T-shirt. She didn't even have a shopping bag. My gosh, she hoped Sarah had a passport. Well, she must have, mustn't she? Jack and Sarah were both wearing dark glasses. And what was that on Sarah's forehead? A bandage. Walking along, they didn't look that abnormal. Like other young people she had seen. But Sarah's hair . . .

"Sarah," she thought. "Sarah."

She was being given her heart's desire, and now she didn't know what to do.

"Thank you, God," she thought. "Thank you, Jesus. I don't deserve this. Help me, God."

She wished that young official weren't there, so bright and smiling. Then it would be easier. She would run over and hug Sarah. But then, heavens, Sarah might slap her or something! What would that young man think? He definitely had that "good dog" expression. He would never get over it if there was a scene. Should she tip him? No. But she wished he would go away.

She got up decisively, walked straight over to the young man and shook his hand, thanked him for his courtesy and praised his success. That meant goodbye. Did he understand? Then she shook Jack's hand.

"Mr. Straw, I'm so glad you were able to make it." (She was watching Sarah out of the corner of her eye. She couldn't see Sarah's eyes beneath those black glasses.)

"Sarah, darling," she said, "you've hurt your head."

"It's nothing, Mother, really." Her voice sounded perfectly normal.

"Oh, Sarah." Mrs. Melmore flung her arms around her daughter. She began to cry. She couldn't stop herself. She sobbed and sobbed. Sarah's body didn't flinch away. She let her mother cry on her shoulder.

"I'm sorry, Sarah, I'm sorry."

"Don't cry, Mummy. It's going to be okay."

"I hope we didn't worry you, being a little late, Mrs. Mel-

more. That bump on Sarah's head—it'll be gone in a day
or so."

"You've got your passport and everything you need?" Mrs.
Melmore asked, pressing her handkerchief to her eyes.

"Oh, yeah. You know me, mother. I don't need much."
Sarah held out her passport. What was that sticking out of it?
Oh, it was a snapshot of Sarah and Jimmy when they were
children.

"Do you want some coffee or something? We don't have
too much time, I think. . . . They have orange juice, too.
Champagne?"

"Oh, not for me," said Sarah. "Champagne, Jack?"

"Sarah, why don't you sit down a minute while your
mother and I get something for you. Orange juice might be
good." Sarah sat down. "You're going to see us off, Jack?"
Sarah asked.

"Of course I am."

He led Mrs. Melmore to the table covered with drinks,
then paused.

"Sarah's really in pretty good shape," Jack said. "That
place on her head—that's nothing. And she's—she's real
clear. That's one thing I've been able to do. Even if it's
only that." He sighed. "I think she's going to talk to you
about everything—sooner or later. Someday. But in her own
way. I wouldn't ask her questions. If you just do what I said
—take her away and be gentle. You know how. She really
loves you, you know."

"I don't know what to say, Mr. Straw."

"Please don't call me Mr. Straw."

"Well—Jack. I don't know what magic you've used. But
whatever it is—I just can't— It's beyond anything. It's way
beyond words. I'm not very eloquent anyway—but perhaps
you know what I must feel—being with Sarah, seeing her
like that. Having my daughter—"

"Mother love," said Jack, "yes, I understand that."

"I don't know what you've done . . . but I can't begin to
imagine any way in which I could ever thank you, ever repay

you. But please, you must ask me for anything you want. Any time. Any way in which I can help you. Whatever it is. Whenever it is . . ."

"About Sarah," he said and paused, "I did that for—well, for love. When I was with you—maybe that was something like it, too, but it was wrong and I'm sorry. Sarah—well, Sarah was different. Sarah's a whole lot different from anything. Maybe it was a good love because it sort of worked or something. Maybe that's why. I haven't figured it out, really. But you could help me a whole lot, right now, Mrs. Melmore."

"Tell me," she said.

"It's sort of embarrassing, but do you have any cash or something on you? I got caught up in this thing with Sarah, and I'm supposed to be down in South America today. And the banks aren't open or anything, and I haven't even got money for a ticket."

"Oh, money," she said. "Oh, gosh. Oh, sure."

She looked in her pocketbook. Wads and wads of French francs. She pulled them all out, all of the little bundles. She gave them all to Jack. Then she laughed. "Carfare home," she said. She reached over and picked up an orange juice for Sarah.

"Well," he said. Then he laughed too. They were announcing the flight. Sarah walked over to meet them. She didn't want the orange juice after all.

"I guess we really should go," Mrs. Melmore said.

"Oh," said Jack. "Just a minute—it's not much, but—"

He gave each of them a long-stemmed red rose. It was like a magic trick. Where had they come from? Had they been in his briefcase?

Jack was giving them both a hug, one arm around each.

"Well," he said, "you two girls know more about me than anyone. Maybe you'll figure it all out someday. I sure can't."

He gave Mrs. Melmore a light kiss on the cheek. "Goodbye, Sis. You're perfect, you know. Just the way you are."

Then Jack kissed Sarah. He kissed her on the mouth, and they hugged.

"Sarah," he said, "I'm going to miss you, God only knows. I love you, Sarah. Wherever you are, remember that."

Sarah raised her hand. She touched her bandage.

"Remember that's true, Sarah, wherever you are."

"*Mesdames et messieurs.*"

The last passengers were walking up the ramp.

"Good luck, Jack."

"I'll write."

"I know how you are about writing, Jack."

Mrs. Melmore shook her head. She was feeling a little groggy. All the strain . . . "Sarah," she said, "We'd better . . ."

Sarah turned and walked up the runway ahead of her mother. She was peeling her rose—pulling the petals off one by one. When she came to the stem, she broke it in two and threw it away. She didn't look back. Mrs. Melmore did. She was afraid Jack might have seen and been hurt. But Jack hadn't stood around to wave.

He was hurrying away—running—in another direction. It was hard to say why, but something in the way he moved made Mrs. Melmore feel that he was happy.

Seat number ten.

"Do you want the window seat, Sarah?"

"Do you like it, Mother? I don't care."

All the signs were lit and the captain was beginning to speak. Mrs. Melmore didn't listen.

They were repeating it in English. The temperature in New York was seventy-eight. There was a pause. Then, "The captain has the greatest pleasure to tell you that in New York it has been raining for four hours."

The passengers clapped their hands and cheered. Mrs. Melmore just squeezed Sarah's hand. And Sarah gave her hand the faintest pressure back. But, when she glanced at Sarah, a few moments later, she realized that her daughter was asleep. She had fallen, quickly and silently, into the deep sleep of a child—free from all the embarrassing noises and unfortunate expressions of sleeping adults.

How beautiful Sarah was, now that her eyes were no longer guarding her face. Her mother gazed and gazed. How extraordinary were her very bones, and the thin flawless white skin which covered them.

Mrs. Melmore felt pierced by happiness—precisely that sort of happiness she had been sure she would never feel again. A happiness mixed with the exquisite pain of regarding perfect beauty. The recollection of perfection . . .

Yes, perfection. If time could only be suspended, if only this journey could go on and on, if only this plane could circle round and round the world, while Sarah slept, and she watched over her.

"That's it," thought Mrs. Melmore. "At last, at the very last, I know the answer."

Mrs. Melmore leaned over and kissed her daughter's cool forehead, next to the bandage. "I love you, Sarah," she said.

A Note on the Type

The text of this book was set on the Linotype in a type face called Baskerville. The face is a facsimile reproduction of types cast from molds made for John Baskerville (1706–75) from his designs. The punches for the revived Linotype Baskerville were cut under the supervision of the English printer George W. Jones.

John Baskerville's original face was one of the forerunners of the type style known to printers as "modern face"—a "modern" of the period A.D. 1800.

Composed by Maryland Linotype Composition Co. Inc., Baltimore, Maryland. Printed and bound by R. R. Donnelley & Sons, Co., Harrisonburg, Virginia.

Typography and binding design by Virginia Tan.